CO

Unable to stop himself, Coulter reached for Josie. Without considering the circumstances of his actions, he pulled her into his embrace. She rested her forehead on his shoulder and clung to his shirt. With a gentle touch, he stroked her back. It had been so long, too long since he'd held a woman like Josie. He buried his face in her long, unbound hair and drank in the clean fragrance. She was everything a woman should be. Everything he'd missed for four long years.

She trembled under his touch and lifted her face from his shoulder. Her eyes were as shiny as blue diamonds. The invitation was there on her face. Her lips parted and Coulter gave in to the need that had been dogging him since he'd entered the jail and heard her voice.

At the first brush of his mouth on hers, he lost the battle to control his emotions. The kiss started out slowly; her lips quivered against his. He tightened his grip and pulled her intimately against him, her thin gown and wrapper no barrier against the strength of his arousal. She clutched his shoulders, her fingers digging into his flesh with an urgency that spurred him to deepen the kiss. . . .

Books by Jean Wilson

SWEET DREAMS
MY MARIAH
COULTER'S ANGEL

Published by Zebra Books

COULTER'S
ANGEL

Jean Wilson

Zebra Books
Kensington Publishing Corp.

http://www.zebrabooks.com

ZEBRA BOOKS are published by

Kensington Publishing Corp.
850 Third Avenue
New York, NY 10022

Zebra and the Z logo Reg. U.S. Pat. & TM Off.

First Printing: May, 1999
10 9 8 7 6 5 4 3 2 1

Printed in the United States of America

To the Renegades, who always believed in this Angel.

Chapter 1

"*Swing low, sweet chariot, coming for to carry me home. / Swing low, sweet chariot, coming for to carry me home. / I looked over Jordan, and what did I see, coming for to carry me home? / A band of angels . . .*"

The words of the old spiritual echoed off the thick stone walls. At the sound of footsteps on the rough board floor, Josie Clark clamped her mouth shut. She swung her gaze toward the door, the bottom half solid wood, and the top, heavy iron bars.

"See what I told you, Coulter?" came the nasal tones of the deputy who had arrested her the previous evening. "She's been caterwauling all night. I couldn't get a wink of sleep."

"Don't worry, Homer, I'll handle her." A different voice, deep, with a soft drawl, rose above the thud of boot heels.

Josie swung her feet to the floor and sat on the edge of the narrow, hard cot. If she couldn't sleep, she was glad

the deputy couldn't, either. Two figures stepped into the
thin beam of morning light that slanted through the narrow window above her. The smaller man she recognized
as the deputy; the other, the one in the shadows, must be
the sheriff.

"Morning, ma'am." He stepped closer and with the
jingle of metal, slid a key into the lock. "Hope you're
enjoying our hospitality."

After a sleepless night, Josie was in no mood for his sick
sense of humor. Her back ached, her throat was dry, and
she felt as if it had been a year since she'd had a bath. The
county jail in the nowhere town of Council City, Kansas, was
the last place she'd expected to spend the night.

"Your accommodations leave much to be desired." She
shot a glance toward her captors, the men who'd wrong-
fully imprisoned her. Her gaze fell on the shiny silver star
pinned to the tall man's black leather vest, then met the
gun tucked at his hip. The rest of him didn't matter. He
was the law. And Josie was his prisoner.

The door swung open and the deputy stepped inside.
"Come on, lady. You wanted to see the sheriff, and he
wants to see you." The obnoxious man didn't even try to
hide the snicker in his voice.

Josie stood and shook out the wrinkled skirt of her once-
crisp traveling suit. The hunter-green broadcloth reeked
of stale beer and perspiration. Thanks to the overzealous
deputy, she felt as bad as she smelled. She lifted her arms
to smooth her wild, golden hair into some semblance of
a bun and felt the rush of cool air under the torn sleeve.
Another casualty in the war against alcohol. Along with
her pert little hat that looked like a dead bird lying on the
bunk. She snatched the feathered creation and plunked
it on her head, hoping it would remain in place. Her best
six-inch hat pin with the pearl head had flown into the
middle of the street during the altercation last evening.

With a determined tilt of her chin, she turned toward

the open cell door. The deputy stretched out a hand toward her. "If you touch me again, Gopher, I'll make sure your right eye matches your left one." She balled her hands into fists to emphasize her words and speared him with a look guaranteed to chill the devil in his own domain.

The deputy covered the side of his face with his palm. If anybody deserved the black eye, this man did. He stood a few inches taller than Josie's five feet four inches, and looked as if he'd just taken a bite out of a big sour pickle.

"See, Coulter, I told you she was a wildcat," he complained, in the same whiny voice that had yelled at Josie all night to be quiet.

"It's all right, Homer." The other man stepped into the dim light. "I'll take care of her." He gestured to the open door. "Ready, ma'am?"

Josie set her jaw and studied the sheriff. He was at least six feet tall; his powerful shoulders filled the doorway. Under the leather vest a blue shirt stretched across his chest. The red bandanna tied at his throat pulled her attention to the sprinkling of dark hair peeking out above the open neck of the shirt. She lifted her gaze and met eyes as dark as the midnight sky.

Never shy, she faced his scrutiny without flinching. Nobody had ever accused Josephine Angelique Clark of being a shrinking violet. She'd learned early to meet both her critics and admirers with equal boldness. She couldn't decide where this man stood. Was he friend or foe? Theatrical people rarely got along with the established law in the local towns, and, as she'd learned, neither did temperance organizers.

Dark whiskers shadowed his square chin and gold flecks danced in near-black eyes. Some women might call him handsome, but his rugged good looks didn't impress Josie. He couldn't have held a candle to Armand's classic features.

The memory of her brother brought a twinge of pain

to Josie's heart. She tried not to think of him or the past. The past was gone. Her life was different now, and she never wanted to go back.

With a haughty tilt of her chin, she stuck out her wrists. "I suppose you're going to need manacles. After all, I might try to overpower you and Gopher and escape from custody."

A crooked smile tugged at the sheriff's wide mouth. "That won't be necessary, ma'am. Between the two of us, we may be able to defend ourselves." He slanted a glance at his deputy and the man's bruised cheek. "Though I understand you pack quite a wallop. We'll go into the office and discuss the situation."

Josie gave her skirt a sassy flip as she passed the sheriff; the pleated hem danced against his canvas trousers. Biting back a caustic remark, she followed at the deputy's heels. Last night she'd been too angry to notice the sheriff's office; now she paused to get her bearings. Two battered desks occupied most of the room, with shotguns and rifles locked in a gun rack on the wall. The aroma of stale coffee and tobacco turned her stomach.

Homer took the chair behind one desk, leaving Josie standing. The man's rudeness was the final straw in her attempt to control a temper on the verge of exploding.

Before she could form a stinging retort, the sheriff came up behind her and offered a straight-backed chair beside his desk. "Please have a seat, ma'am. I'd like to hear what happened last night."

"I can tell you what she did last night, Coulter," Homer said, his lips narrowed to a thin slit in his face. "She attacked me, that's what that wild woman did."

"Attacked you? Gopher, you got in the way when I tried to defend myself against that drunken cowboy." Unable to remain seated, she leaped to her feet. She leaned across the deputy's desk and pinned him with her most intense stare. He cowered away from her.

"Hold it, both of you." With the swiftness of a hungry panther leaping on its prey, the sheriff caught Josie's arm in a viselike grip. He urged her back into the chair. "Calm down, ma'am."

She brushed off his hand and rubbed away the tingles that remained from his bold touch. This man was as impossible as his partner. Exercising her limited self-restraint she managed to swallow back the angry insult that would only cause further problems.

The sheriff propped his hip against the desk and stared down at Josie. "Homer, you can leave. Go home and get ready for church. I can handle Miss . . ."

"Clark," she announced in her most intimidating tone. "Miss Josephine Clark." She tugged on the waist of her basque jacket. In spite of her bedraggled appearance, she strove for a shred of dignity. At this point in her life, that was one of the few things Josie had left.

Homer stood, and moved slowly toward the door. "But, Coulter—"

"Go. I'll take care of Miss Clark." The sheriff waved his hand in dismissal.

Homer flashed a spiteful grin at Josie. She balled her hands into fists to keep from wiping the smirk off his skinny face. On impulse, she stuck out her tongue and turned up her nose. Certainly it was childish, but she couldn't help having the last word, or gesture, as it was.

When she swung her gaze back to the sheriff, she spotted the grin on his face. A hint of amusement lingered in his eyes. He flipped his black Stetson and it landed squarely on a peg across the room. "Coffee, Miss Clark?" He moved to the dented tin pot on the potbellied stove in the corner.

Josie's mouth puckered, and her stomach churned. Although she was starving, the acrid-smelling liquid held no appeal. "No, thank you."

Large, paint-stained hands clutched a chipped mug as he filled it with the thick liquid. He took a sip, made a

face, and lifted his gaze to Josie. "Don't blame you for not
drinking this stuff. It would burn a hole through a cast-
iron skillet."

Josie almost smiled. "A little water would be nice, Sheriff,
if you don't mind."

He wiped out another mug with a rag and filled it from
a wooden cask. Frowning, she took the mug from his hand.
For the briefest of moments, his work-hardened fingers
brushed hers. A strange awareness shot through Josie—
an awareness of tough masculinity, of danger.

"The water's cool and clean, ma'am, even if our
housekeeping isn't quite up to standard." He moved to
the far side of the desk and plunked down his coffee,
sloshing the black liquid onto a stack of papers. "Damn,"
he muttered. Yanking the kerchief from his throat, he
mopped up the coffee, then stuck the damp cloth into his
hip pocket.

His chair squeaked as he eased his tall frame into the
wooden seat. Here in the light, she got a better look at
him. Thin creases etched the corners of his eyes—laugh
lines of a man who smiled deep and often. The lids
drooped as if he'd gotten little sleep the night before.
Probably out on a bender, she thought, like the rowdy cowboys
who had accosted her last night in front of the saloon.
That wouldn't happen to women much longer if she had
her way.

"Well, Sheriff . . ." She tilted one well-shaped eyebrow.

"Steele, Coulter Steele."

The name suited him, she thought. *Strong, stalwart, honest.* The words flashed across her mind. And fair, she hoped.

"Sheriff Steele, what are the charges against me?" Josie
sipped the water, a welcome relief to the cottony dryness
of her mouth.

He set his elbows on the desk and studied her over his
folded hands. "For starters, striking an officer, resisting

arrest, and inciting a riot. Guess those are the most serious charges."

Josie choked on the water and spewed it all over her already-soiled skirt. "Assault? That pompous ass tried to attack me."

"*Tsk, tsk.* Your language, Miss Clark. His name is Homer, Homer Potts."

She folded her arms across her chest. As expected, he took the man's side against her. A travesty of justice, considering she was the victim, the wronged party. "Are you the judge?"

He ran his hand through tousled chestnut-colored hair badly in need of a haircut. "No, ma'am. But if you'll explain what happened, we can settle this thing right now. No need to bother the justice of the peace."

"I would rather talk to him."

"Have it your way. Since today is Sunday, you'll have to wait until tomorrow to see the J.P."

Josie's eyes widened. Wanting justice was one thing; being incarcerated for another day was another. "Will I have to spend tonight in jail?" At the very idea, a cold shiver raced up her spine.

"No, not if you have someplace else to stay." He brushed a large hand across his square jaw covered with a night's growth of whiskers.

"I have a room at the Council Hotel," she said, not even trying to hide the relief in her voice.

He nodded. "Promise you'll show up for court Monday morning at nine, and I'll release you until then."

Grateful to be free, she rose and adjusted her jacket at her narrow waist. "Believe me, Sheriff Steele, I wouldn't miss this circus for the world. Until then, good day." With one long gulp, she finished off the water, set the cup in the center of his desk, and headed for freedom.

Coulter rose and watched the lady sashay through the open doorway. Her head was held high and that little bustle at her rear swayed with every step. She was a looker, that one, with a figure that made men stand up and take notice. And much prettier than most of the saloon girls and whores who came through Council City looking for work. What Homer called "caterwauling" was the sweet voice of an angel.

Something clicked in his head—a dim memory from the past. Had he seen her before? He rarely forgot a face, and one as pretty as hers was hard to forget.

At the window he watched as she lifted her skirts against the dusty street. Under that silly hat that looked like something he'd killed on his last hunting trip, the sunlight turned her curls to spun gold. Of all her feminine charms, though, her best features were her eyes—the bluest he'd ever seen. Like the turquoise stones he and Ellen had found in Arizona while on their honeymoon.

And she was saucy, he thought. She'd stood up to Homer and she'd stood up to him. He couldn't imagine his sweet Ellen even talking back to a lawman, much less taking a swing at him. His little wife would have swooned into a hysterical faint at the thought of spending the night in jail. Not Miss Clark. That feisty lady had not only blackened Homer's eye, she'd threatened to give the deputy a matching pair. Coulter wouldn't have been surprised if she'd tried to give him one, too.

The lady was a handful, he thought, as he took a sip of bitter coffee from the day before. Let Uncle Oscar take care of her. Coulter had all the women problems he could handle at home.

He stretched his arms over his head and yawned. After working most of the night in his studio, he'd hoped to sneak a few hours' sleep before attending church. When he'd received Homer's message that he'd arrested a woman, something told Coulter he'd better postpone his rest and handle the situation. Now he was glad he had. A lady like Miss Clark didn't belong in jail. She belonged snuggled in a man's bed.

The hot coffee went down his windpipe and Coulter choked. Where had that come from? he wondered, shocked at the trend of his thoughts. His gaze followed her across the street to the boardwalk in front of the hotel. Every man she passed stopped and stared at her. Two old geezers ran into each other trying to be first to open the door for her. From the distance Coulter caught her smile and the nod of her head in a thank-you.

A tightening started in the center of his gut, an urge he hadn't felt in a very long time. A longing that had no place in his life.

He knew trouble when he saw it, and Miss Josephine Clark spelled trouble. Trouble with a capital *T*.

The last thing Coulter needed was woman trouble. After one final glance at the lady, he picked up his hat. He would have to postpone his rest if he didn't want to keep Cathy and Miss Bettington waiting. In the two months since Miss Bennington had been in his employ, he'd learned that the housekeeper equated promptness right up there with cleanliness and godliness. He had better hurry if they were to get to church on time.

Two and a half hours later, Coulter entered the First Community Church—the only church in town. His grandparents had been among the first settlers in the territory, and Grandpa Moore had been the preacher from the day he started the church until the day he died, twelve years ago.

Coulter removed his hat and straightened his tie. His badge was pinned to his stiff white shirt, and his gun was tucked under the tails of his dark serge suit. He spotted his uncle, Oscar Marche, in his usual pew—smack in the middle of the church. In fact, almost everybody was sitting in the same pew they'd occupied from the day they entered the sanctuary. He could close his eyes and by location alone pick out every member of the congregation.

Miss Elsie Taylor stepped up to the piano and flexed her fingers. For as long as Coulter could remember, she went through the same routine every Sunday morning. Next, she adjusted the piano bench and flipped through the pages of the hymnal. He wondered why she bothered with the music. Everybody knew she couldn't read a note; she played strictly by ear. Her plump fingers danced over the keys, missing only a note or two, and her gray head bobbed in time to "Blessed Assurance."

Coulter slid in next to Oscar, and Cathy squeezed between them, leaving Miss Bettington on the aisle. The housekeeper claimed that sitting in the middle made her nervous. Homer, black eye and all, sat ramrod-straight in the front pew with the other deacons. The deputy had been so proud to be elected to the board, he'd gone out and bought a new black serge suit and bowler hat.

"Heard there was a little commotion at the Golden Garter last night," Oscar leaned over and whispered.

"Minor skirmish. Homer handled it," Coulter answered over his daughter's dark curls. The memory of Miss Clark's flashing blue eyes skidded across his mind. "You can take care of it tomorrow. By the way, where's Aunt Bertha?"

"Went to meet some new temperance lecturer she'd invited to town. You know Bertha and her causes. She won't be happy until we all quit drinking and smoking and are walking the straight and narrow."

Coulter stifled a grin. Bertha and his mother, Louisa, had been sisters, preacher's daughters who wanted to reform the world. Louisa had fallen in love with the Comanche half-breed, Lucas Steele, and had married him against her parents' wishes. They'd been happy on the little spread where Coulter now lived, until the war came along and both were killed by Quantrill's raiders. That was one of the reasons he'd run for sheriff four years ago. Somebody had to stand up and keep the world safe for innocent people.

"Know what you mean. Next thing you know, she'll be campaigning to get women the vote."

Oscar chuckled. "I saw her list. That's her next mission."

"Shhh," Miss Bettington admonished with an angry glare.

Coulter slanted a glance at his housekeeper from the corner of his eye. Dressed all in black, from the poke bonnet tied under her chin to the hem of her alpaca skirt, the spinster could easily pass for a nun. And she was as strict with Cathy as though the child lived in a convent. But good housekeepers were hard to find in the middle of Kansas, and the woman kept his house clean and his daughter company.

He slipped his arm across Cathy's shoulders. She'd seemed quieter and more subdued than usual. This beautiful child was the light of his life—his reason for living. Cathy had Ellen's sweet nature and pretty face. Her dark hair and eyes were vintage Steele. He squeezed her shoulder in a loving gesture.

Sometimes he felt sorry for his daughter. A series of housekeepers were a sorry substitute for the mother she'd lost five years ago. But Coulter had no desire to remarry. He'd adored Ellen, and he'd buried his heart with her and their son in the Kansas City cemetery. What love he had left, he poured out on his daughter.

Reverend Elijah Harris entered from the side door and mounted the pulpit. After he adjusted his wire-rimmed spectacles on his short straight nose, he opened a songbook. He signaled the congregation to stand and lift their voices in song. The preacher had been with the congregation for two years, and seemed well-liked by the congregation—especially by the widows and spinsters. The tall, thin man was about Coulter's age and had never married.

Being the daughter of a minister, Coulter's aunt thought

the world of the man. Coulter liked the preacher—who wouldn't? But he found the man a little too self-righteous for comfort.

As the first few words of the hymn reverberated through the frame building, somebody flung open the back door and made a noisy entrance down the center aisle. Coulter recognized his aunt's hurried footsteps.

Aunt Bertha stopped at their pew and squeezed past Miss Bettington, who gave an annoyed "Humph," past Coulter, and Cathy. She shoved Oscar over to make room for herself and the woman who followed at her bustle.

"Excuse me, please," a familiar voice whispered. The lady lifted her gaze and stopped cold when she reached Coulter. Blonde curls tumbled from beneath a picture hat, and turquoise eyes met his. Trapped between his pelvis and the pew in front of them stood Miss Josephine Clark.

The soiled dove Homer had arrested was his aunt's temperance lecturer! This same woman had spent the night in his jail. The same woman was scheduled to appear before his uncle the next day.

The woman had the face and voice of an angel, and the temper of Lucifer himself!

Chapter 2

Josie held her breath. Of all the improbable situations. What was the sheriff doing in church?

Stupid question, she admonished herself. . . . But in this pew, where Mrs. Marche had insisted she sit with her family? His eyes darkened to the depths of a starless night and his mouth pulled into a narrow line. She could read the question on his face: *What is this woman doing in church?*

Not at all intimidated by his bulk, or his muscular chest under the black suit, she jammed her elbow into his ribs. He grunted, and she wasn't the least bit sorry if she'd hurt him. She brushed past him, her back against his chest, her rear against his front. Awareness of his hard male body shot strange sensations through her. It had taken mere seconds, yet Josie felt as if she'd been pressed intimately against him for hours. Heat surfaced to her cheeks.

The black-clad woman next to him stopped singing and glared at Josie. A little girl looked up and smiled. She was his child. Josie knew it by the chestnut hair and the dark flashing eyes. By some miracle, Josie managed to get past him and the little girl and fit into the narrow space Mrs. Marche had saved for her. The congregation sang "Amen," and the preacher called for prayer.

After her discomfort of the past night, the service moved at a snail's pace. The song leader sang offkey and the preacher gave a lengthy exhortation on honoring the Sabbath Day and keeping it holy. The little girl grew drowsy and leaned against Josie. With the speed of a serpent's tongue, the woman on the end of the pew snaked a long black-clad arm past Sheriff Steele, and rapped the child on the head. The girl bolted upright. Josie resisted the urge to tap the woman with her knuckles to let her know how it felt.

She remembered what it was like as a child to sit in church after a late show and struggle to stay awake. Her mother, being French, had insisted that they attend mass every Sunday morning no matter how late they stayed up, nor in what town they found themselves. Papa never came with them, but waited outside the church to take the family to a restaurant for dinner. For Josie and Armand, that was the best part of the day.

Did Sheriff Steele make Sundays special for his daughter and . . . ? Was the woman in the black dress his wife? She tried to sneak a glance past him, but all she saw were the sharp angles of his clean-shaven jaw and his gaze slanted toward her. From then on she kept her eyes straight ahead, focused on the preacher. What the sheriff did, and the identity of the woman, were certainly no concern of hers.

Sitting statue-still in the cramped, hot pew, Josie tried to concentrate on the message. The minister was rather nice-looking: tall, with dark blond hair, and warm brown eyes behind his eyeglasses. He was educated and refined, not at all like the crude, ill-mannered sheriff. Why was she thinking about him again? The farther she stayed away from the law, the better off she was.

By the time the preacher pronounced his final "Amen,"

half the congregation was drowsy. The piano player hit the first chord and all over the room heads snapped up, Josie's with theirs. She stood and joined in the last hymn, her voice blending with the others. Sheriff Steele mouthed the words, but no sound came from his lips. The woman at his other side sang loud and out of tune.

As the last note vibrated throughout the building, the pastor held up his hands and asked the people to be seated again. She didn't miss the soft groan that rumbled through the crowd.

"Before we dismiss, I would like to introduce a special guest who's with us today. Mrs. Marche has invited a lady from the Society for the Abolition of Alcohol and Tobacco for a series of lectures. Miss Clark, would you like to say a few words about the meeting tonight?"

Josie stood and glanced from her right where the sheriff's long legs blocked the narrow passage, then to the left and Mr. Marche's paunch. She opted to take her chances with the sheriff. At her nod, he stood. Mumbling an apology, she worked her way past his muscular body, nearly getting crushed in the process. The discourteous man didn't try to help at all. If anything, he stretched out even farther.

Smoothing out the skirt of the navy linen suit, she walked the few feet to the front of the church. Men sat up and straightened their ties. Women murmured among themselves. One little boy remarked loudly, "She's pretty." More than a few shushed him.

"Thank you, Reverend Harris, for allowing me this moment to inform the good people of Council City of our mission," she said, projecting her voice to the rear of the church.

Josie paused and took a deep, steadying breath, just as Mama had taught her to do when she was even younger than the sheriff's daughter. Butterflies danced an Irish jig in her stomach—stage fright—like opening night at the

Grand. *It's only because of the importance of the cause,* she told herself—not because the sheriff was spearing her with an angry look. Her gaze swept over the congregation. Homer Potts sat in the front pew, his face flushed red and his swollen eye purple and blue. She bit back a grin at the colorful hues that contrasted with his black suit and white shirt.

Papa always said the best way to win an audience was to play to one certain person; to find someone, preferably a man, and give him her very best performance. Josie smiled and met Sheriff Steele's hard, assessing stare.

"We all know the evils of demon drink, how alcoholism destroys homes and families. It's up to every one of us, men and women, to fight the devil on his own doorstep. The S.A.A.T. is firmly behind the movement to make Kansas as well as the entire United States of America free from the temptations of drink."

Josie paused to let her words sink in. With his arms folded across his chest, the sheriff remained as stiff as a cigar-store Indian. She swung her gaze around the congregation, but came right back to the sheriff.

"I would like to invite the ladies as well as any interested gentlemen to a meeting this evening at six o'clock here at the church. We will discuss our part in the movement and what each of us can do to make this community safe for our children." She took a step forward, remembering the old adage to always leave them wanting more. "I thank you for your kind attention."

Josie hurried to the rear of the church, the better to gauge her audience, as Papa used to say. The women smiled, while the men grumbled under their breath. She wasn't at all surprised. In the temperance battle, too often men and women took opposite sides. Reverend Harris called for Brother Potts to say the benediction. Homer croaked out a few words and the congregation filed out of their pews.

The pastor clasped Josie's gloved hand in his gentle grip, quite a change from the way the sheriff had grabbed her arm that morning. Flashing a warm smile, he thanked Josie, then stepped into the sunlight to greet his flock. The women who passed told her they would be sure to meet her that evening, while the men merely tipped their hats and mumbled a gruff "Good day."

Mrs. Marche rushed toward her, husband on one arm, the sheriff on the other. The men dwarfed the petite woman. Mr. Marche was a head taller, and the sheriff towered over both. Josie's gaze shifted from the large orange bow tied under the lady's neck to what looked like a bird's nest perched atop her head. All during the service, she'd wondered how Mrs. Marche had managed to keep the yellow canary and red cardinal balanced on the narrow brim of the hat. Over the years, Josie had seen her share of outrageous headgear, but this one took the cake. She stifled a grin. Could be, the lady had one which did resemble a cake.

"Miss Clark," Mrs. Marche called, "I'd like you to meet my family. This is my husband, Oscar—he's our mayor, you know."

The paunchy older man slicked back the little hair that rimmed his shiny head, and smoothed down his long, fuzzy muttonchops that reached clear down to his jaw. He wiped his palm on his coat before he stuck out a huge hand. "Please to meet you, Miss Clark. Hope you'll have dinner with us today."

"Of course she will, Oscar. We have to make our plans for the rally." Mrs. Marche gestured to the sheriff. "And this is my nephew, Sheriff Coulter Steele." Pride and love glittered in the woman's eyes. Though how such a sweet, considerate woman could be kin to this obstinate oaf, Josie had no idea.

Josie removed her fingers from Oscar's and reached toward the sheriff. He enfolded her hand in his and flashed a crooked smile. "My pleasure, ma'am." His palm was warm and hard, with a bit of red paint under the nails. He squeezed her hand and his thumb caressed her knuckles. The touch was far too familiar for comfort. When he didn't say anything about their previous encounter, Josie decided it was best not to mention it, either.

"How do you do?" she asked, surprised at the tightening of her throat.

"Quite well, thank you." Still clasping her fingers in his, he turned to the little girl and the black-clad woman. "This is my daughter, Cathy, and my housekeeper, Miss Bettington."

His housekeeper? That explained the woman's correcting his child. Josie tugged her fingers free of the sheriff's disturbing touch, and clutched Miss Bettington's cold, limp fingers in a brief handshake. Then she stooped down to speak to Cathy. "You're a pretty young lady. How old are you?"

A shy smile curved the girl's lips. "I'm eight, but I'll be nine right before Christmas."

Mrs. Marche tapped Josie's shoulder. "Let's be on our way, my dear. Coulter, will you, Cathy, and Miss Bettington be joining us for dinner?"

The sheriff shook his head. "Cathy will, but I have work to finish at the ranch."

Josie almost breathed a sigh of relief at not having to face him all afternoon.

"How about you, Miss Bettington?" Mrs. Marche asked. "Isn't Sunday your day off?"

The dark-clad woman nodded. "Yes, but I'm dining with Mrs. Potts."

"Give dear Irene our best," Mrs. Marche said. "Her lumbago has been giving her fits for weeks now."

Josie leaned toward Coulter. "Homer's wife?" she whispered.

"His mother." Before Josie could move toward the doorway, Coulter wrapped his large fingers around her upper arm, holding her in place at his side. "Aunt Bertha, why don't you run ahead and get dinner ready? I'll bring Miss Clark along directly. I'd like a word with her."

Mrs. Marche flashed a charming smile. "Certainly, dear. Just don't make her late for dinner. Cathy can ride with Uncle Oscar and me."

Josie watched Mr. and Mrs. Marche stroll away with Cathy skipping along behind them. The older woman flipped open her parasol and twirled it on her shoulder. Miss Bettington scurried after Homer and the tall, thin woman on his arm. Alone with Coulter Steele, she speared him with a haughty stare. "I don't believe we have anything to discuss, Sheriff."

He tucked her arm in his and steered her down the church steps away from the crowd. "I think we do, lady. Who are you, and what are you doing in my town?"

She stopped cold and pulled him up short. "Sheriff Steele, unless you were asleep during the last fifteen minutes of the service, you would be quite aware of my name and mission." Her gaze dropped to his long fingers firmly attached to her upper arm. His strong touch unnerved her, but Josie wasn't about to let him know he had any effect on her at all. "Sir, please unhand me."

Coulter ignored her request by tugging her closer to his side and continuing toward his buggy. "Don't make a scene, Miss Clark. This is the church, not the Golden Garter Saloon."

"Am I under arrest, Sheriff?" she asked, her voice as frosty as a January morning in Boston.

She was a fighter, all right. But there was something about her that didn't quite ring true. She was just too pretty, too smart, and too downright sensuous—yes, that was the word to describe her—to be an ordinary temperance lecturer. There was nothing ordinary about the woman. Her eyes were too blue, her hair too golden, and her body . . . well, he didn't even want to dwell on that dangerous ground.

He tipped his hat to several women who had stopped to stare at him with the temperance worker at his side. To her credit, Miss Clark nodded cordially but didn't speak. It wouldn't have surprised Coulter at all if she'd begun to scream for help. Or blackened his eye.

"No, ma'am, not yet."

The implied threat brought her up short and Coulter almost tripped on his own feet.

"Exactly what is that supposed to mean?"

"The people of Council City elected me to protect them. I fully intend to keep the trust they've placed in me." With a gentle tug, he continued toward the line of buggies and wagons tied under the small grove of cottonwoods.

"Mr. Steele, I'm not with the James gang, or any of the other outlaws that threaten your town. Surely you don't think they're in any danger from me?"

Her wide innocent eyes would have melted a lesser man, but Coulter spotted the mystery behind those long, thick lashes. Miss Clark wasn't quite all she pretended.

"Maybe, maybe not. I just want to find out a little more about you and this organization you claim to represent."

They reached his rig and stopped. He glanced over her shoulder and spotted Homer with his mother and Miss Bettington. All three had their gazes locked on him and Miss Clark.

He'd just turned to Miss Clark when he heard his name coming from a distance. "Sheriff . . . Sheriff Steele."

Turning, he spotted the preacher running toward him, holding his black hat in his hand. "Yes, Reverend. Is there a problem?"

The man stopped, his breath coming in short gasps. "No, no problem for the law. But I've been invited to dinner with Mr. and Mrs. Marche and I would be happy to escort Miss Clark to their home. I understand you won't be joining us today.''

Josie tugged at Coulter's arm in an effort to pull free. Before she could open her mouth to speak, Coulter cut her off. "That's quite all right, Rev, I don't mind at all. I need to know Miss Clark's plans for her rally, and I have some business over that way." He tipped his hat in dismissal. "Good day."

The preacher bowed to Josie and smiled at her. "Then I suppose I'll see you at dinner, Miss Clark. I must say, I, too, am interested in hearing your plans for the movement. This town has been wide open for far too long." He shot an accusatory glance at Coulter. "It's time the law-abiding people ran out the whoremongers and drunks and made the streets safe for our citizens."

Coulter gritted his teeth. He forced a smile. "Rev, that's my job. You stick to hellfire and brimstone, and I'll take care of the criminals. We'll all get along fine." Tugging Josie along at his side, he continued to his buggy, leaving the minister staring after them.

"That was rather rude, Sheriff. The reverend was only trying to help."

In spite of her efforts, he refused to release her arm. "I don't need his advice on how to run my town." Upon reaching the wagon, he released her arm and offered a hand up into the high seat. "Miss Clark."

She narrowed her eyes and set her chin. "It can't be far to the Marche home. I would prefer to walk."

"It's on the other side of town. A cowboy never walks when he can ride." Without giving her a chance for further argument, he set his hands at her waist and lifted the lady onto the seat. For a brief moment, he allowed his fingers to rest on her soft, firm flesh. To Coulter, it was a moment too long. His body's reaction to the touch was unwanted and unneeded. He'd thought that part of him was long dead. He jerked his hands from her. "Slide over," he said, surprised at the harshness in his voice.

Squaring her shoulders, she scooted as far away as possible, leaving the skirt of her navy suit trailing behind her. He leaped up to join her and landed on a tail of fabric. She tugged hard on the material, nearly tossing him to the ground.

"Get off my skirt, you oaf!"

Coulter glanced down and spied a row of lacy petticoats and a pair of fancy leather shoes. His gaze continued up to trim ankles and smooth black silk stockings. He knew silk when he saw it. Ellen had never worn anything else. The gnawing in his gut turned into a giant wallop. Josie tugged again, harder. This time her skirt came loose with the unmistakable sound of ripping fabric.

"Look what you've done," she moaned. Her fingers gripped a handful of blue linen. Pure white unmentionables showed where her top was once connected to her skirt. "This was my best suit."

In one quick motion, Coulter released the hand brake, and flicked the reins. The horses took off at a gallop. The jerky forward movement threw her against his side. She flung her arms around him to keep her balance.

"Now you're trying to kill me," she yelled.

The soft female body crushed against him reminded him of how long it had been since he'd enjoyed the intimate company of a beautiful woman. Too long, and not long enough. A couple times a year, when he felt the urge, Coulter took off for Topeka and the services of an old friend. A bead of perspiration broke out on his forehead. Looked like it was getting to be about that time of year again.

He slowed the team to a steady gait. "Sorry, Miss Clark. But I thought you might want to hurry back to the hotel and change."

She removed her arms and with one hand tried to retain

her modesty, and, with the other, to keep her wide hat on the top of her head. Without her touch, her warmth, Coulter felt a sudden chill, a sense of loss—a sense of relief.

"At the rate you and your deputy are ruining my wardrobe, I won't have a decent thing left to wear. Wouldn't your precious town be shocked if I have to give my lectures in my unmentionables?"

Her words conjured up a myriad of images, all provocative, all delicious. All forbidden. "I'll bet you wouldn't have any trouble getting the men to attend. They might even sign the pledge for you."

"Ohhh," she groaned. "You . . . You *man*."

Coulter tilted one thick eyebrow. "Thank you, ma'am. I hadn't thought you'd noticed. Why, I would even attend a lecture or two, just to watch the show."

The prettiest shade of pink touched her cheeks. It made her look young, vulnerable, innocent. He was almost sorry he'd doubted her. Almost. Not quite.

"Oh, I noticed, all right. You're just like the rest of the male species. You're big, tough behemoths, who think you can run rough shod over all women." She faced him with a boldness few men even dared. "But mark my words, there will come a day when women will have the vote. Then we'll see who's so high and mighty."

"Calm down Miss Clark. Since I'm responsible for the damage to your gown, I'll take it to a dressmaker tomorrow and have it repaired. Meanwhile, you can just change into something else, and spend the afternoon with my aunt and uncle."

"Plus your child and the reverend."

The smile vanished from Coulter's face. Something knotted in his chest. Was it the thought of her being with the minister, or with his daughter? What she did was of no interest to him except where it concerned his child. He slanted a glance into her clear, blue eyes. Yes, he decided, his emotions ruling his head, Cathy would be more than safe with Miss Josephine Clark. But would the reverend? Or Coulter?

In a few short minutes, they traveled the half mile from the church to the main street of Council City. Most of the businesses were closed in honor of the Sabbath, with only the hotel open. He had allowed the cowboys to have their rowdy Saturday night in the saloons and bars, but he'd had the town pass a law against selling liquor on Sunday. After all, even the law needed a day of rest.

As he started down Main Street, Coulter changed his mind and turned the wagon into the alley that led to the rear of the hotel. "You can run up the back stairs and change your gown. I'll wait for you in the lobby. Then I promise to take you directly to my aunt's home." As the wagon came to a stop, she jumped down, landing on the ground with the grace and agility of a ballet dancer.

"That won't be necessary, Sheriff. I'm sure I can find other transportation to the Marche home." With a haughty tilt of her chin, she gripped her sagging skirt to retain her modesty. "Good day, sir," she said as the door slammed behind her bustled derriere.

Coulter removed his hat and fanned his heated face. *Yes, sir,* he thought as she disappeared behind the closed door, *there goes trouble.* But Coulter Steele had never run from trouble, and he wasn't about to start, at the advanced age of thirty-four.

Chapter 3

Josie fumed all the way up the stairs, her temper rising with every step. The man was a backwoods bumpkin with no manners whatsoever. While she rummaged through her trunk for a fresh gown, she blessed him out in every ladylike euphemism in her vocabulary. For good measure she added a few names no real lady would even know.

She pulled out a blue-and-white-striped day frock trimmed with Irish lace and tiny pearl buttons. Like most of her wardrobe, this gown was several years out of fashion, a legacy from a past life where beautiful clothes were important and necessary. Here on the Kansas prairie, few women, if any, would notice that her wardrobe was less than up-to-date. Her clothes were clean and well-made, if now a little frayed around the edges.

Out of habit, she studied her image in the foggy mirror above the bureau. The scooped neckline and short, puffed sleeves were much cooler than the linen suit the sheriff had torn. The insufferable man had her nerves on edge and her temper flaring. He didn't trust her, that much was obvious. Well, she didn't like or trust him, either.

She picked up a straw hat trimmed with blue ribbon to match her dress, and thought about the sheriff. He was too big, too bold, and too attractive. And she didn't at all like the way tingles raced over her skin every time he looked at her with those dark, all-knowing eyes. Or when he touched her arm, even in the most innocent manner. For her sake and the sake of the S.A.A.T., she'd best stay out of his path.

Her hat tied firmly under her chin, she opened the door and paused in the hallway. With a quick glance to the front stairs that led to the lobby where he'd promised to wait for her, she darted to the rear entrance. The livery stable was only a short distance from the hotel and she was certain she could arrange her own transportation—or she would walk. Josie Clark didn't want or need the sheriff's help.

She eased open the door, checking to make sure that his rig was gone. Smiling at her clever move, she hurried down the alley toward the livery. At the end of the building a shadow fell across her path.

"Didn't take you long, now, did it, Miss Clark?" Sheriff Coulter Steele stepped away from the shelter of the building and tossed his cigarette into the street. "Most women take forever to select a gown and change." His dark gaze slid over her with a boldness that bordered on insolence. "I admit, you look most fetching in that dress. Brings out that rosy glow in your cheeks and that blue is the exact color of your eyes."

Taken by surprise, Josie faced him with her mouth agape. "You said you would wait for me in the lobby."

"And you were supposed to meet me there. But I figured you'd try to pull a fast one on me, so I decided to beat you at your own game." He gestured to the wagon waiting a few yards behind him.

Josie growled deep in her throat. She hated to be outsmarted—least of all by an arrogant, know-it-all man. Lifting her skirts, she stalked to his buggy, and without giving him a chance to help her, hauled herself up into the seat. With a brazen flip of her skirt, she tucked the material close to her legs, determined to protect at least one of her dresses against imminent destruction. "Well?" She cast a sullen look in his direction. "I believe your aunt is expecting me to dinner."

A self-satisfied smile on his face, he climbed in beside her. "Yes, ma'am, I believe she is." He snapped the reins and the horses took off at a trot.

The few miles to the Marche home seemed like a hundred to Josie. She gripped the side of the buggy to keep from touching him. A cold silence hovered between them. Josie wasn't about to be the first to speak, and she certainly didn't want to endure any interrogation.

The early-afternoon sun bathed them in its heat, and she was grateful for the wide-brimmed hat; only a parasol would have been better. They passed several small farms, with golden wheat waving in the breeze. Few trees dotted the landscape, mostly along the streams or surrounding the homesteads. Kansas was a flat land, rich and fertile. Josie knew there was still a certain amount of hostility between the cattlemen and farmers, but for now, they were trying to live together. Something told her that Coulter Steele was one of the reasons for the relative peace in the area.

He turned off the road onto a narrow lane. A row of oaks lined the path to a two-story wood-frame house painted white with dark green shutters. Pots of red geraniums and green ferns lined a long front porch. Cathy jumped off the swing and waved at her father. The girl's wide smile brought a twinge to Josie's heart. Josie remembered how much she'd loved her papa and how much she still missed him.

Coulter tugged on the reins. "Miss Clark," he said, his voice harsh.

She swung her gaze to him. "Yes, Sheriff?"

He shoved back his Stetson and narrowed his eyes. "Just a word of warning. The men in Council City like their liquor hard and their women soft. They might not take too kindly to a stranger coming in and trying to change things."

"I'll take my chances. Good day, sir." With that, she leaped from the buggy and strolled to the porch where the child waited. Cathy caught Josie's hand, waved good-bye to her father, and escorted Josie into the house.

At five o'clock that evening, Coulter threw down his brush in disgust. On a long, exasperated sigh, he turned from the painting and lit up a cigarette. Taking a deep draw of the tobacco that usually settled his nerves, he studied his latest painting—not nearly up to the standards he'd set for himself. To an unpracticed eye, the landscape depicting the cowboys seated around the campfire seemed perfect. He'd added all the details, the horses grazing in the background, the sweep of mountains. It was the kind of painting that sold well in the Eastern gallery. But something was missing. For some reason the painting lacked heart, passion.

Since he'd lost his precious Ellen, Coulter had sought solace in his work. He'd always loved painting. Next to his child, his art was his greatest pleasure. Pouring his soul into his brushes, paint, and canvas, he was able to get through the long nights without his wife.

Angry with his inability to complete the task, he studied the sketch that had taken him from his work. Every time he'd reached for a dab of paint, his hand had instead picked up the colored pencil and moved of its own accord over the paper. A pretty face smiled back at him, the blue of her eyes soft and seductive. He saw a worldliness in those eyes—eyes that had seen much more than had most women her age. Instead of the silly hat, he'd sketched a row of feathers in her golden hair. Somehow the ornaments suited her. He only wished he could remember where he'd seen Miss Clark before.

He snuffed out the cigarette, and dropped a cloth over the oil painting. There was no use tormenting himself when the muse wasn't there. On instinct, he folded the sketch and shoved it into his shirt pocket. Given enough time, he would remember.

He'd promised to pick up Miss Bettington and Cathy after the rally at the church. In the next few hours, he faced the host of ranch chores he'd neglected that afternoon. He left the loft and entered the barn. After milking the cow, he changed his mind. The rest of the chores would have to wait. He hurried to the house to wash up and change clothes.

Miss Clark had planned her lecture for six. It wouldn't hurt to keep an eye on the lady. As sheriff, of course, as part of his job. Not because she was so blasted pretty he couldn't get her out of his mind.

An hour later, Coulter joined the other men outside the church waiting for their women. The sun was ending its daily journey across the sky and the evening breeze had chased away the heat of the day. Several farmers were gathered around the bed of a buckboard, passing the time with a poker game. They waved for Coulter to join them, but he declined. He spied Oscar seated on the church steps with Homer.

"Why aren't you inside enjoying the lecture?" Coulter asked, a smile in his voice.

Oscar laughed and shifted over for Coulter to join them. "It's bad enough my wife started this whole shebang. I'd never get reelected if the men saw me inside with them."

From the open windows, the words of "Bringing in the

Sheaves" wafted on the evening breeze. Above the off-key voices of the women, one voice rang out loud and clear. A sweet sensation settled in the center of Coulter's chest. The voice of an angel reached out and gripped him with its power.

Angel? The word hit him like the kick of a mule to his midsection. He knew where he'd seen her before. No, not in person, but a poster, a handbill of a beautiful woman with feathers in her hair. "Well, I'll be hornswoggled," he muttered.

"What?" Homer asked. "What'd you say, Coulter?"

Coulter waved him off. "Nothing. I was just thinking out loud."

After the music ended, Miss Josephine Clark began her planned lecture. Coulter leaned against the wall and listened to her words that carried out into the churchyard. Her impassioned speech denounced the evils of drink and reminded the women of the destruction alcohol causes the home and family. It was their responsibility to rid the town of the demon menace that had invaded it. He halfway listened, his mind on the sketch in his pocket.

"See, Coulter, I told you she was a troublemaker." Homer's harsh words brought him out of his thoughts.

Now Miss Clark was organizing the women. "Meet me tomorrow evening here at the church for further instructions. Do you have any questions?" she asked.

Coulter decided it was time to intervene. A lecture was one thing, but he didn't want trouble. He stepped through the open door into the dim interior. Miss Clark was standing near the pulpit looking every bit like a fiery evangelist on a crusade. Her blue eyes were glowing and a pink tint colored her cheeks. She could pose for a painting of Joan of Arc on a mission.

He stopped for a moment, mesmerized by the passion in her eyes and the fire in her voice. Either she firmly believed in her cause, or she was an exceptional actress. Or both.

"Miss Clark," Coulter called. The heads of every woman turned in his direction. At the front pew, Reverend Harris jumped to his feet. "Are you planning to lead these good ladies on a march through our fair town?" the sheriff inquired.

She squared her shoulders, tightening the front of her softly feminine gown over her bosom. He bit back a groan. Fire flashed from the depths of her blue eyes. "For your information, Sheriff Steele, I am planning a peaceful gathering of women." She slanted her gaze to the minister and granted him a tiny smile. "Any man who wishes to join us, of course, is welcome. Although women may not yet have the vote, according to the Constitution of the United States, we have the right to assemble peacefully."

He shoved back his hat and studied the group. His aunt and daughter were in the front row, and Irene Potts sat in the rear with Miss Bettington. The preacher was the only man in attendance. For a brief moment, Coulter wondered if the man was more interested in the temperance movement or in the temperance lecturer. "Yes, ma'am, I'm aware of your rights. I just don't want any trouble."

As he'd feared, his aunt stood and pointed a finger at him. "Coulter Steele, we aren't looking for trouble. It's the drunks and saloon owners who cause trouble. If you want to lecture somebody, go to the Golden Garter, or to the Longhorn Bar, and do your job. Leave law-abiding citizens alone."

"That's right, Sheriff!" another woman shouted. "Leave us alone and go chase outlaws."

A chorus of female voices bombarded him. Miss Clark remained silent, a smug smile on her face, and her hands folded demurely in front of her skirt. Knowing he was licked, Coulter held up his hands in surrender. "All right,

ladies, just make sure you don't cause any trouble." He
backed away, and returned to the safety of the outdoors.

The men had gathered around the steps, waiting for a
word from Coulter. He shrugged and shook his head. "I
can't stop them from meeting, men. Guess it's up to you
to control your women."

A loud groan rumbled through the crowd. From the
looks of the women inside, he felt sorry for the men who
had to deal with a bunch of fired-up harpies.

"My mother's in there," Homer said. "With her lumbago and her heart condition, this could be bad for her
health."

Oscar laughed. "Don't worry, Homer. Irene's been taking care of herself for nigh onto . . . Well, I don't want to
say how many years." He pulled a liquor bottle out of his
coat pocket. "Here, have a drink, it'll settle your nerves."
After taking a long swig, he passed the liquor to Homer.
"By the way, how did you get that little mouse on your
eye?"

Homer coughed and sputtered. "Went down my windpipe," he muttered. "I got the black eye in the line of
duty." He shot a glance at Coulter. "I was making an
arrest."

Coulter refused the bottle when it came his way. He bit
his lip to keep from laughing. While Miss Clark was inside
marshaling her troops against drinking, the men were outside passing a bottle. Her battle was lost before it had
begun.

A few minutes later, the ladies filed out of the building.
Oscar grabbed the now-empty bottle and stashed it away
under the steps. The men pasted innocent expressions on
their faces and greeted their women.

Coulter stood to the side and waited for his housekeeper
to show her face. She appeared with Irene Potts, both
ladies speaking intimately. He suspected Irene was trying
to match her son with the spinster housekeeper.

"I just don't like it at all, Irene," Miss Bettington was saying, her mouth puckered into a frown. "Homer said she's trying to cause trouble."

"Oh, hush, Harriet, it's up to the women to carry on the fight against drunkenness. We owe it to our families, to our town, to our country." Irene's voice rose with every word. She waved her fist, ready to do battle.

Coulter groaned. His aunt, Miss Clark, and Cathy were the last to exit. Cathy's hand was firmly clasped to Miss Clark's and a look of adoration glittered in her eyes. Preacher Harris followed on her heels. Coulter didn't like it one little bit.

"Ready to go home, pumpkin?" He stretched his hand to his daughter, while striving to ignore the golden-haired woman.

"I guess so, Papa," she said, the smile fading from her lips. "Good night, Miss Clark. Will you come to my house and see me one day? I promise to be good."

Miss Clark brushed a stray lock of dark hair from Cathy's face, a gentle, maternal gesture that made his heart trip. "I don't know where you live, but maybe I can get your aunt to take me for a visit real soon."

"That would be wonderful, wouldn't it, Papa?" she asked turning her gaze to Coulter.

He met Miss Clark's eyes, as deep and fathomless as the azure sea. *A man could drown in those eyes,* he thought, *if he wasn't careful.* But if Coulter Steele was anything, it was careful, especially where women were concerned. "If it's what you want, sweetheart."

"Sheriff, it's nearly dark," Miss Bettington said, pulling his attention from the woman in front of him. "We had best be on our way."

Coulter picked up his daughter. "Papa," she moaned. "I'm too big for you to carry me." In spite of her protests, Cathy looped her arms around his neck and buried her head in his shoulder.

He nuzzled her neck. "Pumpkin, you'll never be too big for me to handle." Glancing over Cathy's shoulder he spied the wistful look on Miss Clark's face. As soon as their gazes met, she turned away and hurried toward Oscar's rig.

"Good night, Miss Clark," Cathy shouted.

"Sweet dreams, love," the lady answered in turn.

Coulter set Cathy in the rear of the wagon and climbed in beside Miss Bettington. He watched as Reverend Harris offered a hand to Josie and assisted her into the seat. He ignored the strange pang in his chest and released the hand brake.

"Are you planning to attend the rally tomorrow night, Miss Bettington?" he asked. With a quick snap of the reins and a loud "Yaw!" the team headed toward home.

If possible, Miss Bettington sat up even straighter. "Absolutely not, Sheriff. I don't believe a woman has any place telling a man what to do. In my opinion, a woman's place is in the home." She let out a loud snort. "You had better keep an eye on that woman. I guarantee she'll cause nothing but trouble."

His hand covered the folded sketch in his pocket. "Yes, ma'am. I intend to do exactly that."

Chapter 4

At promptly nine o'clock the next morning, Josie stepped across the dusty threshold into the sheriff's office. She lifted the ruffled hem of her dark calico skirt to avoid the muddy bootprints that led the way across the floor. She'd specifically chosen the skirt and pristine white shirtwaist, buttoned to her chin and at her wrists. The demure cameo at the throat added the perfect touch for her appearance before the judge.

Years of training had taught her not only how to make an entrance, but the importance of costume to a performance. She'd even taken care to twist her bright hair into the most sedate of buns. Her only other jewelry were tiny pearl earrings, a gift from Papa for her tenth birthday. A pert straw sailor hat completed the ensemble.

Nearly a dozen men crowded the small room, talking loudly among themselves. One by one they swung their glances her way. The murmur of voices dimmed. Those seated, leaped to their feet, knocking over chairs in a chorus of loud bangs. Men tugged off their hats and more than a few combed fingers through their hair.

Coulter Steele and Homer Potts snapped to attention. Homer's mouth gaped open; Coulter rolled his eyes heavenward. The comical looks on their faces almost made Josie laugh out loud. From behind the desk Oscar Marche glanced up. She hid her own surprise with a modest smile.

After a brief moment, he smoothed over his shocked expression and leaped to his feet. "Miss Clark, please come in." He shooed a young man from a chair and held it for Josie to be seated. "To what do we owe the pleasure of your company?"

Coulter nearly tripped over his own high-heeled boots hurrying toward her. "I suggested that Miss Clark stop by this morning for a visit. I'll escort her back to her hotel." He caught her elbow and nearly lifted her from the chair.

Bewildered by the sheriff's strange behavior, Josie kept her seat and waved him off. "Suggested, Sheriff? You ordered me to appear at nine o'clock to stand trial. I believe it's nine, I'm here, but where is the judge?"

On a groan, Coulter gestured to Oscar. "Meet our justice of the peace."

She dropped her gaze to the ornate bronze plaque on the sheriff's desk. There it was: Oscar W. Marche, Mayor and Justice of the Peace. Schooled to control her expressions, she gave Oscar a tiny, shy smile, one guaranteed to win him to her side. How ironic; yesterday Oscar Marche was her gracious host, today he was her judge.

Oscar glared at Coulter over the rim of his eyeglasses. "What's going on, Sheriff? What is Miss Clark talking about?"

"She committed a crime, Mayor," Homer said, shoving a sheet of paper into his hands. "It's right here in my report."

Before Oscar could take the sheet, Coulter snatched it away. "It was a mistake. We're dropping the charges."

Josie, along with the men, watched the show with rapt attention. The paper passed from hand to hand like the ball in a lawn-tennis match. After his stern warning of the day before, Coulter's odd turnaround flabbergasted her.

"You can't do that." Homer made a stab for the paper.

Oscar rapped a large gavel on the desk. "Order. Order in my court!" The room turned deadly silent. Even Homer snapped his mouth shut. "I'll take that report, Sheriff, if you don't mind," the mayor ordered.

With a shrug of his wide shoulders, Coulter passed the paper to Oscar, then propped his hip against Homer's desk. Josie sneaked a glance at him. His mouth curved downward and a muscle twitched in his jaw. Dark eyes shot dire warnings her way. He folded his arms across his chest. He'd rolled the sleeves of his plaid shirt to the elbows, and the sinewy muscles in his forearms bulged with tension. A strange tingle raced over her skin.

"Miss Josephine Clark." At the sound of her name, Josie shifted her attention to Oscar. "It says here you've been charged with disturbing the peace, inciting a riot, and assaulting an officer. These are very serious charges, young lady." He whipped his eyeglasses off and turned to the lawmen. "Which of you officers did this lady assault?" Shaking his head, he answered his own question. "Never mind. Homer, I suppose that's how you got your black eye."

Behind Josie, the men began to snicker and she barely controlled a grin. Homer's hand went to his eye and his face turned blood-red. Coulter merely shook his head.

The twinkle in Oscar's eyes told Josie she had nothing to worry about. "How do you plead, Miss Clark? Guilty or not guilty?"

"We're dropping the charges, Oscar," Coulter repeated, his voice icy.

Again, Oscar banged the gavel. "Sheriff, as long as I'm

in charge, I'll make the decisions." He lifted his gaze to Josie. "What do you have to say for yourself, Miss Clark?"

"Why, of course I'm innocent, Your Honor." She lowered her eyelashes with just the right amount of humility, then lifted her gaze to meet his. Sensuality, honesty, innocence, she rolled them all in one contrived glance. Taking advantage of a receptive audience, she twisted her handkerchief in her fingers, then dabbed the corners of her eyes. The effect wasn't lost on Oscar. But she didn't dare glance at Coulter, certain he saw right through her act.

"There, there, my dear," Oscar said. "Can you tell me exactly what happened Saturday night?"

"I'll tell you what happened, Mayor Marche," Homer interrupted.

Oscar cut him off with another bang to the desk. "Deputy, I was addressing Miss Clark. When I want to hear you, I'll ask. Let me hear your side, Josie, my dear."

A man behind Josie chuckled loudly. "Let's hear how this great, big, tough outlaw beat you to a pulp, Deputy."

"Order!" Oscar shouted. "I'll lock all of you up for contempt of court, including you, Homer."

Josie knew she'd won when Oscar used her given name. She bit back a smug grin. "As you know, Your Honor, your wife invited me to Council City on behalf of my work with the S.A.A.T." A sly reminder of his wife should certainly sway him her way. What man wanted to face an irate crusader like Bertha Marche?

"I arrived in your lovely town last Saturday evening. First I checked in to the hotel, then I decided to have a quick look around—to get my bearings, to spy out the lay of the land, so to speak. As I was passing in front of some noisy saloon, a drunken man staggered into me." For effect, Josie fanned her face with her handkerchief.

She chanced a look at Coulter and the incredulous expression on his face. After clearing her throat, she continued. "He grabbed me by the waist and spilled his beer all over my gown. Believe me, Your Honor, I was mortified. My lovely dress ruined, and I was being mauled by a drunk." With lowered eyelids, she covered her heart with her hands. "I suppose my temper got the better of me— it's a curse, I suppose. My temper, I mean. I swung at him with my reticule. By then another man had come out of the bar, and he shoved the first man away. Before I realized what was happening I was surrounded by men and some-one grabbed for me. Of course, a lady has to defend herself, so I swung with my fists. I had no idea the man who had accosted me was the deputy sheriff—him." She pointed to Homer, who by now had his crimson face buried in his hands.

"Let me understand, Miss Clark." Humor glittered in Oscar's eyes as he struggled to keep from laughing. "You're how tall? Five feet five inches? I admit that's a little tall for a woman, but Homer must top you by at least five inches and he has to have at least twenty or thirty pounds on you. And *you* blackened *his* eye."

Laughter rumbled through the room. A bit of sympathy for the deputy touched Josie. But a reminder of the night spent in the jail cell chased away even that. "Actually, he should be thankful I didn't use my knee."

That brought a series of groans from the men, along with any number of snickers. Even Coulter's lips twitched. "He sure is lucky," someone yelled. "Or Homer would be singing high soprano and walking mighty funny."

"Then he arrested me, and *I* spent the night in jail while the drunk went right back into the saloon."

With that, Oscar came to his feet. "Jail?" All humor faded from his face. He swung toward Coulter and Homer, waving the gavel like a club. "You arrested this young lady and locked her up in that pigsty? This is the woman your aunt invited to Council City as her guest."

"We didn't know," Coulter said between his teeth.

"And I suppose you didn't know she was a lady. A woman

has no business being locked up." He pounded the desk so hard, coffee splashed from his cup onto the desk. "Not guilty. Case dismissed."

A cheer and round of applause rose from the spectators. This time Josie let a wide smile curve her lips, but she resisted the urge to take a bow. She stood and stretched out a hand to Oscar. "Thank you, Your Honor."

Oscar took her hand and patted it gently. He winked at her and said, "Now, you stay out of trouble, Josie, you hear? Bertha and I are expecting you to have dinner with us this afternoon."

She laughed. "Since I won't be incarcerated, I'll be delighted to accept your generous hospitality."

Then, with a proud toss of her head, she glanced at the sheriff. "Good day, gentlemen."

Judging by the look on his face, Coulter Steele would gladly strangle her, and Homer Potts fingered the gun at his hip. Josie knew it was time to make her exit and drop the curtain on this appearance.

She'd barely made it to the door, when Coulter's voice stopped her. "I'll walk you back to your hotel, Miss Clark," he said. "I wouldn't want a drunk or some wild cowboy to accost you again."

"That won't be necessary, Sheriff." She shrugged off his hand. "As you can see, I'm quite capable of defending myself."

He dropped his hand and opened the door. "Oh, I can see that. I meant, I have to protect the men in my town from a well-aimed knee."

Once on the boardwalk, he pressed his fingers to the small of her back and guided her toward the hotel. "That was quite an act you put on for Oscar. I haven't seen so fine a performance since *Romeo and Juliet* in St. Louis. Just one look in those big baby-blues and the prosecution didn't stand a chance."

She stumbled at the mention of a performance. He

couldn't possible know. The Kansas prairie was a thousand miles from New York, and Council City hundreds of miles from Chicago. That world was a lifetime ago. "Are you my prosecutor, Sheriff?"

With a soft chuckle, he increased the pressure at her back. "No, ma'am, I'm just a simple lawman. But if you'd have told me my aunt had invited you to town, we could have saved all of us a lot of trouble."

She stopped in front of Marche's General Store, which was next to Marche's Emporium, and nodded to several women coming out with baskets full of goods on their arms. After the ladies passed out of earshot, she planted her hands on her hips and confronted the sheriff. "I had no idea Mrs. Marche was your aunt. When I go into a town, I expect to be treated like any other woman." Looking up into his strong, handsome face, she asked, "Do you arrest every strange woman who comes into Council City?"

With one long, paint-stained finger, he brushed a stray wisp of hair from her cheek. The unexpected touch brought a tingle to her skin. "No, only the ones who cause trouble and attack the deputy."

Josie groaned. "I'm sorry about that. But Homer asked for it. He wouldn't listen to a word I said. Said I could tell it to the sheriff."

His eyes turned a warm chocolate-brown. "You've made an enemy of Homer. He doesn't take too kindly to being mocked, and I'm afraid when word gets around that you bested him in a fight, he'll be gunning for revenge."

"Sheriff, don't worry about me. I don't intend to remain in Council City long. After I organize Mrs. Marche and her troops, I'll be moving on to another town."

Her own words brought a twinge of regret. After moving from town to town all her life, Josie wondered if it was time to settle in one place—to make a home for herself.

He twisted the stray hair around his finger and studied it. "How long do you suppose that will be?"

His gentle touch had her heart doing acrobats like the trapeze performers in the circus. "A week or so."

Taking her arm in his, he continued down the street. "Then I suppose I'll have to keep an eye on you." He stopped in front of the hotel. "By the way, I believe I owe you a repair job on a couple of gowns."

"I can handle them myself, Sheriff. I suppose I'm as much at fault as you and Homer."

Her arm still locked in his, he continued into the lobby of the hotel. "I gave you my word, and a man isn't anything unless he keeps his promises."

Josie glanced around, thankful that the lobby was empty. "Wait here, and I'll bring them down."

A rumble of soft laughter sent delicious tingles through her. "And have you sneak out the back door again? I'll escort you upstairs."

Knowing it was useless to argue with the stubborn man, she led the way to her second-floor room. At the door she stopped and slid the key into the lock. "Wait here," she ordered. "It wouldn't do my reputation any good if you were caught with me in my hotel room."

Heated sparks flashed in his eyes. "No, ma'am, it wouldn't do mine any good, either."

She hurriedly gathered both gowns she'd left thrown over a chair the day before. Through the open door, she noticed the way he leaned against the wall, his hat shoved back, and his thumbs tucked in his gun belt. The man was just too ruggedly masculine, and she doubted he cared a fig about his reputation.

"Here they are." She shoved her dresses into his hands.

"I'll tell Miss Mabel you need these back as soon as possible, since you're leaving town in a few days."

"Thank you, Sheriff."

"See you around, Angel." With a jaunty tip of his hat, he was gone.

For a long moment, Josie studied his strong back and

long, loose-legged walk as he sauntered toward the rear stairs. His voice rang over and over in her ears.

Angel. He'd called her *Angel.*

Did he know? Or was it only a pet name he'd pulled out of the sky? It didn't really matter. Angel LeClare was gone, and Josie Clark was here working for a worthy cause. In a few days she would be gone. Until then, all she had to do was stay out of Sheriff Steele's path. She suspected that was easier said than done.

Coulter heard the commotion long before he spied the women. The loud boom of a bass drum rumbled above the chorus of female voices raised in song. He stepped onto the boardwalk and waited for the army of temperance workers to round the corner from Elm Street onto Main.

More for their protection than anything else, he'd deputized Oscar and several other men and stationed them along the route from the church into town. He'd chosen to remain near the Golden Garter, which he suspected was their target.

The warm glow of sunset cast long shadows over the dusty street. Pale yellow light spilled from the windows and bat-wing doors of the saloon and bars as they geared up for their nightly entertainment. Several men lounged against the posts outside the general store waiting for the show to begin. Coulter removed the red kerchief from his neck, wiped the bead of sweat from his forehead, then shoved it into his rear pocket. He would rather face the James gang barehanded than deal with a single crusading woman like Miss Josie Clark.

"Bringing in the sheaves, bringing in the sheaves . . ." The rousing chorus filled the air. The lead woman rounded the corner—Josie Clark, as expected. Behind her came the bass drum and several dozen other fire-breathing females.

Reverend Harris and two meek husbands brought up the rear.

Coulter leaned against a hitching post and watched Miss Clark in action. Her head held high, she marched straight for her goal. He wondered about her. What made a pretty and talented woman get mixed up in a reform movement? She simply didn't fit the mold of a crusader.

Seconds later, the female throng reached the boardwalk in front of the Golden Garter. They stopped and crowded the entrance. A couple of cowboys, obviously unaware of the demonstration, halted their horses at the watering trough. They dismounted and started toward the saloon. Miss Clark blocked their way. The bass drum stopped and the singing ceased.

Miss Clark's voice rang clear across the street. "Go back to your homes. This place of evil and sin will lead you down the path to destruction."

The cowboys roared with laughter. "Lady, we like sin and evil and we sure could use some company. How about joining us in some fun?" Taking a step forward, they shoved their way toward the door.

Coulter picked up his pace and crossed the street. With Miss Clark's temper, anything could happen, and he didn't want violence. If Homer's shiner was any indication, the cowboys would come out on the losing end of a confrontation.

The lady stood her ground in front of the other women. Their arms locked together barring the entrance, the women broke out in song. By then Tony Sanders, proprietor of the Golden Garter, had stepped through the batwing doors.

"You're blocking the doors. Get away from here," he yelled above the women's voices.

"Yield not to temptation, for yielding is sin, / Each vic'try will help you, some other to win . . ."

The cowboys laughed and grabbed Miss Clark around

the waist. "Come on, pretty lady, let's do some sinning together."

Josie's face paled. In a clearly reflexive movement, she reared back and with one blow connected with the startled man's jaw. He staggered back several feet, his mouth agape in shock. Coulter reached her the second she lifted her knee. He caught her from the back, staying well out of her line of fire.

"That's enough, Miss Clark. I'll not have a riot tonight."

She swung to face him. "We have a right to be here, Sheriff. This is a free country."

"Get them away from here, Coulter," Sanders shouted behind them. "They're trespassing."

"As long as we remain on the public boardwalk, you can't arrest us for trespassing." She struggled against his grip. The song of the other women died in the threat of a melee.

His aunt stepped forward and placed her hands on her ample hips. "Go away, Sheriff, we won't stop until our town is as dry as the Sahara Desert."

"Bertha, come down from there this instant." Now Oscar had joined the fracas. "I'm the mayor, and I order you to stop this nonsense."

Bertha took Josie's other arm. *"Yield not to temptation . . ."* she sang—loud and out of tune.

Other men gathered on the street and the boardwalk, waiting to see who would win the battle of wills. The wounded cowboy backed away, rubbing his bruised jaw. Coulter raised his voice to be heard above the din. "Ladies, you'll have to move on, you can't block a place of business."

Josie struggled against his grip. "We're staying here until we close down this hellhole and every one like it in the country."

"Then you're under arrest. All of you."

The women stopped singing, and a moan rumbled through the crowd. He glanced over the throng, women he'd known most of his life. Some had been friends of his mother, the younger women had been schoolmates, some he'd even called on a time or two. Besides his aunt, Irene Potts, lumbago and all, was part of the assembly. The reverend was at the rear, cowering in the shadows. All honest citizens, but they were breaking the law, and he'd sworn to uphold the peace.

"Then we'll gladly go to jail to support our cause." Josie lifted her voice. "Martha, hit that drum. We'll march to our destiny."

Head lifted high, Coulter's hand firmly on her arm, Josie Clark led her troop in time to the drumbeat. Undaunted, she began to sing.

"Onward, temperance soldiers, marching as to war. / With the flag of victory, leading on before . . ."

He shut his ears and set his jaw. The woman was certainly proving his prediction. Josie was trouble.

Trouble with a capital *T*.

Chapter 5

Not at all intimidated by the strong-willed sheriff, nor the catcalls of the watching men, Josie led her little army to jail. She hated the thought of these women being locked up, but their cause was worth the sacrifice. Coulter had his hand firmly attached to her arm, as if she would try to escape. A troop of men followed in the street, the husbands scolding their wives for their part in the march. Josie shut her mind to them, and sang even louder.

At the jail, Coulter opened the door and stood aside so the women could enter. As they flooded into the small room, they stopped singing.

"She didn't tell me we would go to jail," someone whispered behind her.

"I have babies," came another voice. One woman began to cry.

Josie threw back her shoulders and addressed her troops. "We have to stand together if we are to drive the devil from our community. Don't let this stop you. We'll spend the night if jail if we must."

"Ladies," Coulter raised his voice. "I don't want to keep you from your homes and families, so I'm going to release each of you into your husband's custody."

Josie stepped forward. "Sheriff, we're all adults; we're ready to stand for our rights."

His eyes narrowed and a muscle twitched in his jaw. "Miss Clark, I would advise you to be quiet while I settle this."

Irene Potts spoke up from the rear of the group. "I don't have a husband, Sheriff. Will I have to stay in jail?"

He sighed, clearly unhappy with the corner he'd been backed into. "No, ma'am. I'll release you to Homer."

"Sheriff—" Josie began.

With one hard look, Coulter cut her off. "I'll deal with you later, Miss Clark."

Josie stood to the side. She didn't want any of these women to suffer the indignity of spending the night in jail as she had to do. One by one the men entered and claimed their women. Each promised to be responsible for his wife's behavior and to keep her out of trouble. Homer glared angrily at Josie as he escorted his mother from jail. Irene's gait, which had been so strong and vibrant while marching, now slowed, and she leaned on her son's arm for support.

Oscar took a reluctant Bertha by the arm. Then he turned to Josie. "I'll take responsibility for Miss Clark, too."

"Thank you, Mr. Marche, but I've been responsible for my own actions for years."

Reverend Harris stepped forward. "Sheriff, I suppose you can release Miss Clark into my custody. I'm willing to vouch for her."

Coulter speared him with a cold stare. "Rev, I believe you were a part of the march. Therefore you're as guilty as Miss Clark or any of the ladies. I'll be glad to release you, but I don't think you need the added responsibility. You may leave."

"Sheriff, I merely went along with the group to offer my protection and support. I certainly do not condone violence." The preacher turned to Josie and took both her hands in his. His palms were smooth, as if he'd never done anything more strenuous than lift his Bible. "I'm sorry things turned out this way, Miss Clark. We'll plan another course of attack against the evils and sin in this town."

"That's quite all right, Reverend. There's more than one way to skin a cat, so to speak." She tugged her hands free.

He slanted a glance at the sheriff then turned back to Josie. "I hate leaving you here in this awful place."

"The lady will be fine, Rev. She's more than able to fend for herself." With the finesse of a barroom bouncer, the sheriff escorted the minister to the door.

Josie looked around and found herself alone with Coulter. He leaned against his desk and shoved his hat back off his forehead. A stray lock of brown hair tumbled toward his thick eyebrows. Josie twisted her fingers together to keep from brushing it away from his eyes. He wrinkled his brow. "Now, what do you suppose I'm going to do with you, Miss Clark?"

She folded her arms across her chest. "I suppose you'll have to lock me up for the night. I don't have a husband and I certainly don't want to burden Oscar or the reverend with a criminal like myself. Besides, I believe women should be able to stand for themselves. I'm an adult, and if women had the vote, I would be quite old enough."

"That presents a small problem."

"Problem?" She lifted one eyebrow.

"You see, if I lock you up, somebody has to stay here overnight. Homer had to take his mother home, and I promised my daughter I'd be home early. I can't deputize one of the men, because they're with their own wives. And I sure as heck don't want to face Oscar again if I do lock you up."

Josie glanced around the dingy jailhouse. She shivered at the thought of spending another night in this place. "You can release me into my own custody. I promise I won't run away overnight."

A wry smile curved his lips. "I'm not worried about your leaving town. What if you should decide to block the Golden Garter again, or cause another riot?"

"Sheriff, I did not cause a riot. I promise I'll go directly to my hotel."

"Nope." He shoved away from the desk. "I have a better idea. I'll release you into my custody. You can come out to my place tonight. That way I can see you don't cause any more trouble."

Josie's heart tripped. "Your place?"

"Don't get the wrong idea, Miss Clark. You'll be quite safe. It'll be perfectly harmless and aboveboard. Miss Bettington and my daughter are at home, two excellent chaperones." In a most gallant gesture, he offered his arm. "We'll pick up a bag from your hotel, and be on our way. I like to get home before my daughter goes to sleep."

"Don't I have anything to say in this matter?"

He tucked her arm in his. "No, ma'am, you don't."

"And if I refuse?"

"I'll simply hog-tie you, toss you over my shoulder, and throw you across the back of my horse."

Josie opened her mouth to protest his barbaric threats. At the stern expression on his face, she changed her mind. She had little doubt he would do exactly that, and nobody in the town would stop him. If anything, the men would cheer him on.

"Oh, all right. I guess it will at least be cleaner than the jail cell."

With a resigned shrug, she allowed him to lead her out

into the fresh night air. He might have stopped her mission tonight, but he couldn't keep her at his ranch forever. *We'll just see who has the last laugh, Mr. High and Mighty Sheriff,* she thought, a wicked grin sneaking across her face.

By the time Coulter drove the borrowed wagon halfway to his home, he'd already begun to doubt the wisdom of his decision. It had been a long time since he'd been alone in the moonlight with a beautiful woman. Even longer since he'd felt the heat stirring in his blood.

Although he hadn't remained celibate in the five years since Ellen's death, his encounters with women had been purely for physical release. He refused any emotional attachment. Yet with this woman, something new, yet as old as time was happening inside him.

Under the full moon, her hair shined like spun gold, and she smelled of rose water and French milled soap. From the brief times he'd touched her, he knew her skin was as smooth as silk.

Next to him, all warm and soft, she hummed the tune she'd been singing all evening. Occasionally, the words slipped from her pink lips. *"Yield not to temptation,"* then something about *"dark passions, subdue."*

She was tempting, all right. As appealing as that ripe red apple must have been to Adam.

More than once he fought back the inclination to pull off the road into a grove of trees and show the lady a thing or two about sin and passion. Of course, he would do no such thing. He'd given his word she could trust him. He tightened his grip on the lines until the leather straps cut into his palms. Anything to make his body obey his mind. Thoughts like that could only get him into trouble, and he had enough trouble with Miss Clark as it was.

As the gnawing in his gut grew unbearable, the lights from his house came into view. Being welcomed by a spin-

ster housekeeper every night was a far cry from having a
loving wife. But Ellen was gone, and nobody could ever
take her place in his heart.

"We're home," he said, stopping the buckboard in front
of the long narrow porch.

The lady stiffened her spine. "It's quite lovely, Sheriff.
Somehow . . . Never mind."

He laughed. "Thought I lived in a soddy, or a lean-to?
My father built this for my mother. I have three bedrooms
upstairs and a spacious living area down."

"Your parents? Do they live here?"

With a hard jerk, he pulled on the brake and tied off
the lines. He tore off his heavy gloves and tossed them on
the seat. "They were killed by Quantrill during his raid
on Lawrence back in 'sixty-three. They'd gone to visit
friends and got caught in the crossfire. I stayed home to
tend the ranch."

Her hand reached out and covered his. "I'm so sorry.
Is that why you became a lawman?"

Her touch offered compassion, warmth. He glanced at
her, trying to read her expression in the darkness. But he
didn't have to see her to know that genuine sympathy
glittered in her blue eyes. "In a way, yes. I do what I can
to protect the people from ruthless outlaws who kill for
the sheer pleasure of killing."

His voice had gotten harder, but Coulter couldn't stop
the bitterness from spewing out. For some odd reason, he
suspected she understood.

"The people in this county are very lucky to have you
as their protector."

"You didn't think that earlier."

She removed her hand. "Believe it or not, Sheriff, we're
on the same side. Only our methods are different."

"I suppose you have a point there." He jumped to the
ground and came around to her side. Without giving her
a chance to leap down on her own accord, he spanned

her waist with his hands and lifted her from the seat. Her hands fell to his shoulders and for a moment he held her suspended in the air, her face level with his. A coyote howled, a cow mooed, and the crickets chirped. But his thoughts were on the woman in his arms. What would she do if he tried to kiss her? Her lips parted, pink and ready.

"Sheriff—Sheriff Steele, is that you?" Miss Bettington's shrill call broke the spell created by the woman in his arms and his own unfulfilled needs.

The hinges on the front door squeaked. Miss Clark gasped, and Coulter eased her to the ground.

"Yes, ma'am." He bit back a groan. He wasn't sure what would have happened if the housekeeper hadn't chosen that moment to step onto the porch. But he sure was willing to find out.

Silhouetted in the doorway, the housekeeper planted her hands on her hips. "What's going on out there?"

"Miss Clark will be staying with us tonight." He caught her fingers and gave her encouraging squeeze. Lord knows, she'd need it, dealing with the straightlaced spinster.

"Staying? Here?" Miss Bettington's voice rose an octave. "Where will she sleep?"

Until now, Coulter hadn't given it much consideration. He escorted the ladies into the parlor. A kerosene lamp cast its yellow glow over Miss Bettington's Bible lying open on the table next to the rocker. Rubbing his hand across his jaw, the day's growth of whiskers bristly on his palm, he thought for a moment.

"I suppose in my room," he said, proud to have come up with the solution.

Both women swung to face him. Both women dropped their mouths open. Both women squealed at once, *"Your* room?"

"Hold it, ladies, before you both have conniption fits." He held up his hands to silence them. "I'll sleep on the davenport, or in the barn. Miss Clark can sleep in my bed—alone."

Miss Bettington folded her hands in front of her chest. "Sheriff, I am not prepared for . . . guests."

"Oh, don't concern yourself, Miss Bettington," Josie Clark said. "I'm not a guest, I'm a prisoner."

The woman's eyes widened, and she screwed up her mouth. "You've brought this . . . this hussy—a criminal— into your home, with a young, innocent child here. Not to mention a God-fearing woman like myself."

Josie set her hands on her hips; fire flashed in her eyes. "I am not a criminal, madam. I, too, am a God-fearing woman. All I did was lead a peaceful march. It isn't my fault that the men in this town are so fond of drink."

"I warned you she was a troublemaker, Sheriff." The housekeeper pointed an accusing finger at Josie.

"Ladies, please." Coulter struggled to control his laughter. As sheriff he'd stopped any number of brawls, but nothing was worst than a catfight between two hostile women. "Miss Clark is only here because . . . because . . ."
Because I'm an idiot.

"I didn't have a husband to assume responsibility for my actions. The sheriff generously offered to keep an eye on me so I wouldn't cause a riot in his quiet little town." She turned toward the stone fireplace and the picture of Ellen on the mantel. After a moment, she returned her gaze to the housekeeper. "I won't get in your way, Miss Bettington, and I promise not to corrupt either you or Cathy with my sinful presence. I'm certain the sheriff will release me tomorrow."

"That's enough, ladies. Miss Bettington, please consider Miss Clark a guest like any other I would invite into my home." He glanced up the darkened staircase. "Is Cathy in bed already?"

"Yes, she is. She was naughty this evening, so I sent her

to bed early. She has to be taught to act like a lady. I won't have her running around like some wild Indian.''

Coulter caught the woman's slur over his heritage, but he chose to ignore it. He didn't bother asking what offense his daughter had committed this time. It seemed that almost every day he received a different report of his child's unsociable behavior. He didn't understand how his sweet, loving daughter could be as disagreeable as the house-keeper claimed. Cathy definitely needed a mother.

His gaze shifted from the spinster in the severe black dress to Miss Clark, whose white shirtwaist and black skirt were every bit as simple. There the resemblance ended. It was like comparing a peacock to a crow. With her bright hair, her pink cheeks, and classic features, Miss Clark would shine in a feed sack. She looked all prim and proper. But he'd seen the passion smoldering in those blue eyes. And his reaction to that fire set his nerves on edge, and his body on slow burn.

"I'll get your bag and show you to your room." He spun on his heels and headed for the relative safety of the outdoors. After a few deep breaths, he told himself he was a fool to entertain any thoughts about Josie. She was nothing like his sweet, innocent Ellen. No woman could ever be as perfect as his wife, or take her place in his heart. Cathy might need a mother, but he sure didn't need a wife. Unfortunately, he couldn't have one without the other.

When he returned to the house, Miss Bettington remained statue-still in the same spot, while Miss Clark had traversed the room. She was studying the sketch of his mother, one he'd done when he was a mere boy of twelve. His father had liked it so well, he'd had the drawing framed and hung it on the wall for all the world to see. She looked up with a question in her eyes.

"My mother," he answered.

"She was very pretty."

He shrugged. "The drawing was done by an amateur; it doesn't do her justice."

She tilted her head from side to side. "A promising artist, I'm sure. Cathy resembles her a great deal."

Ignoring Miss Bettington, he gestured to the stairs. "I'll show you to your room, and pick up a few things for the barn." In those few seconds he'd decided that the loft in the barn was a much safer place than downstairs in the parlor. The more walls separating her from him, the better off he was.

At the head of the stairs, he gestured to his bedroom, the one his parents had shared, where he now slept alone. "The closed door is Miss Bettington's room, the other is Cathy's," he whispered.

He struck a match and lit the lamp on the hallway table. Without so much a glance at his wide bed with the feather mattress and patchwork quilt, he gathered clean clothes and a blanket. Josie had remained in the hallway, her gaze on Cathy's door.

"It's all yours, Miss Clark." He gestured to his room. "Sweet dreams."

"Thank you, Sheriff. Hope you enjoy the night in the barn."

He grunted. Looked like he was in for another sleepless night in the studio. "I'm sure I will."

Chapter 6

Josie waited in the hallway and listened until Coulter's footsteps faded on the stairs. Miss Bettington's shrill complaint, followed by Coulter's deep voice, drifted up to her. It wasn't as if she'd chosen to be there. And it served the insufferable man right if he had to spend a miserable night in the barn with his animals.

If only he trusted her just a little, she would be safely tucked into the hotel in town and he could have his own bed.

She turned toward the large bedroom—*his* room—when a small whimper drew her up short. At first she thought it came from downstairs, or from outdoors, like the sound of a small frightened animal. Straining to hear, she realized the noise had come from Cathy's room.

After a quick glance toward the staircase, she tip-toed to the partially open door, and peeked in. Darkness bathed the room, with only a thin stream of moonlight falling across the narrow bed. A small body lay huddled under the covers, not even a head showing. After hearing another tiny gasp, Josie picked up the kerosene lamp and ventured farther into the room.

Cathy must be having a nightmare, she thought. Quietly, she approached the bed. Sometimes eight-year-old girls needed nothing more than to be held and comforted.

She reached out a hand and touched the covered lump where a head should be. "Papa?" the weak muffled voice whispered.

"No, honey, it's Miss Josie. I didn't mean to wake you."

Cathy shifted the coverlet until only her eyes peeked out. "Miss Josie? What are you doing here?"

"Your papa invited me to spend the night," Josie said, stretching the truth a bit.

Without question, the little girl accepted the explanation. "Is Papa home?" Was that anxiety in the childish voice, or was she merely half asleep?

"He's out in the barn. He thought you were asleep, and he didn't want to disturb you." Josie set the lamp on a table and perched on the edge of the narrow bed. She brushed a stray lock of dark hair from Cathy's forehead. Trailing her fingers down the girl's smooth pink cheek, she felt the unmistakable stickiness of dried tears. Her heart went out to the motherless child. All too well, Josie remembered the nights she'd lain in bed, in a boarding-house or hotel, and wept for her mother. "Sweetheart, did you have a bad dream?"

She shook her head. "I . . . I couldn't sleep." Her voice cracked and one large tear trickled down her cheek.

A band tightened around Josie's chest. "Do you want me to get your papa?"

"No, please don't tell him."

The appeal in her tone bothered Josie. "Do you want me to lie with you until you go to sleep?"

"Will you, please? My mother used to let me sleep with her and Papa whenever I had a bad dream or when I was sick."

Josie stretched out on the blanket next to Cathy. "My mother died when I was a little older than you. Sometimes I still miss her."

"Papa said Mama went to heaven with my baby brother."

A tear burned in the back of Josie's eyes at the news. Her heart melted for Coulter, who had lost both a wife and child. All he and Cathy had left was each other. "Your father loves you very much."

"Will you marry Papa and be my new mother? I promise I'll be real good and you won't ever have to yell at me or give me a licking. And Papa won't have to send me to the 'sylum for bad girls."

Puzzled at the innocent appeal, Josie wrapped her arms around the child to comfort her. As her hand brushed Cathy's legs, the child flinched. "Honey, it's up to your papa who he marries." Carefully, she lifted the blanket. "Did you hurt yourself?"

"Yes," Cathy moaned. "I . . . I fell down."

Concerned for the child, Josie lifted the hem of her short nightgown and glanced at her legs. She stifled a gasp. Even in the pale glow in the darkened room, Josie spotted the marks on the child's white skin. Long red marks, like the ones she and Armand had received in the orphanage. Welts left by a strap. Anger churned inside Josie like storm clouds gathering over the ocean. Who would do such a horrible thing to the little girl? What kind of offense warranted such cruel punishment?

Cathy yanked the blanket to cover her legs. "Please don't tell Papa. I promise I'll be good. I don't want him to send me away."

"Go to sleep, sweetheart. Everything will be all right." But when Josie Clark got through with Coulter Steele, he would wish he'd never seen a strap. "I'll sing a little song my mama used to sing to me." Stretching beside the child, she struggled to keep her distress out of her voice.

"Hush, little baby, don't say a word, Papa's going to buy

you a mockingbird . . ." The words came automatically, but Josie's mind was on the man who had inflicted this pain on his only child. By the time Josie reached the last verse, Cathy's breathing was deep and even. She kissed the child's forehead and eased from the bed. "Don't worry, love," she whispered, "he won't get away with this."

Hands trembling, she picked up the lamp and set it on the hall table. She gritted her teeth to keep from screaming out. Ready to confront the problem head-on, she ran down the stairs into the parlor. Miss Bettington sat in the rocker, her Bible on her lap. Did the housekeeper know about the abuse? Did she condone it?

"Where's Sheriff Steele?" Josie asked, struggling to keep her voice even and calm.

"In the barn, I suppose."

Without even asking the direction of the barn, Josie rushed through the front doorway into the cool night air. It had to be somewhere at the rear of the house. Her cheeks burning with fury, she stepped from the porch and turned the corner of the house. Dark shadows loomed in the distance. The dim glow from an open doorway directed Josie to the barn. Not bothering to watch where she walked, Josie trudged across the yard toward the light. She didn't care what she stepped in or how damp the hem of her skirt got. Coulter Steele had better watch out. Josie Clark was on the warpath.

The smell of hay, horses, and manure assailed her as she entered the barn. Stalls lined the walls of the building, and the moo of a cow greeted her. A black horse stuck his head over a low door, and snorted. She jumped back, totally lost in the foreign place. From somewhere a man was whistling a tune that sounded amazingly like "Yield Not to Temptation."

"Sheriff Steele," she called. "Are you out here?"

His head popped out from one of the stalls. "Miss Clark, what a surprise." Wide shoulders followed, and a chest bare of clothing. Perspiration gave his skin the look of gleaming bronze. A wide smile snaked across his mouth. She'd been right about him being a magnificent specimen of manhood, but Josie knew that beauty was only skin-deep. Some of the most handsome men and most beautiful women she'd known were rotten clear down to their black hearts. Like Sheriff Coulter Steele.

She balled her hands until her nails bit into her palms. "I would like a word with you."

He tossed down a pair of dirty leather gloves and rested his chin on a pitchfork. "Had trouble sleeping alone in that big, comfortable bed? If you give me a minute or two, I could be talked into joining you."

"You low-down, no-good varmint! If I were a man I'd give you a thrashing you'd never forget!"

"What are you getting so riled about?" He puckered his brows and ran a hand through his messed hair. "I was only teasing."

Her gaze dropped to his chest where drops of sweat beaded on the dark hair that swirled around tight male nipples. The strength and power of his body sent a surge of heat through her. Josie quickly extinguished the growing fire by remembering the pain those robust muscles could inflict on a small girl.

She took one fearless step forward. "You don't deserve to wear a badge. Or do you hide behind the law so you don't have to stand up like a man?"

"What the hell's got you in such an uproar, Josie? You still mad because I stopped your march and sent the women home?" Tossing down the pitchfork, he took one step in her direction. By now they were inches apart, eyes locked like gladiators in the Coliseum.

"Oh, you're really good at bullying women and children, aren't you? But I'm not afraid of you." She poked a finger into the center of his bare chest. "And I'm a heck of a lot closer to your size than Cathy."

He shook his head as if to clear it. "What does my daughter have to do with whatever you're talking about?"

"Don't play dumb with me. Or did you think nobody would ever find out what you've done? Why, your poor departed wife would turn over in her grave if she knew!"

With one quick movement he snatched up his shirt and yanked it over his head. "Leave my wife out of this and tell me in plain English what you're talking about."

She was close enough to smell the perspiration and the hay that clung to his hair. "I'll spell it out, plain and simple. I know you've been beating your child with a strap."

He jerked back as if he'd been kicked in the head by a mule. "I *what*?"

Josie moved in, her face inches from his. If he wanted to strike her, she was more than willing to take the blow for the child. "I heard a noise in Cathy's room, and I went in to check on her. She was very upset, and she begged me not to tell her papa. You can't deny you threatened her. I saw the marks on her legs."

"Marks, what kind of marks?" He caught her arms and dug his fingers into the flesh.

Those powerful hands could break her in two if he became angry enough. But Josie wasn't about to back down. "Strap marks, where you beat her with a belt, or more likely a razor strop. I had my share of whippings when I was sent to the orphanage after my parents died. And I know how brutal they feel to a child. The physical pain goes away, but you never forget the humiliation that goes with the beating." The memory of the past, the fear for a beautiful little girl, brought unwanted tears to her eyes.

He shook her until her teeth rattled. "My God, woman, are you mad? What are you accusing me of? What kind of monster do you think I am? I've never laid a hand on my daughter in my life. She's all I have left of Ellen. I love her more than anything in this world." The rawness of his words tore through her.

His eyes darkened, and genuine pain glimmered in the midnight depths. She believed him. In that simple statement, he'd poured out his heart and bared his soul. "Coulter, I saw the marks and her tears."

"Josie, as God is my witness, I've never struck my child."

"Somebody did."

Coulter felt his world crumble around him. He tightened his grip on Josie's arms, his only anchor to reality. The jumble of her words swirled in his brain, then they all came together like the pieces of a jigsaw puzzle. And he didn't like the picture they formed.

"Miss Bettington." He forced her name past the tightening in his throat. "The bitch has been hurting my child."

Eyes wide, Josie stared at him. "You're accusing your housekeeper?"

"It makes sense. Since she came, Cathy hasn't been herself—she's been quiet, subdued. And not a day passes that I don't hear about the infraction of one rule or another." The burning in his gut reached clear to his throat. It was important that this woman believe him. That she support him. "I had no idea she was hitting my baby."

Josie's eyes glittered with unshed tears. "Coulter, what are you going to do?"

"Break the skinny bitch in half." The need for action surged through him. He released Josie, and picking up the pitchfork, flung it with all his strength. It entered a haystack against the wall. He wished it were Miss Bettington's evil heart.

As if a cloud had been lifted from his eyes, he saw the signs that had been staring him in the face for weeks. The woman talked about discipline, of needing to teach Cathy to be a lady. "I've been so caught up in my work, I ignored my child."

"I can't pass judgment on you or your housekeeper, but

I cannot in good conscience allow this to continue. Come up to the house, see for yourself, talk to Cathy." Josie set her hand on his arm, her touch warm and reassuring.

"If what you say is true, Josie, I'm afraid of what I'll do to that woman."

"God knows, I wish it wasn't true. And if I'm wrong, and Cathy hurt herself falling down, I'll spend the next week in your jail."

Coulter shook his head. Gut instincts told him Josie was right, that in his desperate need for a housekeeper he had ignored the truth. He squeezed her fingers and silently prayed for strength. "All right. Let's go."

Hands entwined, he led her toward the rear porch. The lamp still burned in the parlor, and through the open window he saw the housekeeper in the rocker reading her Bible. "We'll go up the back stairs."

Silently they climbed the narrow spiral stairs at the rear of the kitchen. He picked up the lamp and shoved open Cathy's door. His heart constricted at the sight of his daughter curled into a ball, her blanket clutched to her face. He didn't want to wake her, but he had to see for himself—he had to know the truth.

Josie motioned him to silence with her finger across her lips. Carefully she lifted the edge of the blanket.

Curled on her side, her nightgown twisted around her waist, Cathy couldn't hide the red welts on her legs below her short underpants. He recognized the marks for what they were.

Unable to endure the pain at seeing his child's injuries, he hurried back into the hallway and struggled to catch his breath. His skin grew cold and he thought he was going to be sick. Anger coiled in him like a snake ready to strike. Hands trembling, he returned the lamp to the table. Josie closed the door and waited at his side.

"I think it's time I had a little talk with Miss Bettington."

Without waiting for Josie to follow, he took the stairs

two at a time until he landed in the parlor. *Calm down,* he told himself. *Don't do anything rash.* With cold, steel determination, he faced the woman.

She closed her Bible and lifted her head in question. "Would you like a cup of coffee, Sheriff? I left the pot on the stove."

"No, ma'am," he said, determined to control his temper. "May I have a word with you?"

She lifted one narrow eyebrow and cast a glance past his shoulder at Josie standing in the shadows. "If we have something to discuss, Sheriff, I would prefer not to have an audience."

"I'll have a cup of that coffee, if you don't mind," Josie said. She disappeared into the kitchen before Coulter could stop her.

"Miss Bettington, I want to talk to you about my daughter. I would like to learn your views about discipline." Coulter jammed his hands into the rear pockets of his denims. Thankfully, he stood partially in the shadows so the fierce expression on his face wouldn't frighten the woman.

A self-satisfied smile tugged at her narrow lips. "I believe in what the Good Book teaches. 'Spare the rod and spoil the child.' You said I can have a free hand with your daughter. I intend to teach her proper manners and how to behave like a lady."

"I see," he managed to say. "A rod? Do you mean a switch? Or a belt?"

She folded her hands as in prayer. "The Word says that if you beat a child with a rod, he will not die. I use a strap, like Mr. Bettington, my father, used on me. I certainly learned proper behavior. And so will Catherine."

It took all his self-control to remain rooted in place, not to wrap his fingers around her scrawny neck. "Did you have to correct Cathy today? Did she misbehave?"

"Yes. She was playing outdoors against my orders. She

tore her dress and got her shoes filthy. I'd warned her that she was to remain clean until you returned home. I gave her a spanking and sent her to bed without supper. She must learn to be a lady."

"And you used a strap?"

"Actually, a razor strop."

He bit his lip and counted to ten. That didn't work, so he counted to twenty. His hard-earned self-control was inches from snapping. "Miss Bettington, please go to your room and pack your bags. I want you out of my house at dawn. I borrowed a wagon from the livery, and it will be hitched and ready for you at daybreak."

Her jaw fell open. "Pack? Leave? What do you mean?"

Unable to stop himself, he took two steps in her direction. "In two words, you're fired. I don't want you near my child again. Or near my home. I'll give you two months' salary and a ticket back to Kansas City."

"It's her fault." She waved her arm toward the kitchen. "That hussy put you up to this. It's all a plot to get rid of me so she can use you for her own purposes."

"Miss Clark isn't involved in this. I saw the marks on my daughter's legs, and I will not tolerate anyone touching her." Coulter stepped closer. Genuine fear gleamed in the woman's eyes. Probably the same fear she'd seen in Cathy's eyes.

"I told you she would cause trouble. Mark my words, if she moves into your home, your daughter will turn into a hussy exactly like that woman." Head held high, she picked up her Bible and marched to the stairs. Abruptly, she swung to stare at him. "I will not stay where I'm not wanted. But you will rue the day you let that woman into your home."

"Miss Bettington, I already rue the day I hired you."

With a loud sniff, she climbed the stairs and disappeared out of his sight. Just in time. Another minute alone with the harpy and Coulter would have gladly broken her in two. The confrontation left him more drained than if he'd single-handedly battled a grizzly bear. He sagged onto the davenport, propped his elbows on his thighs, and dropped his head into his hands.

"Can you use a cup of coffee? I don't think she'll try to poison us."

He glanced toward the kitchen and spotted Josie silhouetted in the doorway. He couldn't deny that she was a welcome sight for his bruised spirit. "I wouldn't put anything past her." Taking the offered cup from her, he clutched it in both hands to keep from spilling it all over himself.

Josie settled next to him. "I'm sorry Coulter, really I am."

"I'm sorry, too, Josie. Sorry I subjected my child to any form of abuse. I hope she forgives me."

She covered his fingers with hers. "She loves you. She would never blame you."

He glanced down at their entwined hands—hers, white, small, perfectly manicured; his, large, sun-browned, and paint-stained. Yet they seemed a perfect match. "I hired the woman, but hell, it's near impossible to get a qualified housekeeper way out here on the prairie. Most women prefer the city and prestigious positions."

"I'm sure you'll find somebody new. A woman who will take good care of your home and your child."

"That could take weeks, months. I need help now." His gaze lifted to her eyes, warm and soft. "What about you, Josie? Cathy likes you, and you seem fond of her."

She snatched her hand away. "Oh, no, Sheriff. I really can't."

Puzzled, he studied her expression. Her eyes were bright with unshed tears and her mouth pulled into a straight line. "Why? It's all strictly aboveboard." He prided himself on coming up with the perfect solution to his problem. His daughter would have a companion, and he could keep Josie out of town and out of trouble. "I promise to be a perfect gentleman, and I can assure you nothing unseemly will happen."

"It isn't that—I just can't." She stood and walked across the room, the damp hem of her skirt brushing the worn carpet. At the mantel she stopped and studied Ellen's photograph for a second. "I have my work, I'm already committed to the cause."

He moved behind her and ran a finger across the gilded picture frame. "Cathy really misses her mother. She needs a woman in her life."

"You can remarry, Coulter. Cathy needs a mother, not another temporary housekeeper."

His heart twisted at the thought of any woman taking Ellen's place. "Josie, I loved Ellen more than life itself, and when she died, I wanted to crawl right into that grave with her." Taking the picture from her he returned it to its place on the mantel. "Nobody could ever take her place. I'll never fall in love again." He meant every word. After five years, the pain was still there, like an open wound that refused to heal.

Josie turned to face him, her eyes warm and a soft blue like the morning glories his mother had planted around the porch. "I understand how you feel—believe me, I've lost people I love, too. But you have a child to consider."

He turned away, her words too true to face. "Hell, I've told myself the same things a hundred times or more." A bark of bitter laughter sprung from his lips. "But what if I got a wife like Miss Bettington? It wouldn't be so easy to dismiss a wife as a housekeeper. No, thanks. I'll hire somebody to look after my daughter until she's old enough to be on her own."

"Why me? I know you don't trust me. Aren't you afraid I'll corrupt your child's morals?"

"Josie, a while ago you were willing to battle a man twice your size to protect that child. I know you would never hurt her."

"All right, Coulter. I'll do it. I'll stay for two weeks while you look for a housekeeper. But I won't stop my activities. I fully intend to shut down every saloon in your town."

With a shake of his head, he studied her determined look. "Miss Clark, I have no doubt you can do anything you set your mind to. But if you cause any trouble, I'll have to arrest you."

A glint of anger flashed in her eyes. "I won't be much good to you in jail."

"You won't have to stay in jail. I'll have Oscar sentence you to, say, six months, and parole you into my custody."

"You wouldn't dare."

"Try me, Miss Clark. A desperate man takes desperate measures."

She threw up her hands. "You win. I'll stay out of trouble. And you'll advertise for a housekeeper tomorrow."

"Then we have a deal?"

Josie gifted him with a tiny smile. "For two weeks."

Something about her smile sent a flash of heat to his heart. "Or until I find a qualified housekeeper."

She gave her skirt that sassy flip, and started for the stairs. "Whichever comes first."

"Yes, ma'am. Whichever comes first." His gaze locked on her swaying hips. Head held high, back straight, the woman certainly knew how to make an exit. Josie Clark was full of spunk and spun sugar. She would stand up to Satan himself if he got in her way.

He hoped he wasn't making a mistake bringing her into his house. But it wasn't Cathy's safety that concerned him, Josie would never lift a finger to a child. He wondered how he could live under the same roof with a beautiful woman and keep his hands to himself. True, he had no intention of falling in love, but he was still a healthy male with a healthy male appetite.

And Josie Clark was the most tempting morsel to come his way in many a day. Her song ran over in his ears. It was going to take a heck of a lot of strength to *"yield not to temptation"* and subdue the *"dark passions"* she inspired in a very weak man.

Chapter 7

Josie didn't even try to sleep that night. The bed was too big, and smelled of a man—Coulter Steele. Although the sheets were clean and fresh, his citrusy soap permeated the entire room. She tossed and turned, kept awake by the noise from the next room where Miss Bettington banged drawers, and stomped the floor all night, packing to leave.

The tiniest bit of sympathy for the woman touched Josie. A spinster housekeeper had to rely on her employer for a roof over her head and food on the table. Josie knew what it was like to depend on others for her substance. Hadn't Mrs. Johnston taken her in after Armand was killed and she had nowhere to go?

Nowhere any decent woman would go. Terrell Sullivan, lead actor and troupe manager, had offered to take care of her, at a price. He wanted her as his mistress, but Josie had decided she would rather scrub floors and empty slop buckets than sell herself to a man. After all she'd lost, her pride was the only thing she had left.

Considering Coulter was on the verge of murdering her,

he had been more than generous with Miss Bettington. Perhaps next time she could find a home without young children. She had no business being around young children. Her leaving was best for all.

Except for Josie.

Josie moved to the window that overlooked the front of the house. The first glimmer of dawn broke over the horizon, bathing the land with a pale pink glow. From the direction of the barn, a wagon rumbled up to the porch. Coulter sat ramrod-straight, the expression on his face hidden by his wide black hat. She dropped the curtain, and backed away before he spotted her spying on him.

What had she gotten herself into now? she wondered. She had no business letting this man coerce her into becoming his housekeeper, no matter how temporary the job. Being alone with Coulter Steele was like throwing a rabbit into a den of foxes. Every time he so much as glanced her way, she felt his eyes devour her. Her skin tingled, and needs she couldn't identify surged within her. Even if she managed the strength to deny her attraction for him, she had other problems to consider.

Things like her work; her obligations as a temperance leader; her lecture tour; her vow to rid the world of demon alcohol. She'd promised Mrs. Johnston and the leaders of the S.A.A.T. to deliver the messages, and come hell or high water or Coulter Steele, she was going to do it.

A greater problem faced her immediately, however. Josie knew next to nothing about running a household and caring for a child. Coulter had backed her into a corner like a hungry cat after a mouse. He may have the upper hand for now, she thought, but she hadn't given up the fight.

She threw off her nightgown and reached for her clothes. Well, she'd fought her way out of situations worse than this. How difficult could it be to play house for a few weeks? An eight-year-old girl couldn't present too many problems. Surely Josie could act the part and give the performance of her life.

Snatching up the skirt she'd worn the day before, Josie's heart sank at the condition of the garment. Her late-night walk in the damp barnyard had stained and dirtied the hem of still another gown and petticoats. She tossed the skirt aside and pulled a pink day-gown from her satchel. With a quick shake to remove some of the wrinkles, she laid it across the wide bed.

In the growing daylight, she studied the room—his room. The heavy oak furniture spoke of permanence, strength—like the man himself. Coulter's presence permeated every inch of the room. His comb and brush lay where he'd tossed them carelessly on the dresser. On the washstand his shaving equipment waited for his morning routine. A black suit hung on a hook behind the door, and a stack of clean shirts sat on a chair. Next to the bed, the round table held a kerosene lamp and a framed portrait of his wife.

Although she didn't want to disturb any of his personal things, Josie couldn't resist picking up the picture and studying it. The woman was very beautiful. Long dark curls framed her perfect, heart-shaped face, and her eyes were as bright as emeralds. A tear threatened to spill from Josie's eyes. So young—too young to die and leave a devoted husband and child. Like Mama, who'd left Papa and two children. But unlike Papa, Coulter had learned to cope with his loss and had turned his grief into something positive. Papa had turned to drink and lost everything, including his own life.

At the sound of footsteps and a door slamming, she hurried into her petticoats and gown. Nimble fingers hooked the tiny buttons on the front, and tied the dark-rose ribbon into a large bow at her back. After years of changing costumes, Josie could dress and undress, change her hair, and be presentable within minutes. Quickly she brushed out her hair and twisted it into a presentable chignon at the back of her head.

"Sheriff," came Miss Bettington's shrill voice from the hallway, "if you will be so kind as to carry my trunk downstairs, I will be on my way."

More footsteps and a man's heavy boot heels thudded in the hallway. Josie remained behind the closed door. Miss Bettington was Coulter's affair, and it was best she not interfere. But even the walls couldn't dim the woman's censure or her outburst of anger toward Coulter as well as Josie. She hoped the woman would leave Council City in a hurry. Josie had already made an enemy of Homer Potts; she didn't need another adversary trying to undermine her cause.

At the window again, she watched as Miss Bettington, unassisted by Coulter, climbed into the wagon. A dark poke bonnet shadowed her face, but Josie had no doubt she was giving the sheriff a blessing-out, in the most ladylike language, of course. She jabbed a black-gloved finger at him like a dagger. Although Josie couldn't hear them, she knew the words concerned her and her reputation.

It was almost comical, Josie thought. If the woman only knew the truth about Josie's sordid past, she would have enough gossip for months. But nobody in this part of the country knew about her connection with the LeClares; not even Mrs. Johnston, who had been friend, companion, and mentor for the past four years.

Josie's conscience began to prickle at the back of her mind. Surely Coulter had a right to know about the woman he'd put in charge of his child. She squeezed her eyes shut against the pain the memories brought back. Josie knew she would never harm the child. Besides, she would leave as soon as he hired a real housekeeper. Surely she could act the part until then. Housework couldn't be that difficult, could it? She'd watched Mrs. Johnston's maid, and she knew how to wash and iron her own clothes, and make a bed. Beyond that, she could learn as she went along.

On silent feet, she left the room and closed the door behind her. Across the hall, Cathy's room was silent, and at the end of the hall, the open door to the housekeeper's room revealed a room in total disarray. Josie shrugged and started down the stairs.

The aroma of freshly brewed coffee reached her before she entered the kitchen. That was the first thing she would have to learn. Although she preferred tea, Coulter would want coffee to start his day. She paused for a moment at the kitchen door to get her bearings. He stood at the large cast-iron stove with his back to her. Bacon sizzled in a frying pan, and a bowl of eggs sat next to the stove. The tall, broad-shouldered lawman looked perfectly at home with his sleeves rolled up and his dark hair curled around the collar of his blue shirt.

Interesting, she thought. For the life of her, she couldn't picture either Armand or Papa frying bacon or making coffee. Her father and brother loved fine food, but would never venture near a kitchen.

"How many eggs, Miss Clark?" he asked, with a glance over his shoulder.

Josie jumped, lost in her observations. "I'm not much for breakfast, Sheriff, I'll just have a piece of bread."

"I'll fix you one egg, and I usually have four. Remember that tomorrow when it's your turn. Can't expect to start the day on an empty stomach."

Fix his breakfast? That meant getting up at the break of dawn and performing duties she had yet to learn. Chores that included slaving over a hot stove. Better than jail, she reminded herself.

Possessing a quick mind and an almost perfect memory, Josie moved nearer the stove to learn the breakfast preparations. He moved with quick efficiency, cracking eggs into the sizzling grease and flipping them over at precisely the right moment. Not too difficult, she thought. If he could do it, so could she.

"How about pouring the coffee while I get the eggs on the table?" He gestured to two mugs set next to the stove. A large enamel coffeepot waited on the back burner.

Coffeepot, skillet, bacon, eggs, she memorized the order of preparing breakfast. Seems simple enough. She carried the two heavy mugs to the table and proceeded to finish the setting. A drawer on the heavy oak worktable contained silverware, and the shelf above had a set of plain white dinnerware. After setting the small table for two, she filled the mugs with the dark, strong coffee. It certainly smelled better than the coffee in the jailhouse.

The kitchen was large and bright with sunshine pouring in through the window. A red pump sat at the edge of the large sink. She also spied a coffee grinder, an assortment of pots and pans, and other utensils as foreign to Josie as the farm implements in the barn. The room was spotlessly clean, the floor scrubbed and the pots gleaming. Miss Bettington was clearly an excellent housekeeper. Josie swallowed down her apprehension. Even the large wood-burning stove was intimidating.

It was only temporary, she reminded herself. Until Coulter could find a woman who knew how to use the instruments, she would just have to bluff her way through.

"Here we go, Miss Clark. Hope you like them over-easy." Coulter slid one egg onto her plate and four on his. Then he set a platter of crisp bacon between them.

Trying to be useful, Josie carried a loaf of bread and a small crock of butter to the table. She sat at her place and poured fresh cream into her coffee and added two spoonsful of sugar. With a few quick slashes, Coulter sliced the bread. Then he took the chair opposite hers.

Josie spread butter on her bread and took a bit of the perfectly cooked egg. When she looked up, she found Coulter smiling at her. Something fluttered in her chest.

"Is something wrong, Sheriff? Do I have egg on my face?" She dabbed her mouth with her napkin.

He laughed and reached over and flicked a small crumb from the corner of her mouth. "No. It's just been a long time since I've had such a pretty lady at my breakfast table."

Her pulse racing like it had after half a dozen curtain calls, she shrugged off his compliment. "Please don't get used to it. Remember, this is only a temporary arrangement." After taking a sip of the coffee, she glanced up at him again. "Sheriff, I believe we should come to an understanding about a few things."

He tilted one thick eyebrow that reached nearly to the tumble of chestnut-colored hair on his forehead. "What things, Miss Clark?"

For the first time she spotted the dimple that pierced his left cheek when he smiled. "Exactly what are my duties in your home? I feel it only fair to inform you that I have little experience as a domestic or as a governess"

Dark, fathomless eyes studied her for a moment. "You appear to be a well-bred young woman, and most women are taught how to run a household from girlhood, or so I've been told."

Josie took a moment to cover her mouth with the napkin and come up with a plausible explanation. It wouldn't be wise to let him know she hadn't been reared like most young ladies; that she'd never really had a home, or been required to perform domestic chores. "You see, sir, I came from a rather unusual family." That was true, to say the least. When her mother was living, the LeClares were the most popular performers in the music theaters. "We traveled a great deal and I'm afraid my education was greatly lacking in domestic duties. I'm not much of a cook and I'm not sure I can live up to Miss Bettington's standards. And, of course, I know nothing about milking cows or whatever else one does on a farm."

"What exactly did your father do, that you traveled so much?"

A bead of perspiration trickled down her chest and rolled between her breasts. She always broke out in a sweat when she became nervous. Stage fright, her father called it. Josie didn't understand why this performance was so important, but she knew it was. "He was a merchant." *Good thinking*, she complimented herself. "Import and export. And he liked us to travel with him."

He propped his elbows on the table and studied her over his folded hands. Today the paint stains were lighter, washed away by the strong lye soap. "I recall your mentioning being sent to an orphanage. How did that happen?"

There was no harm telling the truth about this part of her past. "After my mother died, my father turned to drink. He was killed in a barroom brawl. My brother and I were sent to an orphanage. We ran away and later I was taken in by Mrs. Johnston, one of the leaders of the S.A.A.T." She missed a few years in telling the story, but he didn't need to know that she and Armand had gone back to the theater until he, too, had been killed—or about Terrell Sullivan, who'd tried to make her his mistress. She'd worked hard to put that safely behind her and start a new life.

Genuine sympathy glittered in his eyes. He reached out and caught her fingers in his strong grip. "I see. I suppose we can work things out. Mainly I need a companion for my daughter, a woman to see that she's fed, clothed, and kept reasonably clean. Between the two of us, we can manage meals, and I'll hire a neighbor boy to milk the cow and handle the outdoor chores."

"That's fine, Sheriff. I'm sure we can manage for two weeks until you hire a qualified housekeeper."

"I'm sure we will, Miss Clark."

The sound of running footsteps drew her gaze to the

door. Cathy rushed into the kitchen and flung herself at her father. "Papa, you're still home."

Josie smiled at the child's attempts to fashion her long curly hair into twin braids. More hair escaped than was bound into the lopsided plaits. Pink ribbons hung loose, falling to the shoulders of her blue calico smock. Her stockings were crooked and her shoes untied. The effect was delightfully charming.

Coulter hugged the girl and kissed her forehead. "Sure am, pumpkin. I'm going in a little late today. I didn't finish all my chores yesterday, so I've decided to hire Charlie Reeves to give us a hand." He propped her on his knee. "Say good morning to Miss Clark."

Cathy lifted wide golden eyes to Josie. "You're really here, Miss Clark. I thought I was dreaming last night." The girl glanced around the kitchen. She lowered her voice and asked, "Where's Miss Bettington?"

Tightening his grip on his daughter, Coulter gave her a loving smile. Seeing him with his child, Josie wondered how she could have ever doubted his love, or even entertained the thought that he would hurt the child. Cathy clearly adored her father.

"Baby, Miss Bettington isn't with us anymore. I've asked Miss Clark to stay with us for a while. I know you and she will get along very well."

Confusion in her eyes, she glanced from her father to Josie. "Miss Bettington is gone?"

Josie reached for her hand. "Yes, love. I'll be staying with you until your father can hire another housekeeper."

"Papa," she said, laying her head on her father's shoulder, "I'm tired of housekeepers. I'd rather have a mother of my own, like the other girls."

"I know, sweetheart. But that's not possible. For now, just enjoy having Miss Clark as your friend and companion." He looked tired and vulnerable, an endearing quality in the big, self-assured man. Even a tough lawman like Coulter Steele had a soft side.

After giving him a big kiss, Cathy scooted off his lap and ran to hug Josie. "I'm glad you're here, Miss Josie. And I'll be real good, I promise. Cross my heart and hope to die." The little girl made an X across her chest and raised her right hand in an oath.

"I know you will, love, and we'll get along famously. Sit down, I'll get you a plate, and maybe your papa will share one of his delicious eggs with you."

Seconds later Josie had another place set at the table and Cathy was eating with gusto.

Josie hoped Coulter's confidence wasn't misplaced—that she could live up to his expectations; that she wouldn't get too involved in the lives of the handsome sheriff and his precocious daughter.

Josie wondered if it wasn't already too late for her heart.

Chapter 8

The day passed in a blur as Josie tried to become accustomed to her new duties. She constantly reminded herself it was only temporary. Cathy was delighted and stayed underfoot all day. Josie didn't object to the child's constant questions or attempts to be helpful. If anything, Josie would have been lost without Cathy's assistance.

Coulter's daughter was a sweet, affectionate child who glowed in any kind of attention. After setting the housekeeper's room in order, Josie moved her things to clear Coulter's room for his use. Although she had reservations about sharing the same roof with such a devilishly handsome man, she knew she had little choice in the matter. He couldn't very well sleep in the barn when he had a perfectly good bed of his own. She would just have to take him at his word as a gentleman that nothing untoward would happen between them.

But could she trust him to remain a gentleman? Looking deep into her heart, she wondered if she wanted him to.

Josie shoved the devastating thought from her mind and concentrated on preparing supper for him.

Miss Bettington had left a large pan of freshly baked rolls on the worktable, and two loaves of bread wrapped in a towel. She also discovered left-over baked ham. The pantry was well stocked with canned goods and dried fruit.

The neighbor boy, Charlie Reeves, had come by that afternoon and brought in fresh milk and collected the eggs. He picked fresh green beans from the garden and carried in a basket of tomatoes and corn. He also made it clear that he would be ready and willing to help in any way he could. By the young man's wide smile and adoring glances, Josie knew she had an ally.

With Cathy's help, Josie managed to boil corn and slice the tomatoes for their supper. Since she had no idea how to prepare the beans, she decided to wait until she got some advice before trying to cook them.

The meal was on the table when Cathy entered the kitchen, her hands behind her back. "Miss Josie," she called, her voice quiet and shy.

Pleased at the results of her first attempt at a meal, Josie glanced at the child. "Yes, love?"

"I have something for you."

"For me? Good, I love presents, don't you?" Josie perched on the edge of a chair at eye level with the child.

Cathy nodded, "Yes ma'am. But these are for you." She stuck out a handful of flowers—roses from the garden, plus daisies and buttercups that grew wild in the pasture.

The little girl's generous gesture shot clear to the center of Josie's heart. She blinked away a tear. "Honey, they're beautiful. Thank you so much." After giving Cathy a brief hug, she stood and glanced around. "Let's get a pitcher and put these in water. They'll look lovely in the middle of the table while we have our supper."

"Oh, no, ma'am, we can't. Miss Bettington never let me

bring flowers in the house. She said they carry bugs and stuff, and when the leaves fall, they dirty up the floor."

Coulter had been right in dismissing the woman, she thought. A child needs love and attention, not rules and regulation. "Then we should be glad Miss Bettington isn't here anymore." Josie filled an empty pitcher with water from the bucket and arranged the flowers as best she could. "See, aren't they beautiful? We'll have flowers every day if we want."

"Do you think Papa will like them?"

Josie smiled at her uncertainty. "Of course he will. The roses make everything smell real sweet. We'll pick some more tomorrow and I'll show you how to dry the petals and put them in your bureau to make your clothes smell good."

Cathy flung her arms around Josie's waist. "I love you, Miss Josie. I hope Papa marries you and you never have to leave us."

Taken aback by the girl's heartfelt plea, she brushed her fingers through the child's thick curly hair. How could she explain to a lonely child that she didn't want to marry, that she was committed to a cause that had put her and the sheriff on opposite sides from the moment they'd met?

"Sweetheart, someday your papa will fall in love with a really nice lady and they'll get married. I have to leave soon to finish my lecture tour and work for the movement."

"I understand. Papa explained all about ladies and men falling in love and getting married, but I wish he would fall in love with you."

She kissed the top of Cathy's head. "Whoever your father chooses will be extra nice. And I'm sure she'll be a much better cook than I am."

Cathy looked up and smiled. "I'll bet she won't be prettier than you."

Josie laughed. "Shoo. I think I hear somebody coming up the drive. Run and see if it's your papa."

When Cathy ran to greet her father, Josie took a moment to check her reflection in the window. She smoothed the stray tendrils of pale hair into the hairpins holding her thick tresses in a sedate chignon. Her cheeks were rosy from being in the warm kitchen, giving her a bright, youthful appearance. Hurriedly she tugged off the soiled apron and shoved it into the pantry.

From the kitchen, she heard Cathy greet her father. "Papa, you're home! Come see what me and Miss Josie fixed for supper."

" 'Miss Josie and I,' " he corrected, a smile in his voice. "I'll be in as soon as I unload the wagon and stable the horses."

Josie glanced out the window and watched him jump down from a wagon. He tugged off his hat and wiped his brow on his shirtsleeve. As if feeling her eyes on him, his gaze swung to the window, She lifted her hand and waved. He signaled her to come out before he moved to the rear of the wagon.

Josie stepped through the living room to the porch door. Coulter smiled at her. "I brought your trunk from the hotel, Miss Clark. Thought you'd be needing your things."

"Thank you, Sheriff. I appreciate your thoughtfulness." Josie bit her lip as a particularly disturbing thought hit her. She hoped when he'd gathered up the few things she'd left loose, he hadn't rummaged through her trunk. Buried at the bottom was her scrapbook full of the details of her former life—pictures of Mama, Papa, Armand, and Angel. Surely he wouldn't, she thought. But if the sheriff distrusted her as much as she supposed, he may consider it his right and privilege. Josie shook off the thought. No use courting trouble, as Papa used to say.

Heaving the heavy steamer trunk as easily as if it weighed nothing, Coulter set it on the porch. "I'll carry it up for you as soon as I take care of the horses and clean up a bit. It'll only be a few minutes."

* * *

Coulter studied Josie across the table. The roses framed her face like a portrait in a fancy frame. A pleasant evening meal with a pretty woman was quite a change from the stern housekeeper who had constantly harangued him about his daughter's behavior. He relaxed and listened as Josie and Cathy gave him a running commentary of their day.

"Isn't our supper delicious, Papa? Miss Josie did it all by herself." Cathy looked up at him with wide-eyed innocence.

Josie smiled and tousled his child's already-unruly hair. "Cathy, a few minutes ago you told your papa you helped me fix the meal, and I'm sure he knows very well that Miss Bettington baked the rolls and the ham. I did slice the tomatoes all by myself without cutting off my fingers."

"The dinner is excellent, no matter who fixed it."

Her lighthearted laughter sent a surge of heat to the center of his stomach. He struggled to extinguish the needs growing inside him. Sitting across from the beautiful woman, he began to doubt the wisdom of inviting her into his home. This time it wasn't Cathy's well-being that concerned him, but this woman's presence wreaked havoc with his hard-earned self-control.

She'd already won his daughter, his aunt and uncle had spent the day singing her praises, and from the report he'd gotten from Charlie, the young man was clearly smitten. Of course, the saloon owners weren't too happy about her mission. And Homer had repeatedly complained that the woman was a troublemaker. Miss Bettington had moved in with Homer and his mother until she could find another position. Coulter wished the woman had left town. His instincts told him the former housekeeper meant nothing but problems.

Cathy finished her ham and shoved the tomatoes around her plate. "Papa, I was real good today. I kept my dress and shoes clean, and I helped Miss Josie all day long. Can you please let her stay with us forever?"

He looked up at Josie and spotted the hint of sadness in her eyes. "Honey, that's up to Miss Josie."

Josie wiped her mouth with her napkin. "Cathy, I explained all that to you today. I can only stay for a few weeks. Then I have to continue with my work. Even after I leave, we can still be friends. I'll write you letters, and you can write to me. When I get back this way, I'll visit with you and your papa."

For some odd reason the thought of her leaving brought a twinge to his heart. Would he be the one to miss her when she left?

Cathy lifted wide eyes to Josie. "But that's not the same. I write letters to my grandmother in Kansas City, and she writes back to me. But it's not like when we used to live with her and Grandfather."

Coulter had no idea Cathy missed her grandparents so much. They loved their only grandchild as much as they hated Coulter. Even four years later, they still blamed him for their daughter's death. "Why don't you finish your supper and we'll go for a ride. You do ride, don't you, Josie?"

"I'm afraid not, Sheriff. In addition to my housekeeping skills, that's another part of my education that's been neglected." She dropped her napkin and stood. "Would you care for a cup of coffee before you leave? I figured out the grinding mill, but I wasn't sure how many beans to use, or how much to put into the basket. I hope it's drinkable."

He smiled at her attempt at modesty. "Then tell us what are you proficient at, besides singing." From the corner of his eyes he noticed the way her hands trembled as she picked up a heavy mug.

"Singing? That caterwauling? What makes you think I can sing?"

"I heard you when I came into the jail. Then I was sitting next to you in church. You have the voice of an angel."

The mug slipped from her fingers and shattered on the cast-iron stove. "Oh, how clumsy. I'm so sorry."

He jumped to his feet. "Don't touch it, Josie. I'll clean it up."

Cathy's face turned pale, and she ran to wrap her arms around his waist. "Please, Papa. Don't whup Miss Josie. She didn't mean to break the cup. You can whup me instead."

His child's words sent a shock through him. "Honey, I know it was an accident. What makes you think I'm going to whup anybody?"

Tears glittered in the corners of her dark eyes. "But, Miss Bettington—"

"Love, Miss Bettington is gone. You know I'll never strike a lady. Miss Josie would probably shoot me right between the eyes if I lifted a hand to her."

Josie draped her arm across Cathy's shoulder. "Come sit down and finish your dinner while Papa picks up the broken cup."

Cathy's dark eyes shifted from Josie to him then back to her plate. "I don't like tomatoes. Do I have to eat them?"

"No. Just finish your ham and roll. And drink all of your milk," Josie said.

Coulter picked up broken earthenware and dropped it in the trash. "I'll pour the next cup. We don't have many mugs to spare." He filled two cups and set them on the table. "What are your specialties, Miss Clark?" he asked over the rim of his cup.

She poured half a cup of milk into her coffee and stirred in sugar. "I'm fluent in French, and I can play piano a little. I would be happy to give Cathy lessons, if you don't mind."

He sipped the coffee and choked on the strong, bitter taste. When he caught his breath, he shook his head. "Making coffee isn't one of your talents. Tomorrow I'll teach you how to make a decent pot."

"And can we teach Miss Josie how to ride, can't we, Papa?" Cathy asked in her childish exuberance.

"How about it, Miss Josie? Do you want to learn how to ride?" He flashed her a smile as he moved to the back door to throw out the undrinkable coffee.

She began to clear the table. "I don't think so. Horses are too big and intimidating. I'll keep my feet on the ground, or ride in a buggy. You two run along, I have some letters to write."

"Don't get into trouble, Miss Josie," he teased. "We'll be back before dark." In spite of his lighthearted comment, Coulter couldn't deny his disappointment that she wouldn't be riding with him and Cathy. For some odd reason he liked being with her. The gentle lilt of her voice stirred something deep inside him. He shoved the feelings away. That part of him belonged to Ellen, and no woman could ever take her place.

"Believe me, Sheriff. I'll be on my best behavior. I have no desire to spend another night in jail."

Cathy propped her fists on her narrow hips. "Papa, you wouldn't throw Miss Josie in that nasty old jail, would you?"

He laughed. "Not if I know what's good for me, I won't." Turning to Josie, he spotted the glimmer of laughter in her eyes. "Sure you won't come with us and let me teach you how to ride?"

She waved him off. "Positive. But if you don't go, it'll be dark before you can even saddle up and ride."

Unable to resist the temptation, he leaned toward her and planted a quick kiss on her lips. Before she could react, he turned on his heel and hustled his giggling daughter out the back door.

* * *

By the time Cathy was safely tucked in bed, Josie was as tired as when she'd performed a matinee and two nightly performances. Coulter excused himself with the explanation that he had work in the barn. She need not wait up for him, as he usually stayed out quite late.

Josie sealed her letters to Mrs. Johnston and the leaders of the S.A.A.T., which explained her progress and her plans for the next few weeks. She also penned a note to Mrs. Marche, asking for assistance in the next phase of their attack on the bars in Council Bluff. If Coulter wouldn't let them march, she had other ways to reach her goal.

She hoped Coulter would take her into town the next day with him, but if not, she planned to ask Charlie to hitch up the buggy for her. After all, she was a housekeeper, not a prisoner.

With Cathy asleep and the house quiet, she went into the bedroom and prepared for bed. After loosening her hair, she passed her brush through the long tresses—and thought of Coulter. The man hadn't been far from her thoughts all evening. She wondered how much, if anything, he knew about her. More than once he'd mentioned Angel. From what Cathy had said, he'd once lived in Kansas City, and she and Armand had performed there in a theater only months before her brother had died. She bit her lip at the possibility that he'd seen her. There she was, courting trouble again. No good ever came out of guessing. She would just bide her time and see if anything came out of his suspicions.

Although she was exhausted, Josie found herself not quite ready for sleep. She slipped her lace-trimmed cotton wrapper over her nightgown and ventured downstairs for a cup of tea. That she knew she could prepare without disaster.

While she waited for the water to boil, she glanced out the kitchen window toward the barn. A glimmer of light came from the loft, where an unusually large window overlooked the pasture. *Odd,* she thought. *What could Coulter be doing up there so late at night?*

A teacup in her hand, she watched as shadows drifted across the lighted window. The grandfather clock in the parlor struck eleven, but Josie suspected she wouldn't be able to sleep until she heard Coulter return to the house. Papa had always said if she had one fatal flaw, it was her curiosity. That curiosity got the better of her, again. Setting the empty cup aside, she knew she wouldn't be able to rest until she learned what was going on in the barn so late at night.

The moon was high and the path to the barn lit by its warm glow. She tied the belt of her wrapper tight around her waist, and glanced down at her thin slippers. This time she watched her toes, careful not to step into any unknown substances.

A chorus of night insects accompanied her on the narrow path. It was a beautiful night, with the moon and stars lighting the way. She slipped through the barn door and stopped, suddenly feeling foolish and having second thoughts about why she was out there. Coulter had a right to his privacy, as she demanded hers. After all, he was probably only moving haystacks or cleaning out debris.

Ready to turn around and run back to the house, the sound of a voice stopped her.

"Josie? What are you doing out here?"

She jumped back a step. "I . . ." *No use lying,* she thought. "I was wondering when you were coming back into the house." Looking around the dark, cavernous barn, she wondered from which direction his voice came.

"In a little while." A long silence hung in the air. "I'm in the loft. Come up. I have something to show you."

At the end of the barn, she noticed a glow of a lamp that hadn't been there seconds ago. She moved toward the light and spotted a narrow ladder not unlike those in the theaters that led up to the scenery and sets. Gathering her gown in one hand, she climbed the rungs with the same agility she displayed when she was performing. At the top, a strong hand reached out and clasped her wrist. With one hard tug, Coulter pulled her into the loft.

Her foot caught on the hem of her wrapper and she lost her balance. She flew into him, catching herself against his hard chest. His arms went around her waist. She clutched his shirt and she felt the pounding of his heart against her fingertips. Lifting her gaze, she spotted the heated sparks in Coulter's dark eyes. For a long moment, she stared up at him, unable to move. She remembered the brief kiss when he'd left the kitchen that evening, and she wondered how it would feel to really kiss him. To know the fullness of his lips against hers. To feel the heat that smoldered inside her body, burst into a wild inferno.

Shocked at the intensity of her feelings, Josie shoved herself out of his arms. With a mumbled apology, she turned away to control the trembling in the pit of her stomach. Taking a deep, steadying breath, she glanced around the loft.

Her eyes widened in surprise. Instead of bales of hay or other farm implements, the loft was cluttered with canvases, easels, jars of paint, and brushes. Slowly she swung around, taking in the strange atmosphere. She would expect to find an artist's studio in Paris or Milan, but this was a ranch on the Kansas plains; and the artist was a rough, masculine lawman.

A particularly beautiful portrait of a young woman caught her gaze. She recognized the face as Ellen, his wife. Josie's breath caught in her throat. The passion and love that came through in the painting brought tears to her eyes. "You must have loved her very much." The words came out in a husky whisper.

"I *do* love her very much."

The pain in his voice brought her up short. She glanced around and spotted a large oil of a Western scene with the mountains in the background and a single, lonely cowboy seated near a campfire. The man looked remarkably like Coulter. "Magnificent," she whispered, afraid to break the spell of the wonderful paintings. "Did you do all these, Coulter?"

He chuckled softly. "Not too shabby for a bumpkin sheriff in the middle of nowhere, don't you think?"

Fire danced in his dark eyes. Passion and pride reflected in his work.

"They're wonderful." Her hand reached out to the solitary figure in the painting, a man so much like the artist himself. "Where do you show your work? You should be in New York or Paris."

"I'm here, where I belong. A New York gallery handles my Western scenes and I put the money away for my daughter's future." He unfolded a sheet of paper. "What do you think about this one?" he asked.

Her gaze shifted to the sketch in his hand. It was her face—or rather Angel's—with a smile on her lips and feathers in her hair. The expression in his eyes said it all.

He knew. He'd learned her secret.

He knew Josephine Angelique Clark was Angel LeClare.

Chapter 9

"What do you think, Angel?"

Coulter watched the play of emotions that skidded across her face. Surprise and shock were chased away by a closed, nonchalant expression.

"I think you're a fine artist who's probably wasting his time as a lawman."

"Don't try to change the subject. I want to know about you. Are you Josephine Clark, or are you Angel LeClare?" He spread the sketch on his worktable and studied the blue, blue eyes that exactly matched those of the woman standing before him.

The likeness was perfect, her portrait would be magnificent. *If* he decided to paint her.

She gripped the lapels of her wrapper as if to close herself off from him. A pretty flush extended from her forehead to where her throat disappeared into the lace neckline of her pristine white nightdress. "I'm Josephine Angelique Clark. I left Angel LeClare behind four years ago. How did you find out?"

He lowered his lashes and studied her through narrowed lids. "I'm not sure. I suppose I saw a flyer when I was in Kansas City or St. Louis. Being an artist, I never forget a face. But it was probably your voice that gave you away. Angel suits you a heck of a lot better than Josie. What are you hiding from?"

"I'm not hiding, Sheriff." She sank onto his high stool and studied the sketch. "Josephine Clark is my given name. LeClare was our stage name. My mother was French, and when my parents began to perform in Europe, they thought LeClare sounded more theatrical than plain old Clark."

His gaze dropped to where her robe gapped and her legs were clearly visible under her thin gown. In his mind's eyes, he pictured her in a gaudy costume that exposed those shapely limbs. The vision wasn't nearly as titillating as the woman seated before him. A fresh, flowery scent wafted from her and started an unbidden fire deep in his gut. He picked up a cigarette to occupy his hands and calm his nerves.

"Angel LeClare was a musical-theater performer and actress. Josie Clark is a temperance worker. Somehow the two don't seem to go together." Striking the match on the sole of his boot, he held it to the tip of the cigarette until it glowed red.

As if suddenly noticing the way her wrapper had slipped open and her legs were exposed to his view, she stood and pulled the garment closer to her body. "Sheriff, I have every reason to hate alcohol and the effects of drink." She brushed a finger across the sketch. "After my mother died, Papa couldn't face life without her. He drowned his sorrow in drink. He was killed in a drunken brawl in Chicago."

The sadness in her eyes brought a twinge to Coulter's heart. For a time, he had considered turning to liquor to ease the pain when Ellen died. But he had a daughter who needed him, and he would never do anything to hurt Cathy. "Is that when you were sent to the orphanage?"

She nodded. "We were only there for a few weeks when we ran away and rejoined the troupe of performers."

" 'We'?"

"My brother and I. We lied about our ages and picked up where our parents left off. We were even able to locate their costumes and material."

"Where is your brother now?"

Her gaze shifted from the sketch to Ellen's portrait. "Times were hard for us, and we found ourselves in a second-rate show. Armand started gambling to make money to buy the things he wanted. I told him I didn't want expensive clothes or jewelry, but he needed them. One night he won big, so I understand. He never made it back to the hotel. The police found his body the next day. All his money and jewelry were gone, and I was alone." Her voice was flat, tired, as if she'd lived with her sorrow for so long, there was no emotion left. "A kind lady in St. Louis took me in and together we began to work for the movement."

Unable to stop himself, Coulter snuffed out his smoke under his heel and reached for Josie. Without considering the circumstances of his actions, he pulled her into his embrace. She rested her forehead on his shoulder and clung to his shirt. With a gentle touch, he stroked her back, like he often comforted Cathy when she was sad or lonely. But this wasn't a child in his arms. Josie was a beautiful, full-bodied woman. Her breasts were crushed to his chest, her softness pressed to his hardness. He groaned at the instant reaction deep in his gut. Heat surged through him like a brush fire in the middle of a dry summer.

It had been so long, too long, since he'd held a woman like her. He buried his face in her long, unbound hair and drank in the clean fragrance. She was everything a woman should be. Everything he'd missed for four long years. The drought in his life had lasted far too long.

She trembled under his touch and lifted her face from his shoulder. Her eyes were as shiny as blue diamonds. The invitation was there on her face. Her lips parted and Coulter gave in to the need that had been dogging him since he'd entered the jail and heard her voice.

At the first brush of his mouth on hers, he lost the battle to control his emotions. The kiss started out slowly; her lips quivered against his. He tightened his grip and pulled her intimately against him, her thin gown and wrapper no barrier against the strength of his arousal. His tongue snaked past her parted lips, seeking entrance to her sweetness. She clutched his shoulders, her fingers digging into his flesh with an urgency that spurred him to deepen the kiss.

He gathered a handful of her hair, the golden strands like smooth, silk thread. When she began to return the kiss, matching her tongue to his, Coulter lost all sense of time and place. Primal needs, deep, hidden desires, took over. He pressed his tongue into the warmth of her mouth, stroking gently to imitate the way he wanted to know her fully as a man knows a woman. One hand dropped below her waist as he eased his swollen manhood against the soft cleft of her body.

She groaned softly, the sound exciting him to an even bolder touch. His fingers left her hair and skimmed the sides of her breasts. Her nipples hardened into tight buds against his chest. He broke off the kiss and grazed a row of light nips along her jaw and throat.

He was ready to take her—the heat in his veins about to burn him alive. "Angel," he whispered, the name catching in his throat. "A beautiful angel, as tempting as Eve."

With a trembling hand, she threaded her fingers through his hair. "Coulter, what's happening to me? I feel like I'm on fire."

Taking careful steps backward, Coulter eased toward the davenport he kept in the loft for when he worked late into the night. He lifted his gaze past her head and spied Ellen's portrait. Her golden eyes seemed to lock with his, and he thought he saw a frown tug at the corners of her mouth. His breath caught in his throat. Sanity stopped him in his tracks. His gaze shifted from his beloved's serene smile to Angel, the woman in his arms.

Passion glittered in her azure eyes, eyes that drew a man and tempted him beyond his endurance. Her skin was flushed; her body warm and ready to mate. Guilt swamped him like a tidal wave. How could he betray his Ellen with another woman?

He caught her arms and held her away from him. Her eyes were glazed with desire. His breath was coming in short gasps. It took a moment before he was able to speak, to offer some kind of explanation. "No, Angel, we can't."

"Can't?"

"I want you, but I can't make love to you."

Josie shook her head to clear away the fog from her mind. From the first touch of his lips, she'd slipped from reality into someplace she'd never been before. "Make love?" She looked into his face, his eyes dark and needy. Of course, that's where they were headed. To the davenport and a night of lovemaking. How had she let things get so out of control?

As if seeing herself through another's eyes, she noticed the way her wrapper had shifted from her shoulders, and how the neck of her gown had opened to reveal her throat and the tops of her breasts. Coulter was standing before her, staring into her face as if he, too, were just coming out of a trance.

"I'm sorry, Josie. I should have known better. It won't happen again." His voice seemed to come from far away.

She cupped her heated face in her cold hands, hoping to gain a tiny bit of composure. What must he think of her? Was she some kind of wanton who had no business in the home of a decent man? Or taking care of a sensitive little girl?

His fingers bit into her arms, holding her in place. "Are you all right?"

It took all her effort simply to nod. "You're right, it can't happen again. I shouldn't have come out here. I'm sorry if I embarrassed you." She dropped her gaze to his hands. "Please let me go, I want . . ."

He released her and she stumbled backward, her knees too weak to support her weight. When he stretched out a hand to help her, Josie shrugged out of his reach.

She hugged her wrapper tight against her body. Moments before, she'd been on fire; now a chill raced through her. "I have to go."

"Wait, let me explain—"

"You don't owe me an explanation, Sheriff. I know what you think of me. I'm nothing but a stage actress with loose morals. You decided you didn't want to dirty yourself with me." The words rushed around the tightening in her throat. She knew all too well what people thought about performers. He would never believe she'd never been with a man, that she'd guarded her heart like the most priceless of gems. After all, it was the only thing she had left.

Josie darted for the narrow ladder. As she stretched a foot down toward the top rung, Coulter caught her arm, and yanked her back into the loft. "Not so fast, Angel. That isn't what I think at all." He pulled her to a halt in front of him. "Listen to me, please."

Knowing it was useless to struggle against his greater strength, she dipped her head to hide the distress in her eyes. "I don't want to hear what you think of me. I'll have my things packed and be ready to leave your home at sunrise."

"Damn, Angel, it's all my fault." He cupped her chin with his finger and lifted her gaze to meet his. "You're a beautiful woman, and any normal man would desire you. I wanted you—hell, I still want you. But I couldn't just make love with you as if it meant nothing. It wouldn't be fair to you. It wouldn't be fair to me." His voice dropped to a deep growl. "I still love Ellen."

She shifted her gaze to the portrait on the easel, then to the sketch of Angel. How different they were, she thought. Innocence and purity versus worldliness and deception. "I understand," she said.

"I don't believe you do. I don't think any less of you since I learned you were a performer. And I don't want you to leave. You'll just have to trust me to control my carnal desires. Believe me, you're the first housekeeper I've been tempted to even look at twice."

Somehow she couldn't imagine him grabbing Miss Bettington and trying to kiss her. "Are you sure you want me to stay? You don't think I'll corrupt you or your child?"

"My daughter is crazy about you and I think you'll be good for her."

"For two weeks, Sheriff. That was our original agreement." Josie looked into the heat that lingered in his eyes and wondered how she was going to live under the same roof with him. Never in all her experience had she been so tempted by a man.

He stuck out his right hand. "It's a deal, Miss Clark."

In a purely businesslike manner, she accepted his gesture. "Thank you, Sheriff Steele." His hand was warm and Josie couldn't help remembering the way those same fingers had felt on her body only moments earlier. "I suppose I should get back to the house. Cathy may wake up and look for me."

"Go ahead. I'll be in as soon as I turn down the lamps and close the windows."

Her gaze fell to the sketch. "Are you going to tell anybody?"

"No, Angel. It will be our little secret."

She breathed a sigh of relief. Life was hard enough for a temperance worker without having a shady past to complicate matters. "Thank you," she said. By instinct she knew when it was time to make her exit. Gathering her gown and wrapper in one hand, she scurried down the ladder and left the tempting confines of the barn.

Chapter 10

"Miss Josie, come see!" Cathy's excited call came from the front porch where she was playing with her dolls.

"What is it, honey?" Josie rushed to the door to see what was the problem.

"Somebody's coming up the drive."

"Is it your papa?" Josie's heart fluttered in anticipation of seeing Coulter. She hadn't seen him since she'd left the loft last night. The kisses they'd shared lingered on her lips and her body tingled every time she thought about the way he'd touched her.

It was all wrong; she should be ashamed of the way she'd responded to his embrace. He was still in love with his wife, and she had her own agenda. A thousand times during the long, sleepless night she'd told herself to pack and leave. But with the light of dawn, she decided to stick it out for one more day—for Cathy's sake. What other reason could she give? The girl needed her until Coulter could find a respectable housekeeper.

Cathy shielded her eyes with her hand and yelled over

her shoulder. "I don't think so. It looks like Reverend Harris." She tossed aside her doll and ran down the drive.

An unexpected pang of disappointment struck Josie. Coulter had left before she arose that morning, leaving only a short note on the table. He wrote he had a busy day and he would try to return home early to take Cathy for a ride. Josie had been disheartened—not because she wanted to see him, but she'd planned to ask him to drive her into town.

Quickly she brushed her fingers through her hair to smooth back the tendrils that had slipped loose while she'd done a few household chores that morning. Stepping onto the porch, she watched as the black buggy came to a halt near the steps.

As expected, the minister was attired in a black serge suit, stiff white shirt, and black string tie. He tied off the lines and glanced around the yard. Cathy ran up the buggy and called out a loud greeting. "Hi, Preacher. What're you doing here?"

Josie wondered the same thing, although good manners prevented her from blurting out the question. "Good afternoon, Reverend," she called. "It's good to see you. Would you care for a cup of tea?"

The minister studied Josie for a moment before he climbed down from the wagon. "Good afternoon, Miss Clark, Cathy." He removed his black flat-brimmed hat, and inclined his head in a stiff, formal bow. "A cup of tea sounds wonderful. And Cathy, you know I often came to visit Miss Bettington."

The child followed in his footsteps and stopped beside Josie. "She ain't here no more. It's just me, and Miss Josie, and Papa. But he's in town, chasing outlaws or something."

Josie smiled at the girl's openness. Her grammar, like her manners, also needed work. The preacher frowned, clearly unhappy about something. Josie had a pretty good idea she'd soon learn the reason for the unexpected visit. Except for the solemn look on his face, the preacher was a rather nice-looking man. His features were softer, almost feminine—unlike Coulter's rugged, outdoorsy looks. His hands were smooth and white. The heaviest work he did was carrying his Bible and delivering the Word.

"Cathy, let the reverend catch his breath. I'm sure he visits all his flock from time to time." She held open the front door. "Please come into the parlor." As they entered the room, she turned to Cathy. "Honey, you can help me serve the tea."

The girl's eyes grew wide. "Can I have tea? Miss Bettington never let me drink any."

"And I won't, either. You can have milk while we have our tea."

After gesturing the minister to the davenport, Josie hurried into the kitchen. Minutes later, she carried a tray containing two cups, sugar, a glass of milk for Cathy, and a china teapot. As if she were greeting a visitor in her own home, Josie poured the tea and offered a cup to the reverend. She hadn't realized what a comforting feeling it was to be settled in a home with a family, although it was only a temporary situation.

For a few minutes, Josie and Reverend Harris exchanged small talk about the congregation, about the town, until the conversation deteriorated to a discussion of the weather. Both had finished their tea, but Josie sensed that the minister hadn't reached the real reason for his visit. He fidgeted with the cup, then he set it on the table beside the divan.

"Miss Clark, if I may be so bold . . ." He cleared his throat and slanted a glance at Cathy. "May I have a private word with you?"

His request took Josie by surprise. Surely anything the

minister had to say could be said in front of the child—
unless it was some kind of trouble. Josie looked down at
the girl who was quietly wiping a white smudge of milk
from her mouth with the back of her hand. "Cathy, would
you mind going out to the barn and seeing if Charlie would
like something cold to drink?"

On a sigh, Cathy rose and turned to Josie. "All right,
Miss Clark. I don't understand why grown-ups always want
to get rid of kids when they visit. Miss Bettington always
made me go outdoors whenever Mr. Homer came to look
for Papa, when he knew good and well Papa wasn't even
home."

Biting back a grin, Josie wondered about the former
housekeeper's relationship with the deputy. They would
make quite a pair, she thought, both so stiff and cold they
could start a snowstorm in July. "Run along, sweetie. I'll
give you a special treat later."

Alone with the minister, Josie settled back on the rocker
and waited for the man to begin. He twisted and shifted
positions several times, and ran his finger under the tight
collar of his stiff shirt. A line of perspiration beaded on
his upper lip. She tilted one eyebrow. "Well, Pastor. Did
you have something to discuss with me?"

Again he cleared his throat. "Um, Miss Clark, I'll get
right to the point. As you know, I was quite disturbed the
other evening when Sheriff Steele insisted you come to
his home after the rally. Then, when Miss Bettington
returned to town and said you were taking her place . . ."
His voice trailed off and he lifted his hands in a silent
plea. "A single woman and a widowed man living in close
proximity can cause quite a bit of concern among some
people."

Josie bit back a caustic remark. *Some people like you, don't
you mean?* She swallowed the words rather than start an

argument. It wouldn't do her cause any good to alienate
the town's minister. "Exactly what do you mean? My position here is only temporary until Coulter—Sheriff Steele
can hire another housekeeper. Did you frame the same
objections when Miss Bettington was working for the
sheriff?"

If he tugged any harder on that collar, he would pop
the button. His Adam's apple bobbed up and down like
a float on the water. "Well, no. But that was different. Miss
Bettington was . . . was . . . Um, she was older than you."
He sighed, as if glad to think up some reason other than
the truth.

Unable to remain seated, she stood and moved to the
mantel. Her gaze fell on the portrait of Coulter's wife. The
minister certainly didn't have to worry about Coulter and
Josie as long as Ellen stood between them. She was as real
a presence and as fine a chaperone as Miss Bettington in
the flesh had been.

"Age should make no difference. I certainly hope you
aren't implying I'm less moral or virtuous than she."

"No, no, not at all." He coughed and Josie began to
wonder if the man had consumption. "It's just that people
in a small town love to gossip."

"And as a newcomer, I suppose 'people' are speculating
about me."

"May I be completely honest with you, Miss Clark?"

She picked up his discarded cup and replaced it on
the tray. "By all means, Reverend Harris." The action
helped calm some of her rising temper. It wouldn't do
her already-tarnished reputation any good to blow up at
the minister. She sank back into the chair and waited to
hear the worse.

"I'm not sure you're aware that Sheriff Steele doesn't
have the most sterling character in town. He's been known

to return home at all hours, often with liquor on his breath."

The reverend's revelation didn't surprise Josie. She knew Coulter wasn't a saint, and he had more than a few reservations about the temperance movement. "Did you get that bit of news from Miss Bettington, by any chance?"

He shifted again, clearly uncomfortable by Josie's bold stance. "Yes, and others have seen him frequent the bars and saloons in town."

"Certainly it's part of his job as sheriff to maintain order in those places." Why she felt the need to defend Coulter, she had no idea. "I admit I'm not pleased that he doesn't support our cause, but surely that doesn't make him any worse than many of the men in town."

"There's more, Miss Clark." He glanced around and lowered his voice in a conspiratorial tone. "The sheriff was seen coming out of your hotel room carrying some of your . . . your apparel." A flush rose from his collar to his eyebrows.

Josie twisted her fingers together in her lap. Nothing escaped the gossips in town. If they knew even a bit about Josie's past, they would have enough material to talk about for a year. "You can tell your informants that the sheriff was merely assisting me in finding a seamstress to repair my torn garments. There was certainly nothing unseemly going on between us."

"Nothing to cause the gossips to trouble themselves, Reverend."

Coulter's unexpected voice brought them both up short. Josie spun around and the minister's flush reached clear to his hairline.

"Sheriff, I didn't know you were home. I didn't hear you ride up." Josie felt like a child caught with her hand in the cookie jar.

Coulter propped a wide shoulder against the doorway to the kitchen. "I took the short cut across the south pasture. Guess I'm too late for your tea party."

Coulter's dark gaze took in the entire scene in one long, hard glance. It was all quite aboveboard and proper, so why the heck did a hint of jealousy prickle at him? He'd met Cathy in the barn, and she'd warned him about the minister's visit.

Josie stood and stared at him. "What are you doing here?" The blush on her cheeks gave her a charming, girlish look. But the minister looked as if he were about to have a stroke. The man leaped to his feet and picked up his hat.

With feigned nonchalance, Coulter shoved away from the door. "I live here."

"I mean, what are you doing home in the middle of the afternoon?"

He shrugged. "Just came to pick up a few supplies. I got a wire from the sheriff over in Goodland. Seems the bank was robbed and he's asking for help in tracking the bandits. I'm taking a few good men and meeting up with his posse."

Coulter moved farther into the room and stretched out his hand to the minister. "Sorry we couldn't visit, Preacher. But I have to get moving, and I'm sure you have other calls to make."

"Yes, of course, Sheriff. I should be running along." He smiled at Josie. "Thank you for the tea, Miss Clark." With a quick nod, he scurried through the front door as if his coattail were on fire.

Coulter tucked his thumbs in his gunbelt and watched the minister drive away. "Preacher giving you a rough time?" he asked.

Josie moved to his side, her violet fragrance drawing his attention to her presence. "You know how small-town people like to talk. They're just speculating about our relationship."

Her words flowed over him like a warm summer breeze. Their relationship. The sound of it brought to mind the kisses they'd shared in the loft the past night—not that he'd thought about much else during the long, sleepless night. But he had no relationship with this woman. He still loved Ellen. "What did you tell him?"

"That they have nothing to worry about; I'm working as your housekeeper. Then he warned me that you're sometimes less than a perfect gentleman."

He laughed. That was one very big understatement, considering the way he felt every time he looked at this woman. "I would advise you to heed his warnings, Angel." Realizing he was treading on dangerous ground, he turned toward the kitchen. "I'd better gather up my supplies and hit the road."

"How long will you be gone?" Josie stopped him with her hand on his bare forearm.

Her touch sent a shot of longing through him. The same longing he'd spent the entire night fighting.

"Not more than a few days. If we don't pick up their trail by then, we might as well give up." He covered her fingers with his own. Her comforting gesture reached clear into his heart. He'd missed having a woman care for him, someone who was concerned for his safety.

"Be careful, Coulter."

On pure impulse, he lifted her fingers to his lips and planted a brief kiss there. "Believe me, Angel, I will." Her sparkling blue eyes met his. He wondered what she would do if he kissed her like he had done last night. He'd wanted her, more than he'd wanted a woman in years. Since Ellen. He dropped her hand and stepped away. Leaving her for a few days was best for both of them. He would use the time to get his libido under control.

"I've asked Charlie to move into the barn until I get

back. He'll do whatever chores you give him, and drive you into town if you need anything."

"Cathy and I will be fine, Sheriff. Don't worry about us."

"I'm sure you will, Angel."

"Do you want me to pack some food for you?"

"A few cans of beans, some bread and coffee. I'll pack the rest of my gear." He took the stairs two at a time.

By the time he returned to the kitchen, Cathy was helping Josie wrap the food in a cloth. He paused for a moment and watched them work together. His heart constricted. His daughter definitely needed a mother. But was Josie Clark the right woman for the job? Or would she up and head back to the theater the first chance she got? He shoved the thought from his mind. He didn't need the distraction of a woman when facing a dangerous mission.

"Guess I'm ready to head out," he said.

Cathy threw herself against him and wrapped her arms around his waist. "I love you, Papa."

"I love you, too, sweetheart. Be a good girl and take care of Miss Josie." He planted a quick kiss on her forehead.

"Aren't you going to kiss Miss Josie, too?" Cathy smothered a giggle with her hand.

He took the food from Josie and met her shy smile. What the heck? A man needed a woman's kiss on his lips when he was riding off on a manhunt. With a swiftness that left her open-mouthed, he planted a quick, hard kiss on her mouth. "See you in a few days."

For a long moment, they remained so close their breaths melted into one. "Take care," she whispered.

Coulter stepped away before he gave in to the impulse to sweep her into his arms and finish the job he'd started last night. "I will."

With one last look into her heated gaze, he hurried through the doorway. He wasn't sure which was more dangerous—chasing bank robbers, or staying in the house with a beautiful, desirable woman.

After one quick glance back at Angel waving from the porch with his daughter at her side, he decided.

The woman.

Without a doubt, the woman.

Chapter 11

With Coulter gone, Josie had time to think. And to worry. Being stuck out on the ranch wasn't doing either her project or her nerves any good. So she developed a plan.

After finishing her chores, she put on a pretty navy suit and a perky sailor hat, then she asked Charlie to drive her and Cathy into town. She'd spent another sleepless night because of Coulter Steele, and she no intention of staying on the ranch and worrying about him all day.

If anything happened to him, word would come into town first. She wanted to be nearby if for some reason he needed her. For his daughter's sake, she told herself. Certainly not because she cared. Besides, she wanted to confer with Bertha without Coulter around to interfere with her cause.

She entered the emporium where Bertha usually spent her days managing her favorite of her husband's many enterprises. Over dinner the past Sunday, Josie had learned how the one-time drummer had come to Council City with little more than a suitcase of wares, and married the preacher's older daughter. He'd opened a general store, then expanded it into a small conglomerate of businesses. In addition to the emporium and general store, Oscar owned the livery stable, the feed and hardware store, as well as having an interest in the hotel, the bank, and several other properties on Main Street.

He'd done well, and Bertha had set herself up as the social leader of the town. Having her for an ally was a real coup for the S.A.A.T. In addition, Josie genuinely liked the woman. Being childless, Bertha clearly adored the sheriff and his daughter.

The emporium was well stocked with the latest fashions and dry goods from back East. Josie stopped and studied an array of colorful fabrics stacked on the shelves along the wall. A glass showcase held an assortment of threads and lace trims for the well-dressed lady.

Josie remembered a time when she and her mother thought nothing of grabbing up bolts of silks and satins, crystal beads, and Venetian laces. Mama always employed the best dressmakers who sewed the latest fashions.

Those days were gone, and Josie's present wardrobe consisted of remakes of the gowns she'd purchased when she'd been a performer. That was before Papa and Armand had died. She shook off the memory of the past and focused on the problems at hand.

Cathy ran ahead and called for her aunt. "Back here, darling," Bertha yelled back. "I'm in the millinery department."

Josie smiled. Obviously Bertha had been to Lord and Taylor or Wanamaker's and had set up her store into various departments, divided by the variety of goods available. Of course, her shop was on a much smaller scale than the Chicago emporiums, but she'd done her best to imitate the larger, elegant stores.

After glancing at the artfully arranged shoes and ready-made dresses hanging in view, she moved toward the rear.

Millinery was Bertha's first love. She bragged that she personally designed and made every hat sold in her shop.

When Josie found Bertha, she was pinning a huge pink feather on a straw hat already covered with enough feathers to fly away on its own accord. She wondered if the local women ever purchased the outrageous fashions. Most ladies at church wore calico sunbonnets or simple straw hats with very few decorations. Bertha, on the other hand, wore her own designs, some even more extravagant than the one in her hand.

"What do you think, Josie? This is one of my most stunning styles. I'll wear it to church next Sunday."

"It's really something, Bertha," Josie said, evading the fact that the hat was ridiculous to a fault. Josie's own headgear had been purchased in Chicago, and was extremely conservative by comparison.

"You know, dear, these red feathers would be lovely on you. I'd love to design something for you. Why, with your pale hair and bright eyes, you would be quite a knockout when you enter church." She waved a huge ostrich plume toward Josie. "I'll bet even my stubborn nephew would notice you in something like this."

Heat rushed to Josie's face. Angel always wore feathers in her hair, and Coulter had already noticed. "Bertha, I have enough problems without attracting further attention to myself."

"Nonsense. A woman needs to be noticed by a man— a special man, that is." She set the hat aside and eyed Josie over her spectacles. "You've raised quite a stir in town by staying out at the ranch alone with Coulter."

"Miss Josie isn't alone with Papa," Cathy said, coming to Josie's defense. "I'm there with them." Picking up the outrageous creation, Cathy placed it on her head and studied herself in the mirror.

With a gentle laugh, Bertha snatched the hat from the child. "Run along, Cathy. Uncle Oscar is working over in the grocery section. Tell him to give you a nickel's worth of candy—my treat."

Josie watched the child skip across the wooden floor and through a doorway that separated the stores. "She's a lovely child, isn't she, Bertha? Is she much like her mother?" Josie asked, curiosity getting the best of her. Cathy was right about one thing. Josie and Coulter were well-chaperoned. Ellen was always right there between them.

"Actually, Cathy is more like my sister, Coulter's mother. Louisa was strong-willed, with a mind of her own. When she met Lucas Steele, she decided to marry him, and nothing and nobody could stop her. It didn't matter that he was half Comanche, or that he had nothing more than a run-down ranch. She loved him and he loved her. They both adored Coulter. What happened to them was a great tragedy for all of us."

The sadness in the older woman's eyes touched Josie. "What was Coulter's wife like?"

"Ellen? She was a sweet, gentle girl. But she was spoiled by her rich parents. Coulter met her when he went to Kansas City to study art. Her parents didn't think an artist was the proper husband for their daughter. Not that they thought Coulter was good enough for their only child. They always thought he was beneath their lofty social circle. But he was what Ellen wanted, and they gave her everything she wanted." Bertha set the hat on the dummy and tied the red bow under the chin. "He switched to law and joined her father's law firm."

The thought of Coulter giving up his art for the woman he loved brought a tingle to Josie's heart. "He loves her very much."

"I know. In Coulter's eyes Ellen was perfect, she could do no wrong. He gave in to her every whim. She insisted on living with her parents, and that's where they stayed. I know Coulter wanted his own home, but Ellen was accustomed to the luxury and servants that Coulter couldn't afford.''

"Was he happy?"

Bertha studied Josie with a strange gleam in her eye. "I suppose so. But Ellen is gone, and it's time he gets on with his life.''

Although Josie couldn't agree more, the sheriff's personal life was none of her concern. "Bertha, I didn't come to discuss Coulter's problems; I wanted to speak to you about our next plan of attack.''

Bertha tilted one eyebrow and slanted Josie a knowing smile. "Actually, dear, Coulter is our problem. He's ordered us not to organize any marches or to block the sidewalk in front of the saloons. He sides with the men on this issue.''

"And the women are on our side. I do have another strategy.'' Josie glanced around to make sure they were alone. Satisfied that the other customers were on the far side of the store, she lowered her voice. "We've learned of two ways to close down the bars. One, we can cut off their supplies of alcohol. But that's rather difficult since we don't know where or when they get their deliveries.''

"Oscar could tell us; he knows everything that goes in Council City. But he likes his nip now and then, and refuses to cooperate. What else can we do?"

"Second, we can cut off their customers.''

A frown tugged at Bertha's full lips. "If we can't block the doors, how can we stop the men from frequenting those places?''

"We can get them to sign abstinence pledges, or we can embarrass them into staying away.''

"How can we do that?'' Bertha tilted a skeptical eyebrow.

"In some cities we station our workers outside the bars with the pledge forms. We also make lists of the men who enter the establishments. Then on Sunday, we read the list in church. These fine, upstanding husbands don't want the congregation to know their habits, and their wives usually can convince them to support the cause."

Humor twinkled in Bertha's eyes. "What an idea! Many of the men are deacons, who certainly don't want their sins announced to the congregation."

Josie fingered the red feather, almost tempted to buy it for old times' sake. She quickly rejected the notion. "On my way here, I noticed the bank is directly across from the Golden Garter. Coulter can't stop me from sitting outside the bank, and from there I can watch the comings and goings in the saloon."

"What about your job out at Coulter's place? I don't think he'll be too happy about this."

"I'm his housekeeper, not his prisoner. If I choose to come into town, he can't stop me as long as I don't neglect his child. Cathy can come with me and identify the men I don't know." The thought of displeasing the sheriff was of little concern. She'd already made it clear she had no intention of giving up her project. In truth, she rather enjoyed the idea of riling Coulter. "Besides, he isn't here. I can get started and the other women can spell me when I'm out on the ranch."

"That's a fine idea. I'll help you when I'm not busy in the store, and, of course, Cathy knows just about everybody in town. The way she feels about you, she'll want to be right at your side."

Josie squeezed the older woman's hand. "I appreciate your support. Since I'm here, I'll get started right away."

"Let's have some tea first. I've gotten the finest imported tea from India, and I'm ready for a break."

Josie couldn't help smiling. "That sounds wonderful." They moved to a small table set up in the corner of the store. "By the way, Bertha, has there been any word from the sheriff?"

"Not yet." Over her shoulder, Bertha cast a sly glance at Josie. "But don't worry. Coulter can take care of himself."

"I'm not worried. I'm only concerned for Cathy." She certainly didn't want the child to lose her father, as Josie had. Yet why did the thought of something happening to Coulter leave a hollow spot in her chest?

"I understand," she said, handing a cup to Josie. Her smile said Coulter's aunt understood a whole lot more than Josie wanted her to—a whole lot more than Josie wanted to admit even to herself.

For the next three days, Josie became a fixture in front of the bank. Glad to be back at work, she carefully jotted down the names of the men who entered the bar across the street. Although few were willing to sign the pledges, she nevertheless felt she was making progress. Cathy thought it was great fun, and waved to everybody who passed on wagon or horseback. Several times a day Homer, whom Coulter had left in charge of his town, passed by, but he steered clear of Josie. The deputy clearly didn't want another black eye, or worse.

Tony Sanders, the proprietor of the Golden Garter, stared at Josie, but since she wasn't actively interfering with his business, he chose to ignore her. From time to time, other women arrived to spell Josie. Since their march had been aborted, they eagerly looked forward to contributing to the cause. As long as it was someone else's husband, not their own, who would be embarrassed, they were happy to take the names.

Every time a horse passed on the dusty street, Josie studied the rider, eager for a glimpse of Coulter. He'd been gone for over three days, and even Oscar hadn't heard from him. By Saturday afternoon Josie wondered if the town should send out a posse for the sheriff.

The streets were crowded with farmers in their wagons, rancher's wives driving buggies, children greeting their friends, and numerous cowboys spending their day off in town. Many of the men entered and left the bars and saloons. Gaily-gowned women lounged on the boardwalks in front of the saloon, encouraging the men to enter and spend their hard-earned wages. Most of their customers were cowboys from the surrounding ranches. Josie carefully noted the names Cathy gave her, including the brands of the outfits where they worked. Men she recognized as farmers and ranchers tugged their hats low on their foreheads, making identification difficult.

Josie was sorely tempted to move her location directly into the doorways for a better view. She abandoned the idea when a bunch of tough-looking wranglers tied up at the hitching post in front of the saloon.

Ignoring the men, she shifted her attention to a rider on a gray horse passing at a slow gait. The man's shoulders were slumped and his dark hat rode low on his forehead. "Coulter!" She jumped to her feet and tried to quell the pounding in her chest. He was back, and he was safe.

Coulter reined in his horse. The feminine voice penetrated his numbed brain. He turned to see the blonde woman standing at the edge of the boardwalk, her hands clutching the post. In that brief instant, a glimmer of hope pierced the weariness that had plunged him into a dark hole. His base instinct had been to go directly home—to her, he was forced to admit. Instead, duty took over and he'd ridden into town to check with Homer.

Was she in town waiting for him? His gaze locked with hers. He propped an elbow on the saddle horn and drank in her beauty like a man lost in a desert, spying a cool, clear lake. As he watched, a movement behind her caught his eye.

Cathy darted past Angel's skirts and flew into the street. "Papa!" she squealed, reaching him on a run. "I'm so glad you're home."

He reached down and clasped his daughter's arms. With little effort he hoisted her into the saddle in front of him.

"Hi, pumpkin. What are you doing here in town? Waiting for your papa?" His words were for Cathy, but his gaze moved slowly over to Josie. She clutched a ledger book in her arms, keeping her eyes locked with his.

The heat was there, as fiery as the sun glowing relentlessly overhead. He wiped the sweat from his forehead with the back of his hand. Suddenly aware that Cathy was speaking, he forced his thoughts back to his daughter.

"Papa, I missed you so much." She wrapped her arms around his neck and buried her face in the front of his dusty shirt.

"Well, did you now?" An unbidden smile snaked across his lips. "Are you and Miss Josie looking for me?"

"I was. I'm working with Miss Josie, but we were watching for you." She leaned closer and whispered, "Miss Josie kept asking Uncle Oscar if he'd heard from you."

A bit of the despair of the failed chase flew away at the thought of Josie waiting for him. "You can quit worrying your pretty little heads now that I'm home. Did Charlie drive you into town?"

"Yeah. And he comes and takes us home. Except last night, Reverend Harris took us home after the Bible study."

An odd twinge of jealousy struck Coulter. He didn't like the minister following behind her. Josie was supposed to attend to Cathy's needs, not flirt with other men. He needed to have a talk with the lady.

"Papa, will I still be able to work with Miss Josie?"

He stopped his horse in front of the general store when he saw Oscar step through the open doorway. "What kind of work were you doing?"

"We're working for the S'ciety." She twisted in his arms. "Hey, Uncle Oscar, my papa's home."

"I see that, Cathy." Oscar reached for out and lifted Cathy from Coulter's arms.

Coulter swung from the saddle and looped his reins over

the hitching post. "Run and tell Miss Josie I'll meet you at home in a little while."

"Okay, Papa. We'll fix a real fine dinner just for you." She took off on a run toward Josie.

Coulter lifted his gaze and spotted Josie where he'd left her in front of the bank. Before he had time to contemplate what kind of work she and Cathy were doing for the Society, Oscar slapped his back in a hearty greeting.

"Glad you made it back, Coulter. Any luck trailing those outlaws?"

"No. We lost them in Oklahoma Territory." The fact that they'd lost the trail burned like acid in Coulter's gut. His instinct told him that it was only a matter of time until Council City would be a target for the bandits. He and Homer had better be on the alert for the eventuality. He shoved back his hat and glanced toward the bank. "We thought we were getting close, but somehow they found a hiding place we can't seem to locate. I think somebody's hiding them not too far from Indian territory." From the corner of his eye, he spotted Homer hurrying toward him. Not trouble, not now, when he was bone-weary. "How's everything in town? Any problems?"

Oscar frowned and gestured to the deputy. "Nothing important. I'm sure Homer will fill you in on all the gossip."

By the look on his uncle's face, he knew something was up. Oscar didn't have much use for Homer Potts, and had advised Coulter against hiring the man who had been his opponent when he'd first run for sheriff. But Homer was an experienced lawman, and Coulter needed a good deputy.

"Sheriff, glad you're back. I told you that woman was nothing but trouble, but nobody would listen to me."

Oscar shrugged and returned to the sanctuary of his store, leaving Coulter alone to face his irate deputy. Without even asking, Coulter was certain Homer was talking about Josie Clark. "Homer, I'm bone-tired. Short of murder or a riot, I'll hear all about it tomorrow."

"Harriet said you'd take her side."

Several men stopped on their way into the store to watch the confrontation. Not wanting his business to be spread all over town, Coulter lowered his voice. "Harriet?"

Homer squared his shoulders, ignoring the bystanders. "Miss Bettington. Mother invited her to stay with us until she finds another position. She warned us that woman would cause trouble."

"You've already told me that. What kind of trouble did she get into now? Not another altercation with you?" Coulter moved past the two men studying the checkerboard resting on a barrel.

At the reminder that he'd come out on the losing end of their last confrontation, Homer's face reddened. He glanced around and spied the men bending their ears to hear his reply. Coulter resisted a grin at the comical expression on Homer's face. The deputy remembered all too well not only being bested by Josie, but Oscar's censure as well—not to mention the snickers of the townspeople over his black eye.

"She's sitting there, by the bank, day after day writing in her book. I told her she'd have to move along, but Oscar said she has every right to sit there."

"Did you try to arrest her?"

George Wright looked up from his daily checker game and started laughing. "He wouldn't dare, Sheriff. That little lady's one tough hombre."

"Nobody asked you, George. I ought to run you in for vagrancy."

"Can he do that, Sheriff?" asked his companion, Russell Allen.

Coulter shook his head. Since he'd returned to town five years ago, the men had spent every day except Sunday engaged in their daily competition. He was certain their wives sent them into town to get the men out of their hair. "It's all right, boys. You're safe as long as Oscar doesn't complain." He started walking toward the jail, a few doors down the street. "John Davis is the bank president. Has he complained about Miss Clark?"

Homer hurried to keep up with Coulter's longer stride. "No, but she's got the other women helping her."

"Exactly what are the women doing?" He stopped at the jailhouse door and glanced back toward the bank. Josie and Cathy had disappeared; on their way home, he hoped.

"Taking the name of every man who goes into the saloons. She plans to read the names in church this Sunday."

Coulter rubbed his forehead at his growing headache. This was one of the times he regretted not taking Oscar's advice. "As long as she doesn't break any laws, there's nothing we can do. But I'll talk to her and see if I can convince her to stay out of trouble."

Easier said than done. Josie Clark had a mind of her own, and Coulter had no idea how to convince her to stay at the ranch when she set her mind on coming to town. He shook his head in disbelief. Since she'd come to Council City, the temperance worker had turned the orderly town upside down.

And she'd set Coulter's peace of mind right on its ear.

Chapter 12

Josie couldn't pull her gaze from Coulter's strong back as he guided his horse down the dusty street. Her heart beat faster at the sight of him. He was dirty and tired but he'd lifted Cathy into the saddle as easily as lifting a rag doll. She hugged her arms, remembering the way his hands had felt around her a few nights ago.

The anxiety of the past days disappeared the instant she'd seen he was safe and unharmed. When he slid down from the saddle, he glanced her way, a warm grin on his face. Did he know she'd been waiting for him to return home? Could he possibly know that she'd spent sleepless nights worrying about his safety? All that mattered was that he was home.

Home? With a start she remembered that within minutes he would return to the ranch, expecting to find a hot meal and bath. Neither was waiting for him. Not only were her cooking skills lacking, Josie had left early and hadn't bothered to start a fire in the stove. After what he'd clearly been through, he deserved more than a piece of cold, stale bread and sliced tomatoes.

For the past few days, she and Cathy had eaten their dinner with Oscar and Bertha. Coulter's aunt would be willing to help, but Saturday was her busiest day in the emporium and Josie couldn't ask her to leave her shop to prepare dinner for Coulter.

She had to think fast. Watching as Coulter spoke with Oscar, Josie's gaze drifted across the street to the City Cafe, the restaurant where she'd eaten several times in the past week. Polly Turner, chief cook and owner, was one of the Society's staunchest supporters and had become a friend to Josie. Like most of the women who championed the cause, the widow had her own reasons for working to abolish liquor. Josie had learned that Polly's husband had gambled away their ranch, then died of alcoholism. She'd been left with three children, including ten-year-old Sally Jane, who was Cathy's best friend. With Oscar's financial assistance, she'd used her cooking skills to operate a successful cafe.

Josie took off on a run, an idea buzzing around in her mind. All she needed was a little help from Polly, and to find Charlie and reach the ranch before Coulter did. She was almost positive Homer had enough complaints to keep Coulter occupied at the jail for at least a little while.

For the time being, Josie's luck held out. Minutes later, Charlie pulled the rig in front of the restaurant and helped Josie and Cathy onto the high seat. The young man had finished his chores early and had returned to town for a few hours of relaxation. At Josie's urging he'd stopped and picked up the clean wash from Mr. Wong's Chinese Laundry. Whatever salary Josie expected from Coulter was rapidly being eaten up by paying for laundry services and ready-prepared food.

They'd barely entered the house when Coulter rode his horse into the barn. With minutes to spare, Josie started the fire in the cast-iron stove and dumped the chicken and dumplings from Polly into a large pot. Cathy ran outside to greet her father. Josie was certain by the time they returned to the house, Coulter would have a full report of their activities of the past days. She hoped he wouldn't be upset at her latest project. A good hot meal would go a long way into calming his ire.

With the food warming on the burner, Josie sliced the fresh bread Polly had set in the basket, and added fresh tomatoes from the garden. In return for the dinner, she'd agreed to give Polly the bushel of green beans that sat waiting in the pantry. It seemed like a fair trade since Josie had no idea how to prepare or can the beans.

After setting the table with the mismatched china, she stepped onto the porch with a clean towel and soap in her hand. Coulter stepped from the barn, Cathy skipping behind him. His long stride seemed a little slower than usual. He glanced up at her, and flashed a crooked smile. A band tightened in her chest. The warmth that flowed over her was much like the times when Papa had winked at her in a gesture of praise for a good performance. Similar, but stronger and different.

He stopped at the pump and grinned up at Josie. "I suppose you won't let me into the house until I clean up."

She returned his smile. "That's right, Sheriff. I spent all day scrubbing the floors and cooking your dinner. I want a clean man at my table."

Mischievous humor glittered in his dark eyes. "Sure you did. And who was that lady sitting in front of the bank when I rode into town? Please tell me it wasn't your twin. One Angel is all this mortal can handle."

And this one man was more than she could handle. She tossed the towel at his head. "Let's just say I have talents as yet untapped."

"Of that I have few doubts." He caught the towel and dropped it beside the pump. In one quick movement, he tugged his dusty shirt over his head. "Cathy, honey, please run in and get Papa a clean shirt?" he asked, as the dirty garment cleared his head.

"Sure, Papa." Cathy ran into the house and slammed the screen door behind her.

"I'll take a hot bath later this evening." Coulter grabbed the red pump handle and stroked it up and down.

Josie flushed at the thought of his naked body soaking in the same tub she'd soaked in last night. The sight before her was equally disturbing—his bare torso gleamed with sweat, the muscles in his arms and chest bulged. It was enough to set her nerves on edge. Yet she didn't dare turn away.

He stuck his head under the spigot and let the water flow over his hair in a steady stream. Her gaze remained locked on him. Splatters of crystal-clear water poured over his shoulders and arms, plastering the dark hair to his bronzed skin. His face glowed with pleasure. His expression reminded her of the way he'd looked a few nights ago when he'd backed her toward the davenport in his loft. Heat surged through Josie, along with feelings she'd spent days trying to understand.

During her years as a performer, she'd heard the women backstage talk about men, about love, about sex. Their giggles and exclamations always made her curious about men and their effect on women. Until she had met Coulter Steele, she'd had little idea what had gotten the women so excited. Now she knew. Simply looking at this man did strange things to her insides.

Coulter stopped the pump and shook the water from his hair. He covered his head and face with the towel. Beads of water drizzled down his body to his lean waist and into the denims tugged low on his hips. Josie's gaze followed the progress of one particular drop to the dark

COULTER'S ANGEL   133

hair that swirled around his navel and lower into his trousers. She gripped the porch post to keep from moving toward him and brushing her hands across his gleaming flesh.

Josie had been around handsome men all her life. Backstage in the theater, she'd seen men in various degrees of dress and undress. But none had ever impressed her like the man standing there beside the pump. Coulter Steele was man, pure and simple—as masculine and appealing as Adam was to Eve; and as tempting as that ripe, red apple that had caused her downfall.

The words of the old hymn echoed through her head. *"Yield not to temptation . . ."* Resisting was getting harder and harder all the time.

His face hidden in the towel, Coulter watched the play of emotions on Josie's face. The pretty flush gave her a look, part innocent curiosity and part womanly interest. She was a woman with womanly needs and passion. His body reacted with a painful surge of desire.

He'd never had a woman look at him quite like that. True, the "ladies" with whom he'd spent an occasional night had offered flowery words of flattery, however genuine or false. Certainly Ellen had never gazed at him as if ready to devour him alive. His wife had always insisted in total darkness when they'd made love. And she'd never dared look at his nudity in broad daylight.

He changed his mind about the hot bath. If he managed to make it through the evening, he would douse his desires in the cool creek that ran a few hundred yards behind the barn.

As he lowered the towel and began to wipe his chest and shoulders, Cathy burst through the doorway waving his shirt like a flag. "Here it is, Papa. Hope you like the blue one."

Josie jumped and spun on her heel. "I'd better check on dinner. Please come in as soon as you're dressed." Her skirts swung in a sassy flurry, showing a petticoat edged in lace, and trim ankles above her leather shoes.

Cathy planted her hands on her narrow hips. "Papa, did you make Miss Josie mad?"

Coulter hurriedly wiped the water from his chest. "I don't think so, honey. Why do you ask?"

Eyes almost the exact color of his own glared at him with childish indignation. "Her face was red and she was looking at you kind of funny."

His face hidden as he slipped the shirt over his head, Coulter smothered his laughter. She hadn't been looking at him half as funny as the way he was looking at her. "Just in case I've offended Miss Josie, let's go pick some flowers. That should make her glad with me again."

"Okay, Papa. I know she likes flowers, and those pink roses by the front porch are her favorites." Cathy jumped to the ground, and shooed away the stubborn hen that made her nest under the house.

Trailing behind his daughter, Coulter couldn't help noticing the difference the past week had wrought in the child. Cathy was humming a song and skipping her way across the yard. His heart swelled at the sight of his daughter, once again the happy, carefree child she should be. He lifted his gaze to the house. He had Josie Clark to thank for the change. But what would happen to Cathy when she left? When Josie Clark reverted to Angel LeClare and took off for parts unknown, to do God only knows what?

"Papa, you cut the roses, while I pick some daisies." She knelt on the ground in front of the flower bed. "Watch out for the thorns."

Coulter pulled his out his pocketknife and opened the blade. Heeding his daughter's advice, he cut through the stem of a pink bud on the brink of opening. The fragrance wafted around him, reminding him of the woman as beautiful as a rose with a temper as prickly as thorns. But there

was no rose without a thorn, and Josie's passion made her
Angel.

He'd thought that being away on the manhunt would
keep his mind so occupied, he would have little time to
think about her. To his dismay, she was never far from
his thoughts. He wondered what she was doing—was she
staying out of trouble? To him, she wasn't Josie Clark, she
was Angel LeClare.

Lost in his thoughts, Coulter jabbed his finger on a
thorn, drawing a single drop of blood. He stuck the injury
into this mouth and muttered under his breath. He'd better be careful around the roses, and he'd better keep his
wits about him with Angel. She could cause a heck of a
lot more pain than any prickly flower. Quickly he cut off
another three flowers and wrapped the stems in his handkerchief.

"Here, Papa," Cathy said. She flashed a sly grin as she
handed him a bunch of daisies. "Did you used to bring
flowers to Mama when you were courting her?"

"I suppose so, honey." But never ones picked in the
meadow. Ellen loved flowers from the florist. His wife had
been as delicate as a hothouse orchid. Josie reminded him
of the wild roses twined around the porch rail.

"Good. Now you can give the flowers to Miss Josie when
you call on her like her suitor."

"Call? Suitor?" Coulter's breath caught, and he choked
on his attempt to speak. "I'm not ..." By the time the
words formed on his lips, Cathy had run up the porch and
into the house. "I'm not calling on anybody, especially
not Josie." His voice trailed off to a whisper.

Coulter's gaze fell to the bouquet clutched in his fist. If
he wanted to be perfectly honest with himself, he would
admit that it was Josie's face he saw when he closed his
eyes at night. It was Josie's voice that called to him in his
dreams. It was Josie's soft body he wanted to join with his

own in love. He cursed his weakness. Ellen was the woman he loved, not Josie.

He wanted to drop the flowers and grind them under his heels. He wanted to deny his attraction to Josie. He wanted to ... He wanted to quit lying to himself. The pretty blonde had reminded him how long he'd been alone. How much he missed having a woman to love. How much he'd missed having a woman love him.

In spite of all his needs and longing, Josie wasn't the right woman. Too soon she would be gone, off to conquer other towns and spread the message of the temperance movement. Or back to the stage.

"Papa, come on." Cathy's voice pulled him out of his stupor. "We're waiting for you."

On a long sigh, Coulter climbed the steps and entered the house. Cathy caught his hand the instant he stepped through the doorway.

"Miss Josie," she called. "Come see. Papa has something for you." She tugged him toward the kitchen.

Josie turned from the stove and glanced at him over her shoulder. She tilted one shapely eyebrow in question. By now her color had returned to normal. The stray hair around her forehead was damp and he suspected she'd splashed cold water on her face.

"Papa has flowers for you. Aren't they beautiful?"

Cathy's motives were as clear to Josie as they were to him. The little minx was playing matchmaker.

"Yes, they are, Cathy. But I have the feeling it was your idea." She jammed her hands into the pockets of her apron as if afraid to reach out for the flowers.

"Oh, no, ma'am." Cathy crossed her arms over her heart. "I promise. Papa thought about it all by himself."

Josie eyed him suspiciously.

"My daughter's right, Miss Clark. It was my idea." He shoved the bouquet toward her. "I just thought you would like them. After all, you said you worked hard all day."

A tiny smile curved her lips—lips the exact color pink as the flowers. Humor twinkled in her blue eyes. "Thank you, Sheriff. They're lovely."

Their fingers brushed as the flowers changed hands. Her gaze lifted and he recognized the heated sparks in the fathomless blue depths. He jumped away as if scorched by her touch. "Something smells mighty good." The words sounded strained even to his own ears.

Cathy giggled and took her seat at the table. "Chicken and dumplings, Papa. Your favorite."

He glanced at Josie, her back to him as she arranged the flowers in a glass. "And if that's apple pie, I'll think I've died and gone to heaven. Miss Clark, I'd say you're a real angel."

She turned toward him and set the bouquet on the table. High color returned to her face. "I still can't make a decent cup of coffee. Would you kindly prepare the pot while I set the meal on the table?"

While he did her bidding, he glimpsed an exchange between Josie and his daughter. They looked like two conspirators plotting a crime.

"Isn't Charlie going to join us?" Josie asked.

Coulter took a large and unfamiliar bowl from her hands and set it in the middle of the table. "No, I sent him home. I think he has plans to go sparking this evening."

"Is that why he was making sheep eyes at Jenny Mae Booker?" Cathy asked, her words drawing both Coulter's and Josie's interest. "I saw them in the livery when I went to fetch him to bring us home. Reckon he's planning to court Jenny Mae." She lifted her gaze to Coulter's, and a wide smile curved her small mouth. He could almost read the question in his daughter's mind. Was he planning to court Miss Josie?

No, his mind shouted. *Never in a million years.*

Josie settled on a chair and spread her napkin on her lap. "Cathy, what do you know about courting?"

Cathy lifted guileless brown eyes and grinned. "I know a lot. I know that when men go courting, they give ladies flowers and candy and they hold hands and make funny faces at each other." Josie's gaze dropped to the flowers in the center of the table. Cathy continued, barely taking a breath. "They dance together and sometimes they go off in the dark. I guess they go sparking or something. But I'm not sure exactly what sparking means."

A wide grin slashed across Coulter's face. His face turned red, as he struggled to keep from laughing. Josie could only stare at the child, dumbfounded.

"I'll tell you about it, pumpkin, when you get to be thirty or forty or so." To his credit, Coulter managed to control his glee. "Let's eat, before this delicious meal gets cold."

The topic of men, women, courting, and sparking was dropped in favor of chicken and dumplings. Coulter shared a little of the manhunt, relaying that the outlaws had gotten away. Josie kept waiting for him to question her on her activities, but he kept the conversation on safe, neutral subjects.

Until he dished out his third helping. "These are some of the best chicken and dumplings I've ever had. They're almost as good as Polly's over at the cafe."

Cathy giggled, covering her mouth with her hand, and Josie choked on her water. He knew. The glimmer in his eyes said he'd seen right through her ruse. Josie squared her shoulders and met his gaze. She'd promised to look after his daughter and provide as best she could. Even if she wasn't particularly adapt at domesticity, the man should be grateful she was at least resourceful.

"Wait until you taste the pie," she offered with a wide smile.

"I'm sure it will every bit as delicious as Polly's."

Josie offered her most charming smile, the one that always won over her audience. "I'll fetch us each a slice." She stood and moved to the stove. "That coffee should be done by now," she said. Holding the handle of the pot with the corner of her apron, she filled two mugs.

She felt Coulter's gaze on her back as she returned to the sideboard and sliced the pie. With a flourish, she set a large piece in front of him, and smaller pieces for herself and Cathy.

Before she returned to her chair, he caught her hand. A surge of heat spread up her arm. "Miss Clark, this is one of the finest meals I've had in quite some time."

A twitter of nervous laughter bubbled from her throat. "Sheriff, considering you've been on the trail for close to a week, I'm sure anything other than beef jerky and sourdough would be welcome."

His rough thumb brushed lightly across her knuckles. "The company is certainly better. Grubby lawmen and cowboys can't compare to two beautiful women across the table."

"You think we're beautiful, Papa?" Cathy asked, lifting innocent eyes to her father.

Grateful for the distraction, Josie slipped her fingers free of his grip. The heat from his touch lingered long after she returned to her chair and picked up her fork.

"The two most beautiful ladies in Council City." He swung his gaze to Josie. "Maybe even in the entire state of Kansas." His heated gaze brought a quiver to the middle of Josie's chest.

A pleased smile danced across Cathy's mouth. "Or the whole United States of America?"

He laughed and tugged on Cathy's slightly askew pigtail. "The whole wide world."

"As pretty as Mama?"

Coulter's laughter died away. A pained look darkened his eyes. "You're every bit as pretty, sweetheart."

"What about Miss Josie?"

"Cathy, quit bothering your father and eat your pie." Josie's hand trembled at the reminder that any woman in

Coulter's life would always be compared to his wife; and she would always come out second-best.

"Well, Papa?" Cathy persisted, ignoring the censure in Josie's tone.

"Almost," he answered. Dropping his gaze, Coulter devoured the slice of pie in a few quick bites.

Cathy ate with relish, unaware of the tension at the table. Her appetite gone, Josie shoved the crispy crust and apple filling around her plate. The child's eagerness to encourage a relationship between her father and Josie had put a damper on the meal. Coulter sat stiff and rigid at the table, and the instant he finished his pie and coffee, he shoved back his chair.

"Do you mind if I leave without helping? I'd like to clean up and I have some chores to finish in the barn."

"Papa," Cathy protested, "I thought we could go riding."

"Maybe tomorrow," he said, his voice unexpectedly rough.

"But tomorrow's Sunday, we have church, then we'll go to Aunt Bertha's for dinner. And we won't get home until late." The child's shoulders sagged and a frown pulled at her mouth.

Josie's heart went out to the child. She resisted the urge to box Coulter's ears for hurting his child's tender feelings. She remembered how much she'd loved doing things with her own papa, and how much she missed him.

Coulter knelt beside his daughter's chair. "Tell you what, honey. I'll take off Monday, and we'll spend the entire day together. We'll do whatever you want, and go anywhere you say."

"Oh, Papa, I love you so much." Flinging her arms around his neck, she kissed her father's cheek in a loud smack. "Can Miss Josie come with us?"

"If that will make you happy." By the gruffness of his

voice, Josie wasn't sure her going with them would make Coulter happy.

"It will, Papa. Can we go on a picnic down by Indian Bluff? We can fish and swim and maybe I'll invite some of the kids from town. We'll have so much fun."

"Sure, honey." Stretching to his full height, he turned on his heel and stalked toward the stairs.

"Sheriff," Josie called to his back. "Do you want me to put water on the stove to heat for your bath?"

He stopped and slanted a glance over his shoulder. "No, thank you, Miss Clark. I'll bathe in the creek."

"Won't that be cold?"

"I sure as hell hope so."

Chapter 13

To Coulter's annoyance, the cold creek water did little to cool his ardor. After his bath in the creek, he'd gone into the loft to attempt a few minutes of work on his paintings. That didn't help one bit.

Whenever he glanced up from his work, he spotted the sketch he'd made of Angel. Then his gaze would drift to Ellen's portrait. Along with the two beautiful women, guilt stared him in the face. He shouldn't desire Josie, but he did. His longing for the woman was wrong, but whenever he looked into those heavenly blue eyes, he couldn't stop his body's reaction. He loved Ellen, he continually re-minded himself. No woman could take her place. But at times a man needed a live woman in his bed. Someone warm and giving. Full of passion and fire. Like Josie.

After a few minutes he gave up trying to paint, and stalked across the yard to the house. The sun had set only minutes before, and a warm, golden glow cloaked the land. In the barn the animals were settled down for the night, and the chickens were hidden away in the coop. Except for the ornery hen who made her nest under the porch. She darted across Coulter's path, squawking loudly, and disappeared under the house. He'd kill the dumb hen and cook her up with dumplings if she wasn't such a good layer.

He smiled at the reminder of the meal Josie had served at supper. She hadn't even tried to fool him. Anybody with half a brain would know she hadn't time to cook the chicken, if she even knew how, which he seriously doubted.

He stopped under the shadow of the large elm where Cathy's old swing hung by one rope. The house loomed ahead, a dark silhouette against the pink sky. Josie hadn't yet bothered to light any of the lamps.

Two harmonious voices were carried on the gentle evening breeze. Josie and Cathy joined in their own rendition of "Yankee Doodle." His heart tripped at the peal of his child's laughter when they reached the last line and Cathy wanted to know why "they called him macaroni." Josie instantly lifted her voice in the rousing melody of "Dixie." He was certain to need another dunk in the creek before the evening was over.

From his vantage point, he watched them sway gently back and forth on the slatted porch swing. The chain squeaked in time to their song. Josie's arm was looped across Cathy's shoulder, and the child was nestled into her side. There was something so right about the scene, he wished he could capture it on canvas. His mind's eye could envision what an emotional portrait the pair would make. He also knew it was a picture he would never paint.

The woman was a mystery. She was beautiful, intelligent, and her voice rivaled Jenny Lind's. She'd revealed a little about her past, but for some reason, parts of it didn't ring quite true, or she was omitting chunks of information. A woman with her talent would be a success in any theater in New York or San Francisco.

As if she sensed his presence, she glanced over her shoulder. The words of the song hung in the air. Even from the distance he spotted the glow of pleasure on her face. She loved singing as much as he loved painting. So why had she given it up? Was she only biding her time before she returned to the stage?

Cathy turned and spotted his presence. "Papa. Come sing with us. Miss Josie knows all kinds of songs. We're having so much fun."

"Sweetheart, you know I can't carry a tune in a bucket." Coulter paused for a moment to gain control of his growing desire. Surely a woman who'd been a performer knew how her smiles and glances affected a man. She'd practiced the art of flirtation and learned it well. Thank goodness Coulter was too wily to succumb to her feminine wiles.

"Miss Josie is teaching me how to sing. She can teach you, too."

Laughing under his breath, he strolled toward the porch. "I'll leave the singing to the two of you. But I think it's about time a certain young lady prepared for bed."

"Who?" Cathy lifted innocent brown eyes to him. "Miss Josie?"

The thought of bed and Josie brought a sharp jolt to the pit of his stomach. He stumbled on his own feet. If just thinking about her aroused him like this, what would happen if he touched her, kissed her, held her? First thing Monday, he would advertise for a housekeeper. An old one. And homely.

"Your papa is talking about Miss Cathy," Josie said. She removed her arm from Cathy's shoulder and stopped the swing with her toe.

"Aw, Papa. Do I have to?" Cathy fluttered her eyelashes and flashed an impish grin. It hadn't taken the eight-year-old long to learn coquettish ways. He would surely have his hands full in a few short years.

Coulter averted his gaze from Josie and smiled at his daughter. "Yes. Run up and put on your nightgown. I'll be right up and tuck you in."

"Yes, sir." She slid off the swing and shuffled toward the door. "Can Miss Josie come up and sing to me like she did while you were gone?"

"I don't see why not." He took Cathy's place next to Josie. "Thanks for looking after my daughter while I was away," he said. The fit on the narrow slatted swing was tight, and he felt her warmth pressed against his side.

"It was a pleasure. She's a lovely child." Josie shifted, trying to put a little distance between their hips.

Out of pure devilment, Coulter stretched out one arm across the back of the swing and toyed with the lacy collar of her blouse. "Besides teaching Cathy to sing, what else did you do while I was away?"

"Not much." She started to get up, but he stopped her with a hand on her shoulder.

"Don't go. I don't bite." *Unless provoked,* he added to himself.

She stiffened her spine. "I know you don't, Sheriff Steele. But I should help Cathy prepare for bed."

His thumb brushed gently against her throat. Her skin was soft and smooth, and she smelled like the roses he'd picked before supper. "No need for that. I'd like to find out what you've been doing in town every day. Why were you sitting in front of the bank? Were you waiting for me?"

She drew a sharp breath, then released it gradually. "Cathy missed you, and naturally I was concerned for your safety."

The sound of that filled him with emotion. He liked having a woman concerned for him, waiting for him. Especially in his bed. As quickly as it came, he shoved the devastating thought from his mind. Simply sitting beside her had his blood roaring through his veins with white-hot heat. Why didn't he move to the steps? Because he liked the feeling, and for the first time in years, he felt alive.

"You could have waited out here just as easily." He was making a big mistake sitting beside this woman in the growing darkness. She was too enticing, and he was too needy. He tugged gently on a loose hairpin, and a gleaming, golden tress curled around his hand.

She shifted slightly, not enough to shake off his hand, only enough to look into his face. "Sheriff Steele, you can quit playing cat and mouse with me. I know full well that Homer gave you a scathing report on my activities over the past week."

Even the dim light couldn't hide the fire in her gaze. "Angel, you can call me Coulter."

"I would prefer being called Josie."

"Angel suits you better." He stroked the silky wave between his thumb and index finger. With his toe, he shoved and started the swing again. Maybe the slight breeze would cool some of the heat that was surging through him with the ferocity of a wildfire in a swift wind. "I want to hear your side." His voice dropped to a husky whisper.

She swiped her tongue across her lips, making them moist and inviting. Her mouth was inches from his, so close their breaths mingled. He shifted his hand and pressed lightly on her neck. One kiss, just one quick taste of that delectable morsel to satisfy the hunger that nagged at his gut. Her eyelids lowered and she moaned softly. His heart pounded as loudly as the squeaking chain. He needed her; he wanted her; and he knew she wouldn't protest his kiss.

"Papa, Miss Josie, I'm ready."

Josie jerked away from him. She widened her eyes and gasped. Snapped out of his stupor, Coulter jumped to his feet. He didn't know if he was happy or miserable at his daughter's interruption. Was it salvation or damnation?

"We'll be right up, sweetheart." He gripped the porch post for balance. For a man called Steele, he felt as weak as a newborn kitten. "Go on," he said over his shoulder. "Tell her I'll be there in a minute."

She stretched out a hand toward him, then let it fall. "Are you all right?"

With a wry grin, he nodded. As soon as he was able to control his runaway lust he would be able to walk properly. The screen door banged shut behind her and Coulter managed to draw a deep breath. His first night back in his own bed and he knew he wouldn't get a wink of sleep.

The sun was a warm glow in the eastern sky when Josie ventured into the kitchen the next morning. She'd gotten little sleep the previous night. So had Coulter, she suspected. Before sunup, his door had creaked open and she'd heard the clatter of boot heels on the stairs.

Reaching into the pantry, she slipped a clean apron over her skirt and crisp white shirtwaist. She'd dressed carefully for church, wanting to make her best impression on the congregation when she revealed the latest strategy in the war on alcohol. The royal-blue suit, a prior casualty in her first battle in Council City, had been expertly repaired by the dressmaker, and cleaned and pressed at Mr. Wong's laundry.

The coffeepot was simmering on the warming burner, but Coulter was nowhere in sight. Her best course of action was to give him a hearty breakfast before they left for church, to put him in a good mood. She had little doubt he'd planned to discuss her activities before they'd been distracted the past night. She also had no doubt he wouldn't be at all happy with her plans.

Reaching for the cast-iron skillet, she glanced out the window toward the barn. A tall figure stood propped against a porch post, staring at the blue morning glories that twined around a white trellis high above his head. Her fingers tightened on the handle as she studied his wide back and the thick, chestnut-colored hair curling around the collar of his blue workshirt. He clutched a white mug in his large hands. Smoke from the hot coffee wafted in the cool morning air. She wondered what would have happened last night if Cathy hadn't called.

He'd wanted to kiss her and she was going to allow him. The butterflies that had attacked her stomach all night took flight again. Her grip loosened, and the skillet clattered to the floor. With a loud gasp, she jumped aside to protect her toes.

The screen door slammed shut with a bang. She looked up to see Coulter standing in front of her, a worried expression on his face. "What happened?"

Josie lifted her gaze and grinned. "Just a little clumsy this morning. No harm done."

She stooped down to retrieve the skillet the same instant Coulter did. Their foreheads bumped and both mumbled an apology. Josie grabbed the handle and found her hand covered with Coulter's long fingers. Gazes locked, they stared at each other for the span of seconds that seemed like hours. His hand was warm, his eyes even warmer. He was as close as last night, when she'd been sorely tempted to throw caution to the wind and fall into his arms.

The chill of the morning turned to suffocating heat. Coulter lifted his free hand and stroked the back of his knuckles across her cheek. His most innocent touch excited her more than the embraces of any man had ever done. Until now, she'd hated the way men had grabbed at her or tried to force their attentions on her. This was far different from anything she'd ever experienced during her years in the theater. She held her breath while awaiting his next move.

"You're so soft," he whispered.

Josie realized she was about to tumble into his arms. She also realized that it would be the biggest mistake of her life. Forcing a laugh that sounded more like a frog's croak, she rose to her full height. For a brief moment he stared up at her. He took the skillet from her grip before he stretched to his feet.

"I'd better get your breakfast started," she mumbled. Not wanting him to notice the high color that burned at her cheeks, she turned toward the stove.

He plopped the skillet on the burner. The clang of metal against metal rang through the quiet kitchen. "That can wait. I'd like to finish what we started last night."

If possible, Josie's face grew warmer. Last night they were about to make love. "What . . . what do you mean?"

"I'd like to know what you're up to."

"What I'm up to?" Her mind spun in confusion. "Coulter, what are you accusing me of?"

"I'm not accusing you of anything, Angel—Josie." He trapped her against the stove with his arms on either side of her waist. "I simply want to hear what you're planning to do with that list of names you've been gathering while sitting in front of the bank."

He was too close to allow her to think clearly. He smelled of clean fresh soap and the bits of straw that clung to his hair. "I'm continuing my work for the Society."

"How?"

If only he would move away, then she could gauge his reactions to her words. His hot breath tingled against the back of her neck. "Sheriff, let's have some coffee and sit at the table. We can discuss the situation like two rational adults."

His hands fell away, leaving Josie feeling strangely alone and cold. "All right. You talk while I fix breakfast."

She felt as trapped as a rabbit cornered by a fox. "I should be preparing your food," she said, in a effort to evade the subject.

He filled a cup with coffee and set it on the table. "After that fine supper you served last evening, you deserve a day of rest."

The mocking tone of his voice racked her nerves. He knew very well she hadn't cooked the meal. For some reason of his own, he seemed determined to go along with the charade. Josie squared her shoulders and bolstered her defenses.

"Thank you, Sheriff. I appreciate your kindness." Aware that she was stalling, she set a pitcher of milk on the table and poured a little into her coffee. "What did Homer tell you?"

With quick, efficient movements, he sliced thick slabs of bacon and dropped them into the skillet. The boldly masculine lawman should have looked out of place in the kitchen. But Coulter was a man comfortable with himself, and his duties—whatever they might be. "Only that you're causing trouble again. He's still afraid you'll . . . Well, the black eye was bad enough. He doesn't want to see what other havoc you could create."

Since he had his back to her, Josie had no idea of his mood or his disposition. "I can assure you, I'm not here to cause trouble. My task is to convince the men to quit drinking and to abolish liquor from your town."

He set the now-crisp bacon on a platter. The delicious aroma made Josie's stomach rumble with hunger. While he broke eggs into the hot grease, she began to slice the bread she'd gotten from Polly.

"How do you propose to achieve your noble ambition?"

"Since you forbid us marching on the saloons and bars, we had to change our tactics. I've had men sign sobriety pledges and I've made lists of the men who frequent the wicked establishments. I'll read the names in church and hope the offenders will repent and renounce their sinful ways." Even to her own ears, the pronouncement sounded pompous and self-righteous.

"How do you think the men will take to being embarrassed in front of their friends and families?"

She held the plates while he flipped perfectly fried eggs from the skillet. "They'll think twice before they go back into the bars or imbibe."

He shook his head in dismay. "Take a word of advice, Angel, and forget it."

"Why?"

He settled on the chair across from her. "I warned you before that the men won't take kindly to an outsider interfering in their recreation. You've already made an enemy of Homer. I don't need any trouble in my town."

She narrowed her eyes. "Sheriff, I explained I'm not here to cause trouble. None of this would be necessary if the saloon owners would voluntarily close down their establishments."

"That isn't likely. It's their livelihood."

"Like it or not, Prohibition is coming. It's only a matter of time until the legislature outlaws liquor in Kansas. And it will be up to you to enforce the law."

"When the time comes, I'll perform my duties. Meanwhile, I want you to stay out of town and out of trouble." A muscle twitched in his jaw.

"Is that an order?" Unable to remain seated, Josie stood and leaned toward him with her knuckles planted on the table.

He jumped to his feet, knocking his chair over with a loud bang. His face was inches from hers. "No, it's a very strong request. I have enough problems without having to watch you all day long.''

Right was right, and Josie refused to back down. "Let's get a few things clear. You are neither my father nor my husband, thank the good Lord—but my employer—my temporary employer. Nothing more. As long as I see that your meals are prepared and that your daughter is happy, you have no rights to dictate how I spend my free time.''

"That may be true, but I can sure dictate where my daughter goes and how she spends her time. I forbid your taking her into town.'' Fireworks glittered in his dark eyes and his breath came in short gasps.

Josie's temper shot up to the boiling point. She glared at the obnoxious sheriff through a red haze of fury. "Do you mean you expect me to stop working for the Society?''

"You finally get the point.''

"Then I quit.'' She folded her arms across her chest and stepped away.

"The Society?''

"No, you! You can find yourself another housekeeper.''

"You can't quit. You gave your word.'' In a few long strides, he came around the table. He wrapped his fingers around her upper arms and hauled her into his chest.

Josie struggle against his grip. She was inches away from lifting her knee and doing permanent damage.

"Then I take it back.'' Her breasts were crushed against his shirt, the buttons digging into her flesh. His mouth was so close, she could smell the coffee on his breath.

"You can't take your word back,'' he ground out between his teeth.

"Oh, yes I can.''

"I'll arrest you and lock you up in jail.''

"You wouldn't dare." Shoving against his chest was like trying to tumble a brick wall bare-handed.

"Lady, I'd dare anything to keep my daughter safe and happy."

"Papa, Miss Josie, what's the matter?" Her face pale, Cathy stared unmoving from the doorway. "Why are you fighting with each other?"

Chapter 14

Coulter tore his gaze from the woman in his grip to his daughter's distressed face. Instantly he dropped his hands from Josie's arms. She staggered and clutched her fingers in his shirt. Her breath coming in harsh gasps, she looked from Cathy to him and back.

"Oh, Lord," she whispered. "What have we done?"

For a long moment nobody moved. Cathy was barefoot and wearing her sleep-rumpled nightgown. One untidy braid hung to her shoulder and the other had long been unraveled. She swiped the back of her hand across her eyes. Coulter's heart leaped into his throat. How much had she seen—how much had she heard?

Josie loosened her grip and stepped away. She covered her flaming cheeks with her palms. Coulter's anger dissolved into a mass of self-reproach.

"Sweetheart, we weren't fighting." He bit his lip against the lie. In truth they'd been snarling at each other like mad dogs over a single bone.

"Yes, you were. I could hear you hollering clear up to my room."

"No, honey, you misunderstood." In a few long strides, he reached his child. Kneeling before her, he gently brushed the hair from her face. "We were just having a discussion."

Cathy's face was a mask of misery. "Why do you want to throw Miss Josie back in jail? If she did something wrong, you can punish me. I don't want her to leave us."

Josie moved toward them and wrapped her arm across his daughter's shoulder. "Love, I'm not going anywhere. Your papa was just . . ." She looked to Coulter for answers, but he had none. "He was just reminding me of my responsibilities, of what he expects us to do together."

"Papa, me and Miss Josie don't do anything wrong." Cathy twisted her fingers in the folds of her nightgown. "After we clean up the house, we go into town and work for the S'ciety. It's so much fun watching everybody coming and going to the store and to the bank. I get to play with Sally Jane and Carol Ann. I like it better than when I used to have to stay out here with Miss Bettington all day long."

The pain in his child's eyes was his undoing. "Miss Josie and I just had a little disagreement. She's agreed to help us out until we get another housekeeper." He shot a glance at the woman, daring her to disagree, or to threaten to quit again.

"But I don't want another housekeeper. I want a mother."

Coulter cringed. He realized how much he'd failed his child. In his obsession with Ellen, he'd neglected to give their child what she wanted most. Now Cathy was suffering for his selfishness. "Honey, we talked about that already. Miss Josie has her work and I'm not ready to get married again."

"Cathy, I promised your papa I'd stay"—Angel shot a

glance at Coulter—"as long as you need me." She wiped Cathy's face with the corner of her apron.

"All right, Miss Josie." Cathy lifted a small hand to her father's face. Her fingers brushed across his whiskered jaw. "And you won't make us stop working for the S'ciety? I like going into town and playing with my friends."

On a long sigh, he cradled his child in his arms. What choice did he have? Against his better judgment, he nodded in agreement. How could he deny his child this simple request when he would be refusing the thing she wanted most in the world? "I'll drive you into town myself." That way he could keep an eye on them and keep them out of trouble.

"I love you, Papa."

Coulter blinked back tears. "I love you, too, baby. Now, come get some breakfast. We have to get ready for church."

Josie moved away, a forlorn look in her expressive blue eyes. "I'm going to finish dressing. Cathy, come to my room when you're ready for me to fix your hair."

Head tall, back ramrod-straight, she lifted the hem of her blue skirt and marched toward the stairs. The small bustle at her rear bounced provocatively with every step.

Coulter couldn't help admiring the woman. She was something—holding her own in their argument and standing up to him for her rights. He was grateful Cathy had interrupted when she had. One minute later and he would have been walking mighty funny into church that morning, and singing high soprano.

He glanced at his daughter and caught her watching him watching Josie. Cathy grinned and turned toward the table. "I'm starved. I'll bet I could eat a dozen eggs this morning."

Laughing, Coulter picked up the skillet and set it on the stove. "Let's start with two. Then you can work your way up to that dozen."

If it hadn't been for Cathy's constant chatter, the ride

to the church would have passed in stone-cold silence. The child sat in the middle of the high wooden wagon seat, with Josie aloof and distant. She'd spoken no more than what was essential after their vocal confrontation. And when Coulter had stretched out a hand to assist her, she'd blatantly ignored his help, and hauled herself into the wagon.

If the haughty lady was expecting an apology from Coulter Steele, she'd better think again. He'd been absolutely within his rights as her employer. As sheriff, he had the responsibility to the town to insist she curtail her activities. Especially if those activities concerned his daughter and the safety of the people. But for Cathy's sake, he was willing to compromise, if Josie was willing to do the same.

Before he tied off the reins and came around the wagon, she'd already leaped to the ground. Her hand entwined with Cathy's, Josie moved toward where Bertha and Polly were chatting in front of the church steps. He'd recognize his aunt a mile away by the outrageous feathered creation planted atop her head. Thankfully the wind wasn't blowing, or Bertha would surely take off and soar like an eagle.

Coulter followed a few paces behind. One eye on the ladies, he stopped for a few words with his uncle. Oscar didn't look too pleased. "Coulter, what are you going to do about Miss Clark?"

"Not you, too? I heard the same thing from Homer. And I'll tell you what I told him. Nothing. Unless she breaks the law, there's nothing I can do." Coulter tore off his black Stetson and slapped it against his leg. "Not that I didn't try. The lady is as stubborn as the most ornery mule I've ever seen."

Oscar tugged him by the arm to a spot under a spreading elm. "Bertha tells me she intends to read the names of the men who went in and out of the bars this week."

"So I understand. She didn't by any chance see you, did she?"

"I wouldn't care if she did, but Bertha would skin me alive. That's not what I'm worried about. If she manages to close down the Golden Garter and the other saloons in town, I stand to lose a mint." He clamped an unlit cigar between his teeth.

Coulter shot a glance at the women, who seemed lost in their own conversation. Cathy had run off and was head-to-head with Sally Jane and Carol Ann, her two closest friends. "What do you mean?"

"I'm expecting a wagonload of good Kentucky whiskey, and stand to make a good profit. Besides, you know I'm Sanders's silent partner in the Golden Garter."

"I suspected you were involved, but I'd hoped you weren't. Does Bertha know?"

Oscar glanced over his shoulder at his wife. "Son, I've been married to that little woman for nigh on to thirty-five years, and if she found out, we wouldn't make it to thirty-six. If you can keep Miss Clark from stirring things up for a few weeks, I'll get out of the liquor-supply business and stick to running my own businesses."

Coulter shook his head. "Oscar, I've tried. But short of locking her up in jail, there's little I can do."

"You can't lock her up. The women would tar and feather both of us." He smoothed down his muttonchops with his fingertips. "Keep her out of town, out on the ranch. Hell, tie her to the bed if you have to."

Coulter let out a bark of sardonic laughter. Thinking about her in bed already had him losing sleep. "Uncle, are you suggesting improper behavior right outside the churchhouse? I'm surprised at you."

Oscar slapped Coulter on the back. "Son, don't tell me you haven't thought about that solution on your own. She's a fine-looking woman and you're out there on the ranch with only Cathy as chaperone. A little loving goes a long way in controlling a lady. Court her, keep her too busy to come into town and cause trouble for me. Marry her."

"Marry her?" Coulter choked on the words. Oscar was the second one that morning to talk about marriage.

"Why not? It would solve all our problems. You need a woman. Even the good Lord said it's not right for a man to be alone."

Unable to control himself, he gaped openly at Miss Josie Clark. At that very moment, she lifted her gaze and returned his stare. Fire and passion; it was written in those heated blue eyes. He needed a woman, but he wasn't about to get hooked up with that spitfire. Plopping his hat back on his head, he tore his gaze back to his uncle. "I'd rather be tied to a stake and burned alive than tied to that harridan."

Oscar hooked his thumbs in the armholes of his plaid vest and stuck out his considerable paunch. "You could do a lot worse, my boy. Don't wait too long to state your intentions, Coulter. I notice the preacher has eyes for the lady in question."

Coulter opened his mouth to remind his uncle that he no intentions toward the lady, honorable or otherwise. The clanging of the church bells calling the congregation to worship drowned the words on his lips.

"Yes, sir." Oscar continued his discourse. "You'd better move fast. If Miss Clark marries the preacher, they'll turn all the men in this town into teetotaling pansies. Then where would my business go?"

"Straight to hell with the rest of us," Coulter murmured to himself. "Let's go and see what kind of fire and brimstone the preacher is going to rail down on us sinners today."

Oscar returned the unlit cigar to his inside coat pocket. "Hope he's not too long-winded. Got home kind of late last night. I didn't get much sleep."

The Saturday-night poker games in the livery stable were the town's worst-kept secret. Coulter suspected that Oscar had been a professional gambler before he'd come to town, claiming to be a drummer. "Another meeting of the town council?"

The mayor shot a glance at his wife and laughed. "No. Last night I had to take inventory at the store."

Coulter shook his head. "One of these days Aunt Bertha is going to catch you and tear what little hair you have left from your shiny head."

"I'll take my chances. Besides a cut for the house, I generally turn a tidy profit every week. Helps keep my wife in those silly hats she fancies."

They paused at the door and allowed the women to precede them down the aisle. Bertha lifted her head for Coulter's kiss and gave him an affectionate pat on the cheek. Miss Clark tilted her nose at a perfect forty-five-degree angle and continued into the dim interior of the building. Only a complete imbecile would consider marrying that woman. Let the preacher have her. They deserved each other.

Coulter followed at a slower pace. If that was how he felt, where did this niggling of jealousy come from? And why was it nipping at his heels like a hungry hound dog?

Josie dashed ahead to be first to enter the pew. She scooted toward the side aisle, leaving the entire bench available for the family. Let that intolerable sheriff sit at the end next to his uncle. She settled on the hard wooden seat and straightened her jacket and skirt. Glancing to her left, she spied Bertha and Oscar joining her. Thankfully Coulter wasn't in sight.

"Excuse me, Miss Josie." From the side aisle, Cathy squeezed past her legs and plopped between her and Bertha.

Josie adjusted the bow in the girl's hair, then reached for a hymnal. Her fingers collided with a large hand sprinkled with dark hair across the back. A quiver raced up her arm.

"Reckon we'll have to share," came a familiar, deep, male voice.

Chancing a glance out of the corner of her eye, she spied the man next to her. While she'd been distracted by Cathy, Coulter had entered from the side aisle and slipped into the pew next to her. He wiggled his hips to make room, pressing his six-gun into her hip bones. With a loud grunt, she jammed her elbow into his ribs in retaliation. If she had to wear a bruise on her hip, he'd have one on his side.

He groaned and looped her arm in his, effectively stifling her movements. Lowering his head, he whispered into her ear, "Try that again, Angel, and I'll turn you over my knee."

"What are you doing here?"

"I don't like this any more than you. My daughter dragged me to this end of the pew. I didn't want to make a scene. Don't you make one, either."

"Shhh," someone whispered from behind them.

Trapped between the handsome man and his child, Josie resigned herself to her fate. The congregation stood for the first song, but Coulter didn't release his grip. All during the service he remained pressed at her side. Standing or seated, he kept her arm locked in his. And Josie didn't hear a word the Reverend Harris said.

From time to time she dared a glance at Coulter. He was a handsome devil in his dark suit with the white shirt that contrasted with his bronzed skin. Josie constantly reminded herself of the adage her mother had quoted time and again: "Handsome is as handsome does." And his actions were far from attractive.

Lost in her thoughts, Josie failed to hear the preacher when he called her to the front. Coulter nudged her gently, and she noticed several heads turned in her direction.

"Think about what I told you," he whispered, as he stood to allow her out of the narrow pew.

Josie clutched her handbag to her chest. All eyes in the congregation were trained on her. Miss Bettington sat ramrod-straight, her eyes shooting poison arrows at Josie. Beside the former housekeeper, Mrs. Potts waved a greeting. In the front pew sat Homer and the other deacons— men she recognized as going in and out of the saloons.

She removed her list from her bag and glanced around the congregation. The woman sat on the edge of their seats, grinning in anticipation. They were happy as long it was somebody else's husband being embarrassed, not theirs. The men squirmed and slumped low in the pews. The children who were still awake fidgeted, wanting to get outside where they could run and play.

Her gaze locked with Coulter's. A warning gleamed in his dark eyes. She nodded to the minister. "Thank you, Reverend Harris." Taking a deep breath, she pasted a smile on her face. "As most of you know, we've been asked . . ." She drawled out the word, and several women stifled their snickers behind their gloved hands. "Sheriff Steele requested that we curtail our marches out of concern for our safety. In spite of a minor setback, it's the intention of the S.A.A.T. to continue the battle against liquor."

The grimace on Coulter's mouth deepened into a scowl. She hurried along, afraid he would jump from his seat and indeed turn her over his knee. "Our next course of action is to list the names of the patrons of the various bars and saloons, to try to persuade the men to give up their drinking and return to their homes and families. I have the list right here, along with a few pledge forms." In a dramatic and totally unexpected move, she folded the paper in half, then half again. "I've decided not to read it aloud—at the present time. Several other ladies, along with myself, will continue making our lists. Those who do not desire to have us read their names can abstain from frequenting the saloons and take the pledge."

An audible sigh rumbled through the building. The most devout temperance workers frowned, but many of the women seemed relieved.

"Remember, like the indomitable John Paul Jones said, 'I have not yet begun to fight.' Thank you for your kind attention." She moved aside and allowed Reverend Harris to conclude the service.

As the congregation filed out into the yard, she waited inside the building and spoke briefly with a number of women. Eager to avoid Coulter, she glanced around for the side door. Before she could reach the exit, a large hand clamped her arm.

"Bravo, Angel. Another sterling performance. Such an accomplished actress never should have given up the stage."

She looked up and spotted a tiny glimmer of admiration in Coulter's eyes. "I believe in the cause, Sheriff. And I meant every word I said."

"Only a rat deserts a sinking ship."

Josie struggled against his grip, only to have him tuck her arm in his. "My ship is far from sinking. It's the saloon and bar owners who are going down in defeat."

"Miss Clark, my aunt is expecting us for a pleasant Sunday dinner. Let's call a truce. All this fighting is liable to give me indigestion." His eyes issued a challenge she couldn't refuse.

"All right, Sheriff Steele. As long as you don't interfere with my project, I'll control my activities. I won't cause any trouble in your town."

He flashed a triumphant smile. "You have a deal." The look on his face was pure male superiority. He may have won the battle, but the war was far from over.

Being the last to leave the church, they stepped out into the bright sunlight and found few families remaining.

Cathy was running toward their carriage with Oscar and Bertha. Coulter tugged her toward his wagon.

"Miss Clark, are you ready?" Reverend Harris settled his bowler on his head as he approached. "Mr. and Mrs. Marche are expecting us."

Josie granted the minister her brightest smile. "Yes, I am, Elijah. The sheriff was kind enough to escort me from the church." She unwrapped her arm from Coulter's unyielding grip. "Wasn't it kind of Elijah to offer to drive me to Bertha's? We'll see you there, Sheriff."

With a haughty tilt of her chin, she accepted the minister's proffered arm and left Coulter Steele cooling his heels alone.

Chapter 15

Cathy pounded on Josie's door before she was fully dressed the following morning. "Come on, Miss Josie. Papa promised to take us on a picnic today." She flung open the door and plowed into the room.

Josie smiled at the girl's enthusiasm. "Calm down, honey. It's only seven o'clock. You told your friends your papa would pick them up about nine. You have lots of time." She sat Cathy on the edge of her bed and passed a brush through the child's thick dark hair. Excited about the outing, Cathy bounced up and down on the feather mattress. "Hold still, sweetie, so I can braid your hair."

"I can't help it, Miss Josie. I'm so glad Papa is going to take the day off. We'll have so much fun. We can go fishing, and if we catch a fish, we'll cook it over a campfire."

The child's happiness more than made up for the problems Josie faced with Coulter Steele. "And just in case you don't, I'll pack you a nice lunch. Your aunt sent some delicious ham home with us last night."

Cathy plucked at the eyelet trim on her smock. "Are you still mad at Papa?"

"Mad?" Josie tied a narrow red ribbon on the end of each long braid. "We weren't mad at each other. That was just a silly, grown-up difference of opinion. We got over that yesterday."

"I'm glad. Papa looked kind of mad when you were sitting on Aunt Bertha's porch with the reverend." She leaned closer and whispered, "I think he's sweet on you, but he don't want anybody to know."

"Cathy, where did you get such an idea?"

"I heard Aunt Bertha tell Uncle Oscar."

The last thing Josie needed was gossip or speculation about her personal life. And certainly not about her and the minister. "Honey, the reverend and I are friends. But I don't think he likes me better than anybody else."

Cathy stood and planted her hands on her hips in an exaggerated grimace of impatience. "No, not the preacher. Papa. I think Papa is sweet on you."

"Oh." Josie moved toward the mirror so the girl wouldn't see the glimmer of pleasure in her eyes. For an eight-year-old, Cathy was entirely too perceptive. In spite of her better judgment, Josie's eyes were glowing with interest. "He's only being nice because of you."

Coulter may be attracted to her, but he clearly wasn't fond of her or her activities. Over the past twenty-four hours he hadn't uttered a dozen civil words. The man had been totally obnoxious. He'd spent most of the afternoon with Oscar, completely ignoring his aunt, his daughter, and Josie. Cathy was dead wrong about her father. He still loved Ellen and there was no room in his heart for another woman.

"Give him a chance, Miss Josie. Papa is too stubborn to admit he's lonely and that he needs to get married. Sometimes when he looks at you, I think he just wants to eat you up." Cathy wrapped her arms around Josie's waist.

Josie laughed softly. "Sweetheart, you have quite an imagination. When your papa looks at me, he sees a woman who can't cook, can barely clean a house, and knows nothing about running a farm. I think he's wishing for a good, home-cooked meal." She kissed the top of the child's head. Lord, she would miss Cathy when she left. An odd sensation pricked at her heart. She had to admit she'd also miss Coulter in spite of his bullheaded ways.

Cathy ran to the doorway. "I'm going to find Papa and make sure he found our fishing poles. Then I'll dig some worms from the garden."

Worms? Josie shivered at the thought of picking up a worm and threading it onto a hook. Thank goodness she was staying home while Coulter escorted the children on their excursion. At a slower pace, Josie followed Cathy to the kitchen. She wasn't surprised that Coulter was nowhere in sight. He was as determined to avoid her as she was to avoid him.

She'd just prepared a cup of tea, when Cathy again ran in calling her name. "Miss Josie, come see, it looks like Miss Polly and Sally Jane."

By the time Josie reached the front porch, the farm wagon came to a stop. Coulter grabbed the lines of Polly's two-horse team.

"Morning, Miss Polly," he greeted with a wide smile. "What brings you out here this time of the morning?"

Polly tied off the reins as her daughter jumped down from the high seat. Sally Jane squealed with delight and ran toward Cathy. The girls darted back into the house, laughter following in their wake.

"Thought I'd save you from having to come all the way into town to fetch my daughter. She hasn't slept all night and I got tired of hearing her ask what time you were coming." She stood and Coulter offered a hand to help her to the ground.

From her position on the porch, Josie watched the

friendly exchange. True, Polly and Coulter had been friends for a long time, and he had every right to flirt with the widow. Ten years older than Josie, Polly was a very attractive woman. More important, she was an excellent cook and housekeeper. She would make a perfect wife for any man. Then why did this smidgen of jealousy nag at Josie as if the man meant something to her?

Laughing, Coulter looped Polly's arm in his and escorted her to the porch. "Cathy's been pestering me all morning to go into town and pick up your daughter. If she had her way, she'd move Sally Jane out here with us."

"Not without her ma, you won't," Polly said with a smile.

"That could be arranged." Coulter flashed a winning grin.

A slight blush tinged Polly's cheeks. "You'd better be careful what you tell a woman, Sheriff, she just may take your teasing seriously."

Coulter winked; his dark eyes sparkled with humor. "I'm not the kind of man who trifles with a woman's affection, ma'am."

"And I would never know if it was me or my cooking you were after," she returned.

"You are the best cook in town, no doubt about that." He lifted his gaze to Josie.

Josie tightened her grip on the teacup. It was the perfect solution to his problem. Polly was a good, kind woman, and her daughter and his were the best of friends. If Coulter were to remarry, he would have no reason to keep Josie as his housekeeper and she would be free to pursue her own endeavors. Away from Council City. Away from Coulter Steele. Away from her heart . . . When had her heart become involved?

Tired of being on the outside of their friendly banter, Josie stepped forward. "Polly, would you care for a cup of tea? Or coffee?"

Polly tucked a stray lock of brown hair under the brim

of her sunbonnet. "No, thank you, Josie. I have too many errands to run this morning. I'm on my way to pick up fresh vegetables from over at the Fisher place, and Mrs. Beckman has milk and eggs for me. If you have those green beans ready, I'll take them while I'm here. Save you a trip into town."

Coulter tilted one thick eyebrow; Josie could read the question in his eyes. "Fine. Charlie left them in the pantry." Ignoring Coulter's look of displeasure, she led Polly into the house. "Sheriff," she called over her shoulder, "would you be a gentleman and carry the bushel of beans out to Polly's wagon?"

He grunted, but complied with her request. Her gaze locked on his muscular back and bulging arms as he lifted the basket with little effort. As usually happened when she looked at him, heat crept up her neck and flutters settled in her midsection. Hurriedly she turned away and reached for the kettle. "Sure you can't stay for a cup of tea?"

Polly grinned. "Sorry, Josie, but I have to get back to town and start cooking. I'm grateful you and Coulter agreed to take Sally Jane off my hands for one day." She lowered her voice. "How did Coulter like the chicken and dumplings?"

"He loved them, of course." Josie couldn't keep the sharpness out of her tone. If she was trying to win Coulter with her cooking, Polly was doing an awfully good job.

"You know a good meal goes a long way in softening a man's heart."

And Polly was sure doing a good job with Coulter's. Josie chose to change the subject. "I'll try to come into town tomorrow to continue taking names. Then I'll call another meeting Wednesday evening after Bible study, to plan our strategy."

"I'll be there. And if you need another meal for a special occasion, be sure to let me know. I'll prepare a dinner so good, Coulter Steele won't know what hit him."

Josie forced a smile. She'd had no idea Polly had set her sights on Coulter. Well, if she wanted him, she was welcome to the obnoxious man. "Thank you, Polly. But I think I'll manage."

"Sure you will, honey. With your looks, you don't need to know how to cook." Polly rushed ahead to the porch. "Thanks, Coulter," she called. "Take that picnic basket from the back. I packed it for your outing, just in case you don't catch any fish."

The woman had left no stone unturned. Preparing the lunch with Bertha's leftovers had been the one thing within Josie's limited abilities. Now Polly had taken that away.

Coulter helped Polly up into the wagon, and stared up the lane until she disappeared from sight. He set the picnic basket on the porch.

"You sold *my* beans?" His voice was soft, with a definite hint of accusation.

Josie backed up a step, surprised at the look of condemnation in his gaze. She felt like a criminal caught in the middle of a bank robbery. "I didn't exactly sell them."

"You gave them away?"

"I bartered."

"Bartered?"

"Don't pretend to be naive, Sheriff. You know good and well that I didn't cook that meal Saturday evening. I made a bargain with Polly. I traded the dinner for the beans. In my opinion, I got the better of the deal. Those beans will go bad in a few days if somebody doesn't cook them." With her head held high, Josie spun to return to the house.

Before she'd taken one step, Coulter was beside her, blocking her way. "The beans weren't yours to give away."

Lifting her gaze, she spotted a hint of mischief in his eyes. "Sheriff, why are we arguing about something so trivial? You enjoyed the dinner. After all, Polly is the finest cook in town; you said so yourself." She planted her hands on her hips. "Besides, by tomorrow Charlie will have another basket of your precious beans, and I still won't know what to do with them."

"You're supposed to can them."

This time it was she who tilted an eyebrow. "Can?"

"You don't know how."

She shrugged. "I haven't the foggiest. Do you?"

"No. Looks like we'll be selling our produce and buying it back this winter from Oscar." He held the door and ushered her into the house. "Let's get some breakfast and see if we can catch some fish for supper."

His humor sent a warm glow over her. He was taking it all rather well. Polly was right. A good meal went a long way in calming an angry man. "I hope *you* know how to cook them."

"Would it surprise you to know I'm an expert at not only catching them, but in cooking, too?"

She grinned up at him. "I also don't clean fish."

He lowered his lashes and his gaze drifted slowly over her. "Exactly what can you do, Miss Clark?"

The heat from his gaze sent delicious tingles across her flesh. "I'm very good at causing trouble for stubborn lawmen, Sheriff."

"More trouble than even you can imagine." With a shake of his head, he gestured toward the kitchen. "Let's get moving. I'll show you how to thread a worm on a hook and how to catch those fine fish splashing in the Council River."

"Ugh. I think not. You can show the girls. I plan to stay right here and catch up on my correspondence."

"No way, Angel. My daughter expects you to come with us, and we won't take no for an answer."

Knowing it was useless to argue with Coulter, Josie resigned herself to fate. After all, she was the one with whom he'd be spending the day, not Polly. "Just don't expect me to touch the worms or those slimy fish."

He caught her fingers and lifted them to his lips. "I

wouldn't dream of dirtying these delicate little hands, Angel. I'll take care of everything."

True to his word, Coulter had the wagon loaded and ready within an hour. He wasn't sure why he'd insisted Josie come with them. If he had a single lick of common sense, he would be grateful for the chance to be away from her, a chance to think about something other than her pink lips, her soft hands, her firm ... There he was, letting forbidden thoughts invade his mind and body.

He stopped at the Lansing place and picked up Cathy's other friend Carol Ann. The three girls sat in the rear of the wagon, laughing and giggling while snitching an occasional doughnut or cookie from the picnic basket. Next to him on the high seat, Josie sat as prim and proper as a lady on her way to an outing in a park. Her simple pink shirtwaist and darker print skirt emphasized her gentle curves and brought out the color in her cheeks. A wide straw hat tied under her chin with a perky bow protected her porcelain skin from the sun's rays. For the moment, Coulter put aside their differences and allowed himself to enjoy the peace of the morning and the companionship of a beautiful woman.

At Cathy's urging, Josie led the girls in song, their youthful voices blending with her sweet soprano. Even Coulter added his off-key baritone to the ensemble. The medley ranged from "Oh, Susannah!" to "Yankee Doodle," with a few hymns thrown in for good measure. She even threw in a chorus or two of "Yield Not to Temptation." By the time they reached the river, the girls had begun making up lyrics and pounding on the wagon floor like a drum, and Josie was imitating various instruments.

Coulter reined in the horses near the banks of the river. "You can stop now," he said. "You don't want to scare off all the fish before Miss Josie gets a chance to try her hand, do you?"

The girls giggled and jumped to the ground. "Oh, Papa, everybody knows fish don't have ears," Cathy said, in her own knowledgeable way. Grabbing her fishing pole and bucket of worms, she headed toward the edge of the water.

"Don't get too close," Josie called after the girls. "We wouldn't want you to fall in."

Coulter jumped down and came to her side. Ignoring her offered hand, he spanned her waist with his hands and lifted her down. For a long moment after her toes touched the ground, he held her close. She lifted her gaze and clutched his shirt with her fingers. She was so pretty, so soft, so inviting, Coulter couldn't stop himself from swiping a light kiss across her lips.

Her fingers tightened, drawing him closer. He deepened the kiss, lost in the wonder of her. Lost in the sweet scent of roses. Lost in the taste of woman.

"Coulter," she moaned against his mouth. "The girls."

It took a moment for her words to penetrate his passion-dazed mind. He'd never had a woman affect him like this. She was a woman who made him lose all sense of time and place when he was near her. Josie was a dangerous woman. For the first time in years, he considered throwing caution to the wind and letting emotion rule common sense. With an effort, he released her and stepped away.

"Remember where we were, Angel," he whispered. "We can pick up here later."

Twin spots of red tinged her cheeks. He lifted his hands to her face but let them drop. Josie was staring past his shoulder. Coulter followed her gaze. He let out a soft, deep groan.

Three pairs of wide, youthful eyes were watching him in wonder. Cathy turned to her friends and announced, "See, I told you so." With a renewed round of girlish giggles, the girls ran toward the water.

"What's that little pepper up to now?" he asked.

Josie let out a long exasperated sigh. "She thinks there's something going on between us."

"Where did she get that idea?" One look into the warm blue eyes staring up at him, and he had little doubt. More than once Cathy had caught them closer to each other than what was considered proper behavior. Especially in front of the girls.

"I suppose I'm to blame. Forgive me, Miss Clark. I should be more careful of your reputation."

"That's all right, Sheriff. Cathy is just a child with a vivid imagination. She wants a mother and she pictures you with every woman with whom you come in contact." She picked up the jug of lemonade and the blanket from the bed of the wagon.

Coulter gathered up the rest of the fishing poles in one hand and the picnic basket in the other. At least with his hands full, he wouldn't be tempted to wrap his arm around Josie's waist and further compromise her reputation.

As they walked toward where the girls were choosing their fishing spot, he was certain Josie was singing "Yield Not to Temptation" under her breath.

Josie spread the blanket in the shelter of a spreading oak near the water's edge. She settled on the ground, her skirt billowing around her like the petals of a pink rose. Coulter flopped down beside her and took a long swig of the lemonade. He gazed up at the clear blue sky through the leafy canopy overhead. Birds chattered and serenaded them from the treetops. A brown squirrel grabbed an acorn and scurried up the trunk.

"This is a beautiful spot, Coulter."

"One of my favorite places. This entire river valley is considered sacred ground to the Indians." He reclined on his elbow and gazed at the nearby bluffs. "For many years, the various tribes gathered here for their annual council and ceremonial rituals. If you're real quiet, you can hear the chanting, and sometimes at night you can see the spirits dancing around the campfires.''

"Your father was Comanche, wasn't he?"

He knew she meant no offense, yet Coulter couldn't stop feeling a bit defensive. "He was a half-breed, and was very proud of his Indian heritage."

"So are you, Coulter. I can see the respect in your eyes whenever you talk about it. It's a proud heritage. Don't ever forget it." Her smile was warmer than the sunshine filtering through the leaves.

"Thank you, Angel. But a lot of people don't share your tolerance. The Comanche have been persecuted, hunted, and relegated to reservations." Old memories haunted him, and the old wounds still hurt. "My father-in-law was never able to forget my background, no matter what I'd accomplished, or what good I'd done."

"Surely your wife didn't feel the same."

He looked into eyes so blue, it was like gazing into the heavens and seeing angels. "Ellen loved me, no matter what her parents thought." Deep in his heart, Coulter wondered if loving him was Ellen's small rebellion against her parents' total domination of her life. Marrying him was the single time she'd disobeyed them and asserted a bit of independence. "That's enough about the past. Later we'll help the girls look for arrowheads and artifacts."

"That sounds interesting."

"Right now, those fish are getting away." He shoved to his feet and stretched out a hand to Josie. "Let's see if we can catch our lunch."

She shook her head and waved him away. "I'll watch from here."

"No, you won't." Wrapping his fingers around her wrist, he tugged her to her feet. "I believe the Good Book says that if you don't work, you won't eat."

Laughing, she hurried to keep pace with his longer steps. "I don't know how."

"I'll teach you everything I know." He stopped near the water's edge where the girls were seated on a rock, working worms onto their hooks. Their boots and stockings were piled on the grass, and their bare feet dangled into the water.

"That should take about a minute."

He snatched up a pole and pressed it into her hands. "I'll have you know, madam, that I'm the champion bass fisherman in the county."

"Forgive me, sir, for doubting your skill and cunning." Humor glittered in her eyes. He liked the way the corners of her mouth curved when she smiled. "If you'll be so kind as to bait the hook, I don't see anything so difficult about dropping the hook into the water. The worm does most of the work."

"But it takes a man's skill to know just when to snatch the line and hook the fish."

"A man's?" Hands planted on her round hips, she issued a challenge with her eyes.

"Well, a man is naturally better at stuff like fishing and hunting and sports."

"If you're such an expert, you won't object to a small wager."

Coulter barely suppressed his laughter. "A wager? Miss Clark, I'm surprised you're a gambler. What will the good ladies at the S.A.A.T. say?"

She straightened the line on her pole and let the hook and floater dangle free. "It's all in fun, Sheriff Steele. Let's see who catches the most fish."

"Let's make it worthwhile. If I catch the most fish, I expect you to cook my breakfast every day for a week, and I want it at five o'clock."

"And when I win, you can wash the dishes every evening for a week."

He stuck out a hand and enfolded her fingers in his. Nothing pleased him more than betting on a sure thing.

Take advantage of this offer to enjoy Zebra's newest line of historical romance novels....Splendor Romances (formerly Lovegrams Historical Romances)- Take our introductory shipment of 4 romance novels -Absolutely Free! (a $19.96 value)

Now you'll be able to savor today's best romance novels without even leaving your home with our convenient and inexpensive home subscription service. Here's what you get for joining:

- 4 BRAND NEW bestselling Splendor Romances delivered to your doorstep every month
- 20% off every title (or almost $4.00 off) with your home subscription
- FREE home delivery
- A FREE monthly newsletter, *Zebra/Pinnacle Romance News* filled with author interviews, member benefits, book previews and more!
- No risks or obligations...you're free to cancel whenever you wish...no questions asked

To get started with your own home subscription, simply complete and return the card provided. You'll receive your FREE introductory shipment of 4 Splendor Romances and then you'll begin to receive monthly shipments of new Zebra Splendor titles. Each shipment will be yours to examine for 10 days and then if you decide to keep the books, you'll pay the preferred home subscriber's price of just $4.00 per title. That's $16 for all 4 books with FREE home delivery! And if you want us to stop sending books, just say the word...it's that simple.

4 FREE books are waiting for you!
Just mail in the certificate below!

If the certificate is missing below, write to:
Splendor Romances, Zebra Home Subscription Service, Inc.,
P.O. Box 5214, Clifton, New Jersey 07015-5214
or call TOLL-FREE 1-888-345-BOOK

SP0599

FREE BOOK CERTIFICATE

Yes! Please send me 4 Splendor Romances (formerly Zebra Lovegram Historical Romances), ABSOLUTELY FREE! After my introductory shipment, I will be able to preview 4 new Splendor Romances each month FREE for 10 days. Then if I decide to keep them, I will pay the money-saving preferred publisher's price of just $4.00 each... a total of $16.00. That's 20% off the regular publisher's price and there's never any additional charge for shipping and handling. I may return any shipment within 10 days and owe nothing, and I may cancel my subscription at any time. The 4 FREE books will be mine to keep in any case.

Name _____

Address _____ Apt. _____

City _____ State _____ Zip _____

Telephone ( ) _____

Signature _____
(If under 18, parent or guardian must sign.)

Terms and prices subject to change. Orders subject to acceptance by Zebra Home Subscription Service, Inc. .
Zebra Home Subscription Service, Inc. reserves the right to reject or cancel any subscription.

"Deal. I'll even show what a gentleman I am, by baiting your hook."

"No, thank you. I've changed my mind. I don't want any nasty old worm in my fish."

Laughing, he reached into the bucket of worms. "You'll never catch anything without the proper bait."

She flashed a smile that would melt a block of ice in the dead of winter. Any male fish caught in that brilliance would jump right onshore for her. "I'll find something in that picnic basket. If it's good enough for us, it should be good for the fish."

Her naïveté was downright funny. He coaxed a fat, juicy brown worm onto his hook and cast the line into the water. From the corner of his eye, he watched Josie digging into the picnic basket and coming up with something. When she returned and settled on a rock twenty feet from him, he could no longer control his glee. "What are you going to use to tempt those fish, Miss Clark?" he asked.

"Chicken. It's right tasty." Swinging the line like a pendulum, she lowered it into the water.

"Chicken? Fish don't eat chicken." He settled on the grass and mentally prepared the menu for the following week. True, she wasn't much of a cook, but she'd learned the fundamentals of eggs and bacon. Most of all, he'd have the privilege of her company before he went into town to work. Damn, her bait was working better on him than on the fish.

A half hour later, the girls grew bored and threw down the poles. "We're going to get something to eat," Cathy yelled.

"Reckon I'll take a break soon," Coulter said. "I'm getting mighty tired pulling in all these fine bass. Looks like we'll have fish for supper, and I'll be served a delicious breakfast every day." He counted the five largemouth bass on his stringer, and saw that Josie had yet to snag her first.

"That's because you're upstream, and you get them

before they reach me. I'll just move over there, and we'll
see who's the winner." With a flurry of skirts, she picked
up her bait and pole, and changed to a spot under a
spreading willow upstream.

"It's skill, Miss Clark. And I'm still the champion."

"We'll see about that, Sheriff."

He reclined on his elbow and watched her. She looked
like a large pink flower amid the grass and trees. Her face
was set in concentration as she tossed her line into the
water with a fresh piece of chicken. He felt only a little
guilty that he'd chosen the best spot for himself—a pool
where he'd spotted the school of bass below the surface
of the water.

"I got a bite!" she yelled, with all the excitement of a
child. "What do I do now?"

"Just pull him in," he yelled. Propping his pole against
a rock, he jumped up to help. He reached her just as she
swung the line and a large bass flopped on the grass.

The girls ran to help. "Boy, that's a whopper," Sally
squealed.

"He's bigger than any of yours, Sheriff," Carol Ann
contributed to the conversation.

"Much bigger, Papa," added Cathy. "I'll bet Miss Josie
caught the granddaddy of them all."

Coulter gripped the line and held up the fish for their
inspection. "He's a beaut, all right. Congratulations, Miss
Clark. Beginner's luck," he said under his breath.

"Skill, Sheriff." Without a backward glance, she jabbed
another piece of chicken on the hook and tossed it into
the water.

For the next hour, Coulter spent more time taking the
fish from her hook than dropping his in the water. Every
time she snagged a fish, the girls hollered with delight,
caught up in the challenge of male versus female—the
age-old battle of the sexes. By the look of her stringer, the
male was losing the war.

Finally Josie dropped her pole on the grass. "Reckon I'll give the fish a break. I think we have enough for you to clean and cook for supper, Sheriff Steele. Any more would just be greed." She flashed him a triumphant grin and followed the girls to the blanket where they'd spread out the food.

Never a graceful loser, Coulter flung his line back into the water. All the determination in the world didn't mean a thing. He didn't get another bite.

At least Josie generously brought him a sandwich, and suggested that he use it for bait rather than the worms. "Gloating isn't becoming for a woman," he growled.

"Neither is arrogance for a man," she replied. Turning on her heel, she strutted to where the girls were digging for arrows and artifacts.

As hard as he tried, Coulter couldn't help admiring the woman. He had a tough time concentrating on fish when she was only a few feet away, running and laughing with the youngsters.

Sally Ann took a stick and poked it into a hole near where Josie was standing. Coulter opened his mouth to tell the girls not to bother the animals, when a shiny black nose emerged from the hole. Sally Ann dropped the stick and ran, but Josie stared into the animal's frightened eyes. Before Coulter could yell a warning, the skunk let loose with its only defense against its enemies.

The spray covered everything within ten feet, Josie his sole human victim. "Help!" she screamed, and the skunk scurried back into its lair.

"Don't move," he yelled, covering his nose with his handkerchief.

"But . . . but it's awful. What am I going to do?"

From a distance, their hands over their faces, the girls yelled instructions: "Jump into the river." "Take off your clothes." "Don't come by me!"

If she didn't look so pitiful, Coulter would have burst

out laughing. "Just stay there. The only thing that works is a tomato-juice bath. Strip off your clothes and you'll get some relief from the smell."

"Strip? That's indecent."

"Get behind that bush and leave the clothes. I'll toss you the blanket to wrap up in."

Her eyes wide with horror, she did as he instructed. Minutes later, he tossed the blanket over the bush. "I'll take the girls home, pick up some tomato juice from my aunt, and come back for you as soon as possible."

"You're going to leave me? Out here? All alone?"

"Believe me, Angel, you'll be safe. No man or animal will come within ten feet of you. Not if they have a lick of sense."

Chapter 16

Josie had never felt so forlorn or so desolate in her life.

Crouched behind a bush, she watched Coulter drive away with the girls in the back of the wagon. He'd left the fish and the picnic basket, and an assortment of birds and animals kept her company from a discreet distance.

She could hardly stand to be with herself. The odor was sickening, and her clothes were ruined. The cool, clear river tempted her to jump in, except she couldn't swim. Fear of being swept away in the current kept her locked to the land and the stench that hung around her like a thick, permeating fog.

With nothing to do but think, she considered the events of the day, and her temper rose with every lonely minute.

It was all Coulter Steele's fault. He'd forced her to come on this picnic. He'd watched while the skunk did his damage. He'd left her alone in this wilderness.

One bright spot in a dismal day was that she'd bested him in the fishing contest. Her fish were bigger and more numerous than his. With a self-satisfied smile, she looked forward to watching him wash the supper dishes for a week. That should bring him down a notch or two.

She plucked at the eyelet-trimmed edge of her drawers. What a sight she must be, sitting out here in her unmentionables. Thankfully, the stink hadn't gone through her outer garments, although her face and arms had received the full force of the spray. The wide-brimmed hat had protected her hair from too much damage. She would hate to have to cut off the curls.

The minutes felt like hours, and only planning a thousand ways to torture Coulter Steele kept her sane. She'd began to doze off when the clop of the team of horses shook her awake.

"Angel, you're still here?" Coulter called.

The blanket securely wrapped around her shoulders, Josie stood and poked her head around the bushes that had been her meager shelter. "Over here. Where could I go without clothes or transportation?"

"Judging by your temper, I guess you're okay." He jumped to the ground and picked up a long tree branch. "Put your things on here; we can burn them when we get home."

"Burn them? You can't burn my clothes."

"Don't have much choice if the odor hangs on." Standing a discreet distance away, he shoved the pole toward her.

As much as she hated to admit that he was right, she followed his suggestion. "Where did you take the girls?" she asked.

"To Polly's. They all wanted to spend the night together. I'll pick Cathy up tomorrow."

Josie tightened her grip on the blanket, hugging it close to her body. A niggling of jealousy nagged her. Here she was, nasty and wrapped in an old blanket, while he'd just seen Polly looking all prim and proper and smelling like freshly baked bread or apple pie. If she knew Coulter, he had probably stopped and enjoyed a piece of that pie. Josie wanted to kick herself for her ugly thoughts about the woman who'd been nothing but kind to her. Polly was Josie's most vocal and ardent supporter.

"What about me?" she asked.

"We'll go home. Polly gave me some tomato juice for your bath." He began to gather up the fish and the remains of the picnic lunch. "Hop into the back where you'll be downwind from me."

Mustering what little dignity remained, Josie stomped toward the flatbed wagon. As she neared the horses, they nickered and shied away. Even smelly old farm horses couldn't stand her. She climbed into the wagon bed and settled on the hard bottom.

His red kerchief over his mouth like a bandit, Coulter set the fish and picnic basket as far away from her as possible. Josie shot him an angry look. Dead fish were a sorry companion.

Coulter climbed into the seat and glanced over his shoulder. "Hold on, Angel. We'll be home in a few minutes."

Gritting her teeth, Josie struggled to keep the scratchy, hot blanket closed for modesty's sake. The wagon bucked and jostled and the sun beat down on her head. Rivers of perspiration poured down her face. She glared at Coulter, who was relaxed and whistling a tune while he drove the team down the narrow dirt road toward his home.

They'd gone about a half mile when another wagon came into view, traveling in the opposite direction. Josie hunched down, burying her head in the blanket. *Please don't let them recognize me,* she prayed. Her reputation wouldn't withstand her being caught in such a compromising position. The men in town would have a field day at her expense, and at the expense of her cause.

"Afternoon, Cyrus," Coulter yelled. To Josie's dismay, Coulter slowed the team and came to a complete stop abreast of the other wagon. "Heading for town?"

"Got to pick up some rope at Oscar's." From under the blanket, Josie dared a glimpse at the man. He was staring right back at her, his eyes wide and his mouth agape. "What you got hidden under that blanket, Sheriff?" Cyrus Miller sniffed loudly and spat ugly brown tobacco juice on the ground. "Looks sorta like that temperance lady that's been causing trouble in town. Smells mighty ripe." The man laughed with a loud guffaw. "Reckon she's skunked."

Coulter shrugged and flashed a grin over his shoulder. "Reckon she is."

Josie shot daggers at his back. By evening, stories of her plight would be all over the county. "Let's go," she growled.

Cyrus stood and stared down at her. "Phew, smells like she spent the night in a hog pen somewhere."

"Thanks to the sheriff, I ran into a small black animal with a white stripe on his back, you idiot. Get me home, Coulter, before I come up there and snatch those reins from you."

Coulter's uncontrolled laughter made her even angrier. She started to stand and the blanket slipped, revealing her full, white breasts overflowing the top of her lace-trimmed chemise. Cyrus Miller's eyes grew wide at the unexpected display of flesh. At the same time, Coulter snapped the reins against the horses' backs and the wagon jerked to a start. Josie tumbled onto her backside with a hard thump. Not only was her reputation in shambles, she would certainly have numerous bruises on her bottom. It was the most humiliating experience of her life.

One hand on the blanket and one on the side of the wagon, she held on for dear life. If she had one more hand, she would have used it to clobber Coulter over the head. She couldn't wait to get her hands around his neck.

They passed several farms before reaching the ranch. In the middle of the afternoon she'd have expected the people to be indoors or busy with their chores. For some odd reason, more than a few were on the road—in wagons, on horseback, or on foot. Everyone yelled at Coulter, and, of course, he slowed and yelled back. When they spotted her in the rear of the wagon, they waved in greeting. She didn't wave back.

After what seemed an eternity, Coulter's home came into view. No matter what it took, she had to rid herself of the foul odor. She jumped off the back of the wagon before he came to a complete halt. "I'm so rank, I can't even stand myself," she grumbled.

"Get into the house— No, go to the back porch. I don't want you to smell up my kitchen. I'll carry the tomato juice and pour it into a basin."

The back porch. Now she was being relegated to the outdoors like a dirty old yard dog. Hugging the blanket to her chest, she marched around the house, the blanket trailing behind her like the train of a disheveled bridal gown. The hen who nested under the porch waddled into her path. "Get!" she yelled. At the angry sound of her voice, the hen squawked loudly and flew toward the chicken coop.

"If that's any indication of your mood, I'll remember to stay out of your way." Coulter stopped at the edge of the porch and set down the box of jars. "You can sponge off all the exposed areas, then I'll get a bath ready for you to rinse off."

"Surely you don't expect me to expose myself out here?"

"We're alone, Angel. Charlie has already gone home, and I promise I won't look." His dark eyes danced with humor—fun at her expense. "I'll even be good enough to heat your bathwater."

Realizing she had little choice in the matter, Josie leaned against the post while he emptied the jars into a large enamel basin. The thick red juice might be appetizing to drink, but the idea of bathing in it was sickening. Though not as sickening as the odor that clung to her skin like the tendrils of a clinging vine.

"I'll fetch a couple of towels and facerags. Meanwhile you can strip off the blanket and any other garments that our friend happened to hit."

She waited impatiently until he tossed the towels on the floor and retreated back into the house. Only when she heard the back door slam did she drop the blanket and begin the disgusting sponge bath in red, sticky tomato juice.

Coulter tried his darnedest not to glance out the window. Josie had looked so pitiful wrapped in the blanket, struggling for some semblance of dignity, he really felt sorry for her. And a little bit responsible. Actually he felt a whole lot responsible. The lady was as much out of place in the outdoors as she was in the kitchen.

Except she'd sure showed him up as a fisherman. He suspected that those were male fish who had jumped on her line, just for a glimpse of those heavenly blue eyes. Like the fish, he couldn't resist her charms, either. His gaze constantly strayed toward where she was carefully dabbing the tomato juice on her skin. Her back to the window, he had a perfect view of her softly rounded bottom and those smooth shoulders where the thin straps of her chemise slipped down her arms.

He forced his attention back to the water boiling on the stove. The blood coursing through his veins was every bit as hot. Looking at her had brought to life all the passion and need he'd tried to subdue. All the desire and love he'd thought he'd buried with Ellen. The tightening in his gut became painful. Coulter didn't know how much longer he could be so near this woman and not give in to his primitive urges.

With an effort, he refrained from indulging his desire to watch her. He busied himself with her bath, dragging the tub into the middle of the kitchen and filling it with hot water. Even the physical effort didn't ease the gnawing in his body. Looking at the water only made his imagination run wild. He pictured her sweet, white body soaking in the tub, her full breasts floating near the surface, her skin growing pink from the heat.

What harm would come from scratching the itch that was slowly driving him crazy? After all, Angel LeClare was no innocent. According to her own confession, she'd spent years on the stage. Everybody knew that singers and actresses didn't have the highest moral character. He remembered the evening in the loft. She'd come into his arms willingly, eagerly. Only his memory of Ellen had kept him from taking her then and there.

He curled his fingers into fists. Ellen was dead. Josie was alive. And he was a man who needed a woman, a wife, a mother for his child. He shook his head to clear away the sensuous fog that had taken control of his common sense. No, he wasn't ready, and he wondered if he ever would be able to let another woman into his heart and into his life.

"Bath's ready," he yelled, without another glance out the window. "Come in when you're finished out there. I'm going to take care of the horses." He stalked out the front and yanked the lines of the team. By the time he passed the rear porch, the screen door had slammed behind that tempting, firm body.

For the next half hour Coulter busied himself in the barn— a fitting place for a man with the appetite of a rutting animal. He considered his painting, but in his present state of mind, he would accomplish little of value. The physical activities, however, did little to take his mind off the woman in his house.

As he cleaned the fish they'd caught, he grumbled under his breath. He'd made a bet, and had lost fair and square.

He didn't like losing, but could it really be a trial to wash a few dishes? It was worth the extra work to have a beautiful woman at his table every night.

He stepped from the barn and crossed his arms over the top rail of the corral. His stallion was stomping and pawing the ground, eyeing the mares in the pasture minding their own business. "Looks like we're in the same fix, boy," he said. "Wanting something we can't have." With a groan of disgust, he pulled a slim cigar from his pocket and jammed it between his teeth. He lit the end and inhaled the sharp, pungent tobacco.

A cup of strong coffee would go good with the smoke, he thought. His gaze wandered toward his house and the kitchen door. She was probably still in the tub, and Coulter was going to respect her privacy if it killed him. Judging by the pain in his gut, it probably would; that meant his kitchen was off-limits for the time being.

What he needed was a separate room for bathing. Coulter promised himself that first thing tomorrow, he would see Oscar about ordering a load of lumber to build an addition to his house. That way, she could retain her privacy, and Coulter could have his coffee.

The thought drew him up short. He was thinking as though she would be staying with him for a while. Their deal had been for two weeks, and one had already gone by with no change in sight. What the heck? The nice, warm bathing room with a large bathtub would be an additional inducement for another housekeeper.

In an effort to be honest with himself, Coulter was forced to admit he didn't want another housekeeper. Neither did Cathy. His daughter wanted a mother, and Coulter wanted . . . No, he did not want a wife.

The back door opened, and he spotted Josie with a bucket in her hand pouring the used bathwater on the garden that grew beside the porch. The woman may have

her faults, but she was never wasteful. Used bathwater went
to watering the plants.

Since she'd come along, the flowers, like everything on
the ranch, had flourished under her care. Even his own
disposition had improved. He actually looked forward to
coming home in the evening. Who wouldn't, with an angel
waiting for him?

The cigar clamped between his lips, he shoved away
from the corral. No use letting her empty the tub alone.
His mother had taught him to be a gentleman. That coffee
would taste mighty good about now.

"I see you're finished," he said, stepping into the
kitchen. His footsteps faltered and his mouth gaped. The
cigar fell to the floor and sizzled in the spilled water.

Josie was leaning over the tub with the tin bucket in her
hand. Her blue cotton wrapper was pulled taut across her
firm, round bottom. She glanced up at him, totally unaware
that the garment had gaped open in front. Coulter stared
at the firm, full breasts that peeked from the folds of the
dressing gown. White lace edging flirted with her smooth,
creamy flesh.

"Coulter," she said, her voice little more than a squeal.
Straightening, she dropped the bucket back into the tub,
drenching her from the knees down. Her eyes wide, she
took a backward step.

Coulter advanced toward her, the cigar forgotten, good
intentions lost in the need that surged like a flash flood
through his veins. "I didn't mean to frighten you," he
whispered, around the tightening in his throat.

Her gaze locked with his, she shook her head. "You
didn't." Damp golden curls floated to her shoulders like
a beautiful silky veil.

Arm's length away, he reached out and twined a shiny
curl around his finger. "You have beautiful hair, as bright
as the sunshine, and as soft as an angel's wing."

She drew a quick intake of air, and swayed toward him.

Her skin was pink and glowing from her bath. The scent of fine French milled soap teased his nostrils. She stretched out a hand and brushed her knuckles across his beard-roughened jaw. For several heart-stopping seconds they remained as still as statues, neither one moving, afraid to break the spell by speaking. Then she moistened her lips with the tip of her tongue.

Coulter's restraint broke. With a deep, painful groan, he closed the distance between them and pulled her hard into his chest. His mouth found hers in a kiss that drove all the willpower from his soul. He fitted her against him, her soft breasts pressed to his shirt. Her sweet, feminine curves matched the contours of his body. His tongue searched and mated with hers; her breath became his. She was soft where he was hard, she was round where he was flat, and she'd started a fire that only she could quench.

He smoothed his hands down her back, cupping her bottom and making a nest for himself in her sweet, womanly folds. He couldn't remember ever desiring a woman with the all-consuming obsession he felt for this angel. His angel. Lord, that sounded good to his passion-dazed mind.

He ended the kiss, then nibbled gently on her swollen lips. "Angel, Angel, feel what you're doing to me. You're a temptation I can't resist."

She threw back her head offering the column of her neck for his sensual exploration. Her fingers tangled in his hair. "Don't resist, Coulter. I want you."

Her words fired his ardor like the blast from a cannon. They were standing in the middle of the kitchen in a puddle of water. Josie's gown was damp, and he knew he must smell like horses, sweat, and fish. None of that mattered. He needed this woman, and she needed him. He scooped her into his arms and carried her toward the stairs.

She twined her arms around his neck and nestled her face into the crook of his neck.

He took one step into the living room, when a noise from the porch threaded into his mind. Somebody was outside, pounding on the door.

"Coulter Steele, are you in there?"

The blood drained from his face and icy fingers clutched his heart. He didn't move, too shocked to even think.

"Coulter, put me down," Josie whispered.

At that moment the door flung open and in stepped an elegantly-clad couple. Behind the black veil of her hat, the woman's eyes grew wide. The man turned beet-red.

Coulter loosened his grip and Josie slid to the floor. From the corner of his eye, he saw her grip the edges of her wrapper in a pitiful attempt to cover herself.

He was caught in the worst possible situation by the worst possible people.

"Miss Clark," he said, in a vain effort to be courteous. "Meet Mr. and Mrs. Montgomery, my daughter's grandparents."

Chapter 17

Josie's knees buckled and only years of battling stage fright kept her from sinking to the floor.

Facing these strangers was worse than performing before a theaterful of demanding critics and hostile hecklers. The woman's penetrating gaze raked over Josie, from the ends of her damp hair that hung in tangles, to her shoulders, to the tips of her bare toes.

As she'd been taught by Mama and Papa, Josie stared right back at the woman without blinking. She was shorter than Josie, the brim of her wide, feather-covered hat hitting the man in the chin. Rich soutache braid trimmed the collar and hem of her stylish violet traveling suit, and a double strand of marble-sized pearls hung to the middle of her ample bosom. Wealth, power, and insolence gleamed in the dark eyes covered by the thin black veil.

Bertha had mentioned that Coulter's wife had come from a well-to-do family. She hadn't indicated they were quite so wealthy. They were so different from Coulter, Josie wondered how he'd ever fit into their world.

Silence weighed heavily in the small, simple parlor. Beside her, Coulter's breath came in rapid, hard gasps. Her own breathing had stopped the minute the people had entered the stuffy room. Coulter stood like a tree trunk, his legs apart and his hands clenched into fists. His shirt was pulled from his trousers, and his hair was mussed from where she'd combed her fingers through the thick curls.

Josie shifted her gaze from the woman to the man. His leering glance was one she'd seen many times over the years, from too many men.

He studied her boldly, his eyes flickering briefly over her face before coming to rest on the center of her chest. She gripped the edges of her wrapper and hugged the garment closed. As quickly as it had heated, his expression cooled, returning to the same stern, condemning look as the woman. Men of his class were experts at hiding their lust behind an austere facade.

They condemned certain women while at the same time enjoying their charms—on the sly, of course.

With an imperious tilt of her chin, Mrs. Montgomery turned her focus back to Coulter. "Is this your so-called housekeeper?" The words shot out like bullets from a Gatling gun. "The woman with whom you're cavorting under the same roof where my innocent grandchild sleeps?"

The heat drained from Josie's body and she tightened her grip on her wrapper to control her shivers. If her reputation had been sullied before, it was now in shambles. She opened her mouth to defend Coulter, but was cut off by his cold, hard voice.

"What are you doing in my home?" Coulter directed the question to the man.

Mr. Montgomery cleared his throat. "We've come to see our grandchild. Where is Catherine?"

"She's in town with friends."

Again the woman turned her gaze to Josie, jabbing a long, black-gloved finger in her direction. "Young woman, please make yourself presentable while we discuss a personal matter with . . . with your paramour."

The color drained from Coulter's face. His eyes narrowed, and the fury in his gaze would melt an iceberg at twenty paces. He sent an unspoken signal to Josie. He needed to handle his in-laws without interference. Not eager to get caught in the crossfire, she darted up the stairs to the relative sanctuary of her room. Tears burned at the corners of her eyes—not for herself, but for Coulter and Cathy. The animosity in the room was so thick, she expected to see lightning flash between the combatants.

She cursed her part in the volatile situation. By being caught in Coulter's embrace, she'd only made matters worse for him. How had she let things get so out of hand?

Coulter struggled to control the anger that threatened to consume all of them with its intensity. This confrontation had been a long time coming. He'd left Kansas City to avoid it; now it had followed him here.

He met his mother-in-law's unrelenting stare with cold, hard fury. If she wanted a battle, he was ready to fight; only, he hated to see Josie hurt by something not of her making. Instinctively he knew Ellen's parents hadn't come for a simple visit. They wanted more.

They wanted Cathy.

"I warned my sweet Eleanora against marrying out of her class," Lillian lashed out, with the venom of a rattler. "As usual, I was right about you, Coulter Steele. You're nothing but an uncouth savage not fit to rear my daughter's child."

Coulter growled deep in his throat, his control about to snap. At that moment he felt less than civilized, a man ready to fight to the death for what he held dear. "Like it or not, Ellen married me, and I'm the father of her child."

"And you killed her because you wanted a son."

The woman's barb pierced with the quick, sure precision of a surgeon cutting out his heart with a razor-sharp scalpel. The hatred of the past ten years spewed from her like a poisoned fountain. She wasn't telling him anything he hadn't told himself a hundred times.

"You have no idea what went on between my wife and I. She wanted another child."

"She did not. Ellen told me over and over how you forced your attentions on her, how you demanded she give you a son."

Nothing could have hurt like the feeling of betrayal that swamped him. Coulter's control snapped. He advanced on the woman, his hands outstretched. Her face blanched under her veil and she backed up a step.

"Steele." Bradley jumped to protect his wife from the impending danger.

Soft, strong hands gripped his forearms, pulling him to a stop. "Coulter, control yourself." Josie's trembling voice brought him up short.

His gaze moved from his former mother-in-law to the blonde woman's pale face. He wondered how she'd managed to dress and return downstairs so quickly.

"Stay out of this, Angel, this isn't your problem." He shook off her grip, but by then he'd regained control of his fury.

"Listen to your woman, Steele. We didn't come to cause trouble." Bradley used the same haughty voice that made his opponents tremble and win judges to his side.

"Why are you here?"

"We heard about your current living conditions, and we wanted to see for ourselves if you were cohabitating with this woman." He shot an accusatory glance at Josie. "I see the rumors were correct."

Beside him he felt Josie trembling. "Miss Clark is my housekeeper and companion for my daughter."

"After what we've seen today, she will be forced to find other employment."

He held his breath, awaiting their next pronouncement.

"We're taking Catherine home to Kansas City with us. Miss Clark, please see that her things are packed immediately."

"Cathy isn't going anywhere." As hard as he'd tried to prepare himself for this eventuality, the thought of losing his child shot terror into his heart. "She's *my* daughter, and she'll stay with me."

"Don't be difficult, Steele. Let her go voluntarily and we'll allow you to visit whenever you wish."

Coulter had watched his father-in-law convince a jury with his calm, reasoning voice. No wonder he was such a successful attorney. Bradley's name had been mentioned for a federal judgeship.

"You have no rights to my child. I'm her father; she belongs with me."

Not willing to be outdone, Lillian waved a hand toward Josie. "We're prepared to sue for custody of our daughter's child. And we'll bring up every indiscretion in your past. And your present."

Josie stepped back as if she'd been slapped. "You can't do that," she whispered.

Lillian's lips thinned to a narrow slash across her face. "We can and we will. My husband has friends in high places, as you well know, Coulter Steele. We'll prove you're unfit to rear a child. Catherine deserves the privileges and advantages we can provide. She should have the life her mother wanted for her."

"Ellen wanted her with me." Coulter choked on the words.

"We shall allow the courts of Kansas to decide." Bradley hooked his wife's arm in his and moved toward the door.

Coulter took one step toward them, but was restrained by Josie's hand on his arm. "Don't, Coulter," she said. "Don't make matters worse."

Worse? How much worse could it get? He wanted to tear the couple limb from limb and stuff their hateful words down their throats. But Josie was right. Physical violence would only play into their hands, give them more ammunition for the battle.

"Get out of my house. I'll see you both in hell before I let you take my daughter."

Bradley paused and flashed a triumphant smile. "We shall see who sees who in hell." He tugged his wife through the doorway. "Let's go, my dear. With a little patience Catherine will be with us where she belongs."

The anguish on Coulter's face tore into Josie's heart with the force of a whirlwind. She hugged her arms to keep from reaching for him, comforting him. Her impulse to hold and be held by him was what had gotten them into this mess in the first place. If she hadn't been in his arms, his wife's parents would have no reason to suspect anything untoward was going on in the house, and they would have no justification to threaten to take his child away.

In spite of the hot afternoon, her bare feet were icy cold. So were her hands. Hurrying to dress, she hadn't bothered with either a corset, petticoats, or shoes and stockings. Her one thought had been to support Coulter with her presence. Now she'd made a total mess out of everything.

She stood beside Coulter in the middle of the parlor, watching until the cloud of dust behind the hired carriage settled to the ground. Neither of them spoke, the *tick-tock* of the grandfather clock in the corner the only sound in the room.

Coulter covered his face with his palms, drawing them down to his chin. He shoulders sagged, and his skin had an unnatural pallor. "I can't say I'm surprised. My only question is why they chose now to make their move."

Josie shrugged, certain she was partially responsible for the problems that plagued him. "Can they do that? Can they take Cathy away from you?"

He turned and took the portrait of Ellen from the mantel. "They can sure try. When I decided to leave Kansas City after Ellen's . . ." His voice broke as if he couldn't say the word. "Bradley and Lillian wanted to keep Cathy with them. They needed a substitute for the daughter they believe I'd stolen from them. An eye for an eye, I suppose."

A huge knot formed in Josie's stomach. Coulter had already lost so much, she doubted he could survive the injustice of losing his child. So far, he'd yet to look at her. Perhaps it was best that she not see the anguish on his face. Surely she would burst into tears that would do neither of them any good. "You were a lawyer, weren't you? Can't you fight them?"

Bitter laughter rumbled from his throat. "I was a lawyer, and a darn good one. But I couldn't compare to Bradley and his courtroom dramatics. The man is an expert in manipulating a jury, and he's personal friends with every judge in the state." He returned the picture to its honored place.

She stretched out a hand to comfort him, then changed her mind. He turned accusing eyes to her. "I'm sorry, Coulter, really I am. If I hadn't come here . . . if I hadn't . . ." Hadn't what? she wondered. Hadn't been attracted to him, hadn't tumbled into his arms, hadn't fallen in love? Josie bit her lip. No, she couldn't love him. She couldn't love a man who couldn't love her back. That would hurt too much.

"Don't blame yourself. They've hated me since the day I met their daughter. Taking my child will be the ultimate revenge." He stomped past her and headed for the door. "I'm going out for a while."

Hands clenched together, she stared after him. She couldn't blame him for wanting to get away from her. In the past few weeks, she'd caused nothing but trouble for the tall, handsome sheriff. More trouble than any decent man deserved.

Coulter's mind spun in confusion. The thought of losing his child—Ellen's daughter—tore at his heart with the force of a tornado ripping through the prairie, destroying everything in its path. Seeking relief from his turmoil, he entered his studio. For long minutes, he stared at the unfinished painting on the easel. He'd always done his best work during times of distress. Why did it take calamity to inspire an artist?

Actually, it took passion. His gaze fell on Ellen's portrait. Since the day he'd met her in college, she'd been his passion. He'd sketched or painted her beautiful face more times than he could count. She was his best model. He opened a pot of oil paint and reached for the right brush to complete the painting of the cowboy at the campfire.

Another sketch caught his glance. This time, blue eyes stared back at him. He'd come so close to making love to her, so close to forgetting his love for Ellen. He sank onto his stool. In spite of everything that had happened in the past few hours, he still wanted Josie. His body still burned for her.

He'd been warned about bringing the temperance worker into his home. But he couldn't deny that his daughter had flourished under her care. After all, Cathy was his first concern. For now. Unless Bradley and Lillian managed to gain custody. He had to think of some way to defuse their ammunition; to convince the court that he could provide the best home for his child.

Tearing his gaze away from the picture of the woman who'd invaded his life, he wiped the brush and dipped it into the paint. It was easy to forget everything when he put paint to canvas. For some odd reason, the muse that had evaded him for weeks came bursting forth like the sunshine after a rainstorm.

Time slipped away as he buried his problems in his work, which was progressing nicely. At this rate, he could ship the painting to the gallery next week. He stretched his arms over his head to ease the tight muscles in his back. The sun was setting, and he would have to light the lamps in order to continue.

He glanced toward the house. A shadow moved across the kitchen window—Josie, probably in her own feeble attempt to prepare supper. She wasn't much of a cook, but she sure was willing to try.

Josie was a special lady, he had to admit. Beautiful, intelligent, and passionate. Something tightened in his chest. He forced the thought of what had happened earlier from his mind. Dropping a clean linen cloth over the painting, he decided it was time to quit. Farm chores still waited, and he still didn't have a plan to defeat the Montgomerys.

Milking the cow and bedding down the animals came so naturally to Coulter, he had time to think. He'd missed the farm chores when he'd lived in Kansas City. His father-in-law had been appalled that a man would prefer the rigorous physical labor of the ranch to the luxurious offices of the law firm; or chasing bandits and outlaws, to prosecuting them in a courtroom.

Coulter stepped from the barn and took a deep breath of fresh country air. True, barnyard odors mingled with the hay and wildflowers, but he loved every bit of it. He belonged here; so did his daughter. While milking the cow, he realized he had a big decision to make. With his legal background, he knew all the charges that would be leveled against him. He also knew what he had to do confront them. What he decided would affect not only his own life, but his daughter's also.

He picked up the milk bucket and headed toward the house. Time was against him, as he was certain Bradley and Lillian would file as soon as they returned to Kansas City.

Josie stepped onto the porch and waited for him. "Coulter, supper is ready."

His gaze locked with hers. He had little choice in the matter. "Angel, you should be the first to know. I'm going to get married."

Chapter 18

"Married?"

The word vibrated through Josie's ears like the clang of a cymbal. She stared at the man gazing up from below, his face unreadable in the shadows of the night. The moon cast only a thin glow over the yard, and the light from the kitchen was blocked by Josie's back. What should have been a happy announcement was made in a flat, emotionless voice.

"You're getting married? But I thought . . ." Thought what? That he'd avoided any mention of the institution. That more than once he'd remarked that he wasn't ready for that kind of commitment. That he was still in love with his dead wife.

"Who's the lucky woman?" The remark bubbled unbidden from her lips.

He let out a bark of caustic laughter. "I'd hardly call any woman lucky to have me. If I'm going to have a ghost of a chance to keep my daughter, she needs a mother. Unfortunately, that means I'll have to take a wife."

Josie's heart sank at his bitter tone. "Coulter, do you have someone in mind? Someone you care for?"

"No." He moved into the light and slowly climbed the steps. Setting the milk bucket on the porch, he propped a wide shoulder against the post where the morning glories grew in profusion. "I need a woman with a good reputation who will be the proper mother for my child. My feelings don't matter one little bit."

"I guess she should be able to clean and cook, wash and iron, milk cows and can beans." Her own words burned in her ears.

"That goes without saying."

Hands trembling, she twisted her fingers in front of her. The woman he was describing was the exact opposite of Josie. She straightened her shoulders and forced away the unwarranted feeling of betrayal. This was best for all concerned. "Of course, taking a wife will solve all your problems. Mine, too." Picking up the milk bucket, she retreated to the kitchen.

He followed at her heels. "As soon as I find a woman, you can move on to the next town and cause trouble for another lawman."

She stopped abruptly, splattering milk on the floor. "That is precisely what I intend to do, Sheriff."

"Then I pity the man." Coulter picked up a dish towel and stooped to mop up the white liquid.

Squatting beside him, she grabbed at the cloth in his hand. "I'll do that. For the time being, it's still my job."

Their heads bumped, and Josie gazed into his eyes, dark with emotion. She knew how much Coulter loved his daughter, and if his in-laws were successful in their quest, it would be partially her fault. He jerked the cloth out of her reach. "I can get it, Angel."

Slowly, she rose, her gaze remaining on his dark head. With utmost care, he cleansed every drop from the wooden floor. Josie resisted the urge to sift her fingers through his hair, to complete what they'd started that afternoon. The tingles were still there, deep inside her, waiting to burst forth in full, heart-stopping passion. That chance was long past, and new and more important problems faced them. Coulter needed a wife, and Josie would help him find the perfect mother for his child.

Even if she broke her own heart in the process.

When he came to his feet, he tossed the cloth into the dishpan. "How about that supper you promised me?"

She offered a tiny smile. "It's leftover ham from Bertha." Josie settled at the table and gestured to the meager meal on the table. "Not nearly as fine as the chicken and dumplings Polly sent the other day."

"It looks good, Angel. Not too many women can compare with Polly." He began to eat the ham and more of the sliced tomatoes of which Josie was rapidly getting tired.

With the mention of Polly came that niggling of jealousy she'd thought she'd defeated earlier. "What about Polly?"

He lifted his gaze from his plate. "What about Polly?"

"You can marry Polly."

"Polly?"

She set down her fork and gazed at him as if he were daft. Didn't the man understand anything? "Moments ago you were singing her praises. She's fond of Cathy. Polly is the logical choice."

"Sorry, that's impossible." His gaze returned to the food on his plate.

"Why? She's everything you need in a wife."

He nodded, his expression glum. "Yes, she is. But Polly isn't available. She already has a husband."

Josie gaped at him in surprise. "I thought . . . I assumed she was a widow. She said her husband was dead."

"She isn't sure. Walt disappeared shortly after he lost the ranch in that card game. Polly thought it best to let people think he'd died. Besides, John Davis has had his eye on Polly for quite some time."

That revelation came as a complete surprise. Who would have thought that the stuffy banker was courting the not-quite widow? A smidgen of remorse curled in Josie's heart. She'd had no reason to be jealous, or to berate the woman who'd been nothing but kind.

"Is there anyone else you care for?"

He stared into her eyes and Josie felt as if those dark, mysterious eyes could see clear into her soul. "Angel, I don't have time to court a woman like a lovesick swain. I need to find someone with the proper credentials and make a decent offer."

"Offer? You make it sound more like a business proposition than a marriage."

"That's exactly what I want. A business deal."

"What about love?"

"Love? I married once for love. One love in a lifetime is more than any man can expect."

Her heart lurched at the forlorn look in his eyes. "Then I suppose we'll have to find a suitable lady who won't mind being a wife in name only."

" 'We'?"

"I'm prepared to assist you in your quest, Sheriff." Josie pasted a smile on her face. She would never allow him to see the pain that stabbed at her heart. Mama had taught her how to play a role and hide her emotions behind a smile. "As you said, this proposition will be advantageous to both of us. I'll make a list of the eligible women in town, and we'll get started on this project in the morning."

He studied her for a moment, his dark gaze almost penetrating her mask of indifference. "I suppose you'll interview them for me?"

" 'Audition' is a better word, Sheriff. If you're playing the part of a husband, you'll need the perfect woman to play your wife. And who better than me to cast the role?"

He threw back his head in a roar of laughter. "Angel, if

you're half as good a matchmaker as you are a temperance leader, I'm as good as hitched.''

Although the thought of him with another woman burned like gall in her stomach, Josie had already decided to help him locate the finest wife in Council County. She would search the entire state of Kansas if need be.

''Exactly how do we go about locating this wife?''

''Very simple. While I'm listing the names of the men who frequent the bars and saloons, I'll make another list of all the eligible women in town. Then we can study their virtues and decide who you want to court.''

''I told you I don't have time to call on a woman and court her for months, even years. I plan to be married in three week's time.''

Josie dropped her fork. ''Three weeks. That doesn't give us much time. But I think I can ensure your aunt's assistance. She knows everybody for a hundred-mile radius.''

He held up his hands, palms out. ''Please, Miss Clark, don't get my aunt involved. I don't have a mind to see my business spread all over the county. This isn't some kind of competition like the cattle or sheep at the county fair.''

With a long sigh, she tossed her napkin onto the table. ''All right, I'll do it alone. Next Sunday, we'll use the Fourth of July celebration to allow you to meet with the ladies and get acquainted in a social setting. That should give you the chance to make your selection.''

She picked up the empty dishes and dropped them into the dishpan. ''I'll ride into town with you tomorrow and begin our common project. I now have an additional reason for sitting in front of the bank every day.''

''Then you haven't given up your project?''

''Of course not. I intend to close down every bar in town and to find you a wife, or my name isn't Josephine Angelique Clark.''

A sly smile pulled at his mouth. ''Your name is Angel LeClare.''

"Josie."

"I like Angel."

As hard as Josie tried to put the past behind her, she rather liked the way he said "Angel," with that deep, smooth voice that curled its way around her heart. She swallowed hard and searched for a safer subject. "Did you clean the fish?"

He groaned. "Yes. I'll fry them tomorrow night for supper."

"Excellent," she said, as she untied her apron. "By the way, Sheriff, did you forget something?" She shoved the red, flower-printed apron at his chest. "Your dishes await. Hope you don't get dishpan hands."

With a good-natured grin, he tied the apron at his waist. "Although I lost the wager, I still expect my housekeeper to prepare my breakfast. I'll meet you here at five o'clock."

Knowing this was his sorry attempt at getting the upper hand, she glared at him through narrowed eyes. "Seven."

"Five-thirty."

"Six-thirty," she countered.

"Six."

"Deal. Then we'll head into town and begin our mutual project."

"Heaven help all of us when an angel gets on the job."

And heaven help the angel who loses her heart to a mortal who can never return her love.

After three days of watching the ladies of Council City frequent the bank, general store, mercantile, and various other merchants, Josie was no closer to finding Coulter a wife than she had been on Tuesday.

Each morning, he drove her into town and warned her to be careful. Except for enduring the taunts from the men before they entered the bars, Josie managed to stay out of trouble. Word about her encounter with the skunk had spread like wildfire through the county. The men snickered and held their noses, while the women offered a bit of sympathy.

Cathy often sat with her and identified the various ladies. Josie had explained she needed to learn about the women for the Society. Little did the girl know that one of these ladies could well be her new mother.

If Coulter would only cooperate.

When Josie presented the lists in the evenings after Cathy went to bed, Coulter summarily dismissed each and all for one excuse or another. Either they were too young or too old. Too fat, or too thin. Too daring, or too sanctimonious.

The one name she refused to add to the lists was her own. That in itself was a challenge. She resisted the urge to offer herself as the most-qualified candidate. In her heart of hearts Josie admitted what she would never voice aloud—that she was jealous of the entire procedure.

She was fond of Cathy, and the child wanted her to stay. Although Coulter professed never to love another woman, he didn't try to hide his attraction to her.

Besides, she loved him.

Those were her pluses. The marks against her as his wife were far more daunting. She had her work for the Society, and her past would always stand in her way. Coulter needed a woman with an impeccable reputation, not a former singer and stage actress. No, she didn't meet any of his criteria. Not only was Josie not a paragon of virtue, neither could she cook or perform the array of household duties demanded of a wife.

So Josie plunged headlong into her effort to find Coulter Steele the perfect wife and Cathy the perfect mother.

In spite of his lack of cooperation, she did have an ace up her sleeve. With the Fourth of July celebration the following Sunday, she and the Reverend Harris had arranged a fund-raiser to build an addition to the church. Word had already gotten around about a "Turnaround

Box Lunch.'' The men were expected to provide a basket lunch and the ladies would bid for the right to eat the meal with the man of their choice.

At first, the women were shocked at the impropriety of actually selecting a man. Then, thanks to Bertha's progressive thinking, the idea took hold, and the women began to take interest in having the upper hand for a change. Polly whispered that she was doing a landslide business taking orders for box lunches.

On Friday afternoon Josie and Cathy were carefully noting the men entering the bars and saloons. She suspected that some of the cowboys were getting an early start of the holiday celebration. Many had gotten paid, and couldn't wait to spend their hard-earned salary on hard liquor and loose women.

The bank, too, was one of the busiest places in town. With so many men going in and out of town, the three men who rode up caused little notice. Cathy said she didn't recognize them, and while Josie studied the strangers, two other cowboys reined in their horses across from the bank and dismounted. Something about them—the guns at their hips, and the trail dust on their clothes—made her take special heed.

Although she had no rational reason for it, an uneasy feeling settled over Josie. An unspoken signal seemed to pass from one group to the other. As the trio slid from their saddles and approached the bank, the pair stood near their horses on the other side of the dusty street.

Perhaps it was her imagination, or maybe she was just being fanciful, but her gut feeling told her to find Coulter. He didn't like strangers skulking around his town, and he usually checked out all newcomers. To get to Coulter, however, it was necessary to walk directly past the bank, and past the strangers.

"Come along, Cathy," she said. "Let's find your papa and see if he would like to get something cold to drink at

Polly's.'' If there was trouble, she wanted the child out of harm's way.

With Cathy skipping along at her side, Josie approached the front door of the bank the same instant the men did. A quick glance told her they meant trouble. Their guns were drawn and one had already pressed into the entrance.

Her gaze locked with one of the men, and before she could move, his fingers grasped her upper arm in a bruising grip. Every nerve within Josie rebelled. Her first and only thought was for the child for whom she took full responsibility.

"Run, Cathy!'' she yelled. "Get your papa!'' Josie kicked out at the man's knees, taking him by surprise. Thankfully, the girl was quick to respond, and took off on a run.

The stranger exploded in a string of angry curses and dragged Josie into the bank. She'd been right. Their guns were pointed at a white-faced John Davis, who was shoving money into a canvas sack. The teller behind the cage was cowering in a corner with a rifle pointed at his chest.

"Don't move,'' the one who held Josie grunted, sticking a pistol into her ribs. "I'd hate to kill a pretty woman like you.''

Her breath caught in her throat, and she was certain her heart had quit beating. The man's brutal grip gave little doubt that he meant business. Part of her prayed that Coulter would arrive, the other part prayed that he wouldn't. By the cold, hard looks in their eyes, she was certain these men would kill anybody who stood in their way.

"Hurry him up,'' growled the man holding Josie. "That kid could get the law here any minute.''

A tall, thin man snatched the sack from John and turned his cold gaze to Josie. "Let's go. They won't shoot if we take the woman with us.'' He ran to the door, and signaled to the others. Shoving Josie ahead of them like a shield, they moved onto the boardwalk. Perspiration rolled down her spine as Josie stumbled on her own feet. The outlaw wrapped his arm around Josie, holding her tight against his leather vest. He smelled of sweat, dirt, and fear.

Or was it her own fear that filled her nostrils with its stench?

From up the street someone yelled, "Bank robbery!"

The bandits fired toward the Golden Garter and men and women raced for cover. Horses neighed and stomped, and Josie was certain she would swoon with terror. The man half dragged, half carried her toward his waiting horse. He yelled obscenities in her ear, urging her to hurry. "If that sheriff shows up, you'll be the first to die," he said.

More shots flew around them, and Josie's worst fears were realized. Coulter was running toward them, firing his rifle as he came. He dived behind a wagon, and when he lifted his head, the outlaw holding Josie got off a shot.

"Hold your fire!" Coulter yelled. "They've got Josie!"

She had to do something before they killed Coulter. They'd reached the outlaw's horse. Time was running out. If the bandit managed to get her out of town, she knew she would never see Coulter again. Taking a deep breath, Josie went limp, sagging in the man's arms like a hundred-pound sack of flour. Her deadweight was too much for him to handle, so he tossed her aside, flinging her to the ground. Pretending to faint, she rolled to the side and hit her head against the watering trough.

Her head swam and everything went dark. Josie's last conscious thought was a prayer for Coulter's safety.

Chapter 19

Coulter's heart dropped to his gut, and his gut dropped to his feet. The bank robbers had Josie.

"Hold your fire!" he yelled. He prayed Homer, Oscar, and the others would hear him over the sound of gunfire. His greatest fear was that she would get caught in the crossfire. One of the few shots he'd gotten off had hit the bandit carrying a canvas sack. The man lay in the dust, the sack flung to the side.

Coulter leaped behind a wagon for cover. Bullets ricocheted off the wooden wagon bed and off the post behind him. With Josie as a human shield, she was in the direct line of fire. He prayed she wouldn't do anything foolish like attempting to fight. These men would kill a woman as quickly as riddling a lawman with bullets.

The buckboard offered little protection, but he had a clear view of their progress. Then it happened. More shots came from the vicinity of the bank, and Josie slumped forward.

She'd been hit. Primitive fury exploded within Coulter.

The man holding her tossed her to the ground where she lay unmoving. Heedless of the danger to himself, he took off toward the man. The shots from his rifle rang out, striking the outlaw who'd held Josie, the man who'd dared touch her, threaten her—hurt her.

By the time he reached her the air was thick with smoke and acrid with the smell of gunpowder. Men were running into the street, firing their weapons. Two of the bandits had managed to mount and were riding hell-bent for leather out of town. Coulter held his fire, afraid some innocent civilian would be injured in the foray.

He knelt on the dusty ground and slid an arm around Josie's shoulders. Her head lolled to the side, and blood matted the golden hair at her temples. Footsteps and dust swirled around him as men gathered to see what was happening.

"Get the doctor!" he yelled. He glanced over her prone body. Except for the bruise on her head and the dirt on her pink gown, he couldn't find anything amiss. She had no wounds, unless she'd been shot in the back. As gently as cradling an infant, he rolled her to her side. Thank God there was no blood, no sign of an injury.

When she fluttered her eyelashes, he began to breathe for the first time since Cathy had run into the general store, calling for him. His daughter had yelled that Miss Josie wanted him at the bank. To his consternation, he was slow to respond, thinking she wanted to discuss another of her likely candidates for his wife. Then somebody shouted that the bank was being robbed.

Oscar was hovering over his shoulder and John had the canvas sack of money under his arm. "Killed one, Sheriff," his uncle said. "Wounded two others. Two got away."

Without looking up from Josie's pale face, he knew that the dead outlaw was the one who'd had her. In his fury his aim had been true and sure. Coulter had gone directly for the kill.

"Angel, are you all right?" he whispered, his face close to hers.

"Coulter?" She lifted her lashes and gazed at him with glassy eyes. "You're all right."

"I'm fine. You gave us quite a scare. Did they hurt you?"

She touched a finger to her temple. "No. I pretended to swoon, then I must have hit my head when I fell."

"You what?" Coulter felt his mouth drop. "Damn, I was scared to death you would pull some crazy stunt."

"I knew he couldn't lift my deadweight, and it worked. Why are you so angry?"

Because I was afraid I'd lost you. The words echoed through his mind. Words he couldn't bring himself to voice aloud. The idea of losing her was too painful to even consider. "We'll talk later. I want Doc to look at you before I take you home."

"I don't need a doctor. I just want to go home."

He stood and cradled her against his chest. Bertha and Polly were at his side. "Take her to the cafe," Polly said. "I'll look after that bump on her head."

Homer stood in the middle of the street, his gun still drawn. "Sheriff, let's form a posse and go after them."

Coulter's gaze swung from the men lying wounded on the ground, to the woman in his arms. "Won't do any good, Homer. They've already gotten a head start on us. Wire all the sheriffs within a hundred-mile radius to be on the lookout. Carry those two over to the jail and get Doc to try to save their lives for the judge."

"I warned you about her, Coulter," Homer hissed between his teeth. "It's her fault they got away. We could have caught them all if she hadn't got in the way."

If Coulter hadn't had his hands full, he would have taken out his frustrations and anger on his deputy. "Later, Homer. We'll talk after I make sure Miss Clark is all right."

"Don't worry, Homer. They didn't get away with the money. Thanks to Miss Clark and Cathy, you got here in time to foil the robbery." John hugged the canvas bag to his chest.

With a long, determined stride, Coulter headed toward the cafe. As he stepped onto the boardwalk, Cathy ran into his legs. "Papa, is Miss Josie hurt? Did the bad men shoot her?" She lifted teary eyes to Josie.

"No, honey. Miss Josie is fine." Coulter was torn between kissing the woman and whuping her. She'd stepped right into the middle of a bank robbery and nearly gotten herself killed.

But he was forced to admit, her quick thinking had not only saved the bank a lot of money, but she'd saved herself as well. None of the other townspeople were wounded, and he doubted the outlaws would try to rob the bank in Council City again.

Inside the cafe, he settled in a chair with Josie on his lap. He couldn't understand how natural and right it felt holding her. She was warm, soft, and, thank God, alive.

"Coulter, let me go," she whispered. In spite of her meager protest, her fingers clutched at his shoulders.

"Sit still, Angel. Let us take care of you."

Bertha hovered over her, dabbing the blood from her hair with a damp cloth. Cathy held her hand, and Polly made a cup of tea. And he simply enjoyed holding the beautiful woman in his arms.

Moments later the Reverend Harris shoved through the crowd gathered at the doorway to the cafe. "Sheriff, I heard Miss Clark was hurt." His words trailed off and his footsteps halted.

Coulter looked up to see the astonished expression on the minister's face. Coulter supposed he should release the woman from his embrace. Instead, he decided to let Josie make the next move.

"I'm all right, Elijah," she said. "Thanks to Sheriff Steele." Her hands loosened their grip, and she shoved gently against his chest.

So, he's Elijah, and I'm Sheriff Steele. Out of sheer orneriness, Coulter refused to let her go. "Lady's got a cut on her temple, but I guess you heard she saved the bank a lot of cash."

"I also heard you killed a man." The censure in the minister's voice brought another wave of fury.

Coulter stretched to his feet, and gently set Josie on the chair he'd vacated. Towering at least six inches over the minister, he stared into the man's face. "Listen, Rev. I don't like killing any more than you. But they would have killed me, Miss Clark, and half this town if given a chance. I figure I saved quite a few lives by killing one outlaw."

The minister paled, and turned his attention to Josie. He caught her fingers in his soft white hands. "Miss Clark, are you sure you aren't hurt?"

"Just a little bump on the head." She looked up at Coulter. "I'd like to go home. I'm filthy, and I feel a headache coming on."

"I'll be happy to drive you and Cathy out to the ranch while the sheriff finishes his business," the minister said.

Before Coulter could protest the minister's interference, his aunt spoke up. "That won't be necessary, Reverend Harris. I'm going to take care of Josie at my house until she feels better." Bertha slipped an arm around Josie's waist and helped her to stand. "Let's go, dear. All this excitement isn't good for you." She turned to Coulter. "You can meet Miss Clark and Cathy for supper. But I'd like them to stay with me for a few days."

"Really, Bertha," Josie protested. "I don't want to cause any more trouble. I can go home."

"No use arguing with my aunt," Coulter said. "We're all going to do whatever she wants, no matter what." He tugged his hat lower on his forehead. At least she wasn't going anywhere with the minister. "Reckon I'd better head for the jailhouse and see if Doc has those outlaws patched up enough for me to interrogate them."

Josie stopped and swung her gaze toward him. "Coulter, you don't suppose their friends will come back and try to break them out of jail?"

He shrugged. "You never know. But Homer and I will be ready for them. Go on with Bertha. I'll meet you later."

She nodded and allowed his aunt to lead her away. To his great satisfaction, Elijah Harris stood with his hat in hand, watching her leave. Where that niggling of jealousy had come from, Coulter had no idea. But he couldn't deny it was there, eating at him like a pesky flea that had latched itself to a dog and refused to let go.

He shot a glance at Polly and caught the beginning of a smug grin on her face. "Reverend, would you like a piece of hot apple pie? I'd just taken it out of the oven before the excitement started. Should be just right to calm our nerves."

The minister removed his hat and settled at the same table he had vacated. "That sounds mighty good, Mrs. Turner."

With Josie under Bertha's care, Coulter was certain the minister wouldn't follow her. He moved toward the door where the crowd was beginning to disperse. As sheriff he had a job to do, and it didn't include sitting around all day eating apple pie.

Early Sunday morning Coulter hitched the team to the wagon and climbed into the driver's seat. He wore his best suit and the new gray hat Oscar had ordered from John B. Stetson in Philadelphia. With the bright sunshine and unusually cool breeze, this should be a nearly perfect day. For the first time in a long while Coulter dreaded being alone. He missed having a companion—a mate—a woman. Josie.

The past two days, he'd spent most of his time at the jailhouse, interrogating his prisoners and making sure their companions didn't try a jailbreak. So far, nothing had happened. The men were mending, and the federal marshal would arrive in a few days to take possession.

Homer had become a real nuisance with his theories about the robbery. He accused Josie of being part of the gang, of being a lookout for them. Why else would she be waiting at the bank every day?

Coulter knew very well why she was watching everybody who came into town, but he had no intention of letting the deputy know that she was helping him find a wife. He dismissed Homer's new accusations like he had all the others. Homer had been finding fault with Josie since she'd come to town and blackened his eye in the melee. He'd never forgiven her for making him the laughingstock of the town. What kind of trouble would the deputy cause if he knew the truth about her background? Coulter shuddered to think what Homer would do if he learned Josie was Angel LeClare, a singer and performer.

Now he was glad Josie and Cathy had agreed to stay with his aunt. After the attempted bank holdup, he'd spent his nights at the jailhouse. He'd convinced them they would be safer in town. But he'd sure as heck missed being in his own home with his family.

A sharp pang pierced his heart. If worse came to worst, this would be his future—a lonely man without a woman or child. He snapped the reins and the team took off in a slow, lazy walk. In spite of her efforts to find him a wife, Josie had yet to come up with a suitable woman.

He urged the horses to a trot. Who was he fooling? The ladies she'd named were perfectly suitable as a mother for Cathy, but totally unacceptable as a wife for Coulter. Those blue eyes and golden hair that taunted him day and night belonged to one woman—the only unsuitable woman, and one not on the list.

Well, he was running out of time to make a decision. It

was only a matter of days until his former in-laws made good on their threat. Marriage was his only option.

After church, the entire town would gather for the Fourth of July celebration on the church lawn. Every available woman in the area would be gathered for the picnic lunch. Word had spread far and wide about the foolish "Turnaround" affair Josie had initiated. The women were all atwitter, and more than a few had asked if he would be attending.

Whoever heard of the men preparing the food, and the women bidding on a man with whom to share their meal? Women had their places and men theirs. Everyone knew it was a man's privilege to select the woman he wanted to court. It was unnatural for a woman to try to take a man's place. Josie's plan was a reversal of the fundamental order of nature. Next thing one knew, the women would be looking for the right to vote. Not that such a thing would ever happen. Not in this century, at any rate.

But he had no doubt that Josephine Angelique Clark would be right in the forefront of the battle.

With a weary shake of his head, Coulter headed toward the church. He couldn't wait for the festivities to begin. Could be, by evening's end, he would know which woman would be the next Mrs. Coulter Steele.

The churchyard was filled with families when he arrived. He was certain many of the single cowboys from nearby ranches would show up following the services. Polly promised to have his box lunch ready in time for the picnic. His stomach twisted with the anticipation and wonder of who would be his dinner companion. He spied Homer assisting Mrs. Potts and Miss Bettington from the deputy's wagon. One thing was sure, it wouldn't be Coulter's former housekeeper.

" 'Morning, Coulter." Oscar pulled one final draw on his cigar before he crushed it under the sole of his shiny new patent-leather shoe. "Any luck getting information from those prisoners?"

Coulter shook his head, a frown pulling at his mouth. "They refuse to talk. Kept saying their buddies would break them out any day now."

"Think they will?"

"Hope they try. I'd like to lock up the whole gang."

Oscar pointed his thumb toward the center of town. "Who's minding the store today, with you and Homer over here?"

"We deputized half a dozen men. They'll take two-hour shifts, and I'll relieve them tonight." Automatically his hand fell to the gun at his hip. "But I don't expect trouble out of the two that got away—not in broad daylight. If they're going to try anything, it'll be at night."

Oscar draped a fatherly arm across Coulter's shoulder. "If you need help, I'll be right there with you, son. You and Miss Clark saved me a bundle when you foiled that robbery. I'd just deposited all my cash that morning, and I sure can't take that kind of loss."

"I'll be proud to have you at my side, Uncle. But I really don't expect trouble." He tipped his hat to a couple of widows who were entering the sanctuary. Both smiled and fluttered their eyes behind their fans, and he wondered if they had designs on him or Oscar. This entire situation was downright embarrassing.

Coulter blinked to adjust his eyes to the dim interior of the church. Immediately his gaze moved to the family pew and to the lady seated beside his daughter. "Looks like the ladies have already made it."

"Humph!" Oscar snorted. "Be thankful you don't have a wife. Bertha is all excited wondering whose box she'll buy and who'll she have the first dance with. You won't have to sit by and watch your woman eat with another man." His uncle slanted a wry smile. "Or will you?"

Coulter shoved ahead to the bench. Oscar's words fed

that pesky jealousy that had taken root in his gut. Who would Josie choose? he wondered. And which of the women would actually pay to eat with him?

He did have a plan. And with his daughter's help, the right woman would be his dinner companion and escort all day. He fingered the red hair ribbon in his pocket. A lot of women were attracted to red. He wasn't sure about angels.

"Miss Josie," Cathy whispered, tugging on Josie's arm. "I know which box belongs to Papa."

Scooting over on the bench, Josie made room for the girl. She'd selected a spot under a tree, near the church porch where Oscar would conduct the auction. "And which one would that be, Cathy? All the ones Polly made look alike."

"The box with the red hair ribbon. I saw him tying it to the box. Are you going to bid to have lunch with Papa?"

Josie bit back a smile. "I'm not sure I'll have enough money. I heard several ladies have their eyes on your papa."

In truth she would like nothing better, but she certainly didn't want Coulter to know how much she'd missed him over the past few days. When he'd settled beside her on the church pew a few hours earlier, she'd tried her best to keep her emotions under control.

His most innocent touch had sent her senses soaring, and his smile had sent her heart pounding out of control. Again she hadn't heard a word of the sermon, her mind on the man who was pressed against her side.

She'd spied the red ribbon sticking out of his pocket, exactly as he'd planned. Did that mean he wanted her to bid on his box and to spend time with him? The thought warmed her more than the sun that filtered through the leaves of the trees overhead.

Cathy flashed a cunning smile. "Can I eat with you and Papa?"

"Honey, the ladies have a table full of goodies for the children in order to give the adults time alone. Surely you want to be with Carol Ann and Sally Jane."

The child glanced around at the table laden with fried chicken, roast beef, and an assortment of cakes and pies. Several children were eyeing the goodies with wide, hungry eyes. "I suppose so. You and Papa need time alone."

Josie's mouth gaped. "Where did you get that idea?" The last thing she needed was gossip about her and the sheriff.

"I'm not dumb, you know. Besides, I heard Aunt Bertha tell Miss Polly that they think it's about time Papa started courting you."

"Cathy, don't you know it's impolite to eavesdrop on people?"

"Sure." She shrugged, not the least bit of remorse in her smile. "But sometimes that's the only way kids can find out what's going on."

Josie laughed. Coulter certainly was going to have his hands full with his daughter. He'd better be careful or the eight-year-old would run roughshod over him and whomever he chose to marry. The reminder brought her thoughts back to Coulter's quest to find a wife. With an effort she tamped down the quiver in her stomach. He needed the proper wife, and she'd agreed to help locate the best candidate for the position—no matter how much her heart rebelled at the thought.

"Run along, honey. The mayor is about to begin the auction."

"The one with the red ribbon," Cathy repeated, as she ran toward the table under a spreading oak.

Oscar Marche stood on the church porch and waved his hat to get the attention of the crowd. From the corner of her eye, Josie noticed Coulter saunter in her direction, followed by a troop of men. The younger fellows marched forward, brimming with confidence; the married men shuffled as if they were unsure of the entire production.

She'd been with Coulter off and on all afternoon. He'd sat beside her while the mayor and members of the town council made speeches which were more political than patriotic. Later, he'd removed his coat and officiated at the footraces for the youngsters. With Oscar as his partner in the three-legged race, he'd won a blue ribbon for first place.

Oscar's voice brought her gaze from Coulter, back to the auction about to begin. "Looks like a fine collection of lunches here, as well as a troop of strong men looking to dine with a pretty lady." He gestured to the women now gathering around Josie. "Ladies, hope you've saved that butter-and-egg money and you're ready to donate it to a good cause." Elijah Harris moved to stand beside the mayor. "All the funds we raise today will go toward adding a Sunday-school room to the church."

A round of applause rang through the crowd. The congregation had already agreed on the fund-raiser, and were using the Fourth of July celebration as an excuse to party. Later that evening, local musicians would provide the music for the dance. Josie slanted a glance at Coulter and found him smiling at her. Quickly she turned her attention back to the ladies waiting impatiently for the bidding to begin. Several were on her list of prospective brides for Coulter—perfectly acceptable women who would make a fine wife and mother.

Josie gritted her teeth, ready to accept the inevitable. After all, she had her own life and she couldn't fit into his and Cathy's world. As the first box went to the man's own wife, Josie felt a band tighten in her chest. Would she ever have a husband and family of her own?

All around her, people were laughing and talking, the ladies whispering among themselves. After the elderly widow Mrs. Songy purchased Oscar's box, Bertha retaliated by selecting a husky young cowboy who worked at a ranch outside of town. As each box was offered, the men made no secret whose dinner was on the block.

So far, Josie hadn't decided whether or not to try to become Coulter's companion. As much as she wanted to be with him, she'd decided to use the picnic as his chance to look over the ladies and choose one to court.

When Oscar held up the box with the wide red ribbon, a murmur rumbled through the crowd. "Bet that's a good one," came a deep, masculine whisper at her side.

At the sound, a tingle that raced over Josie's skin. She didn't even have to hear his voice to know that Coulter was the reason her pulse raced and her skin heated. "It's mighty pretty. But there's no telling the food's any good."

He chuckled into her ear, his breath tickling her cheek. "Set me back a pretty penny. Polly promised a feast to warm the coldest heart." He flicked the ribbon pinned to his shirt. "And he's a blue-ribbon man at best."

"Now, how about this one?" the mayor called out. "Reckon it's all tied up, legal-like. And the lady who gets this box should feel well protected by the man who wears a star. All right, ladies, who's going to bid on this fine, delicious dinner?"

A loud groan rumbled through the remaining spectators. Oscar had all but called the sheriff by name.

An elbow nudged her ribs. "Why don't you start the bidding?" he asked.

Josie barely suppressed a grin. "I really don't need protecting, Sheriff. As you know, I'm quite able to fend for myself."

"Looked like you needed help a couple of days ago when those bandits were in town."

Opening her fan, Josie cooled her heated face. "Hush, now. You're supposed to be looking for a wife."

He let out a long exasperated sigh. "So I am, Miss Clark.

I'm doing my best to find a suitable woman. In fact, I'm tempted to propose marriage to the woman who has the good taste to select my special lunch.''

"Well, that red ribbon must be working. Miss Elsie Taylor seems mighty interested in your box.'' Josie craned her neck to where the church's pianist was standing beside Miss Bettington, Homer, and Mrs. Potts.

Miss Taylor waved an embroidered handkerchief to start the bidding, then, to everyone's surprise, Mrs. Potts upped the bid by five cents. Homer stared at his mother in astonishment, and Josie almost burst out laughing at the expression on his face. She glanced over her shoulder at Coulter. The look on his face was more comical than even Homer's.

Polly got into the act and bid higher. That seemed to spur Miss Taylor, who wasn't about to be outdone. When the price reached a dollar, Homer grabbed his mother and shook his finger at her. Mrs. Potts shrugged his hand from her arm. "A dollar and two bits,'' she called.

"Do something,'' Coulter grunted between his teeth.

Josie faced him with wide innocent eyes. "I don't have that kind of money. You're a very expensive man.''

"Bid two dollars. I'll give it to you.''

"Why, Sheriff. That wouldn't be fair at all. Miss Taylor is a very fine woman. She has a good reputation and she's available. Why, she would make a fine wife and mother.''

The sound of applause interrupted the argument. Oscar's voice drew their notice. "Sheriff Steele, Miss Taylor is your dinner companion. Hope you both enjoy the day. Remember, you're expected to have the first dance tonight with your escort.''

Coulter shot an annoyed glance at Josie, then pasted a wide smile on his face. While they'd been arguing, the woman had come through with the winning bid. Miss Taylor twirled her ruffled parasol at her shoulder and batted her eyelashes at Coulter. Coulter Steele was in for quite a day.

And Josie wasn't the least bit jealous of the elderly spinster.

Chapter 20

Coulter did his best to be gracious to the lady who was his companion. He'd known Miss Elsie all his life. She'd been the church pianist for as long as he could remember, and it was rumored she'd once had her eyes on his father. She'd never married, and had, until only a few years ago, spent her life devoted to caring for her ailing mother.

As he spread the blanket on the soft grass under a tree, he kept an eye on the proceedings. Although most of the boxes had been auctioned, a few remained.

So far, Josie had yet to bid on a single box. He secreted a smug smile. If need be, he and Miss Taylor could share with her. There was more than enough to go around.

While he watched, Josie lifted her voice. When she stood and picked up the box on which she'd bid, Reverend Harris moved toward her. Coulter couldn't believe his eyes.

Josie and the preacher.

The wide smile and proud tilt of the minister's head was far from modest. Elijah Harris was strutting like a peacock with the prize hen at his side. Josie was no better. She slanted a smile at Coulter, and tucked her arm into the preacher's as if it belonged there.

"Is something wrong, Sheriff?" Miss Elsie twirled her parasol and batted her eyelashes.

"Not at all, Miss Elsie. I was just worried if the sun was too much for you. Would you be more comfortable over yonder?" He gestured to the tree where Elijah had settled with Josie. He didn't like her being alone with another man, even if the man was the preacher.

"Oh, no. This is perfect." She bent to settle on the ground and landed with a plop, her skirts bubbling around her like a balloon. "I'm with the handsomest man in town, and that food smells absolutely scrumptious." The lady giggled like a schoolgirl keeping company for the first time. A youthful blush colored her cheeks.

Coulter felt slightly ashamed at the way his thoughts were on Josie and on his desire to be with her, rather than with Miss Elsie. He turned his interest back to his escort. "Polly went out of her way to make this a real feast for a lovely lady like you, Miss Elsie. Hope you like fried chicken, potato salad, and apple pie."

"Oh, yes I do, Coulter." She opened the box and began to spread the food on the blanket. "Don't you think this was a wonderful idea? I mean, the way the men had to provide the food and the ladies were able to bid on the man . . ." She covered her mouth with her hand. "I mean, the lunch of their choice."

Coulter picked up a chicken leg and took a bite. If he couldn't be with the lady of his choice, he could at least enjoy the food he'd provided. "Yes. I understand it was Miss Clark's idea."

Miss Elsie glanced over toward Josie and the preacher, who were talking with their heads together. "Look at her over there with our minister. Don't they make a lovely couple? And they have so much in common, what with the temperance movement and all. You'd better watch out or you may be losing your housekeeper."

A bit of chicken stuck in his throat, and Coulter began to choke. A couple? Losing his housekeeper? At that moment, he realized he would be losing more than a housekeeper; he would be losing his angel. As much as he hated to admit it, Coulter didn't want to lose either one. He would keep her if it meant marrying her himself.

The thought hit him like a bolt out of the blue. Of course! That was the logical solution to all his problems. Since he had no intention of falling in love, he might as well marry a woman he liked seeing across the table every day. There was nothing wrong with having a pretty woman on the other side of his bed, either. She was the perfect candidate for a bride, whether she agreed or not. There was no way he was going to let another man have her.

After finally coming to a decision on his future, Coulter relaxed and enjoyed the picnic lunch, his companion, and the afternoon's activities. Of course, he spend an inordinate amount of time glancing over at Josie and the Reverend Harris. Let the man enjoy her; soon the lady would be unavailable.

A few times during the afternoon, he excused himself to go to the jail and check on his prisoners. The wounded men spent most of their time sleeping, and so far their companions hadn't tried to break them out. Coulter doubted they would come back into town, but he kept a viligant watch just in case.

As the sun sank in the west, pouring gold, purple, and orange streaks across the sky, the evening's festivities began. Caleb Jones broke out his fiddle, and his boys joined their father with an old accordian and banjo. The trio entertained at all the town's functions, and had become quite accomplished musicians. They weren't quite up to big-city standards, but the people in Council City enjoyed the rousing tunes provided by their own neighbors.

The musicians set up on the church's porch, and a grassy area was cleared for dancing. Although Coulter was obligated to dance the first number with Miss Elsie, he fully intended to claim Josie for the rest of the evening.

With all the courtesy his mother and Bertha had instilled in him, Coulter gallantly took Miss Elsie Taylor in his arms and moved in time to the waltz. She smiled and giggled, but before the music stopped, she was panting from the exertion. Coulter escorted her to a bench, and brought her a cup of punch. His duty over, he searched the dancers for Josie.

As expected, she was with the preacher. The dance ended and Josie stepped away from the reverend. By the time Coulter made his way through the throng, the music started up again, and Josie was claimed by a young, robust cowboy. At least the cowboy couldn't hold her close in the energetic polka. For the next three dances, Josie was with one young buck after another. True, she was a beautiful woman—young, and available. But did she have to flirt with every critter in breeches?

Determined to prove he didn't care what she did, Coulter sought out every eligible woman on Josie's list of prospective brides. Although his companions were attractive and suitable, he couldn't keep his mind on any of them. His gaze kept wandering to a certain golden-haired lady. By the time the sun had set, and the lanterns were lit, he'd tired of the game.

He spied Josie near the punch table. In spite of the young men surrounding her, Coulter made up his mind to claim the next dance—and every dance for the rest of the evening.

His mind set, he ignored the men standing on the perimeter of the circle of light and strolled toward the woman of his choice. Just as another of her admirers reached out a hand to her, Coulter stepped between them. "Sorry, the lady promised this dance to me."

As he'd planned, Coulter caught her slightly off guard. Before she could react, he had her hand tightly entwined in his, and he was leading her to the edge of the dance clearing.

Even the musicians were cooperating with him, as they struck up a slow waltz tune. He pulled Josie into his embrace, perhaps a little closer than propriety dictated. By now he didn't give a fig for what was deemed proper. He wanted her, and he wanted her now.

Her hand on his shoulder, Josie tried without success to shove him away. "Sheriff, I don't recall promising you any dance this evening."

Every sway of the waltz brought them farther out of the circle of light. "Sure you did, Angel. Every time you glanced my way you issued an invitation with those beautiful blue eyes."

"I did not. I hardly had time to pay any attention to you. If you'd noticed, I was never without a partner." In spite of her haughty words, a pleased smile curved her lips.

"Oh, I noticed. I hope you noticed that I did exactly as you'd instructed. I danced with every female on your list."

She tilted her head to meet his eyes. In the pale light that filtered through the trees he spotted a hint of pain in her eyes. "Have you decided which lady to court?"

By then they'd left the main body of dancers, and were alone in the shadows of the trees. He stopped moving, but continued to hold her. "Yes, I believe I have."

Her hands rested lightly on his shoulders. "Who's the lucky lady?"

"You'll find out soon enough."

Concealed by the curtain of low-hanging branches, they were hidden from the prying eyes of the crowd. The music surrounded them and the fragrance of wildflowers filled his nostrils. He edged toward a large oak and braced his back against the trunk. Unable to resist the temptation of having a beautiful woman in his arms, he bent his head and planted a tender kiss on her lips.

If he'd expected a rebuke from the lady, it was much milder than anticipated. "Sheriff, are you toying with my affections?" Her words came in a huff of warmth against his mouth.

"No, Angel. I'm dead serious." He effectively cut off any further protest with the force of his mouth on hers. All the pent-up frustration of the past days was released in the pleasure of the kiss. Her mouth opened, warm and moist, offering to be filled. The sweet taste of punch lingered on her tongue, and he kissed her like a man who'd found a spring in the desert.

Coulter dropped his hands low on her back and fit her close to his body. Josie slid her hands to the nape of his neck, her fingers teasing the flesh above his collar. Her touch sent rivers of need coursing through his body. He ended the kiss with a flurry of tiny nips to her cheek and ended at her ear. "Angel, you're making me crazy with desire. Let's go home."

She remained in his arms, neither pulling away nor inching closer. For a long moment she remained silent. Then she lifted her head, and kissed his jaw. "Yes."

Before he had a chance to take advantage of the offer, he heard a rustling noise from the bushes. Just an animal, a squirrel or rabbit, he thought. When the movement came closer, he realized it was somebody else hidden in the darkness. Perhaps another young couple out for a few minutes' privacy from the party.

"Papa, is that you? Miss Josie? It sure is dark out here." Cathy's voice came from a few feet away.

Coulter's heart sank to his feet. With the beautiful woman in his arms, he'd lost track of time and place. If his daughter caught them together, it was only a matter of minutes until Bertha knew, and the whole town would be making wedding plans. He let a smile curve his mouth. Wasn't that what he wanted?

"I'm here, pumpkin. Miss Josie is with me."

Josie gasped and shoved against his chest. "Coulter," she whispered, "we can't let them catch us like this."

"I'll take care of everything," he murmured, not ready to let her go.

A small shape came out of the bushes, followed by two larger ones. "Papa, are you and Miss Josie sparking?"

The loud guffaw that followed could come only from Oscar, and the feminine twitter from Bertha. "Cathy," his aunt said between spasms of laughter, "leave your papa alone. It's time for the singing to start. Then we'll watch the fireworks."

Cathy stood her ground. "But I want Miss Josie to sing with me. We've been practicing 'Yankee Doodle.' "

Reluctantly, Coulter loosened his grip on Josie. "Looks like we got caught," he grunted. "Can't disappoint my daughter."

Josie gripped his arm. "Coulter, I can't sing. What if somebody recognizes me?"

"Don't worry. They've already heard you leading the hymns in the march. Nobody will pay much attention." His arm circling Josie's waist, he moved toward his daughter's small form. "Run ahead, honey, and tell Caleb to get ready."

"He's ready, Papa." Cathy caught Josie's hand and tugged her toward the distant lights peeking through the trees. "Let's go, Miss Josie. I bet you're the best singer in the whole county."

Coulter watched helplessly while his daughter and Josie disappeared in the darkness. Oscar's bulk loomed before him. "We tried to stop her, son. But you know your daughter when she sets her mind to something," his uncle said.

"Just like her father," added Bertha, her laughter dwindling to soft chuckles. "I remember when you were her age, and your parents wanted to get away for one night alone. They left you with me and Oscar. . . ."

On a sigh, Coulter draped his arm across his aunt's shoulder. He twirled a long, hanging purple ribbon around a finger. "Don't remind me of my misdeeds. I got a licking I still feel for leaving without telling you I was going home."

"We spent hours looking for you." Oscar pulled out a cigar and jammed it between his teeth. "Thought you'd been kidnapped by Indians. The posse went to tell your parents, when they spotted you asleep on the front porch."

Coulter laughed. "They'd locked the doors, and wouldn't answer when I knocked. Guess I'm reaping what I sowed."

"Ah-ha," Bertha said. "So you and Josie were sparking."

"A gentleman never tells."

"When did you become a gentleman?" Bertha waved him on while she stopped to speak to a friend.

By the time they returned to the clearing, Cathy and Josie were on the porch with the musicians. Caleb struck up a chord and Cathy began to sing. After a few notes, Josie joined her, harmonizing with the child's youthful voice. Coulter stood back and gazed at them, his heart swelled with pride.

After a verse and a chorus, Josie seemed to relax and get into the spirit of the number. With Cathy at her side, she pranced around the small makeshift stage, her face glowing with pleasure. He wondered if she missed performing, if she wished she could go back to the stage.

After a round of applause, Cathy tugged Josie by the arm and whispered something in her ear. For a second, it looked like the pair was arguing, then Cathy stepped forward.

"In honor of Independence Day, Miss Clark will sing 'The Battle Hymn of the Republic.' "

The crowd gathered closer to watch and listen. Oscar sidled up to Coulter as Josie took a deep breath and began to sing. Silence fell over the audience as her pure, sweet voice filled the air. He'd never heard the poignant words sung with so much meaning and emotion. When she reached the chorus, tears filled his eyes. More than a few men and women dabbed their eyes with handkerchiefs. Even the children had stopped running and playing.

"Angel," Oscar said under his breath. "She has the right name."

Coulter slanted a glance at his uncle. "How did you know?"

"I saw her in St. Louis when I took Bertha on a buying trip about five years back. Thought I recognized her that first day in church. Not many women look and sound like an angel."

"You told anybody?"

"No. She has a right to call herself anything she wants. Guess you knew all along."

Coulter nodded and turned his attention back to the lady on the stage. Pure enjoyment gleamed in her blue eyes. Her face was flushed with pleasure. The audience adored her and she was putting her whole heart into her performance. He wondered how she could give this up, and if she ever regretted not performing. Would she be happy in a small town as the sheriff's wife? Doubts about his decision took root in Coulter's heart.

As the final note of the song faded on the breeze, Coulter put aside his own concerns and began to applaud. The lady deserved the adoration of the people, himself included. One by one, the others joined in until the applause was deafening.

Josie curtsied and lifted her gaze. Her blue eyes were ablaze with pleasure. His heart filled with a sensation he hadn't felt in a very long time—a feeling strangely akin to love. It wasn't love, though. Of that he was certain.

Oscar reached the porch and caught both of her small hands in his large paws. Gradually the applause died away. "Before we have our fireworks display—donated by Marche's Mercantile, I might add—I'd like Miss Clark to lead us in singing 'The Star-Spangled Banner.' " Oscar stepped away, leaving her alone on the steps of the church with the lanterns casting a yellow glow over her face.

"She's very beautiful."

Coulter started at his aunt's voice. He'd been so lost in his own thoughts, he hadn't heard her approach.

"A man could do a lot worst, honey." She nodded past his shoulder.

Coulter glanced around and spied a stern-faced Homer nearby, accompanied by an equally stoical Miss Bettington. The couple looked away to avoid his glance.

"The lady sure is something."

"Something very special. A regular angel, I might add."

Before Coulter could question his aunt on her meaning, everyone was standing for the anthem. Josie's voice rose in song.

By the time the last notes faded, Coulter knew he was fighting a losing battle with his will. All he had to do was convince the lady she was the right woman for his bride.

A hush fell over the crowd as Coulter made his way toward her. He'd almost made it all the way to the porch, when an explosion errupted in the distance. He spun around and saw that Oscar had yet to light the fireworks. Instinctively he knew what was wrong.

His fears were confirmed when Hank Robbins, the man he'd left in charge of the jail, rode into the church yard, shouting, "Sheriff, come quick! Jailbreak!"

Coulter grabbed the reins of Hank's horse. "What happened? How many?"

"Don't know. They pounded on the front door and threatened to blow up the jail. I dove out the back and came after you."

"What about Herman?"

"He followed me out, and he's holding them off from in front of the hotel."

"Sounds like they made good their threat." On a run, Coulter shouted, "Homer, grab your gun and follow me." Without waiting to see if the deputy obeyed the order, Coulter ran to the wagon, snatched up his rifle, and grabbed the first horse he saw.

From the corner of his eye, he saw his uncle and several other men running toward their horses and wagons. At least he would have backup. Gunfire came from the center of town as he spurred the horse into the melee. One quick glance over his shoulder, and he saw Josie with her arms around Cathy. He prayed they would be safe, no matter what happened to him.

By the time he reached the jail, another blast of dynamite had rocked the town. He thought the whole world had gone mad. The music and clatter from the saloons had quieted, and not a soul was in sight. An occassional shot came from behind the water trough in front of the hotel, but most of the gunfire came from the jail.

Thankfully, both of the temporary deputies were safe. Coulter called for his men to halt and signaled them to cover. Through the broken windows of his office, he saw two figures moving toward the locked cells. A few more sticks of dynamite, and the whole building would come down around their heads.

"Hold your fire," Coulter yelled. "You won't get away. Those men are too sick to travel, and at the rate you're going, you'll kill them and yourselves in the bargain."

The outlaws answered with a round of fire toward Coulter. He ducked into the alley between the saloon and hotel. "Keep them busy," he whispered to Oscar. "I'm going around the back."

"I'll go with you," Oscar said. He had started to follow when a bullet ricocheted off the post near his head.

"Stay down. I'll handle this alone."

With his men keeping the bandits busy, Coulter darted across and down the street behind the jail. The rear door was blown off its hinges and hung askew. His office was in shambles, with the desks turned over, and chairs smashed from the explosions. The outlaws had managed to open the heavy wooden door that guarded the barred cells, but so far the iron doors remained locked.

"We've got you surrounded. Throw down your weapons and come out with your hands raised," Coulter shouted.

The man closest to him fired a rifle. Coulter jumped back in the nick of time. He listened until he was certain Oscar, Homer, and the others had them busy. Easing forward inch by inch, he dared a peek inside the doorway.

In the split second before they spotted him, Coulter opened fire, hitting both men. One dropped his gun and threw up his hands, the other returned fire. Coulter dropped to the floor, his gun blazing as he fell. The shots from the outlaws ceased. He rolled over and saw the man lying facedown on the floor. His companion was clutching his arm to stem the bleeding.

"Don't shoot, Sheriff," he moaned. "I'm hurt real bad."

Coulter signaled him away from the doorway. "Hold your fire, men. I've got them covered."

Oscar came into the jail, the others a few feet behind. "Looks like we got all of them," Homer said, waving his gun toward the outlaws. "You get in there with your friends."

"Is that one dead?" Oscar asked.

"Yeah. I shot him." Coulter approached the dead man and gently rolled him onto his back. If the explosion had come as a shock, it was nothing compared to the identity of the bandit.

"My Lord," Oscar groaned. "It's . . . It's—"

"Walt Turner. Polly's husband."

Chapter 21

Josie was certain nobody in Council City got a wink of sleep that night.

The attempted jailbreak had the men on alert for more trouble, and the women stunned at the identity of the outlaw. Nobody had suspected the outlaw who'd tried to rob the local bank was the supposedly deceased husband of one of their respected friends and neighbors.

The shock went further when they learned he was killed by the sheriff.

No one blamed Coulter. The people realized he was only doing his duty as the lawman in the town. He hadn't recognized the masked man as Walt, and had given him ample time to surrender. The sheriff had fired in self-defense.

In a way, Josie blamed herself. If she'd identified Walt in the initial robbery, Coulter may have been able to do something. Being a stranger in town, however, she'd had no idea the man was Walt Turner. Besides, the only man she'd even gotten a good look at was the one who'd grabbed her and was killed by Coulter.

Even the bank manager hadn't recognized the outlaw. John had come to town long after Walt had deserted his family.

Although she hadn't seen Coulter since he'd ridden away during the melee, her heart told her he was devastated by the events of the evening. He was a sensitive man who wouldn't take the death of a former neighbor lightly. Especially since the death was by his own hand.

Before dawn, she'd asked Oscar's handyman to drive her back to the ranch. She wanted to have a warm meal ready when Coulter returned home.

Josie was waiting on the porch when a cloud of dust announced that Coulter had returned. He reined in his borrowed horse when he came even with her.

Dejection and remorse were written on his face. Dark circles rimmed his bloodshot eyes, and grief lined his face. His black trousers were dusty and his formerly white shirt was dirty and torn. He sat slumped forward in the saddle, gazing down at her. He needed comfort—comfort she longed to provide with her heart, her arms, and her body. Whatever he needed, she would give without question and without hesitation. And without regard for her own feelings.

"What are you doing here?" he asked, fatigue in his voice.

"Waiting for you. I have your breakfast ready, and water for a hot bath."

A crooked smile curved one corner of his mouth. "Sounds good. I could use both. Let me stable the horse, then I'll be in."

"Charlie will take care of it for you. Just come on in."
Let me take care of your needs, her heart sang out.

"Charlie? What's he doing here?"

"His chores, of course. He's already milked the cow and

he's working out in the barn." She stepped back when he swung down from the saddle and landed at her feet.

"Looks like you've thought of everything." He moved slowly toward the porch. "Where's my daughter?"

She followed him up the steps. "I left her at Bertha's. She wanted to stay with Sally Jane. Your daughter is a very kind and understanding child."

"I wanted to talk to her about Walt." As if it were the most natural thing in the world, he slipped his arm across her shoulder. "Does she blame me?"

In response, Josie slid her arm around his waist. That, too, seemed the most natural reaction. "No. Oscar told us what happened. He explained you didn't know the man was Walt Turner."

"You're right. I had no idea he was one of the robbers. If I'd known, I'd have tried to reason with the man."

"Do you think he would have listened?" Facing him, she easily read the misery in his eyes.

"I doubt it. Walt never listened to anybody. He had a mean streak as wide as the state of Kansas. You know, he lost the ranch gambling. I also suspect he used to beat Polly and the kids. Not that there was ever any proof. I think she was glad when he took off and didn't come back. Only a few of us knew she'd called herself a widow for propriety's sake."

Josie bit her lip to keep from crying. Polly was always so sweet and kind, Josie had had no idea of the misery the woman had endured in her marriage. "Polly seems to be taking it all very well."

Coulter wrapped both his arms around her back. "She understands I was only doing what was necessary to save myself, as well as countless others. To her, he died when he lost the ranch and walked out on his family. She says she forgives me."

Unable to resist, Josie cupped his face in her hands. The

242   *Jean Wilson*

stubble at his jaw scratched her palms. "I hope you can forgive yourself."

"You see right through me, don't you, Angel? It's never easy to kill a man. Taking a life wrenches me clear through to my soul. It's my problem, not yours."

"I'm making it mine." She planted a light kiss on the tip of his chin. "Come and eat. Then you can take a hot bath and get some rest."

He nestled his cheek against her hair. "Reckon I can use a little tender care about now. Something smells mighty good." He kissed the top of her head. "Besides you."

"Your breakfast awaits, sir." She moved out of his embrace and tugged him by the hand toward the kitchen.

The table was set with what Josie considered their best dishes. She'd set the scrambled eggs and bacon on the warming tray and had fresh biscuits in a bowl covered with a dish cloth.

For a moment Coulter stared at the table and then at Josie. "Don't tell me in the days you spent with my aunt you learned to cook?"

"I had to do something to occupy my time since you forbade me from marching. I haven't spent *all* my time sitting in front of the bank, taking names. I figured I might as well learn to prepare a meal or two. Never know when I might have to take another position as a housekeeper." The teasing timbre of her voice faded away at the thought of leaving Coulter. But no matter how much she cared for him, she would be moving on as soon as he made a decision on choosing a wife.

He chuckled lightly. "I might consider keeping you around for a while."

"We'll talk about that later. Right now, I want you to eat and get some rest." She grabbed the coffeepot and filled his cup. "Don't frown, Sheriff. I also mastered the art of coffee-making. Polly gave me some great tips on household chores."

At the distressed expression in his eyes, Josie covered her mouth with her hand. "I'm sorry. You need to forget Polly, and everything else that's going on in town."

"I'll try. Sit down and eat with me. I like having a pretty woman across from me at mealtime."

Josie's heart fluttered at the heated look in his eyes. He had no idea how much she liked being with him. "As soon as I fill your plate."

He picked up a biscuit and took a bite. "I can't believe you learned all this in one week."

"I've always been a quick study. I could learn entire songs after hearing them once, and pages of dialogue at one rehearsal." She turned to put the plate in front of him and noted a flicker of distress in his eyes.

"Do you miss it?"

Hands trembling slightly, she set his meal on the table. She thought for a moment while she filled a plate for herself. When she returned to her chair, she was able to give him an honest answer. "Sometimes. I was practically born on the stage. It was the only life I'd known until I made the decision to give it up. Since then, I haven't regretted my choice for a minute."

"Until last evening?"

"I can't say I didn't enjoy the praise and admiration of the audience. Papa said the applause gets into your blood and you can never get enough of it."

"Is that how you feel? Are you going back to the theater?"

By the forlorn look on his face, she wondered if Coulter cared what she did or where she went. The thought that her actions mattered brought a smidgen of joy to her heart. "No. I want to do more with my life. I enjoy working for the Society and we're planning to work for other causes in the near future."

Coulter groaned. "Not more demonstrations and marches?"

"If necessary, to change the laws and get equality for all sexes and races." She spread her napkin on her lap and began to eat.

"Angel, I have no doubt you'll accomplish everything you set out to do."

"Why thank you, Sheriff Steele. I hope I've managed to prepare a meal to your satisfaction."

He dug his fork into the fluffy—and, she thought, perfectly cooked—eggs and frowned slightly as he swallowed. Her heart sank. She'd wanted his meal to be a decent homecoming for both of them. Although she knew it could also be a farewell if he'd chosen a woman for his wife. "Is something wrong?"

The beginning of a smile curved his mouth. "Delicious. Even Polly couldn't . . ." His voice trailed off. "I mean, nobody could have done better."

Josie forced a smile she didn't feel. She felt his pain as acutely as if it were her own. "Then prove it by cleaning your plate. I have hot water on the stove for your bath, and I've even changed the sheets on your bed. Charlie and I will see that nobody disturbs your rest."

"Miss Clark, you can be a real tyrant when you choose."

"Sheriff, I'm only doing my duty as your housekeeper."

With a tilt of his head, he studied her for a moment. Josie squirmed under his scrutiny. His expression was unreadable.

"Are you Josie Clark? Or has somebody stolen her beautiful body and turned her into a mild-mannered domestic?"

Heat surfaced to her face. "Don't look a gift horse in the mouth, Coulter Steele. You may not like what you find."

"Then I'll enjoy the reprieve while it lasts."

A companionable silence hovered over the table. Josie couldn't believe how much pleasure she received simply from being with Coulter and seeing him enjoy the meal she'd prepared. Surely she was going to miss him when he married and she would have to leave. The thought of his being another woman's husband cut as deeply as if he'd actually stabbed her in the heart with a knife. But she knew it couldn't be helped.

He'd told her the day before that he'd made his decision—that he'd chosen the woman he wanted to marry. Although her mind told her she couldn't be his wife, her heart refused to believe he had selected somebody else. Especially after the way he'd kissed her under the trees. He was attracted to her, that much was certain. Josie had quit lying to herself about her feelings for Coulter.

She loved him, pure and simple.

"You're awfully deep in thought." Coulter's soft tone interrupted the flow of her imaginings.

She lifted her head and smiled. No use letting him know about her insecurities. Coulter had enough to deal with. Not only were his in-laws threatening to take his child, only yesterday he'd killed a man who'd been his neighbor. The least she could do was give him one peaceful day.

"I'm thinking about what to prepare for your dinner."

He widened his eyes and tilted one thick eyebrow. "You're amazing, Angel. Don't tell me you've learned to cook more than bacon and eggs?"

"I'll have you know, sir, that I can prepare chicken and dumplings, a beef roast, and a pot of rabbit stew. How's that for a repertoire?" Tossing her napkin aside, she stood to refill Coulter's coffee. "Which would you prefer?"

With a swiftness that caught her off guard, Coulter grabbed her wrist and nuzzled her palm with his lips. "A tasty morsel of angel food would do nicely."

A tingle raced up her arm and settled in the vicinity of her stomach. Warmth spread all over her. "Sheriff, behave yourself," she said, in a rasp that surprised even her. "You need your bath and some rest." She tugged her hand free. "If you'll give me a hand with the tub, we can get you clean and into bed."

He groaned softly. "Will you wash my back? Will you tuck me in?"

She planted her hands on her hips in feigned indignation. "Your aunt informed me of the proper duties of a housekeeper, and neither request was on her list."

"I thought your duty was to provide for my comfort and obey my every whim." His forlorn expression was almost laughable.

"Within the limits of morality and propriety, Sheriff Steele."

"Angel, I'm the epitome of convention. My intentions are more than honorable."

"I'll see that they remain so."

Moments later, the tub occupied the middle of the kitchen floor, and Josie had stacked clean towels for his use.

"Did I tell you I'm planning to add a bathing room to the house?" Coulter asked, emptying a kettle into the tub. "I'll even put in running water for our convenience."

"Our?" Josie wondered if he was including her in his plans, or was he merely being polite? "That should make your new wife happy."

"I hope so. I only hope she doesn't expect a long courtship. I don't have time for such nonsense."

Josie's heart twisted and fell to her stomach. "Have you approached the lady? Made your intentions known?"

He grinned at her over his shoulder. "I planned to ask to call on her last evening. But unfortunately, something else came up. I'll speak to her this evening."

His bold declaration struck her right in the center of her heart. She should be happy for him; after all, this was her idea. Yet the thought of him courting a woman hurt as if he'd intentionally rejected her. She had to get away before she let her emotions get the best of her. While he'd been flirting outrageously with her, he was planning to wed another. Although that thought should make her angry with him, she simply loved him too much. She wanted nothing but the best for Coulter and Cathy. That did not include Josie in their lives. "While you're bathing, I'll go out and select a chicken for your dinner."

"Did you learn to kill and clean a chicken?"

At the very idea, her stomach roiled. "No. But Charlie assured me he knows how. That pesky hen had better stay out of my way, or she'll be stewing in a pot this afternoon."

With a shake of his head, Coulter shed his shirt. Josie darted out the rear door before he finished undressing. She was sorely tempted to acquiesce to his request and help him bathe. The way she loved him, it wouldn't take much persuasion on his part to get her into his arms and into his bed.

An hour later Josie ventured back toward the kitchen. Certainly Coulter would have finished his bath, and he should be safely tucked into his bed. She approached the house, a dead and cleaned chicken in her hand. The ordeal of killing, plucking, and cleaning a chicken was a strange experience. If it hadn't been for Charlie, they would be having eggs or bacon for supper again.

She held the still-warm chicken at arm's length, her stomach churning at the memory of its demise. When Charlie had grabbed the squawking bird, she was unable to watch the procedure. She'd turned her attention to lecturing the hen under the porch. As she approached the house, she whispered an apology to the dead bird and informed him he'd given his life to provide a meal for the man she loved.

Humming a tune, Josie pulled open the screen door and stepped into the kitchen. At the sight that greeted her, she stopped dead in her tracks. The chicken slipped from her hand and landed with a splat on the floor. She muffled a cry of alarm.

Coulter hadn't finished his bath; in fact, his head was braced against the back of the large tin tub. Gentle snoring came from his open mouth. Exhaustion had caught up with him. He was fast asleep.

As quietly as possible, she retrieved the chicken and tossed it onto the worktable. Only then did she venture a glance at the naked man. His dark hair was plastered to his head like a skullcap, and drops of water clung to the blanket of black hair on his chest. Unable to stem her curiosity, she stepped closer for a better look.

Her heart skipped a beat, then began to pound against her ribs. He was a magnificently structured man. His tall frame filled the tub, and his wide shoulders were high above the water. Muscular arms lay slack over the rim of the tub to the floor. His arms were a shade darker bronze than his chest. Her gaze slid lower, to his flat stomach. The pale flesh at his navel caught her eye, but she dared not glance lower into that thatch of dark hair between his bent knees.

If she had a lick of sense and decency, she would dart back to the porch and allow him to finish his nap in privacy. But something much more compelling than modesty kept her rooted to the spot.

"Want to scrub my back?"

The sound of his voice snapped her out of her stupor. She jumped back a step and turned her head from him. Had he seen the way she was staring at him? she wondered. Had he seen the lust in her gaze? "I thought you were asleep." Josie backed toward the porch door.

"Don't leave, Angel. I need help."

She spun around. "Help? How?"

"I could fall asleep again, slip under the water and drown."

"I doubt that's possible. You barely fit in the tub."

"What if I'm stuck and can't get out?"

She caught the teasing gleam in his eyes. "I have an idea that you've been bathing yourself in that tub for a number of years. Without my help, or anyone else's." Jamming her hands into her apron pockets, she continued toward the door. "I'm sure you'll be more comfortable in your bed. I'll have your dinner ready when you awaken."

Once outside in the warm morning air, she willed her heart to slow to normal. The words of the old song popped into her head and she began to sing. *"Yield not to temptation, for yielding is sin."* She plucked a blue morning glory from the vine that grew next to the porch. Yielding wouldn't do either her or Coulter any good. She'd best watch her behavior, especially since he was preparing to take a wife.

When Josie finally ventured back into the kitchen, the tub had been returned to the storage room and the kitchen was empty. Coulter must have taken her advice and gone to his room for much-needed sleep. She put the chicken into a pot with the required spices and herbs she'd gotten from Bertha and Polly, and set it to simmer on the stove.

Polly. Again she was reminded of what had happened the past night. Not only did Polly have to deal with the death of her husband, so did Coulter and the entire town. How could Walt Turner have tried to rob the bank where his own wife kept her money, not to mention all his former friends and neighbors? According to Oscar, Walt had always been a vile, selfish man. Oscar said it had been only a matter of time until the man got his just reward.

With the chicken simmering on the fire, Josie picked up Coulter's dirty clothes. Looked like Mr. Wong would have his hands full with the dirt imbedded in the suit. She lifted the shirt and nuzzled her face in the material. Mingled with the perspiration and dirt, Coulter's individual scent clung to the fabric. Tears clouded her eyes. She hoped his new wife would be a good housekeeper who could tend his every need—in his kitchen as well as his bed.

After dusting and straightening the living room, she ventured up the stairs. She didn't want to disturb Coulter, but she should make sure he'd closed the curtains against the light, and that he was resting well. Or so she tried to tell herself. In truth she wanted to see him, to spend a few short minutes simply watching him sleep.

The house was cool and quiet, with only the occasional cow's moo and dog's bark coming through the open windows. After finishing his chores, Charlie had left for the day. Josie stopped at Coulter's door, debating whether to step into his room.

Her heart won and Josie shoved the door open. He was lying on his side, with a light coverlet shoved down to his waist. While she watched, he mumbled something and rolled onto his back. The cover slipped, and Josie gasped at the sight of his bare hips and muscular thigh. She took a step backward. It wasn't right staring at him like a Peeping Tom looking at something forbidden. Yet she couldn't help herself.

It was amazing how his skin changed hues below his navel. The band around his lower hips was almost as pale as her own skin. She stood her ground, drinking her fill. Chances were, she would never see such a magnificent man again. His wife would be one fortunate woman. She hoped the woman was smart enough to appreciate Coulter.

Wanting to leave before she gave in to her impulses and did something foolish, Josie turned to leave. A loud grunt from the bed stopped her cold.

"No, Walt, don't shoot! I didn't want to kill you. . . . I didn't know." The words faded to a deep, heart-rending groan. The covers tangled in his legs and he tossed the pillow to the floor. Without thinking about the consequences, Josie rushed to the bed.

"Coulter," she said, in a voice both calm and reassuring.

She clasped his face in her palms. "Wake up. You're having a nightmare."

"No, no. You can't take Cathy. . . . Don't kill Angel." All his fears were wrapped up into one heartbreaking nightmare.

Taking her by surprise, he caught her by the shoulders and flipped her onto her back. He pinned her to the bed with his body. Josie gasped, too surprised to scream. Glassy, dark eyes gazed unseeing into hers.

He shook her as if trying to drive her into the feather mattress. "Why did you do it, Walt?"

"Coulter, wake up! I'm not Walt, I'm Josie."

"No, no," he groaned. The words seemed to come from some faraway place.

His chest pressed into hers, Josie could barely catch her breath. She shoved at his shoulders, hoping to awaken him to his surroundings. He was damp with perspiration, and his pale face was icy cold. She repeated his name over and over. After what seemed like forever, he blinked, and life came into his eyes.

"Angel?" He shook his head, his damp hair tumbling onto his forehead. "Angel? What? Oh, God, what's going on?" His breath came in short gasps.

Again Josie shoved at his shoulders. This time he rolled to his side and draped his forearm over his eyes. She took a deep breath, filling her starved lungs with air.

"You must have been having a nightmare. I heard you calling out." She rolled to her side and brushed her fingers along his jaw. "I tried to wake you up."

"What was I saying?"

"You must have been reliving the battle at the jail. You thought he was going to kill you."

"Did I hurt you?" He turned to face her, his color gradually returning to normal and his skin growing warm

"No. I was worried about you."

"I'll be all right as soon as my heart returns to normal."

He slid his arm around her, his fingers digging into the flesh at her waist. "I don't know what would have happened if you weren't here to help. You're good for me, Angel."

Josie brushed her hand across his face and threaded her fingers in his hair. She shifted closer, her breasts crushed to his bare chest. In the tossing and tumbling on the bed, her skirt had become tangled around her thighs. Coulter's bare leg pressed warm and heavy across hers. His nearness, his warmth, his strong male body, sent all kinds of emotions rushing through her with the force of a whirlwind.

She'd never lain in a naked man's arms, and Josie wasn't sure if she should continue, or stop before things went too far. She loved Coulter and wanted nothing more than to show that love in the fullest ways of a woman. This would be her only chance before he married and spent his life with another woman. But was it right to want him, when he was all but promised to another?

Torn with indecision, she lay still, not sure what to do. Coulter snuggled closer. "Angel, let me hold you. I need to feel something real and alive. Unless you've killed a man, you have no idea what it does to your insides. I'm torn in a hundred different pieces. I need you to help put me back together."

His words were more powerful and seductive than flowery prose or love poetry from Byron. Josie combed her fingers through his mussed hair. "I'm here for you. I'll do anything I can to help."

He buried his face in the crook of her neck. His lips brushed against her throat, exposed above the collar of her piqué blouse. Delightful sensations stole across her flesh and into the hidden recesses of her body. She'd never imagined how delightful it was to have a man this close, to feel the heat of his body, to feel his growing arousal against her leg. It was forbidden, it was wicked, it was exactly what she wanted. It was exactly what she needed.

"I want to love you, here and now. I need you as I've never needed a woman." Lifting his head, he gazed into her eyes for an answer.

Josie's heart tumbled over and over. To deny him was to deny her own soul. "Yes, Coulter, make love with me."

Chapter 22

Coulter gripped the sheet on either side of the woman lying beneath him. He couldn't believe he had heard the words she'd uttered with so much emotion and caring. After wanting her for weeks, now that she was in his arms, he hoped he could control his desire and give her the satisfaction she deserved. Her eyes were bright with passion; her face was rosy and warm.

Her lips parted and he covered her mouth with his. She tasted as sweet as strawberry jam. Hands shaking, he reached for the tiny buttons that ran the length of her bodice. He needed to feel her next to him and to bury himself in her. In this woman's arms he felt more alive than he had in years.

The front of the blouse parted. His fingers stroked the full, soft breasts overflowing the top of the thin chemise. He continued to kiss her cheeks, her jaw, and down to the flesh that was more tempting than a feast to a starving man. He inhaled the fresh, clean scent of her skin. Without a doubt, she was the most tempting woman he'd ever known.

Her gentle groans spurred him on. Her skirt joined the blouse on the floor, followed by an assortment of petticoats. Clad only in a chemise and drawers, she wrapped her arms around his neck and pulled his face to hers. She returned his kisses, matching his passion kiss for kiss, caress for caress. What he offered, she took, then offered more in return.

When she had shed the last of her garments, a momentary glint of apprehension glittered in her eyes. He leaned back on his elbow and studied her expression. She was so soft and giving, he wondered if he'd gone too fast, if she wasn't as ready for the completion as he.

"Angel, is something wrong?" He struggled with his own needs to consider hers. "Do you want me to stop?" In spite of his offer, he wondered if he could stop, when he was burning up for her.

She ran her soft hands down his back, cupping his buttocks with her palms. "No, Coulter. I'm aching, I need . . . I'm not sure what I need. Show me. Fill me."

He needed no further invitation. He was aching, throbbing for her. Forcing himself to go slowly, he continued a row of kisses to the valley between her breasts. He took first one pink nipple, then the other, between his lips, suckling and nipping until she was writhing beneath him. Only when he was afraid he would burst with desire, did he slip his knees between hers to ease his length into her. He let out a long whoosh of air and closed his eyes for control.

She gasped slightly, and he lifted his weight from her body. Her breath was coming in soft gasps. He fitted himself fully into her, reveling in the tight warmth of woman, of Angel. His heart pounded so loudly, he wondered if she could hear it. He pushed his way past an unexpected barrier, his need spurring him on.

A soft cry came from her lips. He stopped, and took her moans into his own mouth. "It's all right, Angel. Relax," he whispered against her lips.

He paused for a second to calm his racing pulse. She matched her movements to his, groaning softly with a need of her own. He was in heaven, he was with an angel, and he never wanted to return to earth.

When he heard her gasp and felt the tremors deep inside her, he let himself go and followed her to completion.

For long moments he lay in her arms, listening to the sound of her breathing. He could never remember when making love to a woman had filled him with such wonder, with such power. Never had he known a woman so responsive to his touch, so giving and eager to share his love.

He lifted his head to read the expression on her face. Tendrils of damp hair clung to her forehead, and her eyes were shiny. A tear slipped from the corner of her eye. He gently swept the moisture away with his tongue.

"Am I hurting you, Angel? Give me a second to catch my breath and I'll move."

Her fingers dug into the flesh at his back. "No, don't move. I love having you with me."

Coulter rolled to his side and pulled her beside him. He was far from ready to let her go. Her softness and giving heart gave him hope that had been lost in the long, cold years without love. He had no idea what the future held, he only knew he wanted to face it with his very own angel at his side.

He pressed his lips into her hair. "Let's take a nap. I want to just lie here with you in my arms."

She nodded and snuggled into the crook of his arm. "Hmm . . ." she groaned. "I could use a little sleep myself."

With a soft chuckle, he brushed the hair from her eyes. "Then we can start all over again."

"Coulter Steele, you aren't serious. Surely you can't do that again?"

"Care to make a wager? This time I won't lose."

She laughed. "Go to sleep. We'll discuss it later."

His eyes heavy, his body completely relaxed, Coulter shifted to fit her back intimately against his front. He was still hard, he was still needy, but he had a lifetime to fulfill those needs with the angel in his arms.

Coulter wasn't sure what woke him up this time. The last time he'd awakened, they had made love, then slipped back to sleep. It could have been dreaming about making love to his special angel, or the sound of her gentle breathing. It had been so long since he'd had a woman in his bed, he was surprised he'd been able to sleep at all. He swiped a strand of golden hair from where it clung to his whiskers, and listened to the sounds of the empty house.

That was the problem. The house wasn't empty. In his sleep-dazed state, he hadn't noticed the noise from downstairs. Now he recognized the sound of his daughter's running feet.

Instantly he jerked awake, and tugged the sheet over his nakedness and the woman cuddled at his side. Coherent thought evaded him. His mind was numb.

"Papa, where are you?" The words had no sooner reached his ears, than Cathy darted into his bedroom. "What are you doing in bed? It's the middle of the afternoon." His daughter's eyes widened. "What's Miss Josie doing in your bed?"

The voice awakened Josie and she dipped her head under the covers. Heat rushed to Coulter's face. Being caught in a compromising position was bad enough, but getting caught by his daughter was unbelievable. Then it got worse. Bertha stepped through the doorway, her wide hat tilted at a saucy angle.

"Cathy, your papa didn't get any sleep last night. Neither did Miss Josie. They were just taking a little nap." How his aunt managed to keep a straight face was beyond him.

"That's right, honey. We were just resting."

Beside him, Josie let out a sound closer to a sob than a groan.

A wide grin curved Cathy's young mouth. She gazed at the bed with eyes much wiser than her years. "Does this mean you and Miss Josie are going to get married?"

This time Bertha let out a howl of laughter. "Cathy, where did you get such an idea?"

Josie huddled deeper into the covers, her breasts now down around his hips. The effect was definitely upsetting. "Get them out of here," she whispered. Her breath tickled his bare belly.

Cathy took another step closer to the bed. "I'm not a baby. I know that when men and ladies sleep together in the same bed they're supposed to be married. Papa used to sleep with Mama, and you sleep with Uncle Oscar."

"Well, Coulter?" Bertha tilted an eyebrow. She picked up Josie's discarded blouse and tossed it onto a chair. "Shall I plan the wedding for next Sunday after church?"

"No," came the voice from somewhere under the covers.

"Sounds good to me," Coulter said, ignoring Josie's protests. "If you'll leave us alone for a moment, we'll join you downstairs to finalize the plans."

"Certainly, dear. By the way, Josie, I added water to your chicken pot. It was about to burn to a crisp." She wrapped her arm across Cathy's shoulder and steered her toward the door. "Let's go, dear. I'll even get you a new frock for the wedding, if you'd like."

"Thank you, Aunt Bertha." She turned back to her father. "Hurry, Papa; you, too, Miss Josie. We have to make all the plans for Sunday."

Josie wished she could crawl under the floor and never show her face again. Being caught in his bed was bad enough, but now his daughter and aunt were planning a wedding.

Coulter was going to hate her. He'd already chosen a woman for a wife, and Josie was ruining his chance for happiness. "Coulter, what are we going to do?"

"I'll advise you to come up for air. If you get any closer to . . . uh, certain parts of my anatomy, I won't be responsible for what happens. My daughter and aunt will have to wait until . . ."

She jerked upright, hugging the sheet to her neck. Not daring to look at Coulter, she scooted to the edge of the bed and glanced around for her clothes. An embarrassing fire warmed her entire body. By the apparel strewn around the room, any fool would know exactly what had happened in this room, in this bed.

"Coulter, I'm so sorry." She croaked out the words around a sob. "I've made a mess of everything."

"I can't say you were alone, Angel." He caught her arm and tugged her closer to him. "I certainly was an eager participant in what happened here. In fact, I'm rather eager to continue."

If possible, the fever in her blood rose by several degrees. "Let me go. What will your aunt think? I wouldn't be surprised if she ran me out of town on a rail."

His deep rumble of laughter shook the mattress. "I don't think so. She's been trying to get me married off for years; now that she's caught us in this rather compromising position, she's not going to let either of us off the hook."

"How can you think this is so funny?" She shoved against his bare chest, her hand pressed against his pounding heart. "Neither of us wanted to marry. What are we going to do?"

He leaned against the solid oak headboard, a smug, self-satisfied grin on his face. "Get married on Sunday."

"Get married?" Her voice rose to a squeal. She pulled away from him and scooted off the bed, taking the sheet with her. Coulter remained on the bed, totally and gloriously naked; completely unashamed and more than slightly aroused.

"We can't." As hard as she tried, Josie couldn't pull her gaze away from him. Streaks of afternoon sunlight streamed across the bed, bathing his skin with a golden glow.

"Why not? We're both available, and we've proved compatible in the most basic and elementary part of marriage. I need a wife, and, well, now that I've compromised you, it's the only way to protect your reputation."

"What about the woman you were planning to court? Surely she would be a better wife than me." Tearing her gaze from him, she snatched her chemise and petticoats from a heap on the floor. Holding the sheet close to her chest, she knelt down and retrieved her skirt from where it had landed under the bed.

"Let me worry about that." He swung his feet to the floor, inches from her face. "She didn't know, so she won't be disappointed in not being courted for an extended length of time."

Josie didn't dare take her gaze from the floor. Looking up at his nudity would be her undoing. A string of French profanities came unbidden from her mouth. She was forced to reach behind his legs to locate her petticoats.

Another chuckle came from above her. "You'll have to control that temper, Miss Clark. A few people may know the more colorful French phrases."

"Sheriff, please remove your foot from my petticoats. I have to get dressed."

"Since I helped you disrobe, do you want me to help you dress?"

For some reason, he was taking all this with more humor and good nature than she would have expected.

She hugged her clothes to her chest and darted to the relative sanctuary of her own room. As much as she wanted to fight against the situation, gladness had settled in the deepest recesses of her heart. She loved Coulter, and although he didn't love her, she would make him happier than any woman possibly could.

The week passed in a whirl for Josie as she prepared for the nuptials. With Coulter's aunt on the job, Josie had little to do. Bertha was in her prime supervising the entire affair. Josie and Coulter insisted on a simple ceremony following the morning service, and only a family dinner afterward. Bertha, for once, relented, but insisted on being allowed to host a party the following Saturday for the newly-weds. After all, she reasoned, Coulter was sheriff, and his uncle was the mayor. It was their duty to entertain their friends and neighbors with a party. But everybody knew the real reason was to assert Bertha's position as social leader of the town.

Knowing it was a waste of time to argue with her, Josie and Coulter agreed to the plans. The town gossips were kept busy with stories about Josie and Coulter, and about Polly and her husband. Coulter seemed to have adjusted to the killing, although at times Josie heard him pacing the floor into the night.

As far as she could tell, most of the people were happy for her and Coulter, Homer and Miss Bettington being the exceptions. The couple didn't try to conceal their dislike. Josie didn't care what they thought about her. She prayed they wouldn't do anything to hurt Coulter.

Nobody in the community, including Josie, was happier than Cathy. She clung to Josie as if afraid Josie would disappear if she left the child's sight. Coulter's daughter had a hand in every aspect of the ceremony and party. Bertha gave the child a new, ready-made dress and insisted on designing a special hat for Josie. Since Josie didn't want to insult the woman who'd been so generous and kind,

she made up her mind to wear the hat, no matter how
preposterous it was.

Caught up in the plans and preparations, Josie and
Coulter hadn't had a chance to discuss their future, or her
desire to continue her work for the S.A.A.T. On Friday
afternoon, she stepped onto the boardwalk with her new,
resplendent hat in hand, determined to have a few
moments alone with the man she was about to marry. Too
many things needed to be clarified before they tied their
lives together.

She started toward the jailhouse, her mind on the things
she had to say, when she ran smack into a man's wide
chest. Her hatbox flew one way, and her packages the
other.

"I'm so sorry, madam," the man said. He caught her
arm to steady her. "Let me help."

The voice sent a shiver through Josie. She'd heard those
deep, resonant tones before; she cringed at hearing them
again. She turned her head, not wanting to face the man
from her past. Terrell Sullivan had been the lead actor
and stage manager she'd run away from four years ago in
Chicago. "It's all right, thank you."

He tightened his grip, forcing her to look into blue eyes
as chill as the wind off Lake Michigan. "Angel. Angel
LeClare. I knew I would find you here."

"Let go of me. You're mistaken, sir."

"No, Angel. I've been searching for you too long to
make a mistake." He chewed on his unlit cigar, a habit
Josie had always detested. "I can't believe you're hiding
out in this hick town in the middle of nowhere."

"I'm not hiding. I live here." Josie struggled against his
grip. His touch brought back memories, memories she'd
tried to forget. He'd been the one to tell her about
Armand's murder. And he'd offered his help—help that
to him meant she would become his mistress. She recoiled
at the very thought of the man's hands on her.

"Angel, Angel, I've got a proposition for you." He brought his free hand to her face and stroked her cheek with fingertips too smooth for a man. "You're just what I need for my new production. I have tickets to San Francisco for both of us."

"I'm not going anywhere with you. Get away—" Her words were cut off by the thud of boot heels on the wooden planks. Coulter. She knew the sound of his footsteps from hearing them night after night, pacing the floor in his room. Her stomach sank to her feet.

"This man bothering you, Miss Clark?"

Josie's insides trembled at the fury in Coulter's tone. "No, Sheriff. He was—"

Terrell jerked back and raised his hands over his head, a mocking grin splitting his handsome face. "Don't shoot, Sheriff. I was just asking the lady where a man might find some entertainment in your little town."

Coulter's gaze swept from the man to Josie. She averted his glance by stooping to retrieve her packages. "I'll get those, ma'am," he said, as cold and aloof as a stranger.

The bundles in one hand, Coulter helped Josie back to her feet. He returned his gaze to Terrell. "The saloons and bars are across the street. If you need further directions, come to my office. I don't like strangers bothering the women in my town." Taking Josie by surprise, he draped an arm over her shoulder. "I especially don't like men bothering my fiancée."

Terrell's eyes grew wide. Beneath his mustache, a malicious grin curved his thin lips. "I beg your pardon, madam. And congratulations, Sheriff. She's certainly a beauty. As pretty as an angel." He touched two fingers to the rim of his stylish derby and sauntered across the street in the direction of the Golden Garter.

Josie's gaze followed his progress down the boardwalk. As usual, Terrell was dressed in the height of fashion. His coat was tailored to fit his slender build, and his pants creased and pressed. He tipped his hat to several ladies, who returned his smile. If they only knew what a snake the man was, they would run for cover as fast as their legs could carry them.

"You know him?" Coulter asked, when the man was out of earshot.

Josie busied herself taking her packages from his hands. "No. He's a stranger in town."

Coulter stared at her for a long moment before he released the hatbox. "I'll be home early tonight. We have some things to straighten out before we get married on Sunday."

Josie glanced past Coulter and spotted Terrell in conversation with Homer Potts. Her heart sank. There was no telling what kind of trouble that pair could cause for her and Coulter.

"I have to pick up Cathy, and Charlie is waiting to drive me home." She looked back at Coulter, and saw that his attention, too, was on the men across the way. On a sigh, she took a step away from him. Would he still be willing to go through with the marriage when she told him the whole story about her past? Certainly it would be best now rather than later, when he and his child could be hurt.

Why did Terrell Sullivan have to show up now, just when a smidgen of happiness was within her grasp?

Chapter 23

Coulter knew trouble when he saw it. The stranger in town, the man registered at the hotel as Terrell Sullivan, had some connection with Josie. A connection Coulter was bound and determined to discover.

Since he'd run into Sullivan on the street Friday afternoon, he'd often seen the man with Homer. For some odd reason the pair had become rather friendly. Several times he'd caught Homer deep in conversation with the man. When Coulter had approached them, they'd parted without another word.

He'd meant to discuss the situation with Josie, to learn exactly who Sullivan was, and what part he played in her life. Thanks to his aunt, however, he never got the chance. Before Josie could return to the ranch, Bertha had waylaid her with the announcement that it wasn't proper to remain in the house with her intended until after the marriage.

Coulter had almost laughed aloud at the idea. His aunt hadn't mentioned a word about propriety over the past weeks, not even when she'd caught them in bed together. Now she insisted the strictest social protocol.

Coulter put his concerns aside as he drove the buggy he'd borrowed from Oscar to the church on Sunday morning. At least his new wife wouldn't have to ride home in a bouncy buckboard. For the first time in a very long time, he felt that his life was on track again. True, he was only marrying because of his child, but at least the woman was one he found desirable.

So desirable he'd thought about little but her in days. Since that afternoon they'd been caught in bed together, they'd had little time alone, and no time for intimacies of any kind. He would remedy that problem tonight. They were marrying for convenience' sake, but Coulter had every intention of enjoying all the true rights and privileges of marriage.

As he reined the team in under the spreading oaks in the churchyard, he spied Polly and her children stepping down from their wagon. His heart tightened in his chest. Although Polly didn't blame Coulter for killing Walt, he couldn't stop the self-doubt that haunted his conscience. Could he have done differently? Should he have tried?

He jumped down from the seat and hurried to her side. "Polly," he said, "may I talk to you for a moment?"

"Certainly, Coulter. I wanted to offer congratulations to you and Josie." She shooed her children toward their friends and took his arm in her usual, friendly manner.

"Thank you. I wanted to know how you're managing. Are you all right?"

She patted his hand. "I'm the same as ever. If you're feeling guilt over Walt, don't bother. He knew what he was doing when he robbed the bank and then tried to break the other bandits out of jail. As far as I'm concerned, he died eight years ago when he walked out and left me without a home, money, and with three children to rear.

If it hadn't been for Oscar and Bertha, I don't know what would have happened to us."

"You're an amazing woman, Polly."

"What really makes me mad is that when Walt robbed the bank, he was robbing me, his children, and all our friends and neighbors of their life's savings."

"I hope John knows what a jewel you are."

"I remind him every time he eats my cobbler or dumplings. Now that I'm free, we'll follow you and Josie to the altar. After a respectable length of time, of course." She slanted her glance toward Oscar's elegant carriage pulling into the yard. "Speaking of your betrothed, this was certainly rather sudden, wasn't it?"

He laughed. "Polly, you along with most of the town have been pestering me for years to find a wife. I figured there was no use wasting time courting when I could just marry the lady and skip all that nonsense."

"A man of action. And Josie is quite a lady. Beautiful, intelligent, and your daughter adores her."

His gaze followed hers to where the carriage stopped near his buggy. "I just hope I'm doing the right thing."

"Trust your heart, Coulter. You deserve to be happy." They stopped and watched as Oscar leaped to the ground. "By the way, who's that stranger I've seen hanging around town for the past couple of days?"

Without further description, Coulter knew she was referring to Sullivan. "All I know is his name is Terrell Sullivan, and he seems to have become friends with Homer."

She nodded. "They've come into the cafe a few times together."

Coulter followed her gaze to Homer, who was escorting his mother and Miss Bettington into the church.

"There's something about him. I can't put my finger on it, but I'd advise you to keep an eye on him, as sheriff." With a lowered voice, she added, "He could be up to no good."

"I intend to take your advice." His gaze wandered toward Oscar's carriage. At sight of a pink dress lifted above a trim ankle, Coulter lost all interest in Sullivan, Homer, and at that point, even Polly. His heart stumbled as the thought of Josie lying naked in his arms flashed across his mind.

Polly pulled her arm free and shoved him in the direction of the carriage. "Go help your bride. John is waiting inside for me."

Coulter bowed over Polly's hand. "Excuse me, ma'am. I reckon the lady needs help."

He reached Josie in time to set his hands on her slender waist and lift her to the ground.

" 'Morning, Miss Clark," he said, unable to hide the smile in his voice. A grin slanted across his mouth when he spotted the ridiculous hat that sat at a sassy angle above her eyes. His aunt must have emptied her entire collection of feathers, ribbons, and silk flowers to decorate Josie's head for the wedding. A pink bow covered one entire cheek under the thin, crystal-studded veil. He bit his lip to keep from laughing aloud.

"If you laugh, Coulter Steele," she whispered for his ears only, "I swear you'll walk funny for a week."

Coulter tried his darnedest to maintain a solemn expression. He squeezed her waist before he let her go. "That would be a tragedy we would both regret, Angel. Especially on our wedding night."

Her cheeks pinked to the color of the outrageous bow. "Sheriff, behave yourself. We're in front of the church."

"Papa!" Cathy's anxious call drew his gaze back to the carriage. His daughter was waiting, arms outstretched for assistance.

After he set his daughter on the ground, he glanced up at his aunt. Seated on the leather front seat, she flashed a wide, self-satisfied grin. He suspected Bertha had planned this event from the moment she'd laid eyes on Miss Clark.

And last week he'd fallen right into Bertha's trap. Although he should be angry at being coerced into marriage, Coulter couldn't deny he'd been looking forward to the event. His stomach muscles tightened in anticipation.

Bertha stretched out a hand. "Ready for the wedding, Coulter?"

He obliged the woman who'd been like a mother since his own had died. "As I'll ever be." When her feet hit the ground, he chucked her under her chin. He'd been wrong about Josie's headgear. Bertha had managed to save a huge number of wax fruit and vegetables for herself. The resemblance of a bountiful garden sat atop her head. "That's quite a hat, love," he said, with a wide grin.

She tilted her chin to gaze into his face. "Next to Josie's, it's my finest creation. I always strive to re-create the latest designs from my Paris fashion magazines. I'm quite proud to bring a little elegance to the West."

"You've certainly succeeded."

"Thank you, dear. Let's get into the church. I've waited for years to see you marry a lovely young woman like Josie." If Bertha wasn't so dear to his heart, he might take offense at her words. Although they'd never admitted it aloud, he knew his aunt and uncle weren't particularly fond of the Montgomerys. Although Bertha and Oscar had always been courteous and kind to Ellen, he knew they hadn't thought she was the right woman for him.

"You're a born matchmaker." Coulter glanced around and spotted Josie and Cathy standing hand in hand, talking with several ladies. Cheerful congratulations and gentle laughter filled the air. Only Miss Bettington and Homer showed any hostility. The deputy had continued to warn Coulter that Miss Clark would only cause trouble, while most of the men in town offered advice on ways to tone down Josie's temperance activities.

From the corner of his eye, he spotted Terrell Sullivan lurking under the trees near the horses. More than ever,

Coulter was certain the man was up to no good. If only
Coulter had had time to question Josie before the marriage. Cathy turned and signaled for him to hurry.

The Reverend Harris guarded the entrance and spoke
briefly to Josie. When Coulter reached out a hand, the
minister's greeting was as stiff and cold as a dead fish
pulled out of a frozen river in January. He suspected the
preacher was more than halfway in love with Josie himself.
Coulter widened his smile and pumped the man's hand
for all he was worth. " 'Morning, Brother Harris. Nice day
for a wedding, isn't it?''

After a few mumbled words, the preacher freed himself
from Coulter's grip and turned his attention to Oscar and
Bertha. Coulter couldn't blame the man for being jealous;
Coulter would have behaved even worse if their places had
been reversed. As he started down the aisle to take his
place for the service, he felt a lightness he hadn't felt in
years. His first wedding, to Ellen, had been the social event
of the season in Kansas City, with dignitaries from two
states in attendance. This one was more suited to his style.
He slid into the bench between his child and the woman
who would soon take Ellen's place—if not in his heart,
then in his bed and home. He hoped it was enough for
her. It was all he had to give.

Josie's emotions were in shambles. She studied Coulter all
during the service, wondering if she truly knew what she
was getting into. As much as she loved him, she hadn't
planned on marriage. If they hadn't been caught in bed
together, surely he'd never have considered her for a wife.
And she certainly didn't want a husband who didn't want
her. But here she was, waiting for the worship to conclude
so she could say her vows and bind herself to this man for
all time.

She slanted a glance at Coulter. His face was unreadable.

He sat ramrod-straight, his expression solemn as required. The few times she'd met his gaze, she was certain she spotted the heat smoldering in his midnight-dark eyes.

He didn't want to marry her, and was only going through the ritual for his child's sake. A thousand misgivings haunted her over the matter. What if Mr. and Mrs. Montgomery found out about her past? What if they used Josie's reputation as a performer against them? What if Terrell Sullivan interfered? She knew now she'd made a mistake by not telling Coulter all the details of her life, but she'd never dreamed she'd marry the man. Everything had happened so quickly, she'd hardly had time to think. Then Friday, Terrell had shown up on the streets of Council City. Unless he'd changed drastically in the last few years, the man could cause more trouble than a basketful of rattlesnakes.

The minister asked the congregation to stand for the closing hymn, and Josie knew there was no way out, short of embarrassing herself, Coulter, and his family. Truth be told, she didn't want out. She wanted to marry the tall, handsome sheriff.

Their hands collided as they reached for the same songbook. Coulter opened to the correct page, and while holding the book with one hand, he entwined her fingers with his other hand. A thrill shot through Josie. She prayed harder than she'd ever prayed, that she would be a good wife and make him happy.

As the final amen faded, the minister held up his hands again to seat the congregation. From the cold look in his eyes, Elijah Harris was clearly unhappy to have to perform the ceremony. His gaze questioned Josie's reason for the suddenness of the marriage. Josie couldn't possibly confess that she'd been caught in bed with Coulter and shoved into the marriage by his family.

In spite of all her misgivings, she suddenly realized she wanted the marriage more than she'd wanted anything in her life. She loved Coulter and she hoped someday he would care for her.

The Reverend Harris announced the nuptials, and invited the entire congregation to remain to witness the ceremony. Coulter caught her elbow in a strong grip and ushered her to the center aisle. Her gaze shifted to the side, and collided with Terrell's narrowed, pale eyes. She stumbled over her own feet and was only prevented from falling by Coulter's hand on her arm. Her stomach sank. Why would the man be here, except to cause trouble? Trouble for her, trouble for Coulter.

A sparkle of sunlight on Terrell's hand drew her gaze for a long moment. The diamond ring on his little finger was familiar—too familiar. Papa had worn it until he'd given it to Armand. The ring had been missing from her brother's body when she'd identified him in Chicago on that night that seemed like a lifetime ago. Josie's heart raced. Her initial instinct was to rush toward the man and demand answers. A challenging smile curved his thin lips. It was what he wanted, to upset her into doing something rash; to torment her into returning to him as his mistress. Coulter tightened his grip and tugged her toward the front of the church for her wedding.

Josie scarcely heard a word the minister spoke. Her heart was in her throat. Any second she expected Terrell to stand up and stop the ceremony. The flutters in her stomach were worse than any stage fright she'd experienced during her years in the theater.

Coulter's hand was warm and supportive. They were standing in church in front of their friends and neighbors, with a man of God pronouncing them husband and wife. She felt like a complete and total fraud. She didn't deserve this man, this good man who needed a mother for his child. She was a singer, an actress, a player who'd never known a real home. The trembling in her body spread to her arms. Only Coulter's strong grip prevented her from running from the church. He pressed her to his side, and she felt the cold, hard steel of the gun at his hip.

The minister's words droned in her ears. Elijah was far from happy with the marriage, and the expression on his face spoke volumes. When it was time for her to say "I do," it took Coulter's whisper to nudge her into action. She looked up and saw the question in his eyes. She uttered her vows and waited for something to happen. Coulter's voice was strong and confident as he repeated his vows, uniting them together for all time—or until Terrell or somebody else ruined her chance for happiness.

With the short time they'd had to plan their marriage, she hadn't expected him to give her a ring—a symbol of love, fidelity, and eternal devotion. He clutched her hand and started to tug her glove from her fingers. Hands trembling, she removed the glove and accepted his ring. Her doubts fled at the touch of his fingers on hers. The plain gold band was warm from being in his pocket. Tears pooled in her eyes. She lifted her face and met Coulter's heated gaze.

At that moment the love that she'd kept hidden in her heart burst forth with the power of a dozen sticks of dynamite. Coulter Steele was everything a woman would want in a husband, everything Josephine Angelique Clark never had dreamed she would have. He bent and met her lips in a brief, hard kiss.

Instantly they were surrounded by family and friends offering congratulations and best wishes. Bertha started crying, dabbing her eyes with a linen handkerchief; Oscar grabbed Josie and kissed her soundly on the cheeks; and Cathy threw her arms around Josie's waist. Noticeably absent from the well-wishers were Homer, Miss Bettington, and the Reverend Harris. To her surprise, Terrell was waiting patiently in line to greet the newlyweds.

Her hands grew sweaty. In spite of the smile on Terrell's face, Josie knew the man behind the flawless facade. He'd wanted her for his mistress, and he was not a man to give up when he was rebuffed. His cruelty toward his women was well-known in the theatrical troupe, and Josie had wanted no part of him. Fear clutched her heart that he would do or say something to ruin her fragile relationship with Coulter.

She tightened her grip on her husband's fingers. Her husband—the word brought a glimmer of warmth to the chill that had settled in her chest. He would protect her, he would stand at her side.

After a few of their neighbors passed by, Terrell stood before her. His smile was as false as the color that blackened his hair. He stuck out a hand toward Coulter.

"Congratulations, Sheriff," he said, his voice as rich and as deep as when Josie had played opposite him in *Romeo and Juliet*. "Your bride is as beautiful as an angel."

"Thank you, Sullivan. My wife is an angel through and through."

The instant Coulter released the man's fingers, Terrell reached for Josie's hand. She felt as if she'd plunged her fingers into a bucket of ice water. The diamond-and-ruby ring on his finger glittered and teased. She knew he was trying to get a reaction. The ring was Armand's; her insides trembled, and she bit her lip to keep from snatching it from his finger. He bowed gallantly, but didn't try to hide the glimmer of malice in his vivid green eyes. If Coulter hadn't had his hand so tightly entwined with hers, she was certain her knees would have buckled under her.

Sullivan hesitated, as if wanting to say something else, when Coulter swung her toward the next couple in line. Left with no choice, Terrell stepped away. Josie chanced a glance at him and met his angry glare.

Before long, the congregation dispersed, and Josie was alone with Coulter, Cathy, Bertha, and Oscar. She finally breathed a sigh of relief. So far, Terrell hadn't made trouble, but the man was too unpredictable to relax her guard.

"I have a fine dinner waiting at home to celebrate your marriage." Bertha virtually beamed with happiness. "Come along, dears, our guests are waiting."

"Guests?" Josie asked, her heart sinking. She'd hoped for some privacy to confide in Coulter about Terrell. Now that would have to wait until they returned home that evening. "I thought it was just family."

Oscar lifted his hands in surrender. "You know my wife. She considers half the town her family."

"Hush, Oscar Marche. I only invited John and Polly, and her children. She needs to be with family, and she's one of Josie's very best friends." The older woman linked arms with her husband and rushed him toward the door.

"Let's go, Papa," Cathy said. She turned to Josie, her face beaming. "Miss Josie, is it all right if I call you Mama?"

After the anxiety of the past week, the girl's simple request sent a warm glow through Josie like she'd never known. Not even loving Coulter filled her with so much delight. He'd never mentioned love, but his daughter's affection was unconditional.

"Of course, sweetheart. If your papa doesn't mind."

Coulter shrugged. "It's fine with me."

Again Cathy threw her arms around Josie's waist. "I love you so much. You, too, Papa."

"Gee, thanks, pumpkin. Glad I count for something." He tugged on his daughter's long braid. "Want to ride with me and Miss—your new mama over to Aunt Bertha's?"

His words brought a tear to Josie's eyes. For the first time since Papa had died, she felt like she belonged, like she was part of a family. Still, a tiny part of her was still afraid something would happen to prevent her happiness; that her past would ruin her future.

"Sure, Papa. But I'll ride in the back of the carriage so you and my mama can sit together."

The churchyard was deserted when they reached the front door. Even the reverend was gone; probably went

home with one of his parishioners for dinner. A sprinkling
of rain had dampened the ground.

"Wait here, Mrs. Steele," Coulter said. "We wouldn't
want to ruin that fine new hat, running to the carriage."

She touched the overly-ornate headgear and smiled. "It
was your aunt's wedding gift, so I had better be careful."
She huddled closer to the building, under the overhang
of the porch.

"I'll run with you, Papa." Cathy took off on her father's
heels, around the corner toward the trees where he'd teth-
ered the team.

Josie watched them go, her heart full of love and pride.
She'd spent the entire service praying that she could be a
good wife and mother. If only Terrell wouldn't try to ruin
things for her. As if conjured out of her musings, the man
appeared at her side.

"Congratulations, Angel. Looks like you've made quite
a catch."

Her breath caught in her throat. She felt lost and vulnerable with him. "What are you doing here? I thought you'd
gone with your new friend, Homer Potts."

Humorless laughter sent a shiver up her spine.

"That buffoon? But Deputy Potts did offer quite a bit
of information about you, Angel. Seems like you've made
quite a few friends in this little town. Even changed your
name."

"I'm using my real name."

"Does that sheriff know who you are—were?"

"Yes. He knows everything."

"About us?" He moved a step closer, sending her back
to avoid his touch.

"There never was anything between us."

He lifted his hand waving the ring in front of her eyes.
"Surely your new husband would want to know about you
and Armand, about his gambling, and how you offered to
be my mistress after his unfortunate accident."

"His murder, you mean. How did you get his ring?"

"I won it in a poker game."

"You're lying. He won that night, and when the police found his body, his money and jewelry were missing." A new revelation struck her like a bolt of lightning. The evidence was staring her in the face. "You killed Armand and robbed him. It was you!" Anger burst like a firecracker in her head. She advanced on him, ready to scratch out his eyes with her fingernails.

He stood his ground, his smile mocking her. "Meet me tonight, and I'll tell you what really happened to Armand."

She stopped, curiosity getting the best of her. "I can't meet you. It's my wedding— I mean, Coulter ..." The words stuck in her throat.

Terrell caught her arm, his fingers biting into the soft flesh. "Tonight, Angel, or his rich mother-in-law will learn the truth about the woman who'll be raising her grand-child."

Josie's heart leaped into her throat. She had no doubt that he would carry out his threats with lies and accusations she could never live down.

"In the barn at Coulter's ranch. Everybody in town knows where the sheriff lives."

"This man bothering you, Angel?" Coulter's cold, hard voice came from the corner of the building.

Josie jumped and Terrell swung around. Coulter was standing less than ten feet away, his face shaded by his hat. Oblivious to the drizzling rain, he stood with his feet apart, his hand on the gun holstered at his hip.

Terrell lifted his hands and let out a burst of bitter laughter. "Sheriff, I was simply offering my best wishes to your bride. Didn't mean any harm."

His face expressionless, Coulter advanced on the man. "Sullivan, I warned you once about bothering the women in my town. Take a word of advice, and move on. Next time I see you, you had better be on your way out of town."

"You can't order me to leave, Sheriff. I haven't done anything wrong."

With slow, deliberate steps, Coulter moved closer. "Consider it a very strong suggestion, Sullivan. But if I ever catch you talking to my wife again, I'll shoot first and ask questions later." By then he was on the porch steps. "Dinner's waiting, Mrs. Steele, and we don't want to get my aunt riled up by being late." He reached toward her, his expression hard and unyielding.

Hand trembling, she stretched out her fingers. He clutched her hand in a hard grip and all but jerked her from the porch. Heedless of the drizzling rain, he rushed her toward the buggy where Cathy was waiting. Without speaking, he lifted her and deposited her on the seat.

"Coulter," she said, when he joined her in the carriage, "I'm so sorry."

"It's all right, Angel. He won't bother you again."

A shiver crept up her spine. Coulter didn't know Terrell like she did. The man had trouble on his mind, and somehow he'd found out about Coulter's in-laws. She had little doubt he'd had something to do with Armand's death. The ring was all the evidence she needed.

Raindrops pattered on the top of the buggy as they rolled down the rutty road toward the Marche home. Dirt splattered from the wheels, but next to Coulter Josie felt safe and dry. As much as she hated the thought of deceiving him, she would find a way to meet Terrell. She would use anything within her power to convince him to leave her and Coulter alone. She still had a few pieces of jewelry, and she would gladly sacrifice everything she owned to keep Coulter and Cathy safe.

Including her own life, if need be.

Chapter 24

The red blaze of fury that had engulfed Coulter burned hotter than the noonday sun. Sullivan's arrogance and interference were bad enough, but Josie's obvious duplicity cut clear to the bone. The man had shaken her badly, so badly she was abnormally quiet, and whenever his arm brushed hers, he felt her trembling. From time to time she glanced over her shoulder as if afraid they were being followed.

Whatever had caused her distress had something to do with the man and, Coulter suspected, her past. He ignored the drizzling rain and his daughter's constant chatter, his mind on solving the problem at hand. There was no way he would tolerate deception by his wife.

He glanced at Josie, noting the forced smile barely concealed under the sheer silk veil. Tightened his grip on the reins, he wished he could wrap his fingers around Sullivan's neck. The man was slicker than the snake-oil salesman he'd run out of town last year. And he was certain Sullivan was every bit as devious and just as dishonest. It would pay for Coulter to learn why Sullivan had chosen to visit Council City and, more important, when he planned to leave.

"Papa!" Cathy's anxious voice reached through the thoughts that fogged his mind. "Are you listening to a word I said?"

"I'm sorry, sweetheart, guess I was concentrating on the weather. Sure don't want to get your new mama's fancy hat wet before we reach Aunt Bertha's house." He hoped the lie sounded convincing. Josie glanced at him, her expression guarded.

"I want to know if I can spend the night with Sally Jane. Aunt Bertha said you and Mama need to be alone for your honeymoon. When I asked her what kind of moon that was, she said it's when men and ladies go sparking. Is that what you and Miss . . ."—Cathy giggled and covered her mouth with her hand—"I mean, Mama, were doing the other day when you were in bed in the middle of the afternoon?" From her position in the back, she looped her arms around his neck. "Is that what you are going to do tonight? Do you honeymoon outdoors, or indoors?"

Coulter swallowed his laughter. His daughter had the uncanny power to brighten even the gloomiest day and chase away the most depressing thoughts. "You sure are full of questions, young lady. Reckon I'll let your mama answer that one. Sounds like lady-talk to me."

Josie squirmed in the seat beside him, the hem of her pretty dress with pink embroidered flowers, brushing his trousers as she turned to Cathy. "I . . . I suppose some people do it outdoors, but your papa and I . . ." Her gaze slid to Coulter for help.

The embarrassed look on her face brought a smile to his face. Like the gentleman he was, Coulter came to her rescue. "We'll wait and see what we prefer. Who knows where we'll get the notion to spark? It might be in the barn, or the loft, or maybe in the henhouse."

Cathy laughed, the sound chasing away some of the

anxiety of the past hours. Josie's cheeks pinked nearly to the color of the bow on her hat.

"Coulter," she grunted. "What a thing to say in front of your daughter!"

He draped a protective arm across her shoulders. "We're married, Angel. And that's what married people do."

"But . . . but . . ." She sputtered before the right words came out. "We'll discuss it when we're alone."

"Angel, this is the first time I've ever known you to be at a loss for words. Things are improving already."

"Papa," Cathy said, exasperated, "can I?"

"Yes, you may spend the night with Sally, in fact, you can stay until"—he shot a glance at Josie—"Tuesday afternoon."

Josie gasped, but quickly clamped her mouth shut. Looked like he'd finally found a way to get in the last word.

The small crowd gathered at the Marche home shouted a greeting when Coulter stopped the buggy in front of the porch. John, Polly, and her three children stood with Bertha and Oscar. After picking up his daughter and depositing her on the ground, Coulter reached for his bride. The rain had stopped, and the clouds were blessed with a beautiful silver lining. He saw it as a omen of good luck. In spite of Josie's protests, he slid one arm under her knees and the other behind her back. As quick as a wink, he lifted Josie in his arms, cradling her to his chest. She wrapped her arms around his neck. To the cheers and whoops of his friends and family, he planted a solid kiss on her mouth and carried her to the porch.

"Coulter, put me down," she said against his lips.

Instead of obeying, he deepened the kiss until he got the response he wanted. Her parted lips welcomed his touch. Heat surged between them. In that instant, Coulter forgot time and place. Only when somebody slapped him on the back did he come to his senses.

"Save it for tonight, son!" Oscar shouted.

282   *Jean Wilson*

With a sigh of regret, Coulter set his wife on her feet. He clung to her waist for a moment before he allowed his aunt and Polly to smother her with hugs and caresses. "Reckon I can wait," he said on a groan.

"You had best behave yourself, Coulter Steele," Bertha admonished, with a grin. "Or we'll plan a shivaree for you and Josie."

He shrunk back, feigning alarm at the prospect of his friends serenading him and his bride with loud noise, shotgun blasts, and general mayhem. "Not that! Please, have mercy."

Oscar draped his arm across Coulter's shoulder and ushered him into the house. The good-natured teasing made Coulter forget all about Sullivan. Josie, too, joined in the laughter, her mood improved by the friendly camaraderie of the party.

After dinner the ladies gathered in the parlor for tea. Oscar invited the men to his office to show them his new rifle, or so he claimed, with a wink. While the temperance leaders shared a pot of tea, the men toasted the nuptials with a round of good Kentucky whiskey. That alone was cause for another round of laughter. When the women called them back to the parlor, Oscar quickly stashed the bottle.

Although Oscar was convinced he was putting one over on his wife, Coulter knew Aunt Bertha too well. Oscar got away with only what Bertha allowed. Coulter had the feeling his uncle's drinking days were numbered.

Josie glanced up when the laughing men entered the parlor. By the gleam shining in their eyes and their jovial manner, she suspected they'd been drinking. Bertha shot an annoyed look at her husband. Coulter winked at Josie and joined her on the davenport. She shifted to make room for him on the soft cushion. Her insides quivered when he pressed his hips to hers.

"I know Josie didn't have time to prepare a trousseau,

so I wanted her to have something special," Bertha said. She placed a large, gaily-wrapped package in Josie's lap.

"Bertha," Josie protested, "you've already done so much. I can't accept a gift." Tears misted in her eyes at the goodness and kindness shown by Coulter's family and friends. She felt like such a hypocrite, undeserving of their affection.

"Oh, pish. It's only something that should rightfully belong to Coulter's wife." She gestured to the silver ribbon holding the paper closed. "Go ahead, open it."

Josie looked at Coulter, a question in her eyes. He shrugged. "I know better than to argue with my aunt," he said.

Her hands trembling, Josie slipped the bow open and carefully removed the paper. Inside was the most beautiful quilt she'd ever seen.

"A double wedding ring." Josie stroked the tiny, even stitches with the tip of her finger. Small patches of colorful scraps formed the intricate pattern. "It's wonderful, Bertha. But I can't accept it."

"Nonsense. My mother made it as a gift to be handed down to her children. She gave it to me when I married Oscar. Since we don't have children, we consider Coulter our own. I want you to have it; then you can hand it down to Cathy. See, I embroidered your name and wedding date on the corner."

Coulter's fingers brushed her own as he opened the quilt. His touch was warm and encouraging. Along one edge were Oscar's and Bertha's names, and on the other, Coulter's and Josie's. She let the tears flow. It was a gift to last a lifetime. But she wondered if her marriage could survive beyond the honeymoon. In that moment Josie determined to do anything in her power to stop Terrell from ruining the happiness she'd found with Coulter and his family.

Polly gave her a set of embroidered pillowcases with her

and Coulter's initials. With all she'd gone through in the past week, Polly cared enough to make the special gift for Josie. Josie hugged her friend and didn't even try to hide her tears.

"That's enough crying for one day," Oscar announced. "Let's toast the newlyweds." He set a decanter and wineglasses on the polished rosewood table in front of the davenport.

"Oscar," Bertha gasped.

"Don't get into an uproar, dear," he said, planting a quick kiss on his wife's cheek. "It's only apple cider. I won't tempt you ladies with strong drink. I wouldn't want to be responsible for any trouble you might get into." The men joined his laughter, while the children merely rolled their eyes at the antics of the adults.

Bertha filled the glasses and passed them to the guests, including the children. Cathy settled beside her father, proud to be included in a grown-up ritual.

Oscar offered the first toast. "To Coulter, the son I always wanted, and to Josie, the loveliest lady to grace our town"—he glanced at his wife—"since I laid eyes on Bertha. May you have all the happiness we've had."

After one sip, John lifted his glass. "Hope all your wishes come true."

Polly slipped her arm around John's waist. "For now and always."

Josie glanced at Coulter and found his gaze locked on her. Sparks flashed between them. He touched his glass to hers. "To Angel." The simple words matched the fire in his eyes. "Drink up, everybody. I'm feeling mighty fatigued." He winked at Josie. Heat rushed to her face. "Man needs to get his rest, you know."

A loud roar of laughter made Oscar's stomach quiver. "I doubt you'll get much sleep tonight, son."

"Oscar!" Bertha's reprimand was gentled by her own muffled giggles.

"Tell me, Josie," Oscar asked, his eyes gleaming, "are you going to give up your work for the S.A.A.T. now that you're a married lady?"

She looked from the expectant gleams in the women's eyes, to the pleased looks in the men's. "No," she answered.

"Yes," Coulter replied at the same time. He shot her a gleam of pure male arrogance. Heat surfaced to her cheeks. This was one of the topics they hadn't been able to settle. But she wasn't about to be intimidated by Coulter, as sheriff or husband.

Always the diplomat, John intervened. "Why don't you discuss it when you're alone? You know, sometime tomorrow."

Coulter nuzzled her neck. "Excellent idea."

"Papa and Mama are going on a honeymoon," Cathy whispered to Sally Jane, loud enough for all to hear.

"Oh," the other girl replied, tossing her blonde braid over her shoulder. "Are they going to do all that mushy kissing and stuff? Mama and Mr. John do that all the time."

Six pairs of adult eyes shifted to the girls. Not to be outdone, Cathy added, "Wait till I tell you what I saw the other day when I went home with Aunt Bertha."

"Honey." Coulter leaped to his feet. His struggles to contain his laughter made his shoulders shake. "I think you'd better forget what you saw. You're embarrassing your new mama."

Josie didn't see a speck of humor in the situation. She'd been railroaded into marriage and everybody was speculating on her wedding night. Even the children thought it quite funny. Nobody realized just how nervous the entire prospect made her.

Coulter tugged her hand and pulled her to him. She stumbled and fell into his arms. "See? She can't wait to get me home."

"I'll have a talk with these two tonight," Polly said. A

flush tinged her face. "You two can run along. Cathy can stay with us as long as you like."

"Coulter Steele," Josie muttered between her teeth, "you and I are going to have a little talk, too."

Not at all deterred by the censure in her tone, he swept her into his arms. She wrapped her arms around his neck for balance. The beautiful quilt fell to the floor. "Talk, talk, talk, Angel, that's all you do. I'm tired of talking."

She kicked her feet to no avail. "Put me down this instant."

Like the leader of a parade, Coulter stalked to the buggy, the others following in his wake. With little care for decorum, he tossed her onto the seat. Her bottom hit the leather seat and her skirt flew up in an array of petticoats. Protests of indignation only brought about more raucous laughter from the spectators. Bertha set the quilt in her lap and Polly handed up the pillowcases.

Cathy ran from the house, an array of feathers and silk flying from her hand. "Here, Mama. Don't forget your hat."

Josie plopped the hat on her head and struggled to straighten her dress. Coulter kissed his daughter and climbed onto the seat beside Josie.

"Hold it, Sheriff." This time it was Oscar who stopped them. With a wide grin, he shoved a basket at Coulter. "Just a snack so you can keep your strength up." The men all laughed when he emphasized the word "up." "Don't want your new bride to have to spend all night cooking."

"Thank you very much, Uncle. Mighty considerate of you." Coulter caught the basket in his hand and stowed it behind the seat. "Let's go home, Angel."

The horses took off at a trot amid the shouts and laughter of friends and family. In spite of her embarrassment, Josie couldn't help smiling at the gaiety of the group. For too long she'd been alone, without the support of family, and few close friends. Not since Armand had she had somebody to love, somebody to love her. The memory of her brother brought to mind Terrell and his schemes.

Josie hugged the quilt to her chest. For the first time in her life, she had everything she'd ever wanted within reach: Coulter, Cathy, the prospect of other children; friends who cared, her work. And it could all be snatched away by a specter from her past.

She wasn't going to let it happen—she couldn't let it happen. Tonight she would get rid of Terrell once and for all.

"They were only teasing, Angel." Coulter slipped his arm around her waist. "No use getting upset."

At his light banter, she realized her smile had turned into a frown. With an effort, she brightened her grin. "Sorry. Guess it's just the wedding-day jitters. You know, all brides are supposed to blush and stammer over what awaits them at home."

He tugged her close. "No need to worry. We already know how compatible we are in bed. Now, if the rest of our lives goes as easily, we should do all right."

Warm and secure in his embrace, she could almost believe him.

Almost.

What seemed only minutes later, they reached Coulter's ranch. The sun had dropped behind the hills, sending a pink glow over the sky. He stopped the buggy near the porch and leaped to the ground. A wide grin on his face, he reached for Josie. "Reckon it'll soon be dark enough for that sparking and cuddling you promised me."

Feigning indignation, she dropped the quilt and stood. "Sheriff, I don't remember promising any such thing."

His big hands spanning her waist, he swung her down from the high perch. "Already forgot all those vows you made in church? In front of the preacher and the whole

congregation?'' When she was eye-level with him, he
stopped. His gaze dropped to her lips, and she knew he
was going to kiss her. The brims of their wide hats stopped
their faces inches apart. "One of these hats has to go,
Angel, or we'll never get down to business."

Without hesitation, Josie tore the silly creation from her
head and tossed it back into the buggy. Then she shoved
his hat back off his forehead. "Now, Sheriff," she said,
her mouth against his, "no excuses."

Their lips met in a kiss sweet and full of promises of
more to come. The need was there, in full bloom, ready
to burst forth in total passion. Without breaking the kiss,
Coulter swept her into his arms and carried her up the
porch. Sneaking a peek, she tugged the screen door open.
The heavy wooden door swung in and he stepped into the
parlor. Ever so slowly, he lowered her feet to the floor,
careful to maintain the intimate contact of their bodies.

Her breathing was erratic, her pulse quickened. The kiss
went on and on until Josie was breathless with desire. He
ended the kiss and continued to hold her close to his
chest, his heartbeat pounding against her chest. "Is it dark
enough yet?" she asked, gasping for air.

He ran a row of tiny kisses across her jaw. "In a hurry,
Mrs. Steele?" A wide, sensuous smile crossed his lips. "I'm
afraid you'll have to wait until I tend the horses and unload
the wagon. Then you'll have me at your mercy all night
long."

A delightful thrill raced over her, settling in the secret
part of her stomach. "Only tonight?"

With a groan, he set her away from him. "For as long
as you want me, Angel. But remember, I'm only a man."

She smiled, a heady feeling of power sweeping over her.
"I'll be careful."

"Hold that thought. I'll be back in two shakes of a lamb's
tail."

Alone in the parlor, Josie removed her lace shawl and

laid it across the arm of the worn davenport. The pale evening sunlight cast a welcoming glow over the room. Slowly she wandered around the room. Her home. A smile curved her lips. She fingered the curtains at the window. From her vantage point, she watched Coulter lead the team into the barn. Her love for her husband grew every time she looked at him, every time she saw his smile, felt his heated gaze on her.

She let the curtain fall and moved to the portrait of his mother. The pencil sketch showed so much heart and promise. Coulter should devote all his time to his art and give up the danger of being sheriff. He could have been killed the past week, before they even had a chance for a relationship. She shifted her gaze to the pair of rockers that flanked the fireplace. Someday she hoped to rock her babies to sleep in front of the blazing fire.

Her gaze lifted to the mantel where the photograph of Ellen watched over the parlor. Ellen, the woman Coulter loved. Stretching out a tentative finger, she touched the woman's face. Coulter had loved his wife more than life itself. A sadness touched Josie's heart. How could she ever take Ellen's place? An inner voice said she couldn't. But she could make her own place in his heart if he would let her. He may not love her, but she had enough love for both of them. Enough love to mend his life and make him happy.

Chapter 25

Coulter paused in the doorway between the kitchen and parlor. He'd hurriedly stabled the horses and rushed into the house to Josie. She'd been constantly on his mind since the afternoon they'd made love. He'd missed her terribly since she'd been staying with his aunt. Now he could hardly wait to move Josie's things into his room—and her sweet body into his bed.

She was standing in front of the fireplace, staring at Ellen's photograph, a strange look on her face. His wives were as different as sunshine and moonlight. Josie, with her golden hair and blue eyes, was bright, bold, and brave enough to face a band of outlaws single-handed. Ellen had been soft, subdued, and shy. The moonlight was a pale reflection of the sun. True, Josie could never replace Ellen in his heart, but that didn't mean he couldn't enjoy his new wife in the fullest sense of the marriage pact.

As if she sensed his presence, Josie spun around and faced him. "Back already?"

The tremor in her voice brought a smile to his face.

"Charlie finished all the chores while we were in town, and everything is secure for the night."

"Then I suppose . . ." She shifted her gaze to the stairs.

As much as he desired her, Coulter wanted to take things slow and easy. After all, he'd practically railroaded her into marriage. She deserved to be treated with respect and consideration. "Why don't we see what treats Oscar packed for us?" He gestured to the davenport and set the basket on the low table.

Josie smiled shyly and moved toward him. "I am a little hungry."

"Come sit beside me, Angel." He patted the cushion in the center of the couch. Then he dug into the basket and pulled out a covered bowl. "Smells mighty good." Next he found a bottle and two glasses. "Well, how about that? Wonder where Oscar got the champagne?"

Her eyes widened, then narrowed suspiciously. "I wonder. Probably from that stash in the storeroom behind the general store."

It was Coulter's turn to be surprised. Nothing got past those beautiful blue eyes. "How did you know?"

"Bertha and I aren't as naive as you men think we are." She lifted the bottle and inspected the label. "French. And a fine vintage. I must congratulate Oscar on his taste."

Coulter smiled. He would learn not to underestimate his bride. "How do you know so much about champagne?"

"I make it my business to know my enemy. Besides, Mama was French, and Papa always treated her to the very best. He allowed me an occasional sip on special occasions."

"Isn't our marriage a special occasion? Will you try a little? Just a toast to our happiness?"

"Well . . . You know I'm not against an occasional drink for a special occasion. Our movement is about temperance. The problem is that most men can't drink in moderation, therefore we wish to ban alcohol entirely."

He held up his hands. "Angel, I don't need a lecture. One little glass won't turn us into drunks. And I can't think of a more auspicious occasion than our marriage."

Heat flashed in her eyes. "I agree." She lifted the two crystal glasses.

Her easy compliance amazed him. With a quick twist, he tugged the cork from the bottle. The champagne bubbled out, overflowing the bottle and filling the glass in her hands. Laughing, she sipped at the bubbles before they poured onto her fingers. "Excellent. As fine as any I've tasted." She held the other glass for him. "Of course, it's been years since I've indulged."

"Of course." He lifted his gaze and met her eyes, all bright and shiny. And she'd yet to take a real drink. His new bride was a delight. Simply being near her sent his pulse racing and his heartbeat pounding out of control like a runaway team. Their fingers brushed together as he took the glass from her hand. A spark sizzled between them. His love for Ellen had been sweet, gentle. But just the thought of making love with Josie was like getting zapped by lightning.

He touched his glass to hers. "What shall we toast to, Angel?"

"I thought we'd said everything at Oscar's." Her voice was a sensuous whisper, a suggestion of dim lights, perfume, and soft sheets. And promises of joys to come.

"Let's drink to us. You and me. Together. A family. Forever."

The word swelled his chest to overflowing. "Forever" was what he'd thought he had with Ellen. "Forever" was a promise nobody could make. He would do his best to make it forever.

"Thank you, Coulter. That's what I want, too." Eyes locked, they sipped the wine.

In that moment, something special passed between them. He wasn't sure what to call it. Affection, desire, passion, love? Whatever it was, Coulter knew it was stronger than anything he'd felt in years. More than he'd ever hoped to find.

She wrinkled her nose against the bubbles. Unable to stop himself, he leaned forward and planted a light kiss on her mouth. Her eyelids lowered, accepting his offer. She tasted of champagne, deliciously intoxicating. He pulled back, wanting to take the evening slow and easy. They had all the time in the world—the rest of their lives.

Josie sipped the wine, and let the warmth flow through her. She didn't understand why she was so nervous. Her insides were quivering and heat settled deep in her abdomen. Was it anticipation, or something else? She'd already made love with Coulter, so she shouldn't have a virgin's hesitation. Still, she held tight to the stem of the glass to stop her hands from trembling.

Coulter leaned back and stretched his arm across the back of the davenport. His hand rested at her nape, the caress exciting in its gentleness. "You have beautiful hair, Angel. It's a shame to keep it bound in that tight knot." With a few deft movements, he tugged the pins from her chignon. She shook her head and the tresses tumbled to the middle of her back. He combed his fingers through her hair. The intimacy of his touch brought a thrill to her heart. He lifted the hair to his face and inhaled. She'd never even imagined such a sensuous gesture.

His fingers tangled in her hair, drawing her face closer to his. Afraid of spilling her drink, she set the glass on the table. She shifted closer to him, ready, eager to accept whatever he offered. The sun had set, and the room was bathed in the soft shadows of early evening. Josie put everyone and everything out of her mind and concentrated on Coulter, only Coulter. Pleasing him was all that mattered.

This time when his lips met hers, the kiss was long and slow, sweet and coaxing. His mouth slanted over hers like a violinist making his instrument sing to his touch. He was an expert, a genius, a master. His tongue slipped between her teeth, taking possession of her mind and her heart.

In a bold thrust, she met his searching tongue with her own. His touch stoked the embers firing her blood with need. Her body was hot and melting like wax around the candlewick. Coulter was the flame that consumed her with passion.

He shifted slightly and snuggled her onto his lap. She wrapped her arms around his neck to keep him close as he released her mouth for a breath of air. Their breath came in short gasps. His hand cupped her breast, sending another delightful flurry to her lower stomach.

"So sweet, so much woman, so much angel," he whispered, working his way across her jaw with tiny kisses.

She threw back her head, giving better access to the sensitive skin of her throat. Her fingers threaded in his hair. "Not an angel, only woman." A deep moan tore from her mouth as he thumbed the nipple into a hard, tight bud. Through their layers of clothes, she felt the fullness of his arousal against her hip.

His lips continued their sensual descent to the scooped neckline of her bodice. He released her breast, and she groaned in protest. His light chuckle tickled the hollow of her throat. "Why do women have so many little buttons on their clothes?" he asked, with a frustrated groan.

She released the breath she'd been holding. "To make you men appreciate our hidden treasures."

Coulter chuckled softly as his nimble fingers loosed the buttons, exposing her entire bosom to his perusal. "What a treasure I've found in you, Angel." His eyes turned dark with unbridled passion.

Eager for all he had to offer, Josie shrugged out of the bodice, leaving it gathered about her waist. "Is that better?" she asked, her words a whisper against his hair.

"A little." He nuzzled aside the camisole straps and stroked his tongue along the mark left on her shoulder.

"The finest China silk can't compare to your skin. I've never felt anything so soft, or that tasted so good." His mouth closed over the silk-covered breast. He stroked his tongue, wetting the tip through the sheer material.

She held her breath as he sucked and nipped. The tugging of his mouth reached clear to the center of her womanly parts, the place only Coulter had ever known. The place no man but he would ever touch, as no man would ever touch her heart.

Her fingers reached inside his shirt, exploring the smooth and abrasive textures of his skin. She wanted to touch him, to feel him, to know every inch of her husband. The word *husband* fired another spark of heat within her. "I want you, Coulter. I want you so bad I'm on fire."

He lifted his head. In the pale moonlight his eyes were shiny with passion. "Not half as much as I want you." In a quick movement, he surged to his feet and lifted her high in his arms. "On your wedding night you deserve a fine, soft bed with silk sheets. I want you to have it, Angel. I want to give you everything."

She snuggled her lips in the crook of his throat. "Yes, all. Everything." A deep and primal need surged through her. With Coulter, the man she loved, she would have it all. At least for the night.

Hours later, Josie lay snuggled in Coulter's arms, warm and content. Tears burned behind her eyes as she tried to keep her breathing even and steady. Their wedding night was everything she could have desired, and more. Although no words of love passed between them, she knew Coulter cared. His passion, his strength, his overpowering need, could only come from a man who cared for a woman. If he only loved her half as much as she loved him, her dream would be complete.

Only one dark cloud loomed on the horizon. A shadow

from the past that could ruin her happiness, and destroy Coulter: Terrell Sillivan was bad news wherever he went. From the time she and Armand had joined his troupe, he'd caused nothing but trouble. She was convinced he knew more about her brother's death than he let on. And if he told Coulter's in-laws about Josie's past, Coulter wouldn't stand a chance of keeping Cathy.

As much as she hated being near the man, she had to meet his demands. Terrell hated being thwarted. If nothing else worked, she would give him her last pieces of jewelry to get rid of him. Coulter would never understand her relationship with the man. Not that there was anything between them. Terrell had believed she and Armand were married rather than brother and sister. Upon her brother's death, she had been considered fair game for the lecherous man. If any of her past came out, she could hurt Coulter and Cathy. That was the last thing she wanted.

The clock in the parlor struck twelve, and Josie knew she had little time to spare. Terrell had threatened her with exposure if she failed to meet his demands. Josie couldn't afford to challenge him. For the past few minutes, she'd been slowly slipping away from Coulter. At the edge of the bed, she felt cold and alone.

Silently she sat up, placing her bare feet on the wool rug. By the pale moonlight, she glanced back at her husband. He was sleeping soundly, his arm thrown across his eyes. How she hated the idea of deceiving him. But she had to get Terrell out of their lives once and for all. Within moments she retrieved her nightgown and wrapper from the wardrobe where the garments waited, unneeded and unwanted. She slipped on her soft slippers, and on silent feet moved to the doorway.

The bed squeaked and she stopped in mid-stride. Her heart in her throat, she waited until Coulter stretched and rolled over. His steady breathing resumed, and he fell back into a deep sleep.

Cursing herself every step of the way, she moved to the next room, where she'd stored most of her things. Inside her trunk, she lifted the secret compartment and pulled out a small leather bag. When Armand had won at cards, he'd been overly generous. The last of her jewelry, a diamond pendant, was the one piece she'd kept as a reminder of her brother. Now it would be going to a greedy man in exchange for his silence.

Before starting down the stairs, she checked on Coulter. A narrow beam of moonlight slanted across his chest, angling down to his stomach. She swallowed back the sudden spark of desire at the sight of his naked body.

Thankfully, he was still fast asleep. She prayed he wouldn't miss her.

She didn't dare carry a lamp that would alert Coulter. The moon cast enough light to guide her across the yard. Only the occasional sound of a barn owl and the distant howl of a wolf invaded the quiet night. As she shoved open the barn door, she spotted the man seated on a bale of hay, a cigar clamped between his teeth. A lamp hanging from a nail lit one side of his handsome face. Quickly she closed the door.

He dropped the cigar to the floor. "About time you got here. I was about to bang on the door and wake up that husband of yours."

Josie kept a safe distance from the man, hating the idea of being anywhere near him. "I came as soon as I could. And I only came to find out about Armand."

He stood and took one step toward her. Automatically she backed away.

"Is that any way to greet an old friend?"

"We've never been friends. Tell me what you know about Armand's death. Were you there?" The thought that had been hovering in the back of her mind burst forth. "Did you kill him?"

His face was wreathed in anger. "Do you think I'm a

fool, to tell you that? I was in the game, and I won his ring. He was still playing when I left.''

Terrell was such an accomplished actor, she had no way of knowing if he was truthful. And after all this time, she knew she couldn't prove his guilt. Only the ring on his finger connected him with her brother.

She hugged her arms to her chest to ward off a chill. ''Are you saying you don't know who killed Armand?''

''Your husband was alive the last time I saw him. But he was cheating at cards. Could have been a sore loser, or somebody who didn't like cheats.'' His eyes narrowed. ''How do I know *you* didn't have something to do with it? You weren't sleeping with him; in fact, everybody knew he was carrying on with half of the women in the troupe.'' His face was shadowed by the lamp behind his head. ''A jealous wife is capable of anything.''

His words shook her clear to her toes. ''Jealous? I had no reason to be jealous.'' She bit her lip to keep from revealing the whole truth. As long as everybody had thought she was married to Armand, she had had the protection of a husband. Single women were fair game in the theatrical world.

Terrell caught her arm in a steely grip. ''If you didn't love him, why did you run away when I offered to take you in? Together we would have been the top act in this country, or any other. With your beauty and voice, I could have made you the toast of a dozen countries.''

''I didn't want anything you had to offer.'' She shrugged out of his grasp. ''I still don't. If you don't know who killed Armand, we have nothing to discuss.''

Terrell moved to stop her retreat. ''We still have to talk about your new husband's mother-in-law. One word from me, and the sheriff will never see his daughter again.''

Fear made her voice a husky grunt. ''How do you know about that?''

''I know a lot about what's going on in this town. I met

a lawyer in Chicago who was asking questions about a performer called Angel. By his description, I was certain it was you. It only took a few drinks to learn why he wanted to know about you. It's entirely possible the sheriff could lose his little girl because of you."

"What do you want?"

He ran one perfectly manicured finger along her cheek. "Simple, Angel. You."

A chill raced over her like the touch of an icicle pressed to her flesh. "No. Never."

"Then I'll go to that lawyer and tell him the whole, shameless truth."

"You can't." She dug into the pocket of her wrapper. "Take this, it's very valuable. And leave me alone." Holding the chain, she dangled the diamond in front of his face.

His greedy eyes narrowed. "That trinket is nothing compared to what we could get from one performance together."

"No. I don't want to perform. I'm married now, and I intend to stay here."

He snatched the pendant, leaving the broken chain suspended between her fingers. "What would that fine, upstanding sheriff think about his wife if he knew the truth?"

"Your version of the truth, you mean." Terrell grabbed her arms and hauled her into his chest. "Let go of me."

"Not until I get what you've already given to the sheriff." The feral gleam in his gaze frightened her. He tore at the neckline of her wrapper. "You're still a beautiful woman, Angel."

She shoved at his chest, dropping the chain onto the floor. "Get your filthy hands off me." Catching him off balance, she pushed him backward. He landed on the ground, striking his head on a post. Josie stepped back, ready to run. He gripped the post to steady himself.

The kerosene lamp slipped from the nail and fell to the hay strewn on the floor. Rooted to the spot, Josie watched in horror as the kerosene poured out of the bowl onto the dry straw. The flame licked the fuel, spreading the fire across the dirt floor.

"Grab a bucket!" she yelled, spurned to action by the disaster. "We've got to put it out!"

Terrell shook his head. "Get out. This thing will go up like a tinderbox."

"Help me." Josie grabbed a bucket and doused the flame. The fire smoldered, but the water did little to stop the flames that continued to spread on the dry floor.

"I'm getting out of here. You haven't heard the last of me, Angel."

Josie looked around for another bucket of water. Terrell raced to the door, and shoved it open. Swearing under her breath, she searched for more water. Within minutes the fire would consume the entire barn, animals, Josie and all—her gaze flew to the loft—including Coulter's work. She couldn't let that happen.

Chapter 26

Coulter wasn't sure what woke him up. He rolled to his side and reached for Josie, only to find the bed cold and empty. Trained to be alert for trouble, he came awake instantly. Where was his wife?

Something was wrong. He wasn't sure what caused the hair on the back of his neck to stand up like a cat's in danger. A distant sound reached him from the window. If Oscar had kept his promise of a shivaree, he would wring his uncle's neck. In one quick movement, he stood and shoved his legs into his trousers. He took the stairs two at time, landing in the parlor with a bound.

"Josie! Angel!" he shouted. She had to be here. Only minutes ago she'd fallen asleep in his arms.

Racing through the kitchen, he halfway expected to find her seated at the table, having a cup of tea. He banged his foot on a chair, but ignored the pain. Where the heck was Angel?

His gaze flew to the window. An orange glow lit the dark

sky in the direction of the barn. The mooing of cattle and
scream of horses sent an icy chill down his spine.

Sprinting across the yard, he spied a figure running in
the direction of the trees. The barn door was flung open,
and he spotted Josie inside. His heart stopped beating. She
was beating at the flames with a horse blanket. Alarmed, he
raced toward her. Her hair was flying wildly about her
shoulders, and the hem of her wrapper was soiled.
"Angel," he yelled.

Like a woman possessed, she continued without a backward glance. The flames were spreading toward the cows
and the mares in the stalls. "Get the animals," she called
over her shoulder. "We've got to put out the fire."

"Get out. I'll do it." He grabbed her by the waist and
hauled her to the doorway and safety.

She kicked and squirmed and begged him to let her
help. Coulter's heart was in his throat. If anything happened to her, he couldn't bear to think of what he would
do. "No, Angel, it's too dangerous." He deposited her on
the ground and raced back into the burning barn.

He'd no sooner reached the horse stall, when she darted
past him. "Angel, stop."

"You take care of the animals, I'll get your paintings."

"Leave the damn paintings. Get out of here."

The horses were kicking at their stalls, and the cow was
moaning in terror. A wall of fire shot up between him and
the ladder to the loft. Through the smoke and flames, he
saw her scurry up the ladder and disappear into the loft.

Coulter knew he had only minutes to save his stock. He
prayed Josie had the presence of mind to jump from the
upper window when the holocaust reached the loft. Smoke
choked off his breath as he opened the stalls and chased
the horses from the inferno. Frightened by the heat and
flames, the cows took more work. Using all his strength,
Coulter coaxed the animals into the barnyard. Although

the fire jumped from haystack to haystack, the conflagration had yet to reach the loft.

He ran to the side of the barn where the windows overlooked the meadow. He saw her there, tossing his paints, supplies, and canvases to the ground. "Angel!" He cupped his mouth and yelled. "Get out of there! The whole thing can go up in seconds." He searched for the rope that hung from a hook outside the loft. A large painting flew past his head and landed with a plop on the ground. Grabbing the rope, he prayed the rusty hook could hold his weight. "I'm coming up."

"No," she called back. "I've gotten them all. I'm coming down." Silhouetted in the window, she stepped to the edge. "I'll land on that haystack. Get out of my way."

Horrified, he watched a lick of fire ignite the hem of her robe. She noticed it at the same time, and shrugged out of the garment. A large canvas in her arms, she teetered at the window. Coulter held his breath and prayed as he'd never prayed in his life. The second she shoved off and flew through the air, he realized how much this woman meant to him. She was his heart, she was his life. Time seemed suspended as she floated down to the haystack. She landed in a flurry of white nightgown and pale legs. He was at her side instantly, scooping her up in his arm.

"Did you rescue the animals?" she asked, her voice coming in harsh gasps.

"Yes, they're all out. Are you hurt?" As fast as his legs would carry them, he raced a safe distance from the inferno.

"No, I'm safe." She handed him the painting. "So is Ellen."

Not even looking at the portrait, he tossed it aside. Unable to control his emotions, he kissed her hair, her face, her mouth. She smelled of smoke and perspiration. Her gown was torn, hanging about her like rags. She was the most beautiful sight he'd ever seen.

She was safe in his embrace.

Both were breathing hard when he settled them on the damp grass. A thousand questions bombarded him, but they were all meaningless in the face of the close call they'd both had. He'd nearly lost the angel who meant more to him than his own life.

"Coulter, I'm so sorry," she whispered. She snuggled under his arm, her face pressed to his bare chest.

Stroking her back, he pressed his lips into her hair. Together they watched his barn go up in flames. The dry timbers cracked and sputtered, the smoke grew thick and acrid. He hugged her close just to make sure she was all right. He buried his face in her hair. "I can rebuild the barn, Angel. But I would have died if you'd been hurt. Why did you go back?"

"Your paintings. I couldn't let your work burn. I know how much they mean to you."

"You risked your life for my paintings?" He followed her gaze to the last portrait she'd rescued.

"I couldn't let Ellen's picture burn. You love her so much."

"Baby, those are things. You mean more to me than any paintings, any barn."

Her tears traced sooty streaks down her cheeks. "Coulter, I love you so much."

Their first words of love made his heart flutter with emotion. "I love you, too." To his great relief he realized how much he meant it. Why did it have to take a near tragedy to realize how much this woman meant to him? He hugged her closer, afraid to let her go.

Before long, the roof collapsed, the burnt timbers spewing ashes into the air. Framed against the dark sky, the pyre cast an eerie glow over the yard. The chickens scurried and fled for safety. Even the imperious old hen dashed under the porch. Sparks flew in all directions, but surprisingly, in the still air the fire remained confined to the barn. With the rain the day before, the yard was wet and muddy, keeping the fire from spreading to the surrounding fields. As they watched, the flames died to red, glowing embers.

Only then did Coulter dare to take a deep breath. His land was safe, his stock was safe, but more important, he and his woman were safe. As long as they were together, they could rebuild.

Next time, his studio would be separate from the barn. He dropped his gaze to Josie. She was shivering in the chill night air. "Get back to the house, Angel. I want to make sure the animals are okay."

She stood and hugged her torn nightgown to her bosom. "I'll make a pot of coffee."

He nodded. Now that the danger was over, he needed answers. How did the fire start? He glanced at Josie, her shoulders slumped, her footsteps slow. What was she doing in the barn trying to put out the fire alone? And whom had he seen running from the fire?

Josie trudged back to the house, weary of body and soul. In her foolish attempt to protect her reputation, she'd burned down the barn and almost gotten herself and Coulter killed. A shiver raced up her back. If he'd been injured, it would have been her fault. Her fault for not being honest. Her fault for not telling the truth.

Terrell was right, she didn't deserve a fine man like Coulter.

She glanced back and found her husband staring at her with a quizzical expression on his face. A thousand questions flashed in his eyes. He wasn't going to be put off; he deserved to know the truth about the woman he'd married.

With a defeated shrug, she climbed the steps in the darkness. Once inside the house, she turned up the lamp and stoked the stove. Only then did she realized how sooty and disheveled she was. Her nightgown was soiled and torn, and she shivered in the chill morning. She slipped on one of Coulter's shirts. From the washroom, she retrieved his workboots and another flannel shirt. In the confusion, he'd gone outside barefooted and shirtless. The least she could do was keep him warm.

Coulter was stacking the paintings on the porch when she stepped through the doorway. "Coulter," she called. "You're going to catch cold."

He held a painting in his hands—Ellen's beautiful picture. The way he looked at his deceased wife made her heart ache. "Thanks for thinking about my work."

"You and Cathy lost her once. I couldn't let it happen again."

The look in his eyes changed when he glanced up at her. "I almost lost you."

She shook her head. "No, I wasn't in danger. I knew I could climb down that rope or leap into the haystack."

He set down the portrait and took the garments from her hands. "Thanks, Angel. I'll be in for coffee in a little while."

The pink glow of sunrise had blanketed the land by the time Coulter came in for his coffee. From the window, Josie had seen him stomping out the glowing embers to prevent a flare-up. She'd taken the time to wash, braid her hair, and change into a shirtwaist and skirt. He stopped at the pump and doused his head and arms with water.

His eyes red-rimmed, he entered the kitchen and settled at the table. Josie filled two mugs from the pot she'd kept hot for hours. "Would you like something to eat?"

He shook his head. "Sit down, Angel. We need to talk."

Her heart dropped to her stomach. She'd tried to prepare herself for this moment, but nothing had prepared her for the look of defeat in his eyes. Settling across from him, she waited.

He dug into his pocket and dropped two items on the table. "I found these in the ashes, along with an overturned lamp."

Her eyes grew wide. The half-smoked cigar could only come from Terrell, and she'd dropped the broken chain when the fire began.

"How did you happen to make it out there before me? You were already in the barn when I woke up." His voice turned hard with accusations. He was no longer her lover, he was a lawman seeking to solve a crime. "Did you go out there to meet somebody? A man who smokes cigars?" He fingered the cigar butt. "Sullivan?"

He'd cornered her as neatly as a fox corners a rabbit. "Yes. You're right on all counts," she gasped, her gaze on the incriminating evidence.

"God!" He jumped to his feet. The chair toppled to the floor with a loud bang. "On our wedding night you leave my bed to meet another man?"

"Coulter, it isn't what you think." This time she looked up into his pain-glazed eyes.

"You have no idea what I think." He braced his hands on the table hovering over her. "Truth, Angel. It's time you told the truth about your past, and just who the hell is Sullivan?"

Her heart ached for him. And for herself, as well as the future they could have had together. Her gaze fell to her finger where only hours ago he'd put his ring. "I don't know where to start," she whispered, around the lump in her throat.

His gaze followed hers to her ring. "Start anywhere. Start with around midnight when you left my bed to meet your lover."

"No, Coulter, no." She stood and reached for his arm. The muscle was hard and unyielding under her touch. Thankfully, he didn't shake her off. "Terrell isn't my lover, he never was. I love you."

Disbelief sparked in his gaze. "Then why did you go to him?"

The truth was so ridiculous, she could hardly believe it herself. "I did it for my brother."

"Isn't your brother dead?"

"Yes. He was murdered and I've never learned who killed him." Memories of Armand brought back the pain even time couldn't heal. "Please sit down, Coulter. I'll explain everything."

"How does Sullivan fit into this?" He moved to the chair next to hers and reached for his coffee.

She swallowed down her trepidation. "After our parents died, Armand and I spent a few months in an orphanage. But we ran away and continued to perform. Because we were underage, we pretended to be husband and wife. We thought that would protect me from unwanted attention from the men. It usually worked, but Terrell was more persistent than most. He was the lead actor and company manager of the troupe. He was constantly pressing his attentions on me. Armand didn't like it, and threatened to leave the show and join another company."

"I don't suppose Sullivan liked that."

"Not at all. Armand often played cards after the show. One night he didn't come back to the boardinghouse. The Chicago police found his body in a dark alley. His jewelry and money were missing."

Coulter swore under his breath. "That was all the opening Sullivan needed to move on you." A hint of understanding gleamed in his eyes.

"Yes. As soon as I buried my brother, I ran away to St. Louis. I met a kindly lady who took me in. She and I began working for the temperance movement. I took on my birth name, and never looked back."

"That doesn't explain why you went behind my back to meet Sullivan."

"When I saw him at the church yesterday, he was wearing Armand's ring—the one Papa had given him. He said he had information about my brother's death. He also said that if I didn't meet him, he would go to your in-laws and tell them about my past."

"My in-laws?" He squeezed his eyes shut and shook his head. "What does Sullivan have to do with them?"

She shoved her coffee away. Her words were as bitter as the coffee. "He claims that he met a lawyer in Chicago who was looking for a performer named Angel. The lawyer led him here. I don't know how the lawyer knew about me."

"Only a handful of people know about the custody battle. Bertha and Oscar, Polly and John, maybe Homer. Get back to last night. What happened in the barn?"

"We argued, and Terrell knocked the lamp from the nail. He ran when the fire started." She studied Coulter's face, trying to read his reaction. If he didn't believe her, if he didn't forgive her, Josie felt she would die right on the spot. "I tried to put it out. I swear, I didn't want anything to happen to your barn, to your animals, to your work." Reaching across the table, she covered his hand with hers. His gaze dropped. One rough finger brushed lightly over the tiny blisters on her arm. She'd barely noticed the burns in her concern over Coulter.

"You burned your arm." His expression changed. Something akin to sympathy washed over his face. "I have something for it."

She clutched his fingers. "I'm all right. They don't hurt."

He tugged his hand free. "We don't want infection or scars." Moving quickly to the shelf over the counter, he pulled down a small tin and returned to his chair. "This should take care of the stinging and protect your skin."

Automatically she pulled back her arm. She wrinkled her nose against the smelly black salve. "What's that stuff?"

Ignoring her protests, Coulter turned his chair and straddled her legs between his thighs. He caught her arm in his big hand. "An old remedy that always works. The smell goes away, and it prevents infection."

Josie studied his face while he dabbed the salve on the red marks. He bit his lip in concentration. His eyes were hidden behind lowered lashes. "The burns aren't deep and they'll heal quickly," he said, his tone soft. When he lifted his gaze, a new look glittered in the dark depths.

"I suppose I made a mess of everything," she said.

He nodded, his hand still holding hers in a strong, warm grip. "You should have trusted me to handle Sullivan. I'm your husband. It's my place to protect what's mine."

His words chased away some of the chill from her heart. In spite of all that had happened, he still wanted her. He still believed in their marriage. "I know, Coulter. But I didn't want to involve you in my problems."

"Angel, when I married you, I made certain promises. I intend to keep those promises. I'll love you, I'll cherish you, and I'll protect you."

He lifted his hand to her cheek, gently stroking the smooth skin. She turned her face and buried her lips in his palm. "I love you, Coulter."

"Then let me take care of you. Sullivan won't bother you again."

She wished she could believe Coulter. But she knew Terrell wouldn't give up without a fight. And the man always fought dirty.

Coulter slid his hand to her nape and tugged her head forward. His lips moved closer until they brushed hers. His kiss was soft and giving. Soothing and comforting. He must love her. Why else would he be willing to forgive her, willing to keep her in his life? He ended the kiss but kept his cheek pressed to hers. The night's growth of whiskers scratched, but she didn't care. For several long moments neither moved. Maybe, just maybe, Josie had a chance at happiness.

If only she could keep predators like Terrell Sullivan at bay.

Chapter 27

By mid-morning, Coulter was tired, hot, and angry. The last thing he'd expected to be doing the day after his marriage was to be clearing smoldering embers from where his barn had stood the day before. If he got his hands on Terrell Sullivan, the man would think twice before he threatened another woman. Especially Coulter Steele's woman.

He swiped his sleeve across his forehead. Dirt, sweat, and cinders came away on the chambray workshirt. Josie had worked beside him most of the morning, until he'd sent her to the house to fix something cold to drink.

The sound of a horse's hoofs and flurry of dust behind the rider weren't exactly welcome, considering his annoyed state of mind. Hell, he should be upstairs in his cool, comfortable bed with his wife, not tossing burnt lumber into a stack.

Shielding his eyes with his hand, he watched as the familiar horse slowed to trot. He'd hardly expected to be bothered by his uncle. The previous afternoon he'd made it clear he was taking the day off to be with Josie.

He stepped from the ashes of the barn and waited until his uncle slid from the saddle. "Hell's bells, Coulter. What happened?" Oscar stared in disbelief at the rubble.

"A little accident, Uncle, is all."

Oscar shook his head. "I'll order up a load of lumber from the sawmill as soon as I get back to town. And I know Bertha will organize a barn-raising to get you back in business." He shifted his gaze to the horses in the corral. "Lose any stock?"

"No. I managed to get them all out. Thankfully, I'd left your fine buggy in the yard overnight."

Shifting the toe of his shiny boot in the ashes, Oscar asked the obvious. "How did it start?"

It wouldn't do to make accusations and cause his uncle worry. "Not sure. I could have left the lamp in the barn in my hurry to get to my new bride." Coulter tugged off his gloves and shoved them in his hip pocket. "What brings you out here? Nobody knew about the fire."

"Let's go up to the house, son. I have to talk to you."

By the tone of his voice, Coulter knew Oscar wasn't the bearer of good news. His uncle still wore his grocer's apron over his pants and shirt, as if he'd left in a hurry. "We'll talk here. Did something happen? Is it Cathy? Bertha?" Fear lodged in Coulter's chest like a stone.

"No, no, none of those. We got visitors in town today. Mr. and Mrs. Montgomery showed up with Judge Dunbar. They're looking for you."

Every profanity Coulter had ever heard leaped to his mouth. He clamped his teeth to keep from spewing them forth like a volcano. "Damnation!" he grunted. "Did they say what they want?"

Oscar took out his handkerchief and wiped his forehead. "Nope. Said they wanted to talk to you. Today. Homer wanted to deliver the message, but I thought it better to come from me.''

Coulter pressed his hands to the small of his back and stretched. ''Thanks, Uncle. I'd better get into town and face the music.''

''Coulter, another thing.''

What could get worse? He lifted a questioning eyebrow.

''They found Cathy at Polly's. She told them about your marriage to Josie. They want to meet your new wife, too.''

Coulter's heart sank. He'd hoped to keep Josie out of this. The Montgomerys had already caught them together in a rather compromising position. They sure wouldn't be happy that he'd married Josie. ''Thanks for the message. Can you tell them we'll meet with them and the judge for dinner this evening at the hotel?''

''Want me and Bertha to join you?''

''Not necessary. But I'd appreciate if you'll testify for me if the time comes.''

''Goes without saying.''

''How about a cool drink before you head back to town?''

With another sad shake of his head, Oscar stuck out his hand. ''I'd best get back to the store. Bertha was fit to be tied. She's ready to give Lillian and Bradley Montgomery a piece of her mind.''

''Wouldn't do much good. They never did care for my family.'' Coulter squeezed his uncle's fingers in his. ''But I wouldn't trade you and Bertha for a dozen of their kind.''

''You're like a son to us, Coulter. We'll always be on your side. And if you need money for lawyers, just let me know. Whatever I have is yours.''

''Thanks. But I don't need money. What I need is a little luck to convince the judge my daughter is better off with me and Josie.''

''Humph. Just one look should convince him where the girl belongs.'' Oscar slapped Coulter on the back. ''I'll deliver the message." He climbed into the saddle. "Give Josie our love."

Coulter waved to his uncle, then turned his gaze to the house. Josie was watching from the porch, her hands shoved into the pockets of her apron. He shook his head. One day into marriage, his barn had burned down, and he had to fight his in-laws to keep his child. How much was a man expected to take?

That evening Coulter hitched up Oscar's buggy for the ride into town. At first Josie had rebelled against meeting Coulter's in-laws and the judge. She was certain her attendance would do more harm than good.

She'd dressed carefully to portray the right look. This was the performance of her life and she had to look the part of a demure, straitlaced bride. Her navy suit was pressed and her sailor hat was cocked at a perky angle. The sheriff's wife had to be the epitome of propriety and decorum. The thought almost made her laugh. One word from Terrell, and her future would be dashed into as many shards as a crystal goblet smashed against stone.

What if Terrell had already told the Montgomerys about her past? He was a fine actor and could easily convince the judge that Josie was morally unfit to be a mother for a young girl.

Coulter, too, had taken care with his grooming. Under his new gray Stetson hat, his hair was neatly combed, and he'd shaved so close, he'd nicked his chin. She wished she could kiss away the drop of blood as well as the lines that puckered his brow.

After Oscar left, Coulter had explained the situation. Josie knew he was worried, but not any more than she was. At any cost, he couldn't lose his child. Losing Ellen had almost destroyed Coulter. Josie couldn't be the cause of his losing his daughter, too.

As he helped her into the buggy, Josie felt like a condemned felon on the way to the gallows.

"Don't look so worried, Angel." Coulter's smile was
forced. "Nothing's going to happen tonight. We're just
going to talk and see what develops. We just have to assure
the judge that we're kind, loving parents."

"I hope you're right." She squeezed his arm, more to
reassure herself than him. "Coulter, what do you intend
to do if you spot Terrell Sullivan?"

He slanted her a glance. "What I'd like to do is beat
the bastard to a pulp. But I won't, for now. I can't afford
a confrontation in front of the judge. It wouldn't do my
case any good to be portrayed as a violent man."

Josie breathed a sigh of relief. But she couldn't let down
her guard. She didn't trust Terrell, and wondered what,
if anything, she could do to remedy the situation.

The remainder of the ride passed in silence, each lost
in their own thoughts. By the time they reached Council
City, the town was bathed in the pale pink glow of evening.
Coulter maneuvered the buggy past the horses tied in front
of the bars where the loud piano music flooded the street.
Josie stiffened her back at the thought of the revelry and
drinking on the premises. Given a little more time, she
was certain she would have been successful in her mission.
But with all that had happened—her marriage, the barn
burning down, the custody battle—she'd sorely neglected
the reason for her visit to this part of Kansas.

Being a Monday night, the hotel restaurant had few
customers. Josie tightened her hold on Coulter's arm as
they paused at the doorway. She took the moment to study
the audience. The Montgomerys were talking to a short,
portly gentleman at a large table with two empty chairs.
At another table sat a man with a thick mustache and
long sideburns. Josie blinked, and stared at the stranger—
Terrell Sullivan disguised in stage makeup. She'd been in
enough performances to recognize the fake hair when she

saw it. She hoped—she prayed—Coulter wouldn't take notice of the man.

Mr. Montgomery, and the man she assumed to be the judge, stood when they spotted Coulter and Josie at the entrance. Squeezing her hand, Coulter led Josie into the dining room. Although most of her meals were taken at Polly's, Josie had eaten a time or two at the hotel. A glittering gas chandelier cast a glow over the fine china, crystal, and silverware set on the starched white tablecloth.

With a practiced eye, Josie studied her opponents like a fighter studies his adversary. Bradley Montgomery wore a stern expression, but she easily spotted the quick flicker of interest in his gaze. Lillian, on the other hand, didn't even try to hide her condemnation. Not to be outdone, Josie studied the older woman with her own bold assessment.

Mrs. Montgomery was a handsome woman who clearly took pride in her appearance. Her rose silk faille gown was the latest fashion from Paris, very likely a Worth original. Josie felt vastly underdressed in her simple navy suit—or, as she preferred to think, Lillian was vastly overdressed.

As they approached the table, the sound of running feet came from behind them. "Papa, Mama!" Cathy flew into them and wrapped her arms around her father's waist.

Startled, Coulter released Josie's arm and gazed down at his daughter. From the corner of her eye Josie spotted Coulter's aunt. Bertha winked and turned to leave. Josie nodded her approval. The confrontation would be averted as long as the little girl was with them.

Coulter didn't look at all pleased. "What are you doing here? I thought you were spending another night with Sally Jane."

"Aunt Bertha said I could have dinner here with you and my grandparents. It'll be so much fun." Cathy released her father and turned to her grandparents. "Good evening, Grandmother and Grandfather,'' she said, dipping into a small curtsy.

The severe expression on Lillian Montgomery's face eased into a stiff smile. "Come give me a kiss, Catherine." The older woman opened her arms.

Cathy went to her grandmother, who placed a quick kiss on the girl's cheek. "You certainly look better this evening than when I saw you this afternoon."

"Thank you." Cathy stepped back to her father. "Aunt Bertha let me wear the new dress I got for the wedding. She even fixed my hair."

Coulter set his hands on Cathy's shoulders. A possessive light gleamed in his eyes and a muscle twitched in his jaw. Above his narrow black necktie, the veins in his throat throbbed as if he were desperately trying to control his temper. Josie clutched his fingers to offer what little reassurance she could. Not that she had much to give. With Terrell nearby, she was certain no good would come of the meeting.

Bradley Montgomery nodded a brief greeting. "Steele, Miss—I beg your pardon—*Mrs.* Steele, I'd like you to meet Judge Dunbar." At the glimmer of triumph in his eyes, a wave of apprehension swept over Josie. Montgomery was very sure of success.

"I remember Coulter from his days in my courtroom. We miss your brilliant rhetoric." After a brief handshake, he turned to Josie and took both her hands in his. "I'm very pleased to meet you, and, of course, you, too, Catherine." He granted her a warm smile. "Mrs. Steele, I understand you and the sheriff are newlyweds. May I offer my best wishes." His hands were warm and his gaze was steady.

"Thank you, sir," Coulter answered in her stead.

Not to be put off, the judge stared at Josie for a moment longer. After Montgomery's hard stare, the judge's gaze was a welcome breath of fresh air. "Mrs. Steele, please don't think I'm being brazen, but have we met before? Have you ever been to Kansas City?"

Again Coulter spoke up, not allowing her to answer. "My wife was a temperance organizer, Your Honor. She's traveled extensively in Kansas and Missouri. Perhaps you've attended her lectures."

Judge Dunbar shook his head. "No, Sheriff, I'm afraid I haven't." A wide smile pulled at his lips. "But if I'd known the temperance workers were so pretty, I'd be tempted to attend a lecture or two, and maybe even be persuaded to take the pledge."

"Thank you, Judge," Josie said, before Coulter could put words into her mouth. "I have a pledge in my handbag, if you're interested in joining our crusade."

He chuckled softly. "I'll give it strong consideration, my dear."

Josie had long ago learned to read faces. Although this man may hold their fate in his hands, she read honesty and fairness in his gaze. She prayed she was right. It would kill both Cathy and Coulter to be separated.

The pleasantries over, he released Josie's hand and gestured to the chairs. Before they reached the table, the waiter had added another setting. Coulter sat between the judge and Josie, and he settled his daughter next to her grandmother.

Josie glanced up and found Terrell's gaze on her, a sly smile on his mouth. He knew she wouldn't expose him to Coulter, not with so many important people in attendance.

Alert for trouble, Josie heard little of the dinner conversation. The men talked about the economy, about the state government. Judge Dunbar made an occasional reference to Coulter's days as a lawyer. Mrs. Montgomery said little, her gaze on Josie and her grandchild. With an insincere word of apology, Mr. Montgomery ordered a bottle of wine. Josie sipped water, and even Coulter refused to drink.

By the end of the meal, Josie was so tense, she jumped

when Cathy touched her arm. The child leaned over and whispered that she had to use the facilities. Fortunately the hotel was quite up-to-date, and sported indoor plumbing. Grateful for a moment's relief from the strained atmosphere, she excused herself and Cathy. While waiting for Cathy, she stepped into the garden to clear her head.

So far, the evening had been cordial, if strained. The subject of a custody hearing was never mentioned, thanks to Cathy's presence at the table. Lost in her thoughts, she didn't hear the man approach until he spoke.

"Bravo, Angel. Looks like your performance is a success as usual."

She should have expected Terrell to follow her. Whirling around, she faced the man who threatened her happiness. He was close to her, too close for comfort. Josie clutched her hands into fists.

"What are you doing here, Terrell? My husband knows you burned down his barn, and if he finds you talking to me, he'll arrest you, or worse."

He laughed, the sound a wicked snicker. "Don't worry, he's deep in conversation with his father-in-law and the judge." He stroked his fake mustache between his thumb and forefinger. "That's a very pretty little girl. It would really be a shame if anything happened to her."

A icy fear latched onto her heart. "You wouldn't hurt a child."

"Me? Of course not. But a few well-placed words, and that kid would be snatched away to a big house in Kansas City." He pulled out a cigar and studied the tip with rapt attention. "And that sheriff will never see her again."

"Coulter would never let you get away with that."

"He wouldn't blame me. It would all be your fault, and he would hate you because he lost his daughter." Even in the dim garden, she spotted the self-satisfied gleam in his eyes.

"You would lie about my past?" she groaned. The thought of losing Coulter hurt like a knife to her heart. But the thought of his losing Cathy and blaming Josie was worse than death.

"Angel, you know I always get what I want. I want you to come back to the troupe, and I'll do anything to get you back." He struck a match on the sole of his leather shoe and held it to the end of the cigar. After several long puffs, he continued. "I have contacts in San Francisco. We could be the toast of the West Coast: Sullivan and Company."

Josie shivered under his stare. The idea of being back in his clutches was worse than going to prison. "And I'm the company?"

Terrell shrugged, waving the cigar like a baton. " 'Sullivan and Angel.' How does that sound?"

"I'm not interested in you or anything you have to offer. I'm married, and I intend to stay right here with Coulter."

"Without the kid."

"They wouldn't believe a word you said."

"Don't bet on it. I can be very convincing, and when I get through with you, Angel . . ." He took a puff on the cigar. "That upstanding sheriff won't even give you a second look."

"What do you want? I don't have any money."

"I already told you, I want you. In exchange for my silence, I want Angel LeClare."

Her stomach churned and she was afraid she would be ill. Angry words burned in her throat, but she swallowed them down. There was no use agitating him further.

He caught her arm in a steely grip. "The stagecoach leaves tomorrow at eleven o'clock. I have an appointment with the judge at ten. If you aren't here, packed and ready to leave . . . Well, I don't have to tell you what will happen."

"I can't leave my husband."

"Think about this: I heard that Mrs. Montgomery hired

a woman as a nanny for the kid. You know, the woman who hangs around with Deputy Potts. What's her name?''

Her knees began to tremble. ''Miss Bettington?''

''That's the one.''

Josie couldn't be the cause of that woman getting her hands on the child again. She would give her own life to keep it from happening.

''Josie, Cathy? Are you out here?''

At the sound of Coulter's voice, she spun around. Oh, Lord, what was she going to do? She couldn't let her husband catch her with Sullivan. Coulter would probably try to kill the man. Terrell dropped his hand. She stepped from the shadows toward the doorway that silhouetted her husband's tall frame. Her mouth dry, it took a few moments before she could call out.

''Here, Coulter. I'm over here.'' A quick glance over her shoulder, and she saw that Terrell had disappeared deeper into the garden.

''Where's Cathy?'' he called out, worry in his voice.

''I'm here, Papa. I was chasing some fireflies,'' Cathy called from the garden.

''I'm sorry, Coulter. It was such a pretty night, we both were enjoying the fresh air.''

He lifted his hand to her face. ''Is something wrong? You look pale.''

Josie forced a smile she was far from feeling. ''Nothing's wrong. It's just that . . .'' *I have to leave you forever.* ''The strain of the evening just got to me.''

''I know what you mean.'' His thumb stroked the line of her chin. ''I'm so tense, I'm about to snap in two.''

Unable to help herself, she turned her mouth to his palm. How she loved him. How she was going to miss him. But Josie knew she had little choice. She couldn't, she wouldn't be, the cause of his losing his child. Not only would Coulter not forgive her, she wouldn't forgive herself.

Her decision made for her, she kissed his palm for the last time. By tomorrow night, she would be miles away from Council City. Miles away from Coulter and Cathy. With only her broken heart for company.

Chapter 28

Josie eased out of Coulter's arms early the next morning. For a long moment she rested on her elbow and studied the strong line of his jaw, his straight nose, his thick, dark eyebrows, and the long lashes lying on his cheeks. She resisted the urge to smooth his hair from his forehead. His peaceful sleep gave little testimony to the turbulent night of lovemaking.

They'd spent most of the night in one passionate embrace after another. With an almost desperate need, they'd made love as if it were the end of the world. For Josie, it might as well have been.

She brushed her fingers across his warm, muscular chest. His heartbeat was steady and strong. She loved him more than anything. Loved him enough to give him up so he could have what he wanted most in the world. Although she couldn't guarantee that Coulter would keep his child, at least she wouldn't be the cause of his losing his daughter.

Untangling her bare leg from his, she pulled the quilt

over his naked body. She planted a light kiss on his chin and prayed she could go through with her plan.

On silent feet, she moved to the bedroom that had been hers before her marriage. In their rush to marry, she'd left most of her things in that room, along with her trunk. This way, she could be all packed to leave before Coulter awoke.

She had little doubt he would try to stop her. He wasn't a man to take rejection lightly. He would hate her, but no more than she hated herself.

Quickly she splashed water on her face and passed a brush through her unruly hair. Within minutes, Josie was attired in a simple shirtwaist and skirt. Her matching jacket lay on the bed. Her hands trembled as she packed everything she owned into the trunk and satchel. She set aside the ornate hat Bertha had made for her wedding. The one thing she didn't need to take was another memento of her marriage. The pain in her heart was souvenir enough.

"Angel." Coulter's sleep-thickened voice came from his bedroom.

The dreaded moment had arrived. The moment when she had to face Coulter. They were to meet the judge at nine, then she had to find Terrell to keep him from ruining everything for the man she loved.

She took a deep breath to calm her nerves and wiped her damp hands on her skirt. She'd performed before hard audiences, but this act was going to have to be the most convincing in her life. If Coulter thought this was anything but her idea, he would be on Terrell faster than a chicken hawk on a fat hen.

Snapping the lid of the trunk, she turned to leave. She lifted her gaze and spotted Coulter in the doorway, completely and gloriously naked.

His gaze swept over her in one quick glance, stopping when he returned to her face. If he saw half the misery she felt, he would be floored by the sight. "What are you doing?"

She jammed her hands into her pockets to steel her reserve for the task at hand. "Packing."

Heedless of his nudity, he took one wary step toward her. "Why? Where are you going?"

She tried not to look at him, to not see the questions in his eyes, or the frown on his face. Most of all, she didn't want to look at his body, the body that had given her so much pleasure, so much passion and joy. He'd awakened needs within her she'd never even believed existed. He made her feel alive, like a woman. Leaving him was like being consigned to the bowels of hell for eternity. Never again would she glory in his embrace. Never again would she feel that kind of love or desire.

"Away." Bolstering every bit of the bravado she possessed, she tilted her chin at a proud angle.

"What are you talking about?" He took a step closer.

"Coulter, please don't make this difficult. I've decided to return to the theater—where I belong. I hadn't realized how much I've missed the stage, the costumes, the performances, the applause." She bit the inside of her lip to keep the lie going. In that instant, Angel LeClare the actress took over. Josie Clark disappeared, as dead as the cold ashes of her heart.

"This is because of Sullivan, isn't it? He wants you back." Taking a step closer, he stopped within an arm's length of her.

From the short distance, she could feel the warmth of his body, smell her perfume on his skin. "Coulter, did you honestly think I would be satisfied to live in this nowhere town? That I could be happy cooking and cleaning?" She tossed her long waterfall of hair over her shoulder. "I tried, but now I know I'm completely out of my own element. I'm Angel LeClare. I was born into the LeClare family. I belong to the world. I need the admiration of my audience."

"Bull!" he shouted, his face red with rage. "You're my wife. You belong to me."

"Don't be stubborn. I've made up my mind. I'm leaving on the eleven o'clock stagecoach."

He caught her arms, digging his fingers into the flesh. Josie struggled not to flinch.

"With Sullivan?"

"That doesn't matter. I'm going."

"What about the promises you made in front of that preacher?"

The muscles in his neck strained with his effort to control his temper. His breath was coming in short gasps. Josie's gaze lifted to his mouth pulled in a hard line.

"I can't keep them. Everything happened so quickly, I didn't have time to think. You shouldn't have rushed me into the marriage."

He squeezed so hard, he lifted her feet from the floor. Her breasts were crushed against his chest. "You said you loved me."

The reminder of her love was almost her undoing. Josie wanted to hold him, to show him how he'd filled her life and her heart. But she couldn't let him know. He had too much to lose.

"I lied."

"And when you made love to me, was that a lie, too?"

"Of course I enjoyed your lovemaking. You're a strong and skilled lover."

He ground his pelvis into her stomach, his arousal evident in spite of his anger, or perhaps because of it.

"Let go of me, Coulter." Her voice quivered with fear.

Frustration gleamed in his eyes. In one quick move, he picked her up and tossed her onto the bed. Her breath whooshed from her lungs. Before she had time to recover her shock, he fell on her, pinning her to the mattress. Primitive fury lined his face. "I'll show you what kind of lover I am."

Terror riveted her to the bed. Words of protest stuck in her throat. He covered her mouth with his, using his tongue like a weapon against her. She shoved against his chest; she twisted her head to throw him off. "Stop. Don't."

He twined his fingers in her hair to still her face. His naked body lay heavy above her, his rigid manhood pressed into her stomach. "Don't what, Angel? You're my wife. You belong to me, and I'll take what I want." His free hand reached for her skirt, tugging it high on her legs.

Terrified, she bucked to throw him off. His eyes were glazed over with lust. "Coulter, stop. This is rape."

"You're mine." Twisting his fingers in her hair, he forced her face to his. Again his mouth claimed hers in a kiss that was demanding and cruel.

Something inside Josie snapped. Had she driven this good, loving man to commit this despicable act? Knowing her efforts were useless against his greater strength, Josie stopped struggling and resigned herself to her fate.

Coulter felt Josie go limp under him. He opened his eyes and saw the terror on her face. As if he were watching from afar, he viewed the scene in which he was a player. He had a woman, his wife, pinned to the bed with his naked body; in one hand he gripped her hair, and with the other he was tearing at her underclothing. Revulsion rolled through him. How could a man rape a woman, any woman? How could he hurt the woman he loved? Moments ago he'd been on fire, his manhood aching for relief; his pride aching for vengeance.

His insides revolted against his actions, his hands went slack, and he rolled away from her. Disgusted with himself, he sat on the edge of the bed and buried his face in his hands. He heard her rapid breathing behind him, but she didn't move or speak. Finally in control of his emotions, Coulter stood and moved on leaden feet to the doorway.

"If you want to leave, just go. I won't try to stop you. You should be a great success as an actress. You sure as

hell had me fooled." In saying the words, Coulter was
giving up his last chance of happiness. He'd buried one
wife in a Kansas City cemetery; the other was walking out
on him. Both were lost to him forever. Ellen couldn't help
dying, but Josie chose to leave. Her going tore the heart
right out of him.

"Coulter, please listen for just a moment." Her voice
was hesitant and tight.

He halted, but didn't turn around.

"I'll go with you to meet Judge Dunbar and I'll tell him
what a wonderful father you are. Together we can convince
him not to take Cathy away from you."

"And do you think it'll do any good when he sees you
walk out of our lives forever?" He heard the bed squeak.

"You can tell them I had to leave to care for a sick
relative. Then, after Cathy is safe with you, you can file for
an annulment."

Bitterness rose like bile into his throat. "I don't suppose
I have a choice, do I? I certainly don't want the judge to
know I married a notorious stage actress, who lies, cheats,
and deceives everybody she meets."

"Coulter, for what it's worth, I'm sorry."

Shoulders slumped, he paused at the doorway. "Do you
know what the ironic part is, Angel? It's my fault more
than yours. You were the woman I'd chosen. You were the
one I'd planned to court." He let out a bark of bitter
laughter. "That should give you and Sullivan something
to laugh over when you're lying in bed together."

At exactly nine o'clock that morning, Coulter ushered Josie
into Judge Dunbar's hotel suite. The man had chosen his
rooms for the informal hearing to keep the curious away
from the confidential nature of the suit. Coulter's heart
was so heavy, he could barely climb the stairs.

It had taken all his willpower to sit beside the faithless

woman on the drive into town and not tear her limb from limb. In spite of his anger, however, he knew he would never hurt her. He'd known from the beginning who she was and what she was. She'd tried to warn him, but like a fool, he'd listened to his heart, not his head.

Never again, he vowed. From now on when he wanted a woman, he would simply shuck out a few dollars for a couple hours' pleasure. No way would he get his heart involved.

She'd said little, her face a mask of indifference. He was right about one thing. She would be quite a success on the stage. Not only had she fooled him, but everybody in town—with the exception of Homer and Miss Bettington. He hated to think they'd been right.

As they approached the suite on the second floor of the hotel, she gripped his arm a little tighter. "Coulter, please wipe that frown from your face. For the next hour, we're a loving couple eager to make a proper home for your daughter. Don't let the judge guess otherwise."

He shot her a disgusted look. Happy? She'd yanked out his heart and stomped it worse than a thousand cattle in a stampede, and she expected him to pretend that all was well? He thought about Cathy and how Josie's leaving would affect her. In the past few weeks she'd come to love the woman she called Mama. That alone made him hate her even more. But, for his daughter's sake, he would pretend all was well with his marriage.

The grin on his face felt like a grimace. "Is this better? I'm not the accomplished liar you are."

A pink tinge crept over her face. Behind the thin veil of her hat, he glimpsed red-rimmed eyes. Quickly she turned away and fumbled with her handbag. "Yes."

He lifted his hand and knocked lightly on the wooden door. Almost immediately, it swung open. Judge Dunbar, dressed in a black suit and stiff white shirt, ushered them into the parlor. Coulter removed his hat and gestured Josie in before him.

"Good morning, Coulter, Mrs. Steele. Come in, please." He waved them to the davenport and chairs surrounding a small table. "Would you care for some coffee?"

Coulter bit his lip. No, damn it, he didn't want coffee, or greetings, or mindless chitchat. He wanted to know if this man was going to take his child away from him. Instead, he followed Josie to the couch and sat beside her. If it killed him, he would play the loving husband to his traitorous wife.

"Thank you, sir," she said, in a warm, friendly tone. "We would love some. It was quite dusty on our ride in from the ranch this morning."

The judge smiled as Josie took the role of hostess and filled three china cups from the silver pot. Dunbar leaned back in his chair, his gaze locked on her. Coulter smothered any semblance of jealousy from the man's bold appraisal of his wife.

"Sheriff," the judge said after taking a small sip of the coffee, "as you know, this isn't a formal trial and my decisions can always be appealed. But I've convinced Mr. and Mrs. Montgomery that in the interest of all, I felt it best we handle this problem without the courts involved. I've found handling such cases as this in a relaxed atmosphere is often advantageous to both parties, and especially to the child."

Coulter nodded. "I appreciate your candor, Your Honor. I only want what's best for my daughter."

"Yes, I see that both you and Mrs. Steele love the child very much, and that she is very fond of you. However, I have other matters to consider." He set down the cup and steepled his fingers in front of his face. "To be perfectly honest, when this case first came to my attention, I leaned toward the grandparents. After all, a girl needs a woman's influence and care in growing into a lady. But you seemed to have taken care of that concern. I've talked to several people in town, and they testify that Mrs. Steele is indeed a paragon of virtue.''

Coulter almost choked on his coffee at the assessment of his wife. If the man only knew the truth, Cathy would be lost to him in the blink of an eye. ''Yes, sir, she is,'' he lied.

The cup rattled against the saucer in Josie's hand as she muttered a quick thank-you.

''However,'' the judge continued, ''I have other concerns. I had a disturbing talk with your former housekeeper and your deputy.''

Alert for trouble, Coulter sat forward, his attention riveted to the judge's words. Josie gasped, but remained silent.

''Miss Bettington claims that you'd beaten your child and blamed her. Then you dismissed her so you could take Mrs. Steele, then known as Miss Clark, into your home. Deputy Potts confirmed the story, and he also claimed that there was something unsavory in Mrs. Steele's past.''

''Your Honor,'' Coulter said, his fury at both his former housekeeper and the deputy he'd thought his friend, making his voice husky. His hands trembling, he set aside his cup to keep from crushing it in his fingers. ''Miss Bettington is a bitter woman because I fired her. Believe me, I've never laid a hand to my daughter. You need only ask Cathy, she'll tell the truth. I didn't like Miss Bettington's severe manner of discipline and I felt it best to relieve her of her duties. Since I needed help, I hired Miss Clark to be a companion for my child. As for my wife's past, I'm sure all of us have done something of which we're less than proud.''

At his side, Josie twisted her hands in her lap. ''Judge Dunbar, I—''

''That's all right, Mrs. Steele. I've known Coulter for years, therefore I had my doubts as to the stories. And

Catherine did nothing but sing your praises. I plan to interview a few more interested parties this morning, then I'll render my decision this afternoon."

"Who?" Josie asked, her voice a strangled moan.

Judge Dunbar stood in obvious dismissal. "Mr. and Mrs. Montgomery, of course, a Mrs. Palmer, Mr. and Mrs. Marche, and a Mr. Sullivan."

"Mr. Sullivan?" Coulter asked, afraid he'd finally lost the battle.

Josie remained seated, her face as white as her shirtwaist.

"Yes, the man claims to have information that could be important to the case. I'll speak to him in a few minutes."

A volcano of anger erupted inside Coulter. If Sullivan ruined things for him, he would kill the bastard with his bare hands.

He caught Josie by the elbow and helped her to her feet. She was trembling so badly, he was afraid she would sink to the floor.

"Judge Dunbar," she said, her voice weak. "I have to leave on the eleven o'clock stagecoach. I have a sick relative in . . . in San Francisco who needs my attention. I realize this is an inopportune time, but it can't be helped."

Judge Dunbar reached out a hand to Josie. "I'm sorry to hear that, my dear. I hope all is well and that you'll return soon."

"Thank you, sir."

Coulter stretched out a hand to the judge. "Thank you, sir. You can find me in my office at the jail after I see my wife off."

Something in the way the judge gripped his fingers, gave Coulter a modicum of hope. Not much, but hope was all he had left.

The instant the door closed behind them, Coulter released Josie's arm. He couldn't stand to touch her for another minute. "What's Sullivan got to do with this?"

Her footsteps faltered and she gripped the edge of a

lamp table. "Coulter, he promised not to say anything that will hurt you."

"And you believe him?"

She nodded. "If he tells the truth about me, it would ruin all of us."

His eyes narrowed and he studied the distressed look her veil couldn't conceal. "Did you make a deal with him or something? Did he threaten you?"

"Of course not, I make my own decisions. He simply reminded me of all that I'd missed."

Coulter mumbled under his breath. "I should have killed the bastard when I had the chance."

"Coulter, don't say that. You aren't a murderer." She touched his arm, then jerked back her fingers as if she'd been scorched.

"That's true. I've been trained to uphold the law. But believe me, lady, nobody—and I mean nobody—is going to take my daughter away from me."

"I know you're going to win. Just believe."

He wanted to laugh aloud. He'd already lost so much that day, he didn't have anything left in which to believe.

A man passed them on the stairs, the same man he'd spotted in the dining room the past evening. The man avoided Coulter's glance, his gaze locked on Josie. For a brief, almost indiscernible second something passed between them. Her knuckles turned white as she gripped the banister. Only when the man paused to knock on Judge Dunbar's door did recognition hit Coulter.

Sullivan. The damned actor was sporting a mustache and muttonchops, and walked with a limp. The disguise had fooled everybody but Josie. Again Coulter wondered if she'd made a pact with the devil. Hell, Coulter would sell his own soul if it meant keeping his daughter. Had she done the same?

He shook his head to clear away the confusion. Her

motives didn't matter now. She had already purchased her ticket, and his wife was leaving on the eleven o'clock stage.

And by this afternoon, he would know if his daughter also would be leaving forever.

Chapter 29

Josie had never felt so desolate and alone in her life. She stepped from Polly's comfortable cafe onto the wooden boardwalk, and waited for the stagecoach driver to load on her luggage. She'd already made her good-byes, and wiped the tears from Cathy's eyes, with the promise to write every day and to return as soon as her "sick relative" recovered.

She was certain Polly and Bertha saw through the ruse, but they kept silent. Polly squeezed her shoulder in reassurance, while Bertha recited a litany of instructions. Cathy clung to her hand as if afraid to let her go. From Oscar, she'd learned that Terrell had testified that he'd known Josie in St. Louis, as a dedicated temperance worker who was highly regarded by her peers. For that she was grateful. If only his testimony swayed the judge, her sacrifice would be worthwhile.

So far, Terrell hadn't appeared. The only other passenger awaiting the stagecoach was a rather disreputable chap in dingy coveralls with a stooped back. Josie locked her gaze on the man. Of course; it was Terrell in another of his disguises. He certainly didn't want to tangle with Coulter.

Coulter. She hadn't seen him since they'd left the judge's suite. He'd gone directly to his office while she'd spent the past hour with Polly and Bertha. She was grateful he'd chosen to stay away. Josie didn't think she could bear the pain of seeing him and saying good-bye.

"Where's my papa?" Cathy asked, releasing Josie's hand. Before anyone could stop the girl, she darted away toward the jail. Josie's trunk was already lashed to the boot of the stagecoach, and the other passenger waited inside. The driver turned to Josie and gestured to the door. After one last hug for her friends, she stepped into the dusty street.

"Wait, Mama!" cried a young voice. Cathy was running toward her, her father in tow. Josie's heart almost stopped beating. "You have to kiss Papa good-bye." She skid to a halt inches from Josie, with Coulter a step behind.

Confused, Josie gazed into eyes dark with pain and misery. He stepped closer and set his hands on her shoulders. Josie realized she wanted, she needed, this one last kiss from the man she loved. The memory of it would warm her cold nights for a lifetime to come. She leaned into his chest and whispered, "We're supposed to be newlyweds about to be separated. Make it look real."

Not stopping to consider the consequences, she looped her hands around his neck and pulled his head down to hers. His lips were stiff and unyielding against hers. Standing on tiptoe, she pressed closer, putting all her love into the kiss. Her tongue pressed against the seam of his lips, forcing its way into the warm recesses of his mouth. She stroked across his teeth, until with a deep groan, he opened to her and met her bold invasion with equal fervor. His fingers tightened on her shoulders, and Josie's heart sang with emotion. If only she could explain, if only she could

let him know that her profession of love hadn't been an
act, but was the most genuine thing in her life.

Tears gushed from her eyes, making the kiss salty and
sweet. She savored the feel of his strong body, the smell
of his soap, the taste of him, like a condemned woman
offered her last meal.

"Ma'am," came a faraway male voice. "We got to go.
Got a schedule to keep."

Coulter set her away from him. Through misty eyes, she
thought she spotted a like moisture in his dark gaze. "Take
care of yourself, Angel," he whispered.

Somebody—she wasn't sure who—clasped her elbow
and helped her up the step into the high stagecoach. She
settled on the leather seat, and watched as the door closed
behind her. Outside was everything in this world she'd
ever wanted. And she was leaving it all behind for a life
that meant nothing to her. Tears flowed like a river from
a burst dam. She waved to her friends, and kept her gaze
on Coulter until he was no longer in view. Still she kept
looking.

"Excellent, Angel. A finer performance I have never
seen." The sound of applause emphasized the man's caustic words. "You almost had me convinced you loved the
man. Save some of that emotion for *Romeo and Juliet*. You'll
win the heart of the most cynical critic."

"Shut up, Terrell," she said between quiet sobs. "I did
as you asked. I don't need to listen to your babbling."

He chuckled, a sound that sent a shiver down her spine.
"Angel, how rude. Did you learn that kind of rudeness
from that bumpkin of a sheriff?"

She stabbed him with a hard stare. "Leave Coulter out of
this." With her linen handkerchief, she dried the moisture
from her eyes. She'd spent too much time in self-pity. It
was time to face her future, as devastating and uncertain
as it was.

"Of course. We have to discuss our future. We'll spend

the night in El Dorado, then take the train to Wichita. From there we'll head for Denver. I hear they're hungry for fine entertainment. You'll be bigger than Lola Montez. Those rich miners will shower you with gold. They might even give us a mine or two."

" 'Us'? What about the rest of the troupe?"

"I got rid of that bunch of no-talent hangers-on. From now on it's just you and me: Sullivan and Angel." The greedy gleam in his eyes disturbed her.

"Terrell, I agreed to your terms, and I'm going return to the theater with you. But let's get something straight between us." She leaned forward and punctuated her words with a hard stare. "I did not agree to be your mistress, not now, not ever. You will not force your attentions on me, and I won't be forced to kill you. Am I understood?"

He lifted his hands in surrender, but his smile was as phony as the mustache and sideburns he wore. "Angel, I only want to help you, protect you. And you talk about killing me?"

"I still think you know more than you're willing to admit about Armand's death. And before I board the train, I want his ring." Where that came from, she had no idea. But if she was ever to keep him at bay, she had to make sure she had the upper hand. If Terrell got too sure of himself, all would be lost.

She may have given up the man she loved, and the family she craved, but she wasn't going to lose herself. She'd freely given herself to Coulter; she would never want another man to touch her. Least of all, Terrell Sullivan.

"You're in no position to dictate terms to me. I could still make trouble for Steele."

"By now, the judge has made his decision, either for or against Coulter. I'm out of his life, so there's nothing more you can do."

"You aren't going to double-cross me and go back to him, are you?"

She wanted to laugh to keep from crying. "After the way I left him, Coulter would never want me back. It's time for me to go on to where I belong."

"Just to show my good faith—here." He slid the ruby-and-diamond ring from his finger and passed it across to Josie. "With you in my show, I'll make enough to buy a dozen of those."

Josie held out her hand and let him drop the ring into her palm. A little of the chill in her heart melted at having this piece of her brother back. But she knew she had to remain on guard with Terrell. He never did anything without a reason. And he never gave anything away.

Enfolding the ring in her palm, she settled back and accepted her fate.

It was late afternoon when they reached the stopping-off town of El Dorado, Kansas. Several stagecoach lines intersected at the railroad station. Terrell offered her a hand as they disembarked the coach. She shook out her simple gray skirt and adjusted her hat. Her back ached, and her legs were stiff. But her physical discomfort was nothing compared to the pain in her heart.

El Dorado was larger than Council City. It boasted several buildings over three stories tall, and a variety of shops lined the main street. She'd passed through here on her way to Council City. It seemed like a hundred years ago, not the few months it had been.

As she stepped onto the wooden boardwalk, a tall figure appeared in her path. She gasped. By his size and manner-isms, she had thought the man was Coulter. But when she lifted her gaze, she found a different man staring down at her. The only semblance between the blond-haired, blue-eyed man and her husband was the silver star pinned to his black leather vest.

"Ma'am," he said, touching a finger to his hat. "Are you Josephine Clark, also known as Angel LeClare?"

Alarmed, she felt her heartbeat accelerate. "Yes," she answered, wary to say more.

"I'm Sheriff Donaldson, ma'am. You're under arrest."

Chapter 30

"Swing low, sweet chariot, coming for to carry me home. / Swing low, sweet chariot, coming for to carry me home. / I looked over Jordan, and what did I see, coming for to carry me home? / A band of angels . . ."

The words of the old spiritual echoed off the bare jail-house walls. At the sound of footsteps on the rough board floor, Josie clamped her mouth shut. She swung her gaze toward the barred door and waited for her jailers to show their faces.

She'd spent another uncomfortable night in jail, unjustly incarcerated again by *another* stubborn sheriff. Against her protest, he'd steadfastly refused to tell her the reason she was being jailed. When Terrell had issued a protest, the lawman had threatened to jail him, too.

At least this man wasn't nearly as rude as Homer had been when he'd arrested her. Sheriff Donaldson allowed her to keep her valise and he'd arranged a pitcher of warm water for washing. He'd also delivered a delicious dinner, and this morning his deputy had brought her coffee and biscuits. Still, the cot was lumpy, and the cell stifling. And her anger made her hotter than the halls of Hades.

Terrell had promised to come in the morning to secure her release. Perhaps he'd succeeded in clearing up whatever misunderstanding had caused this injustice.

The footsteps drew closer and two tall, wide-shouldered men stood in the shadows—one was Sheriff Donaldson, but the other man was definitely not Terrell. "This her?" asked Sheriff Donaldson.

"Yep." The reply was a guttural grunt.

"Want me to release her?"

"Yep."

Not at all pleased with the turn of events, Josie stood and moved toward the door. The cell was a small, enclosed room, with thick brick walls and the only light from a small window high above her head. The upper half of the solid wooden door had one-inch-thick metal bars. She gripped the bars with her fingers.

"Would one of you *gentlemen*, and I use the word loosely, tell me why I've been accorded the hospitality of your jailhouse when I've committed no crime?"

"I see what you mean. She sure is a spitfire." It was Sheriff Donaldson again. "But she didn't give me any trouble. Came real peaceful-like."

The other man made only a noncommittal grunt. He was dressed all in black, and blended into the shadows.

"Gather your things, ma'am. I'm going to release you."

"It's certainly about time," she replied. "I have a train to catch." Not giving the men a chance to change their minds, she picked up her jacket, her handbag, and her satchel.

She stepped into the hallway that ran the length of the jailhouse, and saw that the other man had disappeared. It didn't matter who he was; she was out of jail at last. The sheriff gestured her into the office, and stepped in behind her. Across the small room, the black-clad man stood with his back to her.

"Coffee?" he asked.

"No . . ." Her words faltered and her knees grew weak. It couldn't be. That voice. The tall, muscular body that two nights ago she'd spent loving until she'd learned every hill and valley, every texture and every inch of his flesh. "Coulter?"

He turned, his dark, unreadable gaze locked with hers.

"I'll take care of that other piece of business, Coulter," Sheriff Donaldson said.

The outside door opened and closed; still Josie remained rooted to the spot. A thousand fears flooded her. Judging by the dark circles under his eyes, and the harsh set of his jaw, something terrible must have happened. "Coulter, what's wrong? Is it Cathy? Bertha? Oscar?"

He propped his hip against the desk. His nonchalant manner unnerved her worse than if he'd ranted and raved. "No, they're all fine."

"The hearing? Cathy—is she . . . ?" Josie couldn't bring herself to finish. "Is that why you're here? To take out your anger on me?"

"Although Bradley thought he had the judge in his pocket, he didn't reckon that Oscar and Dunbar were old friends. They'd been drummers together many years ago. And, of course, he'd always liked me, too."

Taking one sip of the coffee, he frowned and set the mug aside. "The judge said he didn't see any reason to take Cathy away from me. Seems he was a widower himself, with a daughter to raise. He didn't believe a word that old biddy Bettington said about me, and when he learned Lillian had hired her as a nanny for Cathy, he nearly blew his stack."

Afraid her legs would no longer support her, Josie sank into a chair. "Thank God."

"For what it's worth, he said he was very impressed with

my wife, especially a lady who would leave her groom to tend a sick relative."

She squeezed her eyes shut against the sight of Coulter, the man she loved and couldn't have. At least something had come out all right. Now she could leave in good conscience, knowing she hadn't ruined the little girl's life.

The loud whine of a train whistle broke into her reverie. She leaped to her feet. "Is that the train to Wichita? I'm supposed to be on it."

He folded his arms across his wide chest. "Doesn't look like you're going to make it. You're still under arrest."

Panic struck her anew. "But Sheriff Donaldson said I could go."

"No. He released you into my custody."

"Coulter, I've got to make that train. I promised Terrell—that if he . . . then I . . ." Coulter would never understand.

"Don't worry about Sullivan. Mike Donaldson is this minute escorting Sullivan to the train. I've already given him fair warning that if he ever sets foot in Kansas again, well . . ." He rubbed his knuckles, red and bruised. "Next time I won't be responsible for what happens."

The heat drained from her face. "Coulter, you didn't fight with Terrell, did you?"

A pleased grin spread across his face. "I wouldn't exactly call it a fight. You inflicted more damage on Homer when he tried to arrest you that time."

She shook her head against the confusion. "I don't understand any of this. Did you have me arrested?"

"No, I was too darn mad to think straight. Oscar sent the telegram to Donaldson."

"Oscar? Why did he want me in jail?"

Coulter slid off the desk and took one step in her direction. "He figured that if you got on that train, it might not be so easy to locate you. So he just kept you here until I came to my senses and came after you."

"Why?"

"You didn't think I was going to let you go so easily, did you? You're my wife, and I don't like losing what's mine."

"I wouldn't be, if Bertha hadn't interfered, if she hadn't forced you to marry me."

He shook his head. "Angel, you should know by now nobody can force me to do anything. I married you because I wanted to."

Josie's head was spinning. "You want me back? Why?"

"Hell, Angel, isn't it obvious? I rode half the night to get here. I would have beaten Sullivan to a pulp if Donaldson hadn't stopped me, and I'm here laying my heart at your feet for you to dance on." His voice dropped to a husky growl. "I love you."

"No, Coulter. You don't love me, you love Ellen." All the misery of the past few days finally caught up with her. She bit her lip to hold back the tears.

"Ellen's dead. When I saw you in that loft trying to save her portrait, I realized how wrong I'd been to close off my heart from you. I love you, Angel. I want you in my life, in my bed, even in my kitchen." He opened his arms, inviting her to take the last few steps.

That was all the invitation she needed. Josie wasn't sure her feet touched the floor as she ran into his embrace. She pressed her palms against his chest; the quick pounding of his heart matched hers. "Coulter, I love you so much. I couldn't bear it if I'd have been the cause of your losing Cathy. That's why I agreed to go with Terrell, so he wouldn't lie about my past and hurt you and Cathy. You would hate me forever if you lost your child."

He buried his lips in her hair, shoving aside her hat. "I saw right through that act of yours. You're quite the actress, but you weren't acting when you made love with me. All that fire and passion could only come from a woman in love. I figured I'd let you play out your little performance and see just how far you would go. I didn't expect you to actually go away with Sullivan. That's when I got mad."

"I had to, Coulter. I promised."

"You also promised to love, honor, and obey me."

"I do, I always will."

"Sweetheart, you put both of us through hell for nothing. I could never hate you, and if this battle comes up again, we'll fight it together."

She lifted her face and met his heated gaze. "I never wanted to return to the theater. I want a home, a family, and I can't think of a better place to live than in Council City."

Coulter rocked her back and forth. "How would you like to spend a couple of days here at the hotel? Our honeymoon was interrupted by a barn fire, a custody hearing, and a runaway wife."

"What about our daughter?"

"The Montgomerys wanted a little time with her, so they're staying a day or two in Council City. Bertha and Oscar are there to look after things."

"Is Homer minding the sheriff's office?"

He stilled. "No. I fired Homer. I won't have a man backing me up that I can't trust. He's been jealous of me since I was elected, and he hates my wife. Mike Donaldson loaned me a deputy until I get home."

"Looks like you have everything all worked out, Sheriff."

She felt his grin against her cheek. "Sure do, lady. And I intend to keep you so busy you won't have time for temperance lectures, or organizational meetings, or anything but me."

"Don't be so smug, Coulter Steele." She flashed a haughty smile. "I've already planned to give up my work with the S.A.A.T."

"Praise the Lord."

Sliding her hands up his chest, she stroked her fingers across his whiskered chin. "I've decided I can do more good working for women's suffrage. After we get the vote, then Prohibition will be easy to accomplish."

On a long, deep groan, Coulter lowered his face to hers. "We'll just have to see about that."

"Yes, we will," she returned, lost in the wonder of her husband's kiss. "Later, much later."

ABOUT THE AUTHOR

Jean Wilson lives with her family in Louisiana. She is the author of three Zebra historical romances. She is currently working on her fourth, *Christmas Homecoming*, which will be published in December, 1999. Jean loves to hear from her readers and you may write to her c/o Zebra Books. Please include a self-addressed stamped envelope if you wish a response.

BOOK YOUR PLACE ON OUR WEBSITE AND MAKE THE READING CONNECTION!

We've created a customized website just for our very special readers, where you can get the inside scoop on everything that's going on with Zebra, Pinnacle and Kensington books.

When you come online, you'll have the exciting opportunity to:

- View covers of upcoming books
- Read sample chapters
- Learn about our future publishing schedule (listed by publication month *and author*)
- Find out when your favorite authors will be visiting a city near you
- Search for and order backlist books from our online catalog
- Check out author bios and background information
- Send e-mail to your favorite authors
- Meet the Kensington staff online
- Join us in weekly chats with authors, readers and other guests
- Get writing guidelines
- AND MUCH MORE!

**Visit our website at
http://www.zebrabooks.com**

ROMANCE FROM JANELLE TAYLOR

ANYTHING FOR LOVE   (0-8217-4992-7, $5.99)

DESTINY MINE   (0-8217-5185-9, $5.99)

CHASE THE WIND   (0-8217-4740-1, $5.99)

MIDNIGHT SECRETS   (0-8217-5280-4, $5.99)

MOONBEAMS AND MAGIC   (0-8217-0184-4, $5.99)

SWEET SAVAGE HEART   (0-8217-5276-6, $5.99)

ROMANCE FROM FERN MICHAELS

DEAR EMILY   (0-8217-4952-8, $5.99)

WISH LIST   (0-8217-5228-6, $6.99)

AND IN HARDCOVER:

VEGAS RICH   (1-57566-057-1, $25.00)